# *the* silent gift

**Center Point
Large Print**

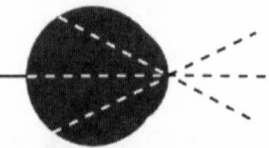

**This Large Print Book carries the Seal of Approval of N.A.V.H.**

# *the* silent gift

## MICHAEL LANDON *JR.*
### AND CINDY KELLEY

CENTER POINT PUBLISHING
THORNDIKE, MAINE

This Center Point Large Print edition
is published in the year 2010 by arrangement
with Bethany House Publishers,
a division of Baker Publishing Group.

The text of this Large Print edition is unabridged.
In other aspects, this book may vary
from the original edition.
Printed in the United States of America
on permanent paper.
Set in 16-point Times New Roman type.

ISBN: 978-1-60285-690-5

Library of Congress Cataloging-in-Publication Data

Landon, Michael, 1964-
The silent gift / Michael Landon, Jr. and Cindy Kelley.
    p. cm.
ISBN 978-1-60285-690-5 (library binding : alk. paper)
1. Single mothers--Fiction. 2. Mothers and sons--Fiction.
    3. Children with disabilities--Fiction. 4. Large type books. I. Kelley, Cindy. II. Title.
PS3612.A5484S55 2010
813'.6--dc22
2009039933

# Chapter One

## *Rural Minnesota*
## SUMMERTIME 1930

SHE APPEARED TO BE FLYING—silvery wings swept upward and proud chin thrust into the stormy Minnesota night. The tiny lady's arms stretched out, embracing the unknown as she emerged through the rain and fog, then disappeared again. Her shiny steel made her more visible than the black 1929 Packard on whose hood she rode. The sedan sped hazardously along a narrow two-lane road that more typically would have suggested shady trees and leisurely Sunday drives. But the darkness, split by two brave headlights, held pounding rain and a monstrous wind that seemed intent on obstructing the vehicle's progress by sheer force of will.

Sheets of pelting rain made visibility nearly zero as Jerry Sinclair frantically peered through the windshield, trying to keep the Packard on the road. The huge oak and maple trees, heavy with foliage and looming like giant sentries when lightning flashed, dipped and swayed in the wind. Furthering his panic was the sound of his young wife's cries from the backseat.

The summer humidity in the closed car made it smell musty and stale—the air almost too thick to breathe. He knew at this speed he was taking chances, but with the urgency of any new father-to-be, Jerry kept a heavy foot on the accelerator to get to the doctor before his child made its entrance into the world. He blamed the false alarm just two days prior for his all but ignoring his wife's urgent request earlier in the day to take her to the hospital. Only seventeen, Mary Godwin Sinclair's teeth had chattered when admitting to her twenty-one-year-old husband that she was scared about the unknown experience of childbirth. Though Jerry may also have been scared, he would never have admitted it to his wife—or to himself.

The beat of the windshield wipers was a metronome for Mary's voice calling to him over the wind's roar. "Hurry, Jerry! Hurry, Jerry!"

He clutched the wheel and careened around a bend. "I'm going as fast as I can!" he shouted over his shoulder. He could barely hear her painful groan.

Jerry rounded another curve, and the car skidded onto the muddy shoulder before he regained control. Mary once more cried out from the backseat, and Jerry turned to look as lightning rippled across the sky. He could see her face contorted in pain.

"Hang on," he yelled, "only a few more miles."

"I . . . can't. It's . . . it's coming! The baby—"

He blew out his cheeks and swung his attention

back to driving just in time to glimpse a small fawn standing in the road, its eyes caught glassy and fixed in the headlights of the Packard. In a split second he calculated the risk of hitting the animal, determining it was too small to even slow them down.

"Your loss, stupid animal!" he shouted in frustration. The startled fawn, legs splayed, held fast like a small statue.

Out of nowhere a large doe bolted into the beam of the headlights and shoved her baby out of harm's way. Jerry cursed loudly and Mary screamed as the Packard slammed into the doe— and the animal flipped up over the hood of the car and crashed against the windshield, cracking the glass. The doe rolled off the hood while the sedan swerved off the asphalt, crashing through a barrier of cattails and wild chokeberry bushes and down the embankment toward a small lake. Jerry frantically pumped the brakes, but the wheels locked up as the car gained momentum and slid down the rain-soaked slope.

In moments the car reached the bottom and rolled right into the dark lake. The flying lady went under first, and the deer's blood washed away as water sloshed over the hood ornament, back over the silver wings, and rippled up the hood. Steam sizzled around the submerged engine, and as the water rose through the floorboards, Jerry could hear himself yelling. He felt the wetness swirl around his ankles, then creep up over his knees.

His frenzied but futile attempts to open the door increased the panic that had him by the throat. Finally bracing one hand on the steering wheel, he used the other to turn the crank and lower the window. His apprehension overpowered all reason as the front end of the car dipped even lower and Mary started to scream his name. In waterlogged clothes and shoes, he struggled to maneuver out the driver's window.

His limbs felt like lead as he lurched and slid on the slick muck. He grabbed the back-door handle and hollered at Mary, "I can't open it! Roll down the window!"

She screamed again, and he could see the water enveloping her belly and rising up her thin cotton dress. Her hands, encased in white cotton gloves, were splayed over the blue material like clouds. He pounded on the window. "Listen to me, Mary! Open the window!" He watched as she caught her breath between labor pains and saw her reach toward the window crank, but then almost immediately cry out again. Her hand clenched in a fist against her belly as the steadily rising water moved farther up her body.

He fought to stay near the car as the water inched up to her chin, but the weight of his soaked shirt, pants, and shoes pulled at him too as the car slipped farther downward. For one brief moment, he could see her terror-filled eyes through the watery glass. He saw her spit out the lake and tip her head back to keep her face in the small pocket of air near the roof of the car. He fought to lift his shoes from the sucking lake bed as he turned and slogged his way toward the shore, collapsing on its edge in the mud.

As water finished filling the last few inches of space in the car, Mary was finishing the journey of her pregnancy even as her world went completely black.

Raindrops splashed into the lake—tiny pits silently marring its smooth surface. The wind that churned the air was nonexistent from below, lending an eerie calm to the water. The world above was muffled, a surreal distance that seemed impossible to reach.

The moon slipped out of its shroud of clouds just as a tiny infant broke through the surface of the lake, cleansed from birth by the water, held in the strong, protective arms of his mother.

**MY STORY IS AS UNIQUE AS MY BIRTH—and so is the fact that I could not tell it to you until now. But even as I give you this account, it isn't me I want you to focus on—rather, it's my mother. My mother is where the heart of this story lies.**

# Chapter Two

*Brewster, Minnesota*
## January 1938

HE CAME INTO VIEW LIKE A BIRD in flight against a wash of cerulean blue. Dark eyes fringed with black lashes above red apple cheeks stared up at the sky. A tuft of dark hair hung below a green woolen cap, and a long scarf streamed out behind him. Once again the pendulum motion sent him skyward, then, giving gravity its due, he flew back the other way only to reappear seconds later.

Hand-knitted green mittens, matching the cap and scarf, enveloped the small hands wrapped tightly around the steel chains. As the swing changed course, his dark eyes closed against the motion, but a small smile played on the lips of seven-year-old Jack Sinclair, flying as high as his mother could push him. As she shifted her boots in the snow, the swish of the swing was interrupted by the crunch of ice crystals under her feet.

Brewster Community Park was filled with children and parents enjoying a mid-January thaw that was nothing short of glorious. A beguiling sun in the winter sky lured the hardy outside with the promise of more warmth than it could actually deliver. But its brightness elevated moods and broke the hold of cabin fever that had claimed the whole town for weeks. The large thermometer outside Lundberg Bank on First Street read thirty-four degrees—positively balmy after many days of subzero temperatures.

Mary Sinclair held the chains of the swing until it stopped, then helped Jack off the wooden seat. Several young mothers standing at the far end of the swing set occasionally glanced in Mary's direction as they talked quietly among themselves. Their children played boisterously together nearby—running in the snow, packing snowballs and hurling them at each other, squealing with the sheer freedom of being outside. Mary paid neither group any heed—her full attention was on her son as she took his mittened hand and walked him from the swing to the slide, then to the merry-go-round that groaned and creaked from the cold when she ran in circles to keep it moving. Jack smiled as he watched the world spin past, his face turned into the wind, the earflaps of his green wool cap flapping in the breeze. Mary laughed as she pulled the merry-go-round to a stop.

"Let's make snow angels," she said as she helped him down. She sat in the snow and gently pulled him onto the sugar-like crystals that covered the dormant winter grass.

"You lie there," she said, motioning with her hands as she lay down on her side next to him, "and move your arms and legs like this." She shifted his left arm and leg back and forth until he got the rhythm and began to move his right arm and leg in the same way.

She grinned at him. "Look at you. You're making wings." She plopped back on the snow and made her own snow angel.

Jack stilled beside her, staring straight above him as a cloud skimmed along on a wave of wind. Mother and son stayed motionless in the snow, ignoring the cold that seeped through their coats.

"It's so pretty," Mary said quietly, her eyes too on the sky. She watched her breath as she blew out a puff of air that quickly turned into its own tiny cloud in the cold, then evaporated into the atmosphere. *Like so many things in life—there one second, gone the next.*

She felt the chilly wind on her cheeks as it ruffled her long hair, the same color as her mother's, like dark cherrywood. It had escaped her own woolen hat and fanned out on the snow. In that moment, as she sat up and grabbed her son's hand, she felt like a young woman in love with life. She pulled Jack to his feet and smiled at him, laying a gloved finger on the tip of his nose. He smiled back, and she drew her finger up the bridge of his nose to his forehead, then traced a heart around his face.

"I . . . love . . . you." His eyes never left her face as she knelt to brush the snow from his jacket. Tiny diamond glints of ice sifted to the ground beneath them as she got to her feet and again slipped her hand around her son's.

"Let's go home where it's warm, Jack," she told him as a shadow passed over the park. She looked up to see the sky becoming an ambient winter blue dotted with heavy, wet clouds. The day had drifted toward evening when she wasn't looking, and she shivered at the dropping temperatures. She pushed up the sleeve of her coat to look at her watch. "We'd better get going," she told the boy, giving a little tug on his arm.

He went along compliantly—the two of them making their way back across the park as the shadows above broadened over the ground. It started to snow, the flakes big and fat as they swirled around, eventually settling on their shoulders and coating their hats and scarves with lacey patterns. But Mary's lightheartedness deserted her with each step that brought them closer to home.

"Watch your step, Jack. It's getting pretty slippery," she warned. Her hand tightened around his as they crossed a street in an industrial section of town. The new snow whirled around them in the wind, covering the streets and frozen ground. Her cheeks felt tight from the cold. "I think we'll have hot chocolate at home. Sound good?"

They made a turn from the street into an alleyway, a shortcut Mary didn't normally use but now welcomed in light of the weather. They moved past trash receptacles and double doors of corrugated metal. The two neared a large truck, where a man, the brim of his gray fedora catching the snow, prepared to lift the rear door of the vehicle. Metal screeched against metal, startling Mary at the jarring sound, but Jack didn't flinch. A stocky, barrel-chested man with neither cap nor jacket carried an upholstered ottoman from the delivery doors of the building to the now-open truck bay.

"This it, then?" the stocky man grunted as he hefted the ottoman to join several other pieces of furniture, protected by green felt moving blankets.

"For now, but we've gotta wait on a chair that won't be ready till seven-thirty," the other man answered as he rolled the metal door down with a bang. "We'll leave after that."

"*Seven-thirty!?* We're gonna be driving all night long now," the stocky man objected.

"Stop yer complaining. At least we got jobs," the man in the fedora shot back. He tipped his hat as Mary moved past with Jack.

"Afternoon, miss," he said, "and little mister." Mary nodded at him with a quick smile, and she hurried her son down the alley that put them just one street away from their own neighborhood.

By the time they had completed the shortcut and arrived at the front of their small house—no more than a cottage, really—on Cedar Avenue, the fresh snow had already covered the ground and made the old gray soot-marred drifts look white again. From the sidewalk, Mary could see a note tacked to the front entrance. At the door she pulled it off quickly, as she would a bandage stuck to her skin, and shoved the paper into her pocket while hurrying Jack into the house.

They stood on a rug near the front door while she helped Jack pull off his galoshes. She quickly toed off her overshoes and shrugged out of her coat, leaving her gloves on. He patiently stood motionless while she began to remove his cap, scarf, and mittens—and then she realized she was shivering.

"It's nearly as cold in here as it is outside," she said with a shake of her head, hurrying Jack back into his outerwear. "We'll keep our coats on awhile." She slipped back into her own wrap and went to a thermostat on the wall, where she could see the mercury stuck way too low under the hard plastic. She gave it a firm rap with her knuckles, the noise muted by her gloves, and was rewarded with a weak sound from below as the gas furnace kicked on.

"Crummy old furnace," she grumbled. "I'll be battling you all night just to keep you going." She led Jack into the kitchen and seated him at the small Formica-topped table with a pile of wooden blocks. "Here you go, Jack," she said, leaning down to catch his eye. She saw a spark of interest as she placed one block on top of another. "Do it just like I showed you before." She took his hand and curled his fingers around a block—then lifted it to help him stack it on another block. "See there. You did it." She watched as he moved by rote, grabbing another block and stacking it on the first two. Though never sure if or when he might follow her lead, she now smiled her satisfaction and made her way to the Frigidaire to pull out a bottle of milk.

Most days, Mary wished for simple conversation, but she settled for music. She clicked on the Philco on the counter, and immediately the strains of Bing Crosby singing "Pennies from Heaven" filled the small room. While she heated milk on the stove, she put a few squares of a Hershey's candy bar on a plate near the burner, which quickly pooled into a melted puddle. She mixed the milk and melted chocolate into two mugs. Putting one of them in front of Jack, she sat down with her own and felt the paper crinkle in her coat pocket. She sighed, pulled it out, and smoothed it against the table.

She rubbed at her forehead, feeling the lines furrowed there. "Just read it," she chided herself aloud. "Waiting won't change the words. Pick it up and get on with it!" She snatched up the note and read the message—twice. She shook her head slowly, the rush of uncertainty and fear she'd been battling for months attacking with renewed vigor.

"What are we going to do? What?" Preoccupied,

it took her a few moments to realize Jack wasn't drinking his hot chocolate but was holding on to the tip of his tongue. With a pang, she reached for his mug and took a tentative sip.

She quickly jerked it away from her mouth. "Oh, buddy, I'm sorry." She blew on the milk several times and took another sip before sliding the mug back to Jack. "It's okay now. Mommy's so sorry." Jack watched her a moment, then lifted it to his lips.

After a quick glance at the clock on the wall, she pushed back from the table.

"I'm sure it's just the two of us for supper again tonight," Mary said as she got to her feet. "So maybe we'll have tomato soup and cheese sandwiches. They're your favorites—right?" She ran her hand through Jack's dark hair and tipped his chin up to make sure he saw her smile before answering her own question. "Right."

The winter shadows of evening had draped themselves over the house, and it was still chilly in spite of the heroic efforts of the furnace. Having removed their coats and dressed them both in wool sweaters, Mary settled Jack on the sagging couch in the living room and tucked a blanket over his lap. She knew he'd be content to sit there beside her, and for the moment she didn't fight the way he seemed to retreat into himself, disappearing into his own mind to a place she didn't understand but nonetheless had learned to accept as a big part of who he was.

She curled a leg beneath her and sat down beside him, finally giving in to the nervous tension that had been building since she'd come home to find the note. She glanced at her watch and figured she had two or three hours to think of the least inflammatory way to start the conversation with her husband. His workdays recently had extended into long evenings, and most nights she was already in bed feigning sleep when he came home.

Jerry didn't like bad news; in fact, just the thought of having this conversation with him made her heart race. Somehow he would find a way to place the blame squarely on her shoulders. But taking the blame for all the things Jerry thought were wrong with his life didn't bother her anymore. She would gladly be the scapegoat as long as it kept his anger and frustration from being directed at their son. *That* was something she'd never allow Jack to experience.

Mary tried to think of the right way to tell Jerry about the note, how to phrase the news so he wouldn't get as mad as she was expecting. For a moment she longed for the Jerry she'd met years ago, when she worked at the Lakeside Theater. The tall, good-looking twenty-year-old had smiled tentatively the first time he'd come to her window to buy a ticket to the matinee showing of *The Iron*

*Mask.* The next day he was back and must have gotten up the nerve to ask her name when he bought another ticket. The third day he slid a quarter across the counter and said, "Mary me."

Her jaw dropped, and he offered a charming smile. "Mary, me need a ticket to *The Iron Mask.*"

It was a fast courtship, and though Mary was only sixteen, she knew she was completely in love with Jerry Sinclair.

"We're gonna have a great life, Mary," he'd promise when they would talk about the future. "I can sell rice to a Chinaman and snow to an Eskimo. I'll be the best salesman Minnesota has ever seen!"

"I know you will, Jerry."

"Tell me your dreams, and I'll make them all come true." He took her gloved hands in his own.

"I want a house of our own and a yard filled with children. Children who'll never know what it's like to be sent from one foster home to another. Children who will always feel loved and safe and will know we'll never leave them—no matter what," she said. "That's my dream."

Jerry had squeezed her hands and smiled. "That's it? That'll be a snap."

Mary believed him.

She had always found it both ironic and sweet that it was during a double-feature intermission one Saturday when Jerry leaned over to hand her a bag of popcorn.

"I want you to marry me," he said quietly.

She smiled. "I *want* to marry you."

Jerry looked down at the popcorn, and Mary followed his gaze to a gold chain lying across the top—a chain looped through a gold wedding band.

"I know you can't wear a ring on account of your hands—and the gloves," he said, his voice low. "But if you wear the ring around your neck, everyone will know you're mine."

The wedding was a quick affair at City Hall, and then ten months later—Jack. Baby Jack born on a stormy night in stormy circumstances.

"He's our little miracle boy, Mary," Jerry used to say, leaning over the tiny infant's cradle to watch him sleep. "He's going to be special someday. You mark my words. He's going to do great things."

Mary now reached for the chain around her neck and slowly lifted it from beneath her sweater. The gold of that wedding band seemed to have dulled over the years, though at one time it had been her most cherished possession. But it was at present simply a reminder of all that had gone wrong—the world shattered for Jerry—for both of them—while they stood in a doctor's office.

*"You were right to be concerned, Mrs. Sinclair. . . . He's profoundly deaf. . . .*

*"No effort at communication at all . . .*

*"Most likely a mute . . . other problems as well. Some kind of faulty connection in his brain . . . we*

*don't know why. Possibly due to the strange circumstances of his birth . . .*

*"Do you give him plenty of love? Spend enough time with him? Or maybe you've spent too much time with him—coddled him?*

*"There are facilities for people like this. The state can assume the burden. He'll never be able to lead a normal life. . . .*

*"To be frank—it's a complete mystery."*

It had been the beginning of the end of their marriage. While Mary fiercely nurtured and protected her son, Jerry withdrew. As her heart expanded with love for Jack, Jerry's seemed to harden. He stopped holding Jack's hand, stopped sitting with him or looking into his eyes. As far as Jerry was concerned, it was almost as if Jack had stopped existing. Jerry was a different man than the one she'd married.

*Or is he really different? Maybe I just saw what I wanted to see. . . .*

Outside the wind was howling, and there was something else. Mary heard an automobile engine—then two round orbs of light passed across the front window.

"He's home early," she whispered as she pulled Jack from the couch. "Sorry, buddy, but it's early to bed for you tonight." She led him across the small living room, and they stepped over the threshold of his bedroom just as the front door banged open. Even from the back of the house, she could hear Jerry blowing noisily on his fingers. She drew in a steadying breath, finished hurrying Jack under the covers, then materialized back in the living room.

"You're home early," Mary said, keeping her tone neutral.

Jerry stamped his feet and brushed the snow from the lapels of his overcoat as he looked over at her and smiled. "Yep." He took off his coat and folded it over his arm.

For a moment Mary was taken aback by his uncharacteristic smile. But she quickly recovered and moved across the room, her hand outstretched, to hang up the coat as she did every evening.

"I've got it." He brushed past her to the coat closet.

She dropped her arm, tugging the sleeves of her sweater over her gloves. As he strode across the threadbare rug, Jerry squared his shoulders in the neatly pressed blue suit and ran a hand over his already smooth hair.

"It's cold in here," he noted as he hung up the coat.

"I'm pretty sure it's the thermostat again," she said carefully. "It's still not working right. . . ." A pause. "Maybe you could take a look—"

"I'll warm up in a hot shower." He quickly closed the closet door.

"I'll have your supper ready by the time you're cleaned up—"

"Don't bother." He headed toward the bathroom. "I'm really only home to throw a few things into a suitcase."

"Suitcase? Where—?"

"A golden opportunity, Mary." He turned to face her from the hallway. "I got a lead on a company that's looking for a new insurance agent. I'm not wasting any time on this. Figure I'll head a hundred miles down the road and be the first rep there when they open their doors tomorrow morning."

"Another business trip?" she dared ask. "How . . . how long will you be gone?"

He shrugged. "Long as it takes."

"So things are good—with business, I mean?"

"Same as always." He loosened his tie and pulled it out of his collar. "I'm gonna take that shower now." He turned back toward the bathroom.

Mary walked toward him and pulled the note from her cardigan pocket. "Wait, Jerry," she said. "You need to see this."

He blew out a sigh. "I'm in a hurry, Mary. . . ." But he stopped and faced her again.

She held the piece of paper out to him. "We got another note from Mr. Carmichael. He's pretty steamed this time. He says we've got to come up with the past three months' rent, or he'll evict us in ten days."

"That old coot is full of hot air," Jerry scoffed.

"He's not going to toss out tenants he's had for six years."

"Yeah, I'm afraid he will," Mary said quietly. She looked again at the note trembling in her hand, then back at Jerry. "If things are okay at work, how come we can't pay the rent? Where are we going to live if he kicks us out? It's not just us, Jerry. We've got Jack to think about." She blinked quickly against threatening tears. Jerry hated it when she cried.

Jerry rolled his eyes. "Is there a single stupid minute when you're not thinking about him?" He swore at her. "Isn't it enough we've built our whole existence around a kid who doesn't show any more emotion than that chair over there? He's like that blasted thermostat—broken and useless."

Mary knew he was just getting warmed up. *Let it go, let it go. . . . Don't make him mad. . . .*

But she had to know. "Don't we have the money for the rent?" Her heart pounded at the confrontational sound of the question and what it might provoke.

"Quit worrying about it," he shot back. "I'll take care of it."

"But if we don't have the money . . . ?"

He marched down the hallway into the living room and threw a hand toward the front window. "If we didn't have the money, do you think I'd have been able to get *that?*"

Mary followed him and looked out . . . at a shiny blue Cadillac parked by the sidewalk.

"Whose car—?"

"I traded in our old Ford and picked up that baby for a song," he said easily.

"You bought a . . . a *new car?*" She was so shocked she couldn't keep the incredulity from her voice.

"How do you expect my clients to take me seriously if I'm driving around in an old heap? What does that say about Jerry Sinclair? That he can't even afford a decent vehicle. You gotta spend money to make money. Besides, the old car was always breaking down. You don't want me out on the highway in something that's unreliable, do you?"

Jerry stepped out of his black wing tips, wiped at a few wet spots from the snow, and crossed the room to place them carefully by the front door.

"I can't believe you bought a new car when we—"

He moved back to the hallway and the bathroom, waving a dismissive hand around the simple room and worn furnishings. "I'm tired of settling, Mary—and for what?" He shook his head. "Besides, I don't have time to talk about this right now. I need a shower before I leave. I hope you haven't used up all the hot water bathing Jack."

"It was too cold to give him a bath," she said

quietly, trying to hold her emotions in check. "That's why I was hoping you could take a look at the furnace. . . ."

"Don't start whining, Mary," he warned, finger pointing at her. "I'm in a good mood, and I hate it when you spoil my good mood." He whirled away from her to the bathroom and slammed the door.

Mary heard him start the shower and the familiar ping as the pipes in the walls expanded. She stood in the middle of the small living room, hands held stiffly at her sides.

She glanced once more out the window at the new car, then walked quickly to the closet and pulled out Jerry's overcoat. She felt inside the pockets, and her hand shook as she withdrew a set of papers folded neatly into thirds—along with a postcard. The picture on the front showed a man and woman, each pulling on opposite sides of a wedding band while the words above proclaimed *Six Weeks in Nevada! Divorce Court Made Easy.*

Now her whole body trembled as she turned the postcard over to read words written in a confident feminine script: *If you want me—here's the answer. AJ.* It only took a second for her to open the papers and realize they were legal documents petitioning for divorce. "AJ" had even helpfully filled in some of the blanks.

Her stunned mind raced with the revelation and all it meant for her—and Jack. She shoved the papers back into the coat pocket and forced herself to check the other one. The white envelope was fat and heavy, and when she opened the flap, Mary was staring at more cash than she'd ever seen in her entire life.

Mary was sitting on the edge of the sofa when she heard the shower stop. It was still cold in the room, and her cardigan did little to ward off the chill, though she hardly noticed it now. Jerry was whistling some tune behind the bathroom door. "The only good thing about having a deaf kid is I never have to be quiet," he'd told her once. "You could drop a bomb right next to him, and he'd never even notice it."

Mary's legs bounced nervously while she waited for her husband, but when he finally entered the room, she stilled her nerves with practiced skill and hoped her smile looked sincere. She didn't have to search for a compliment—he was dressed as meticulously as always.

"You look very nice, Jerry," she said, getting up from the couch and crossing the room toward him. Her sweater was missing some buttons, but it was easy to hold closed with her hands pressed into the pockets. She reminded herself to stand up a little straighter. She knew he hated it when she slouched.

"Jerry, I was wondering—"

"Gotta go." He moved to the closet door, opened it, and pulled out his coat in one fluid motion. She caught her bottom lip in her teeth and made herself move closer.

"Are you sure you have to go?" she asked in a hopeful tone, hoping to distract him. "We never get to spend much time . . . you know . . . alone together anymore."

He paused and raised his brows. "What are you saying?"

She dropped her gaze shyly and smiled. "I just mean that I . . . I miss you sometimes." Tentatively, she withdrew a hand from her pocket, her sleeve riding up, and reached over to take his.

She saw his eyes stare in surprise when he felt the bare skin of her hand on his. He yanked it away as if he'd been burned and looked down to see the red tips of her fingers barely visible under the sleeve of her sweater.

"Why did you do that? You never . . ." He stepped backward, shaking his hand as if trying to get rid of his repugnance.

Mary curled her fingers up under the sleeve and pushed her hand back into the sweater pocket. Her eyes filled with tears.

He shook his head. "Gotta go."

"You'll be back, though . . . won't you?" She kept her voice as even as she could. Anything that sounded plaintive usually triggered an outburst—or worse.

He drew his brows together as he plucked his

wool scarf from the radiator by the door. "What kind of a dumb question is that?" Without looking back, he stepped outside and closed the door firmly behind him.

# Chapter Three

MARY SAT FOR A FEW MINUTES on the sofa and stared at the closed door. A deep breath, then she stood and moved as quickly as she could, putting a few necessities for both of them into a small suitcase before waking her son. She had a fleeting moment of thankfulness that the house had been too cold to put Jack in his pajamas. He was still wearing his clothes and warm wool sweater as Mary bundled him into his jacket.

Her heart was fluttering like a bird escaping a cage while she wrestled Jack into his boots and pulled on her overshoes. She picked up the suitcase, scooped up Jack's hat and scarf she'd left to dry near the front door, and rushed out into the frigid night.

The streetlights along the road shone small amber circles on the snowy ground as Mary stepped off the front porch, took a quick look up and down the street, and hurried Jack down the sidewalk. Even in her rubber overshoes, she nearly fell twice on the icy pathway. Gulps of cold air burned her lungs, and she forced herself to slow down as she held tightly to Jack's hand.

*Jerry's long gone. We'll be okay . . . we'll be okay . . . we'll be okay* swirled round and round in her head.

And then she heard the revving of an engine a few blocks behind them. A frantic glance over her shoulder revealed a car sliding around a corner and coming to a halt in front of their house. With her heart sinking, she watched as Jerry yanked open the front door and disappeared into the house. She pulled Jack off the sidewalk. For once she was grateful he couldn't ask her any questions as they stepped behind a neighbor's house.

In the next silent space, she heard Jerry bellow her name.

"Mar-ree! You got something of mine! Get back here—now! I'm not kiddin' around. I'm counting to five. One . . . two . . ."

She could hear the hammering of her heart as she pulled Jack through adjacent backyards in a crouch. Jerry was still counting, his voice carrying through the quiet, cold night. A car door slammed, then the sound of the engine as it moved forward.

The two darted between neighboring houses from shadowed patch to shadowed patch. Several houses later, they crouched under a fir tree with broad, snow-covered branches near a detached garage. She could see two circles of light slowly advancing up the street toward her, then stopping in front of the house next door.

Mary watched in terror as Jerry left the motor

running and got out. He walked around to the front of the car and stood in the beam of the headlights, his silhouette rigid as he scanned the area. The moon had claimed its place for the night and shed ambient light on the yard, revealing new footprints pressed in the snow. Jerry put his hands on his hips and stepped out of the cylinder of light, becoming nothing but a dark shadow.

"Mary! Quit foolin' around and come home with me," he called as she saw him start to follow the footprints. He obviously was making the attempt to sound conciliatory. "C'mon, honey, this is crazy. I know you're confused 'bout the stuff you found in my coat. Let's go on home and talk about it before poor Jack catches his death of cold out here."

Quietly Mary inched her way with Jack and the suitcase toward the back of the house, fervently hoping there wasn't a watchdog that might give her away.

"You there!" A man's voice bellowed from the front of the house. "What're ya doin' in my yard?"

Her heart nearly stopped till she heard Jerry's smooth answer. "I'm just out looking for my dog. Confounded animal got out, and wouldn't ya know, my son is crazy for the mutt. If I could just look around in the back—"

"I don't give nobody run o' my yard—not dog or man," the man said with finality.

"I'm not looking to stake a claim. Just want to find my dog!" Jerry snapped.

Mary recognized the change in Jerry's voice. He'd gone from a reasonable tone to an irritation he couldn't hide.

Jack sneezed. Any hope of a stealthy escape dissipated with it. She grabbed him up and ran as fast as she could toward the next backyard, suitcase bumping awkwardly against her legs. She heard Jerry's stream of curses and the old man's reprimand about language—and then the car door slammed again. She ran through the last yard on the block and made a dash for the street. The added weight in her arms slowed her steps, but the adrenaline pumping through her veins gave her strength and purpose beyond any she had ever known.

She didn't know what direction to head—only that she had to run as if their lives depended on it. The consequences of Jerry catching them gave her another burst of strength. She couldn't—*wouldn't* let him lay a hand on Jack.

She slid and nearly fell again around an icy corner. But it was cloaked in welcome darkness, and she saw she was at the end of a long street of industrial businesses with loading zones out front. Mary's legs felt like Jell-O and her side ached. She set Jack back on his feet and tried to catch her breath. The street appeared to be deserted—*normal families are home eating their dinner together like they should be* flickered through her mind. She felt her lips turn up in a rueful grin. *Normal. What do I know about normal?*

Mary pulled Jack toward the first building they came to—Remington's Auto Body Shop. She tried the door, but it was locked. They ran to the next business just as two headlights rounded the corner at the end of the street. She jerked on the door of Beltway Tractors as the car started toward them. She waited, flat against the building, and watched as the car moved under a streetlamp. A blue Cadillac.

The Caddy stopped—engine idling, its driver no doubt taking stock of the street. Mary kept a firm hand on her son's shoulder as they pressed themselves into the shadows and waited to see what Jerry would do. After a moment he started to back up—away from them.

Her relief was short-lived.

"Hey, lady! Lady!" Her head snapped around as she looked toward a man in a worn-out overcoat. He carried a brown bag that barely concealed a bottle of whiskey and staggered toward them through a golden puddle of streetlight as if he were wading through butter. "Can ya spare a few bucks for a fella down on his luck?"

Mary vigorously shook her head and glanced back toward the Cadillac still backing up. "No, please go away," she said as urgently as she could manage.

"C'mon, lady. Even two bits'll help," the man slurred ingratiatingly.

She moved her gaze off the Cadillac. "Leave us alone! Please—I don't—"

And then the revved-up pitch of the car's engine as it made a fast U-turn—and she knew Jerry had spotted them. She reacted in an instant. Holding fast to Jack's hand she sprinted on.

*Don't look—just run—run—run!* But she couldn't help herself, and she turned to see the headlights heading straight at them, relentlessly pinning them in Jerry's sights against the street ahead. *No, no, no, no, no, no!*

Frantically she looked right, then left, and realized they were only steps away from the shortcut they'd used earlier that day. Adrenaline once more screamed through her body, and she pulled Jack with her as she scrambled into the alley behind the buildings. The brake lights cast an eerie red glow as the car fishtailed over the icy street, the tires spinning before the vehicle was under control.

It seemed heaven-sent; the big truck she'd seen earlier that day was still parked halfway down the alley. The back end was wide open to the night and to anyone who might want to clamber inside and hide in the depths of the furniture shrouded in blankets and shadows. There was no sign of the men who'd casually greeted her that afternoon, so she pushed Jack up inside, threw the suitcase behind him, and climbed in herself, all the while listening for the Cadillac and the angry tone of Jerry's voice.

She knew he wouldn't give up easily, knew he was out there searching the streets even as she practically dragged Jack past the maze of furniture toward the wall that abutted the cab of the truck. She set down the suitcase and lifted one of the moving blankets from a settee, then sank into the cushions of an oversized chair and pulled Jack onto her lap. She billowed out the blanket—like a sheet over a bed—and let the weight of the material conceal them both.

She barely had time to get her ragged, spent breath evened out before she heard the sound of Jerry's velvety smooth voice.

"Mary? Are you in here?"

The blanket plastered itself to her face when she pulled in a heart-stopping breath.

"Come on now, hon . . . I just want to put this whole ugly misunderstanding behind us. That money is for the rent. I'm taking care of that tomorrow."

She felt the truck shift and knew he had climbed inside. His voice grew quieter but sounded just as soothing. "Mary? I'm not mad—really. I know we both want to make sure Jack has a place that's safe and warm—right?" The soles of his shoes scraped like sandpaper over the accumulated dirt and grit on the metal floor.

Her heart was pounding so loud she was sure he

could hear it, but Mary remained motionless with her son under the blanket. She had no idea what Jack understood of their situation, but for once she was grateful for the long spaces of time when he was as still and quiet as a granite statue.

She heard Jerry heave what sounded like a long, frustrated sigh, then an expletive followed. "Where *are* you?" he muttered.

"You wanna take the first shift—or should I?" A man's voice carried loudly through the walls of the truck.

"I'll do it," another voice answered.

"Okay, let's load 'er up and get going," the first one said.

Mary heard the men grunt and then another shift in the truck as something heavy settled on the metal floor. *"The chair won't be ready till seven-thirty . . ."* she remembered from the afternoon.

"Okay, lock it up," one of the men yelled. The metal door rolled down into place with a thud. Mary peeled back the edge of the blanket and peered out, seeing nothing but inky blackness. She hugged Jack a little closer and hoped he couldn't feel her tremble as she heard the doors to the truck cab open and then slam closed. She didn't even realize she was holding her breath, but when the engine started, she slowly exhaled. *Jerry must have gotten out—somehow he got out before they saw him. . . .*

"Okay, Mary—last chance," Jerry's disembodied voice slipped out of nowhere. She swallowed down the scream in her throat and pressed herself farther back into the cushion of the chair. "If you're in here, you'd be better off telling me than letting me find you."

*Quiet, quiet, quiet . . . don't move. Don't breathe . . . don't blink. . . .*

The truck slowly started to move, and Jerry's curses began somewhere to her left. "I don't need to see to find you in here, Mary," he said with a chuckle that frightened her more than his words, making the hair on the back of her neck stand up.

"*I* can't see, *Jack* can't hear—*you* obviously can't think straight or you wouldn't be running away. We're quite the family—aren't we?"

She could hear him cursing when he lost his balance with the truck's movement and an elbow or shin connected with the furniture. Slapping at the blankets, sweeping his hand over some piece, knocking his fist on a table—the shuffle of his feet grew louder as he moved toward the cab of the truck.

"This is crazy," he hissed into the air. "Completely nuts. I hope for your sake you're not in here or you'll regret it. You—will—regret—it." Each word felt like a hammer blow against Mary's thudding heart.

Mary could tell by the sounds in the dark truck that Jerry . . . *closer* . . . was going through the space systematically—moving blankets . . . *closer*

. . . poking at furniture, narrowing down the search . . . *closer* . . . one square foot at a time. And then she could smell his cologne. He was so close now she felt the air around her move as his hand flailed about to connect with something. It slapped down on the back of the chair just a hairsbreadth from her shoulder. *Too close! Too close! Bend down.* . . . She curled herself over Jack just as Jerry's hand again swept through the air above their hiding place. Then the truck suddenly braked, and she heard Jerry crash against something to a long string of expletives. She tightened her hold on Jack as she heard Jerry scrambling to his feet.

"What kind of bloomin' idiot parks his car across the end of an alley?" The voice carried clearly from the cab through the walls of the truck.

At the blare of the horn, Mary jumped.

"Move!" she heard the driver yelling. "Move the durn car!"

Jerry was still, and it was completely silent in the back of the truck. The total quiet, the lack of movement nearly undid Mary—he could be standing an inch from her, and she'd never know from under the blanket.

"Honk again!"

"I think I'll just ram it," the driver said. "That'll move 'im."

"Hang on—" the other man cut in. "I'll go talk with the guy." The cab door opened, then slammed.

"Hey!" she heard the man yell. "There's no one in the car!"

"We got a ten-hour drive ahead of us! Move the stupid thing!"

Jerry swore again, his voice startling her. *Way too close.* Suddenly he was banging on the tailgate of the truck, pounding on the sides—kicking out at the latch.

"Open up! Open up!" Jerry yelled.

The door started to roll up, and Mary pulled the blanket tighter and scrunched down as far as she could with her arms wrapped securely around Jack. Though it had seemed like forever, it couldn't have been more than a few minutes since they'd climbed into the truck, but Jack hadn't moved a muscle.

"Who the blazes are you?" Mary heard one of the men demand. "And what are you doin' in there? You a stowaway?"

"That's my Cadillac, moron. Why would I need to stow away?"

"Well, now, *that* makes sense," he answered, sarcasm dripping. Then, "Hey, Herb! Call the cops! I think we got us a thief in here."

"I'm no thief either," Jerry said quickly. "I was looking for my handicapped kid. Thought he mighta climbed in here—he's deaf and dumb."

"That right? Then I guess the nut don't fall too far from the tree, mister. You're not deaf—but you're sure 'nough dumb. Now, get outta my truck!"

"Fine," Jerry snapped. "I've searched the truck, and he's not in here anyway."

"Imagine that? Some kid doesn't want to climb into a dark truck in the freezing cold? I'm stunned. Now, you gonna move your car, or do we let a tow truck do the honors?"

"I'm going," Jerry rasped.

Though she couldn't see Jerry leave, Mary could *feel* just the tiniest of shudders as he leapt off the back end.

"That was weird," she heard one of them say. "Didn't you think that was weird, Herb?"

"I think I'm cold, and I wanna get on the road," Herb grumped. Mary pulled back the corner of the blanket in time to see the car's brake lights disappearing around a corner.

"Lock it up. *Again.*"

The door rumbled down for a second time. This time the darkness was like another blanket—a welcome, comforting relief. She hugged Jack tightly to her breast and kissed his cheek. Her beloved son was safe in her lap. Jerry was on the other side of a locked door, hopefully well on his way to wherever he was going, and she had the money. As the truck swayed its way out of the alley, she had no idea where they were headed—but she was sure it would be better than where they'd been.

# Chapter Four

SHE STRUGGLED TO OPEN HER EYES against the bright light. A man was silhouetted against a backdrop of sunshine. Trembling from the cold, Mary squinted to try and make out his face, her heart pounding as she tightened her arms around Jack's body.

Another man, this one in a fedora, came into view and slapped the first one on the back. "Hate these night runs," he said. "Takes everything I got to stay awake."

"You were snoring pretty darn loud for a guy who was awake," the other man replied. "Good thing *I* was driving the last hundred miles."

"That wasn't me. The transmission on this old crate rumbled pretty good." He chuckled as he reached to grab the leg of the chair nearest the door. "Let's get this thing unloaded, and I'll treat ya to some hot cakes."

Everything came rushing back in a blur. Running from Jerry the night before, hiding in the truck—the long ride in the cold, dark space.

The men hefted the chair out to the ground, and Mary watched carefully until they'd disappeared from view. She grabbed the suitcase and hurried Jack between furniture to the wide-open end of the truck. She jumped down, turned to swing her son into her arms, and paused only a moment to look around at their new life.

• • •

Hugging the corner of a brick building, body rigid with nerves, Mary looked over the area near the truck that had carried them away from their small town. She kept a hand on Jack at all times while she scanned about for Jerry or his blue Cadillac. But after only a few minutes she felt herself relaxing just a little.

"You know what I think, Jack?" she said softly into the cold air. "I don't think your dad followed us. I think if he believed we were in that truck, he wouldn't have gotten off without his money."

With the thought of the money, she shoved her hand into her pocket and felt the envelope of cash with a rush of relief. It wasn't all a dream—it was real. She'd left her husband. Left a man who over the years had proven time and time again that he didn't care about anything or anyone—except himself. She'd left a man who only last week had proven he would strike his only child when frustrated if she hadn't been there to stop him. Jerry had been planning to leave them penniless, leave them without a roof over their heads or even a means of provision. *But I left before he could do that to us. . . .* Mary knelt in front of Jack so he could see right into her eyes, and she smiled. "We're going to be okay, buddy. From now on, everything is going to be okay."

She slowly came to her feet. The enormity of what she'd done was gradually becoming real.

She stood there amazed at her own courage—and uncharacteristic good luck. All the things that had unfolded, one on top of another, to get her to this place. If the weather hadn't turned cold, she never would have taken the shortcut through the alley and seen the truck. *Was that a conscious thing or was something else leading me to that spot? And having our sweaters on because of the old furnace . . . ?*

She shook her head at her own reflections— knowing in her heart that it *had* to be luck because it *couldn't* be God. She was sure He'd written her off years ago, was ashamed of her on so many levels. *I was due for a break—that's all. Finally it was my turn for some good luck. . . .*

A blast of cold wind sliced through her coat and pulled her back from her ruminations. Jack shivered against her, and she wrapped her arms around him as she looked beyond the truck to once more take in their surroundings.

*Jerry's not the only one who doesn't know where we are,* she told herself as she watched two more trucks pull into what looked to be a warehouse district. She looked up at the building where they stood, noting it was over ten stories high. The clamor from the city seeped into her consciousness—a train whistle blasting in the distance against a background din of cars, trucks, and horns. Another gust of icy air sliced across her cheeks, and she knew they needed to get to someplace warm. *"Hot cakes are on me. . . ."* Her own stomach was growling, and she was sure Jack must be hungry.

Mary took one more careful look around, then stepped away from the building. "C'mon, sweetie, there must be at least a couple diners in this town," she said, snugging his mittened hand into her own. They moved around the building and down an alley, and then stepped onto a sidewalk parallel to a busy street. *Make that hundreds of diners in this city,* she corrected herself as they blended into the flow of pedestrians and moved along with the tide. In spite of the cold—and the unknown—she felt a ripple of excitement. All the years of waiting and watching and gauging Jerry's moods, trying to anticipate his next one so it wouldn't include those humiliating slaps, saving pennies at a time in case she and Jack needed to escape—but inevitably having to spend the money for food, heat, or a doctor's visit.

Now, somehow, she'd managed to turn the tables. *Jerry's escape money turned into our escape money,* she told herself. The irony hit her squarely between the eyes, and she laughed out loud on the crowded sidewalk. *For once I did something to make things change!*

# Chapter Five

## *Chicago, Illinois*

"YOU KNOW WHAT'S BEST about today, Jack?" Mary asked as she stirred the last stubborn bit of a Hershey's bar until it too melted into the pan of chocolate on the hot plate. "The best thing about today is that we've got each other." She turned from her task, standing at the end of a long bureau, and looked across the small room at her son. Jack stood with his eyes fixed on rows of tiny pink roses that ran up and down the wallpaper.

"In all of Chicago, I'll bet there's not one other mother with a son like you and not one other boy who has a mother like me. That makes us unique, little man. It makes us special."

She poured the chocolate into a mug she'd already filled with milk and stirred it together. "Now we just have to get someone else to *see* that we're special. We have to get someone to figure out that Mary Godwin and son will be a help to their business." She'd already decided that anything she signed, any time she had to write her name—or Jack's—that she'd use her maiden name. No more Mary Sinclair. She was gone—and good riddance. She carried the mug over to a small, low table, then went to Jack and held his shoulder to turn him from the wall. Bending so she could see right into his eyes, she smiled as she touched the tip of his nose, ran her gloved finger up the bridge, and formed a heart around his face.

"I . . . love . . . you . . . little man."

She waited for that spark of recognition that she practically lived for. *And there it is.* The clouds in Jack's eyes cleared long enough for him to return his mother's smile. Her own widened in response.

"Hey, buddy, *there* you are," she said softly. All too soon Jack's smile receded, and she led him to the only chair in their rented room at Etta Cassidy's Rooming House and gently pushed until he was sitting down in front of his favorite treat.

"Of course another best part of today is that we've got heat," she said lightly, reveling in the fact that she didn't need to wear a sweater. "Warmth is good."

She crossed back to the bureau to turn off the hot plate she'd also rented from Etta Cassidy. Just the thought of the landlady made Mary smile. She looked like a sweet old woman—but Mary had quickly learned that Etta had more than her share of business sense and knew how to turn a profit when half the country was barely surviving. It had only been five days since she and Jack had climbed the front steps of number twelve and a half on Shady Oak Drive—a blue two-story clapboard house with a shingled roof and enough birdhouses around the yard to start an aviary. It was Etta Cassidy herself who had answered the ring of the bell—and she'd done so with a scowl on her face.

"I don't buy from traveling salesmen—or women," Etta had said curtly.

"I'm not selling anything," Mary told her.

"You got a suitcase in your hand," Etta observed. "No books or periodicals or kitchen utensils I don't want in there?"

Mary shook her head. "No. Just our clothes. I'm supposed to say that Melly sent me."

Etta's nearly white eyebrows lifted. "You friends of Melly's?"

"More like customers," Mary admitted. "We met her in Hank's Diner this morning."

"That's how I know her." Etta nodded. "Good little waitress. Always brings my coffee hot and my club sandwich sliced without the crust."

"She told me you might have a room to rent. . . ." Mary tried to keep her voice steady.

Etta's eyes narrowed. "You in any kind of trouble?"

Mary shook her head. "No. We really just need a place to stay right now."

"You got a job?"

"Not yet, but I plan to start looking immediately."

"You might still be looking six months from now. How do you plan to pay for a room?"

"I have a nest egg to see me through several months."

Etta digested that information, then cut her eyes to Jack. "Well, I'd take you on in a minute, but I don't rent to anyone with kids. Too much mess and too much noise."

"Jack isn't like that, ma'am. He can't—he isn't able to hear. And he's never said a word. Not even a peep—didn't even cry as a baby. I promise he won't make any kind of noise or mess. He's a very good—"

"Huh. Never met a deaf-mute before. He *looks* normal." She was staring at Jack, who was staring at something behind the woman.

Mary let the comment go. "How much is the room?"

Etta took a minute to answer, her eyes still on Jack. Finally she gave her attention back to Mary. "Two dollars a week—payable in advance," she said. "You got any linens?"

"No, I wasn't—"

"Sheets, blankets, and pillows are fifty cents extra a week," Etta added, "but for that price you get them laundered on Saturdays."

"Fine."

"I don't allow hot plates in the room—unless they belong to me," Etta went on.

"How much to rent the hot plate?"

Etta actually smiled. "You're a smart girl. It's another quarter on top of the two-fifty. Still interested?"

"I am if you'll throw in the hot plate."

"I'm already having to change my policy on account of the kid."

"Maybe so, but you'll only have to change it to 'no kids allowed unless he or she happens to be a deaf-mute.' "

"Got me there." Etta grinned a little as she eyed Jack once more. "You want a piece of candy, boy?"

Jack merely stared at her.

"Just checking." Etta's smile widened. "You're a pretty good salesman, young lady. Especially selling to someone who isn't usually buying."

Etta took them up to their room. Simple and clean, it held a brass bed, an oversized braided rug on the hardwood floor, and a bureau with a pitcher and basin for washing. Etta allowed limited use of her icebox in the kitchen on the first floor, she told Mary. "No charge to store your perishables."

The room was small but had a window with a view of an oak tree. The brass poles on the bed were tarnished, and the chenille bedspread was threadbare along the edges—but everything was spotless. And all theirs. A door with a lock, and an address Jerry didn't know.

"I've got three other boarders," Etta had explained. "I know them 'bout as well as I know you, so I wouldn't be leaving anything valuable lying around in your room. No sense tempting anyone in these hard times, if you get my drift. You'll rotate days for the bathtub—sign-up sheet is outside the door. Besides the no-kid rule—

which I've already broken for you—the one rule I'll never break is that you always have to pay for the room a week in advance. No rent money—no room—no exceptions."

Mary couldn't believe she'd been lucky enough to meet Melly that first morning they'd arrived in Chicago. Melly, a chatty waitress at the first diner they'd seen, who just happened to know a woman who happened to rent rooms within walking distance of the downtown area. While she'd been lucky to meet Melly and Etta, she still hadn't had any luck finding work.

While Jack sipped at his chocolate, Mary spread the classified ad section of the newspaper out over the bedspread and perused the job postings. In the past four days she'd been to sixteen different businesses—four calls a day had proven to be her limit. And Jack's. She had applied for various kinds of employment—waitressing, housekeeping, clerking. . . . She couldn't remember them all. But every place she went she heard the same thing. Sometimes the rejection was blunt; sometimes it was couched in sympathy.

*"Look, miss. I just can't hire you because I can't have you bringing your kid to work. It's not a place for children."*

*"Have you considered finding someplace to . . . to take your son? Just for a while. Just until you get on your feet? 'Cause if he wasn't in the picture, I'd hire you in a second."*

*"I need someone with experience . . ."* And no son, Mary had finished in her mind.

She also heard, *"Someone with at least a year of college . . ."*

*"Can you type sixty words a minute?"*

Mary smoothed the paper and ran her finger down the column. She couldn't help but be concerned that she hadn't found a job yet, but she was not desperate. The budget she'd made for herself was detailed—right down to the nine-cent loaf of bread she planned to buy once a week and the nickel every other week for a roll of Lifesavers for Jack. If she followed her plan, she would be able to last five months and twenty-seven days at Etta's rooming house. She'd escaped with more money than she'd ever had at one time. Three hundred and fifty dollars. A windfall. A boon. *A reason for Jerry to hunt me down and take it back if he could find me.* She frowned, then deliberately forced the thought from her mind. She was on a lucky streak, and today was the day she would find a job. She circled four different job listings that she thought were accessible by bus or on foot, then looked up at Jack. He had a thin ribbon of chocolate froth riding his upper lip. As it always did, the sight of Jack having a *normal little boy moment* lifted her heart just a bit.

"You know what I wish, Jack? I wish there was a hot chocolate factory in Chicago. I'd make it, and you could test it. We'd be a great team!"

• • •

Mary and Jack stepped out of the Chicago Laundry and into the crisp winter air. It was the fourth business she'd been to that day—and the fourth rejection she'd had to endure. The fourth time someone had said no while looking at Jack.

*It doesn't matter—I'll find something. Something better—something that pays more and doesn't involve inhaling pieces of wet lint all day long.*

She snuggled the collar of Jack's coat around his neck and gave his shoulder a squeeze. "I didn't want that job anyway—did you? Who wants to iron clothes that you or I won't ever get to wear?"

She opened her pocketbook, moved aside a clean pair of white gloves, and dug for the roll of Lifesavers. "End of the search for today, buddy." She grabbed the candy and peeled a red circle from the end. "You want a piece?"

She looked down at Jack, but he was completely focused on something else—neck craned back as far as it would go, eyes on the top of a tall building across the street. She waved the red Lifesaver in front of his eyes, but he didn't blink—didn't move—didn't show any interest at all. She followed his sight line and thought she could tell what was captivating him; on the roof of the building she could see people—small figures looking down on the world. The way his mind worked fascinated her. What captured his attention, made him do something different, something she thought of as inspired.

"Let's go see," she said aloud, then folded her hand over his and gently tugged. He went along docilely, as he always did—but he kept his head tipped back and his eyes on the roof until they were inside the Babcock Towers.

The observatory was on the roof—right above the thirtieth floor.

"It's ten cents for you to go out onto the obser-vatory floor," the elevator operator told them, "and kids are free."

Mary opened the silver clasp of her pocketbook and withdrew a dime from her coin purse. A splurge to be sure—*but worth it if it makes Jack happy*, she thought as she carefully snapped the clasp shut and looped the pocketbook back over her arm. When they stepped off the elevator, they walked right out to the island in the sky. It was the highest she'd ever been in her life, and she felt a little queasy as she led Jack to the middle of the rooftop, then waited to regain her sea legs before venturing farther. A four-foot-tall barrier ran along the edge of the roof. The intricate pattern of iron latticework hung about a foot in the air between steel posts and looked as if someone had put one pretty garden gate after another on the edge of the world. Jack stepped closer to the latticework until the tips of his shoes stuck out under the steel.

Mary was right behind him and peered down at the spectacular view: cars, people—she could even see a park in the distance.

"Oh, Jack! Look how beautiful it is up here—no wonder you wanted to do this!"

The wind had picked up, and Jack turned his face right into it and smiled—he loved the wind, but Mary felt a little unnerved. She could have sworn the building swayed just a bit as they stood there. Jack reached out to grab the top of the barrier and rose up on his toes to look over. "All right, buddy, that's high enough," she cautioned.

"It *is* a long ways down, isn't it?" But as she said it, she realized Jack wasn't looking at the ground—rather he was staring at a flagpole jutting out below them perpendicular to the building. It was filled with pigeons, and Jack was actually smiling at them. She watched him for a moment, saw the animation in his eyes as he watched the birds. The moment lasted long enough to fill her with gratitude that they could share it. Finally, he glanced away, his eyes caught by something else. She grinned down at the birds.

"Crazy birds. Don't you know you're supposed to fly south, where it's warm?" she said.

And then a child's voice, "Mommy! Mommy! Look at me!"

Mary dropped her hands from Jack's shoulder to turn a half circle toward a little girl running full speed toward the barrier on the adjoining side of the roof. Even though she knew the ironwork would stop her, Mary's heart clutched as the mother of the little girl ran right after her. "Stop right now, Carol Ann!" she shouted. "You stop right now!"

*Imagine being able to call to your child when there's danger and know she hears you,* Mary thought as the little girl suddenly stopped just inches from the edge.

Her mom by now had caught up to the girl and grabbed her, shaking a finger in her face. "Don't ever do that again!" Several people had stopped to watch, and Mary saw their relieved smiles when the little girl apologized contritely to her anxious mother.

Her own smile in place, Mary turned back to Jack, and her heart lurched to a stop. He stood with the toes of his shoes wedged into the lattice-work of the barrier and was now waist-high over the iron.

"Jack! Get down!" She thrust both arms out to wrap them around his waist—and remembered too late that her pocketbook had been hanging on her forearm. It slipped off—and out into space. She snatched Jack off the barrier and, with her arms still wrapped around him, looked over the side just as the small dot that was her pocketbook crashed to the sidewalk below. *All our money! No, no, no . . .*

She grabbed Jack's hand and dashed for the elevator—but it was between runs.

"Hurry, hurry, hurry . . ." she mouthed—maybe even said the words out loud. She didn't care. The doors to the elevator finally opened after what seemed like hours of waiting, and she rushed inside.

"Down—please, we need to get down. Hurry!"

"There's just one speed, ma'am. Can't do any better than that," the elevator operator said patiently. He stepped outside the elevator and looked around. "Anybody else going down?"

"*Please,* can you just get it started down," Mary pleaded. "I dropped my pocketbook over the side of the building. . . ."

He stepped back inside, hit the button for the lobby, and glanced at her with a sympathetic expression. "You got any money inside?"

She nodded, feeling sick to her stomach. "Quite a lot."

"Hmmm, not good."

"Maybe it'll still be there," she said.

He shook his head. "Desperate times—you know?"

She did know, even as she prayed to someone, anyone, that her times weren't about to get a lot more desperate. *Let it be there. Just let it still be there. . . .*

She shoved her way between the elevator doors before they even opened all the way and dragged Jack with her, sprinting through the lobby and out onto the street. She wound her way through the foot traffic on the sidewalk and then couldn't believe her eyes when she spotted her black pocketbook lying in the gutter next to the sidewalk.

In seconds she had scooped it up. The silver clasp had come undone, the old leather was scuffed and dirty, but otherwise it was intact. With shaking hands she opened the bag and looked inside—gloves, Lifesavers, photo of Jack, bus pass for the rest of the week. She bit her lip and tried to stop the tears welling in her eyes when she realized the envelope with the money was gone.

*"Desperate times—you know?"*

# Chapter Six

MARY AND JACK STOOD at the bottom of the steps of the blue house, their small suitcase between them. The day was cold and gray and the sky looked like snow. She tried to smile at Etta Cassidy, who stood in the open doorway shaking her head in frustration.

"I wish I didn't have to do this, Mary," she said sincerely.

"You've already let us stay three days longer than I've paid for, Etta."

"I wish I woulda told you to keep your money in the bank," Etta grumped to herself.

"Probably wouldn't have listened." Mary forced another smile. "Jerry—well, I was always told not to trust banks."

Etta sighed. "You know I'd let you stay if I could. But I just can't afford to let you have the room for free—my brother needs round-the-clock nursing, and that costs a heck of a lot of money. And since I got another boarder who can move in right away . . ."

Mary felt her chin start to tremble, but she didn't want to cry. "I know, Etta. It's okay."

"If you find yourself employed, and if I've got an extra room again . . ."

Mary nodded. "I'll check back with you."

"Don't forget what I told you about getting Sally Ann benefits," Etta added. "I'm pretty sure the place is over on Eighth."

"Thanks. I'll try there."

Etta hesitated. "This world stinks, don't it?"

Mary swallowed hard, nodding silent agreement. Another wobbly smile and she picked up the suitcase, took Jack's hand, and never went back to number twelve and a half Shady Oak Drive.

A tattered-looking line of people stood in front of a door that proclaimed The Salvation Army— Soldiers of Christ. Mary didn't know where the term "Sally Ann benefits" came from—and right now she didn't care. She had sold her wedding ring for two dollars the day she lost her money, but that was already gone. Now what she needed was a warm place to spend the night and some food for Jack. They took their place in line behind a shivering older man wearing nothing but a thin cotton shirt and pants. Mary could hear his teeth chattering, and she couldn't help but shrink back from the sound.

As the sun slipped toward the horizon, the door opened and a woman in a long navy skirt and high-necked tunic smiled at the line of people so clearly in need. Her hair was tucked under a plain navy blue bonnet, and the white-edged collar of her tunic was offset by shoulder epaulettes adorned with double silver bars.

"Please. Come inside," she offered with another warm smile. She stepped to the side and handed out a small ticket to every person who passed. Mary and Jack made their way through the door and the woman nodded, then held out two tickets, looking down at Jack with an expression Mary could not interpret.

"We serve supper next door about an hour from now," she said. "Stone soup and bread." She lowered her voice. "Don't wait too long, because we'll run out, and I wouldn't want your little boy to go hungry tonight."

Mary swallowed the lump in her throat and nodded her thanks. She remembered her mother putting a heated stone in the cooking pot to keep the soup warm. She squeezed Jack's hand in anticipation of a nourishing meal in his tummy. The woman leaned in a little closer. "I'd set up at the far end of the room, away from this door—it's warmest over there."

"Thanks," Mary managed.

"God bless you," the woman offered sincerely with another glance at Jack.

*Someone who truly cares . . .*

Mary took a moment to look around the room. It wasn't as large as she'd expected. The cots were scattered haphazardly against walls, into corners—any way the small space could be made as personal as possible for the twelve hours the cot would be someone's home. She took the woman's advice and led Jack across the room to the corner farthest from the door and staked her claim to two cots that she pushed together. There were blankets folded neatly on the ends of the cots, and she busied herself making up their beds, working her son's jacket from his small frame—anything to distract her from having to face the truth that they were homeless.

When the evening meal was behind them, Mary led Jack back to their cots and sat down on the edge. While Jack fastened his gaze on some point in space, Mary looked around the room filled with strangers. Besides those like her who needed a bed for the night, there were four people dressed in the distinctive uniform of the Salvation Army. *Okay, Sally Ann—it's Salvation Army.*

Mary watched as the woman who'd been so kind to her now approached one of the uniformed men. He smiled and looked at her in such a loving way that Mary felt an immediate stab of envy. *They're in love. Anyone can see that he adores her—and she trusts him completely.*

The woman brushed her hand over his jacket sleeve, letting it linger there for just a second, then moved on. Mary felt overwhelmed by loneliness. Not that she was lonely for Jerry. The only good thing about this particular evening was that he was out of their lives. She couldn't define the aching, hollow feeling in the pit of her stomach—she didn't know what it was or how to fix it.

"Excuse me?"

Mary looked up into the kind eyes of the same woman she'd been watching. A book was tucked against her waist and a cookie was in her outstretched hand.

"My name is Captain Grace Jamison," she offered.

"I'm Mary Sin—uh, Godwin, and this is my son, Jack."

Grace held out the cookie. "I thought maybe your little boy might want this."

"Oh. Thank you." Mary passed the cookie in front of Jack's eyes and he refocused. She placed the cookie into his hand, and he immediately took a big bite.

"Jack is very handsome," Grace said. "You must be so proud of him."

"I am."

Mary looked away toward the man she'd seen Grace talking to earlier. "Is the man dressed in uniform your husband?"

Grace followed her gaze. "Yes, for almost ten years now. Victor and I met when we were going through our ministerial training."

Mary was surprised. "You're both ministers?"

"All officers in the Salvation Army are ordained ministers," Grace explained. "When we join we dedicate our lives and service completely to God. In fact, marriage is permitted only within the ranks."

"And children—do they, well, permit you to have those?"

"We may have children, but my husband and I don't have any. I . . . I am not able to, the doctor says." Grace's smile was now etched with a hint of pain. "But I still feel so blessed knowing in my heart that this is what I was meant to do."

Mary glanced at Jack and saw cookie crumbs all over his lower lip. She brushed her gloved hand gently across his mouth.

"Things are hard for so many people these days, as you well know," Grace said quietly. Mary nodded as she looked at several families scattered throughout the room.

"I'm not sure if you're aware of the places, besides ourselves, that offer assistance," Grace went on. "There are relief programs for some food such as milk—essentials. We can put you in touch with the right agencies."

Mary sighed. "All I want to do is find a job so I can continue doing what I was meant to do—care for, love, and protect my son."

"Jobs are pretty hard to come by," Grace noted, looking between her and the boy. "You've been out looking?"

"Every day now for nearly two weeks, but I've been turned away more times than I can count."

"Are they giving you a reason? Something that's stopping them from hiring you?"

Mary turned her eyes toward her son. "Usually it's Jack."

"Has he always been deaf?" Grace asked.

Mary nodded. "He's never heard or spoken a word his entire life."

"His father?"

Mary could only shake her head. Grace looked reflectively at Jack, as if she were assessing the situation.

"Would he benefit from school? Maybe a school for the deaf? There are places available—"

"No, he doesn't respond like other children who can't hear," Mary said. "And though it's been suggested a hundred times, I'll never put him in an institution."

Grace nodded in understanding. "So you need a job where they'll let you bring Jack with you to work."

"That's the problem."

"I can see where it could be. . . ."

Grace moved to kneel in front of the little boy and spoke quietly. "The world can be a cruel place for children like Jack." She turned and smiled at Mary. "That's why you need to keep fighting the good fight."

"I'll never stop."

Grace sat on the cot across from Mary. "I believe you. I believe you know how special he really is—that he's a gift, your silent gift from God."

For the first time in her entire life, Mary felt as if someone truly understood Jack, and her heart welled with a quick rush of gratitude toward this virtual stranger. Grace had managed to capture in just a few sentences exactly how Mary felt about her son. Her eyes filled with tears, and she blinked them back.

Grace reached over to lay a hand on Mary's knee. "The problem is getting someone else—just one person, one employer—to realize how special Jack is. To know they'd be fortunate just to be in his presence," Grace finished succinctly.

"Something I couldn't get even his own father to see." Mary sighed. "I'm out of ideas . . . out of answers."

Grace lifted the book she was holding and turned it so that Mary could see it was a Bible.

"Maybe your answer is in these pages." Grace held out the Bible toward Mary. "Please—take this as my gift to you."

Mary put her hands in her lap and shook her head. "Thank you, but I think you should give it to someone who will actually . . . well, open it."

Mary could see her answer had surprised Grace. That hadn't been her intent—she simply didn't want it.

"You won't open it, read it?"

"My mother read to me every night when I was little," Mary said. "Book after book—every chapter and verse."

"That sounds like a nice memory."

"It was."

"Then something happened . . . ?"

Mary glanced down at her hands in their cotton gloves. "I stopped wanting the words."

"What made you not want them anymore?"

Grace's voice was so gentle Mary didn't feel the woman was prying. "They caused too much pain," she answered, her voice low.

"How so?"

Mary hesitated, then looked over at Jack. "We've had a really long day, and I know he must be tired. I think I should get him into bed now."

"Of course," Grace said graciously. She put the Bible down on the end of Mary's cot. Mary thought she'd move on, but instead Grace reached over and took Jack's hand. She closed her eyes and began to pray aloud.

"I ask right now, Lord, that those who see little Jack here will see God. Those who touch him, come in contact with him, will realize that he is special. A gift. Amen."

Mary sat quietly while Grace opened her eyes and smiled warmly at Jack. "Good night, Jack." Then she turned to include Mary in her smile. "I can't believe the words in the Bible are responsible for causing your pain, Mary. They're life-giving truths that bring hope to the hopeless, life to the dead, significance to the meaningless. In Matthew, Jesus said, 'I thank thee, O Father, Lord of heaven and earth, because thou hast hid these things from the wise and prudent, and hast revealed them unto babes.' When I told you your son was special, I meant it." She rose and said kindly, "Good night, Mary."

"Good night."

Watching Grace move on to the next one in need of comfort, Mary got up with the intention of tucking Jack into bed. But almost as to a magnet, her eye was drawn to the Bible still lying on the end of her cot. She couldn't look away, couldn't seem to ignore the fact that it was there. *"I don't believe the words in the Bible are responsible for causing your pain, Mary."*

Mary, with Jack beside her, did not even feel the cold wooden bench beneath her as she sat in the nearly deserted park the following day. The morning stretched into afternoon. The cold, gray sky matched her mood after another fruitless day of searching for a job. She knew there were still hours left and that she should be moving on to the next possible job—the next diner looking for a dishwasher or a waitress, a hotel that needed a maid, or a store looking for a clerk. But she couldn't will herself to do it one more time, couldn't find the energy to tell her feet to get moving—just so one more person could shake his head at her, another could say no. She had no idea how long they'd been in the park—half an hour, an hour maybe? *What day is this? . . . don't think . . . need to wash our clothes—don't think . . . is it possible—don't think—not to think? . . . did I figure out what day this is? . . . I said, don't think . . .*

A brisk gust reminded her that she wasn't alone in her misery, and she glanced beside her. But Jack now sat in a nearby sandbox, dragging a stick back and forth. Though he always seemed oblivious to the weather, she knew he must be as cold as she was. She shook her head, disgusted at her own inability to provide for her son. They didn't have a door to walk through, a bathtub to bathe in, a kitchen where she could heat a warm cup of cocoa—let alone a bedroom they could sleep in and forget the world was such a hard place. Jack suddenly looked up at her—one of his clear moments—and she noticed his nose was running.

"Oh, sorry, buddy. Hold on a second." She crouched down beside the sandbox and opened the suitcase. "I've got something to wipe your nose." She rifled through its meager contents, moving aside her new Bible to pull out an extra white glove. She turned to wipe his nose, but Jack's attention was back on the sand. She followed his gaze.

"Looks like you're drawing a picture," she said as she studied the sand. She frowned. "Wait—not really a picture, is it? It looks more like . . ." She kneeled on the sand and stared at the pattern of the marks, cocking her head to the side. Jack turned and looked at her again, and she met his gaze. "Maybe I can help you finish?"

She moved closer beside him and put her hand over his on the stick. Together they traced the marks he'd already made, but with Mary's help the sand etchings became clearer, more defined. She stared at them, sitting back on her heels.

*They're numbers. Five, four, four, one, four? Five, four, four, one, four . . .*

"Get offa me!" a man yelled loudly from across the way.

Mary looked up from the sand to a scruffy-looking man wrestling with two police officers. The man's clothes were in tatters, and his arms were wrapped around a woman's handbag he had clutched to his chest.

"C'mon now, give it up," one of the cops ordered, yanking the handbag away from the man. He staggered backward, and even from Mary's vantage point, it was easy to see the man was drunk. "I'm hungry and I need money to eat! Is that a crime?"

The officers laughed. "Well, yeah, moron. It's called stealing."

"God help me, I haven't eaten in three days. What's a man to do? Tell me!"

As Mary watched the man, she felt a wave of panic that she might be witnessing her own future, her own desperation. *I can't let that happen—I can't!* She couldn't bear to watch as they pulled the man's hands behind his back to handcuff him. She turned her attention back to the sand, back to Jack's numbers. *Five, four, four, one, four.* She shifted her focus to her son, who was still watching her. She forced a smile she hoped looked reassuring and then glanced at her watch. She knew they needed to leave plenty of time to get back to the mission. Once the place was full, the doors were locked and didn't open again until the next morning. It was the only rule, Grace had told her, besides the fact that one could only stay three nights during a seven-day stretch. No exceptions. *We have tonight and tomorrow night and then . . . don't think about then. . . .*

"We've got to get back to the shelter, little buddy," she said urgently, reaching for the open suitcase behind them, where the black Bible lay prominently against the white background of one of Jack's shirts. She closed the suitcase, got to her feet, and helped Jack to his—then hurried past the officers as they led the handcuffed homeless man from the park.

"Grace!" Mary called.

Grace smiled as she made her way to their cots. "Mary . . . Jack. You made it back," she said. "Any luck?"

Mary shook her head. "No, I'm afraid not. But I've been waiting for a chance to ask you about something."

Grace sat down opposite Mary and Jack and smiled again when she saw the Bible in Mary's lap. "I'm so glad you decided to read it."

"You said I'd find answers," Mary told her, looking down at the open book.

"That's right, I did. It may take a little patience. . . ."

Mary leaned toward her. "I think I've already found an answer."

Grace raised her brows. "Really? That's wonderful."

"Something . . . remarkable—no, I think *miraculous*—happened today," she said. "And I need to be able to say it out loud to someone. Talk it through. Do you have time?"

"Of course. It's my turn to supervise tonight, so I'm here until tomorrow morning."

Mary nodded and tightened her grip on the Bible while she gathered her thoughts. "It's about Jack," she finally said. "He did something today when we were in the park."

"Really? What did he do?"

"I want . . . I want you to keep an open mind."

Grace smiled her agreement. "I believe I can do that, Mary."

"Remember when you prayed for Jack—that people would realize he's special?"

Grace nodded. "I remember."

Mary looked around to be sure they would not be overheard. Grace leaned toward her as Mary went on, "He *is* special, Grace. I've always known it—but today he did something that shows it. Proves it."

Grace shifted her eyes to Jack. "Tell me about it."

"Well, like I said, we were in the park—and I don't mind admitting I was pretty discouraged, so at first I wasn't paying much attention when he sat down in a sandbox and started dragging a stick through the sand. After a while, I noticed he wasn't just dragging the stick—he was actually making specific marks in the sand. At first I thought it was some kind of a drawing"—Mary's voice rose with her excitement—"but then when I put my hand over his on the stick and we traced the marks together, they became more clearly defined."

"What were they?"

"Numbers."

"And he doesn't usually write numbers?"

"He's never drawn or written anything before."

Grace beamed at the boy. "Wow. Good for you, Jack. That's really something!"

"He wrote five, four, four, one, and another four."

"That's impressive—very special."

"The specialness is not that he *wrote* the numbers—it's what the numbers mean," Mary said carefully.

Grace looked puzzled. "I'm afraid I don't understand. . . ."

"I started wondering if the numbers might be his way of communicating, so I started counting out the numbers using the alphabet as a guide—*A* would be one, *B* would be two, and so on. But it only spelled out gibberish—'eddad' or something."

"So what do you suppose Jack was trying to tell you with the numbers?"

"When we got back here and I opened our suitcase, he picked up the Bible. The only thing I could think of was that he wanted me to read to him—even though I knew he wouldn't hear a word. So I started to read every word, every number of every chapter, and every number of every verse. And that got me thinking about Jack's numbers again. Maybe the Bible had something to do with the numbers. I tried to combine his numbers—but there were too many for it to be just the chapter and verse. Then I started to count how many books are in the Bible, beginning with Genesis as book one and went all the way through—and that's when it occurred to me that maybe the first number or numbers were the book, then the chapter and the verse. So I've been working through all the different possibilities, and I finally came to this combination—the book of First Timothy is the fifty-fourth book in the Bible." Mary flipped to a page she had marked with a piece of paper. "Chapter four, verse fourteen: 'Neglect not the gift that is in thee, which was given thee by prophecy, with the laying on of the hands of the presbytery.'"

"So . . . what exactly are you saying?" Grace asked, her eyes on Jack.

"Last night you laid your hand on him and prayed."

"Yes . . . ?"

"I'm wondering if it's that Jack isn't special just to me, Grace. That he really is . . . special. You prayed that others would recognize it. Maybe they'll—well, they'll recognize it by his numbers. For Scripture passages . . ."

Grace smiled kindly. "That's a fascinating theory," she said. "Very intriguing, Mary."

"Time for lights-out, folks!" a man's voice called out over the quiet conversations in the room.

"Oh, it's getting late," Grace said as the overhead lights turned off. The room was dark except for a dim light illuminating the hallway that led to the two bathrooms.

"Can we pray?" Grace asked, reaching in the darkness for Jack's hands. Mary bowed her head, wondering what Grace was thinking about Jack's gift.

"Heavenly Father, I ask your blessing on Mary and Jack, and on Jack's special abilities—on his numbers, whatever this means. I pray that *all* of the chapters and verses in your Book will have great meaning in their lives. Amen."

"Mary? Time to get up now." The woman's voice was accompanied by a gentle shaking of her shoulder. Though the residue of sleep still made things fuzzy, Mary sat up quickly and looked into Grace's kind eyes.

"It happened again." Mary's voice sounded tentative even to her own ears. She reached for the Bible still next to her cot. "Last night . . . Jack's numbers. It . . . it happened right here in this room." She found the page she was looking for and looked up into Grace's face, trying to determine her openness. She held up the open book for Grace to see. "I was reading Proverbs and got a pencil from my pocketbook to underline a verse that has a special meaning to me. Then Jack—he put his hand on mine and started to move the pencil across the page."

Grace leaned forward and Mary pointed at numbers written in the margin. "Nine, one—twenty-seven?" Grace read aloud. "That kind of dispels your theory, doesn't it? I'm not exactly sure where the book of Proverbs falls, but I'm sure it's long after the ninth book—"

"Proverbs is book twenty," Mary explained, "but Jack wasn't writing numbers because of the page I was reading—he wrote these because of something he was seeing."

"Mary, I know Jack is special, but are you sure you have this right?" Grace's tone was gentle but puzzled.

"I'm pretty sure," Mary said. "Let me show you," and she thumbed through more pages. "The ninth book is First Samuel. I looked up the first chapter and the twenty-seventh verse." Mary then read aloud, " 'For this child I prayed; and the Lord hath given me my petition which I asked of him.' "

She looked up from the page at Grace. "No one but me ever touches Jack—but you have. Just last night. And now this." Mary held up the Bible. "I know *I'm* not pregnant"—she gave a little smile—"so I'm wondering . . . if maybe this is meant for you. . . ."

Grace's eyes filled with tears. "I told you the other night that it's not possible. So I don't know . . ."

"I'm not saying this to cause you any pain," Mary added quickly. "It's just that I really believe these numbers are something Jack saw and can't communicate to us any other way."

Grace took a long breath, wiping away the tears. "It's time now to get your things together."

"Just maybe . . . ?"

Grace shook her head. "I can't bear another disappointment, Mary. I know you mean well, but we both realize Jack's numbers could mean anything."

"That's true. But still I can't help but wonder . . ." She didn't finish when she saw the sorrow on Grace's face. "Anyway, I want to thank you for your kindness and for the Bible."

"You're welcome. God's blessing on you today. I'll be thinking of you both and praying you find a job."

# Chapter Seven

IT WAS CLOSE TO DUSK when Mary exited the Blue Moon Diner with Jack in hand and stopped on the street to get her bearings. *So close!* She'd been so close to having an actual job.

"Sure thing, young lady," the owner of the diner behind them had told her. "Got an opening for a waitress, and a looker like you might earn me some repeat customers." He chewed the end of a stubby cigar while she choked out the next bit of information that surely would send them packing. It always did.

"My son, Jack, doesn't go to school. He's deaf and can't speak. He'd need to come with me to work every day. I can't leave him. . . ."

The unlit cigar rode up and down on his lip while he chewed and took stock of Jack. "He's a good-looking kid. People like happy endings to hard-luck stories," he mused. Finally he shrugged. "I got no beef with you bringing your boy. Now— fill out these papers while I take care of a few customers. I'll be back to look 'em over and give you your schedule."

Speechless with relief, all Mary could do was nod. A little over an hour later, he passed a uniform across the counter. "Okay, honey," he said, "here's a blouse, a skirt, and an apron."

"I'll need to wear my gloves," Mary said as matter-of-factly as she could. And she told him why. The owner took back the uniform and wished her luck.

Standing outside the diner, Mary blinked back tears and tugged the glove of her right hand a little higher on her wrist. It hadn't been Jack this time—her own hands had been her undoing.

The weather had grown progressively colder throughout the long, frustrating day, and now they'd wasted so much time in the diner it would be a miracle if they made it back to the shelter before it was full for the night, the doors closed. She looked up at the street sign and realized they were several blocks away from the Salvation Army building.

The thought of Jack going without supper was hard, but the thought of trying to sleep on a park bench made her heart hammer in her chest. "C'mon, little man. We've got to run."

They arrived breathless—and she felt sick. The door was closed and the posted sign read, Sorry—Full for the Night. *"The doors are locked once we're filled to capacity. There are no exceptions—doors don't open again until seven a.m."*

"This can't happen," she whispered aloud. "I can't let this happen."

*Is Grace inside? Will she hear me and let us in?*

She raised her hand to knock on the door, but an old man sitting on the sidewalk, back propped against the building, waved listlessly at her.

"Don't bother," he said. "They won't answer."

"But I know someone inside. I know Captain Grace, and she—"

"It don't matter." This from a man sitting next to him. "You could know the pope himself, but they won't let you in. It's the daggone rules of the place."

"The rules aren't going to keep us warm tonight," Mary whispered, fighting tears. Jack slumped against her, and she put her arm around him to keep him on his feet.

"Ain't a good night to've missed it neither," the first man said as he spat a stream of tobacco juice on the sidewalk. "Some mighty fine smells comin' outta that kitchen tonight 'fore they closed the door. Real meat—not just some watery soup with a cabbage leaf in it. I heard someone call it a celebration meal 'cause they had some celebratin' news. Called it a real miracle. Everybody in them Sally Ann uniforms was grinnin' like Cheshire cats. Talkin' 'bout some 'boy prophet' who predicted the impossible—a baby or somethin'—and it's comin' true."

"Boy prophet?" Mary stared at the man.

"That there's the scuttlebutt." The man nodded sagely and went back to his own cogitations.

In a daze Mary took Jack's hand and led him back up the street. Her thoughts mulled over her conversation with Grace that morning. She glanced over her shoulder at the door to the Salvation Army. *A baby . . .*

"Maybe it's because of you, Jack, that they're eating meat tonight," she murmured. "You *are* special—and now maybe others are going to know it too."

Sleet came down in waves as Mary pulled Jack along the busy downtown streets. Her mind raced with worry about where they would spend the night—and finally she remembered a movie theater about a mile down the road. *If we can sneak into the lobby and then up into the balcony, maybe we can hide out until morning.* It would be warm—and safer than sleeping on the street. Her stomach ached from hunger, and she couldn't even bear to think about how Jack must be feeling. Wet, cold, and miserable, she pulled Jack into a storefront doorway. At least for a while they'd stay out of the sleet and hope for a break in the weather. *If misery was measured like money—we'd be rich.*

She looked down at Jack shivering against her, then out at the cars on the street, at the people who all seemed to have someplace to go. She crouched down so she could put both arms around her boy. *But, Jerry—we couldn't have stayed. . . .*

Mary watched a long burgundy-colored Rolls Royce slide to a stop at the curb just a few yards away. She could see the front tire had gone flat. A reed-thin man in a uniform and billed cap climbed out of the driver's side. He hurried around the front to the spare tire, attached in its special receptacle on the passenger side.

Mary could barely see through the sleet streaking the car's windows, but she could make out the figure of a woman in the backseat.

Olivia Edmunds looked the part exactly—elegant, privileged, rich, and certainly immune to the everyday worries of money and food and shelter. Wrapped in fur with diamonds sparkling at her neck, she sat in the back of the Rolls waiting for her driver, Phillip, to change the flat tire. The sleet pinged against the back windows of the car, but her eyes were fixed on a woman and a little boy who were huddled in the doorway of a business long since closed for the day. She hadn't taken her eyes off them since the car had stopped.

The Rolls shifted as the tire was changed, the minutes ticked past, and the sleet never let up, but the woman and her child remained under the umbrella of concrete—not moving. After Phillip stowed the jack and the flat tire in the trunk, he slammed it closed, opened his door, and started to climb into the driver's seat. But Olivia stopped him.

"Here, Phillip"—she reached over the seat—"would you please give this to that lady over there?"

Phillip took the bill with alacrity. "Yes indeed, Mrs. Edmunds."

It took only a few steps for the man to arrive in front of Mary and Jack. He held out a five-dollar bill. "My employer would like to offer you this money," he said without preamble.

"Sorry?" Mary questioned.

He frowned. "Just take the money, miss. She wants you to have it. Maybe you can get a meal or two and a room for the night."

"I . . . I can't just accept a stranger's money," Mary said, even as she eyed the five dollars.

The wind picked up, and in the blowing sleet,

the driver shrugged down into his coat. "I'd take it if I were you," he suggested. "Pride won't keep your boy warm tonight."

Mary hesitated, then finally held out her hand. He slipped the bill across the palm of her glove.

"Please . . . please thank her for me."

"I will," he said, turning immediately for the car. He slid back into the driver's seat, and Mary heard the engine start. She picked up her suitcase, took Jack's hand, and started past the car. Ducking her head to keep the sleet out of her eyes, she turned toward the back window as they passed. She hesitated for just a moment to look through the window at the generous woman in the backseat.

"Thank you," she mouthed carefully and saw a slight nod from the woman behind the glass. Mary started walking, head still bent against the wind, and heard the car pull away from the curb.

They hadn't gone more than a dozen steps when the Rolls backed up along the curb just past them—and stopped. The back window rolled down.

"Please—won't you get in," the lady invited. "It's awfully stormy out tonight. I can take you wherever you need to go." She opened the back door partway, then slid over to the other side of the backseat.

Mary barely hesitated before she climbed in with Jack in tow. For a second she could do nothing more than relish the heat in the car.

Feeling like a drowned rat, she tried to smile at the lovely woman, who looked as if she'd just stepped out of a fairy tale.

"I'm Mary . . . and this is Jack," she said. "I don't . . . I don't normally take money from strangers—or rides, for that matter, but I'm in a bit of a bind right now and my son—"

"I'm Olivia Edmunds," the lady said. "I'm happy to be of help. Where can I have my driver take you?"

"Oh, uh, well, I don't know. The Salvation Army shelter is full tonight, and they told me about a few other places—"

"A hotel, then? There must be something suitable."

Mary looked down at the now-damp bill still in her hand. "Yes, thank you," she said softly.

Olivia leaned forward. "Phillip, we need to find a hotel. Something clean—affordable."

"Yes, Mrs. Edmunds. I think I know just the place."

The car moved smoothly into the traffic. Mary looked out at the mix of rain and snow splashing against the glass.

"So, Jack"—Mrs. Edmunds turned toward him—"I have a little girl at home who might be close to your age. She's ten. How old are you?"

"He's seven," Mary answered.

"Oh, seven is a great age. Do you like to play with cars or read books, Jack?"

"He likes blocks," Mary said. "And I hope you won't think him rude, but he's . . . he's been deaf since his birth. He doesn't speak."

Mary saw the flicker of sympathy in the woman's eyes as she looked at Jack. *And now she sees him differently than just a little boy. Just once, just once I wish someone else would see what I see when I look at him. . . .*

"Oh, I'm . . . sorry," Mrs. Edmunds said.

Mary slipped her arm around her son and pulled him closer. He relaxed into her side but stared straight ahead. "No need to be sorry. Jack is exactly who he was meant to be—a very special little boy."

Mrs. Edmunds turned her gaze from Jack to Mary. "I'm sure that's true."

"No, I mean he's truly . . . special. He has a . . . a gift."

The woman hesitated, then, "That's wonderful. I think all mothers need to recognize their chil- dren's unique gifts—no matter what limitations they might have."

"That's . . . that isn't what I mean," Mary said as Mrs. Edmunds smoothed out her fur coat. "Jack has a divine gift—a gift from God."

Even in the semidarkness of the car, Mary could see Olivia Edmunds's eyebrows lift. *Keep going— say something. I can explain it . . . I think.* "Sometimes Jack can touch someone's hand and . . . and 'see' things," Mary hurried on. "He communicates what he sees by writing numbers, and they correspond to a chapter and verse in the Bible."

The eyebrows rose a little more before Mrs. Edmunds offered a still smile and leaned just a bit away from Mary. "That's . . . very interesting," she said. "Certainly not something one would hear every day."

Mary was very aware that the woman's expression had gone from sympathetic to wary. *Now she thinks I'm crazy . . . she believes I'm a crazy woman with a deaf-mute son. What was I thinking?* Mary gave a tiny shrug and smiled. "I guess it's like you said. A mother can see her own child's uniqueness. I'm sure you can see all kinds of special gifts your little girl has."

"Yes, that's true." Olivia Edmunds smiled. "As her mother, I would champion her to the moon and back."

Mary returned her smile. "That's a *mother's* gift."

At Mrs. Edmunds's nod, Mary relaxed. The three in the backseat shifted a bit as the driver made a turn.

"Do you mind if I ask you a question, Mary?"

"No—"

"I'm just wondering how you ended up in your . . . present circumstances."

Mary drew Jack even closer. He'd closed his eyes, his chin resting against his jacket, suggesting he was asleep. She turned and looked Mrs. Edmunds in the eye. "My—well, my present circumstance is as much a nightmare as a surprise to me," she began. "No one ever expects to be standing on a street without a bed or roof over one's head. But with no job, no money, I can't provide my own son with something as basic as food and shelter."

"So you've been looking for employment?"

"Yes, of course, but no one will hire me, since I need to keep Jack with me at all times. He cannot stay alone, and I can't afford to hire someone to look after him."

"What kind of work are you looking for?" Olivia asked.

"Anything, really," Mary replied. "I've answered waitressing postings, clerking positions in stores . . . I can cook, clean, do laundry, iron, scrub floors and windows. I tried for two different maid positions, but as soon as I mentioned Jack, they turned me down."

Olivia turned away toward the window for a moment. When the car started to slow, she looked over at Mary. "I have a maid—Matilda . . . but she *is* getting on in years. She could probably use some help." Her musings seemed more for her own benefit than for Mary's. She sighed as she looked intently at Mary's face. "You're a lovely young woman, Mary. It's possible you aren't going to get a maid position easily because some women might feel threatened with someone so attractive in their homes."

"Thank you for the compliment," Mary said, feeling rather awkward. "But I'm a hard worker," she added, trying not to read anything into the woman's musings about her maid Matilda.

"You know what they say," Olivia observed as she glanced at Mary's gloves. "You can tell a lot about how hard someone works by looking at their hands."

"I suppose that's true, but I . . . I have to keep my gloves on all the time."

"And why is that?"

Mary curled gloved fingers into her palms. "My hands . . . they were burned when I was a little girl. They're scarred and ugly—it's hard for people to see them."

"But they don't stop you from everyday tasks? No pain or anything like that?"

"No, nothing like that."

Phillip spoke from the front seat. "Ma'am, this is the hotel I was thinking of."

The car pulled over to the curb and stopped in front of the Lamplight Hotel. Even though the sleet had all but stopped, the place looked cold— sad and forlorn.

"I don't know how to thank you," Mary said, gently moving Jack. "For the money—the ride . . ."

"You know, I don't think you'll want to stay here." Olivia peered out at the hotel.

"Oh, Mrs. Edmunds, this is more than fine," Mary assured her. "I had no idea where we'd be sleeping tonight. This is—"

"I'd like to offer you a position," Olivia put in, turning back to face Mary. "I believe we have a place for you—and for Jack—at our house. Matilda might take some convincing. . . ." Her voice trailed off, but then she smiled. "But that's not for you to worry about."

Olivia was still speaking, but Mary couldn't think past the fact that she'd just been offered a job. She wanted to shout for joy—maybe even hug the woman. But she couldn't move. Couldn't comprehend how this day was turning out. The offer of money—a ride—and now a job! She focused on her new employer's words.

"You would work Monday through Saturday," she heard Olivia say. "Some evenings and Sundays if necessary. Does this sound acceptable to you, Mary?"

Mary tried to refrain from laughing hysterically, tried to hold in check the tremendous relief that rolled over her. "Yes. Yes, thank you. I'll work anytime—all the time. Whatever you need."

"Room and board will be included in your wages," Olivia added.

*Does that mean we live with her? A job* and *a place to live!*

"And you may leave your gloves on while you

work," Olivia said. "I'll see to it that you have several pairs."

Olivia eyed the battered suitcase holding all of Mary's and Jack's worldly belongings. "Is that it, then?" she asked. "Nothing else we need to pick up? Someone to notify?"

Mary shook her head. "That's it. There's nothing . . . no one."

"I assume you will be able to start immediately—well, I mean after you get settled in and all?"

Mary smiled and felt a thousand worries slip from her shoulders. "It just so happens we can, Mrs. Edmunds. How can I ever—"

"Good," Olivia said briskly. "Phillip, let's go home."

## Chapter Eight

THEY LEFT THE LIGHTS AND BUSTLE of downtown Chicago and headed northeast toward Lake Michigan. The traffic thinned out, and from what Mary could see through the darkness, the scenery grew more rural. In the backseat of the Rolls, Mary felt as if she were dreaming, as if she were gliding, soaring effortlessly out of one difficult, sad world and into another filled with light and hope. She didn't let herself question the events of the last hour—her confidence in the future was too tenuous, based on an offer from a virtual stranger. *Is this really happening? It must be, for here we are!*

Mary tried to concentrate on the small talk from Olivia. "Mary? Did you hear me?" Olivia asked.

"I'm sorry, Mrs. Edmunds—what was it?"

"I asked if you were from Illinois."

"I grew up in a small town in Minnesota," she said.

"Any family still in Minnesota?" Olivia wondered.

Mary shook her head. "No. No family anywhere. It's just Jack and me."

Olivia shifted in her seat, adjusted her necklace. "Then you and Jack are blessed to have each other."

Mary smiled. "Yes, we are." *And thank you for not asking about Jack's father. . . .*

The estate of Richard and Olivia Edmunds was impressive by anyone's standards, but to Mary, it looked like a palace lit from the inside. At a time when most people were doing their best just to get by, the Edmundses seemed to be doing extremely well. The weather had cleared, and the inviting glow of the light from the huge windows drew Mary toward the lovely, comforting sight of the sprawling red-brick three-story colonial. The vehicle had stopped in the circle drive, edged in jade green shrubbery and lit by tall lamps. Mary helped Jack from the car as she took in the massive rectangle at the center of the structure with solariumlike breezeways extending on either side to the smaller two-story wings. A white dormer, perched like a crown on the slate roof, drew Mary's eyes to the starry sky above. *People actually live like this.* . . .

"Follow me," Olivia invited as she moved past Mary and Jack toward the wide steps that led to a columned portico framing the large front door. It opened as if on its own accord the moment Olivia placed her foot on the top step, and they followed her inside, Mary clutching Jack's hand.

The massive foyer opened up to a magnificent staircase from the middle of the intricate parquet wood flooring, widening as it fanned out onto the second floor. Brass sconces on the walls sent light in all directions, and Mary followed Jack's gaze to a twinkling crystal chandelier high above in the center of the foyer.

Olivia walked toward a round table not far from the door and placed her pocketbook beside a large, beautiful arrangement of fresh flowers in a crystal vase. A grandfather clock chimed eight times, and Mary's only thought at the moment was *It's perfect.*

Olivia turned to face Mary and Jack. "It's late, and I'm sure you both are tired. We'll get you settled quickly." She waved them toward the stairs, talking as they went. "We have two children. Douglas is fifteen and in his first year at the Lake

Forest Academy—his father's alma mater. He'll be home on holidays, of course."

A voice from behind them said, "I didn't hear you come in, ma'am."

Olivia paused at the bottom of the staircase and looked past Mary. She turned to follow Olivia's gaze to an elderly woman in the foyer behind them, gray hair set in close pin curls all over her head. A starched white apron circled her ample waist, and a pink lace handkerchief formed a triangle to peek out of a pocket on the bodice of the gray dress.

"Matilda—there you are. You'll be glad to hear I've brought reinforcements," Olivia said cheerfully.

Matilda arched an appraising eyebrow, and Mary watched her take in their shabby clothes, their neglected appearance.

"Reinforcements?" Matilda repeated, turning her attention back to her employer.

Olivia nodded as she pulled off her satin gloves. "Yes, this is—"

"Mother, you're *never* going to guess what Susie said today!" A girl bounced into the foyer and stopped short when she saw Mary and Jack. "Oh, sorry. I didn't know we had company."

"Not quite, dear. Mary, this is our daughter, Anna. She's ten. . . ." Olivia drew the girl into the circle of her arm.

Mary could quickly see the mother in the

daughter's face. Anna's brown hair was cut into a stylish bob. Eyes wide with curiosity, she looked at both of them frankly—especially at Jack, who stared back at her without expression.

"Anna, Matilda—this is Mary and her son, Jack. Mary is going to be helping you with your duties, Matilda," Olivia said.

"As live-ins?" Matilda asked.

"Yes, that's right."

Mary offered a smile in Matilda's direction, but the older woman looked anything but happy.

Anna leaned closer to her mother. "*He's* going to live here too?"

"Yes, darling, with Mary in the servants' wing," Olivia said quietly. Then to Matilda, "I think the room across from yours will work well, don't you think?"

Anna looked at Jack. "What grade are you in?"

Matilda sighed. "I'll make up the bed, then."

"Hey there, hello?" Anna said to Jack. "I'm in fifth grade—how about you?"

"I can make the bed," Mary offered. "Just show me where the sheets are—"

"They're called *linens*," Matilda said firmly.

Anna stood on her toes and whispered loudly, "Mother, he's being rude. He won't answer my questions."

"Jack is not able to hear you"—Olivia laid a hand on the girl's shoulder—"and he can't answer you."

Mary explained quietly, "He's called a deaf-mute."

Anna's eyes grew wide and she looked at Jack with a new interest. "Mute—like muting sound?"

"Yes, that's right. Jack doesn't speak," Olivia explained. "He's . . . special."

"*Really?* You mean like a mime?" she asked, taking a step toward Jack.

Mary started, "No, not like—"

"Like Charlie Chaplin!" Anna exclaimed. "I love Charlie Chaplin films. *Modern Times* is his latest. He's so funny when he plays the Little Tramp. Have you seen it?"

"Um, no . . . I haven't."

"Anna," Olivia said, sounding like she was trying to curb some impatience, "it's different for Jack. He's not like Charlie Chaplin."

Anna drew her gaze up and down Jack's worn clothes. "He sure looks like he could be Charlie—"

"*Anna!*" This time her irritation with her daughter was plain. "Please apologize immediately. That was uncalled for, and you must say you are sorry."

Anna's eyes flickered between Mary and Jack. "But even if I apologize, he can't hear me," she muttered.

"It's okay," Mary put in quickly. "We do look a little . . . ragged."

"I didn't mean anything by it," Anna argued. "And I *was* comparing him to a character I *love* in the film," she finished defensively. She looked at Jack again. "Can—you—read—my—lips?"

"No, he is not able to do that either," Mary said.

"Olivia?" a man called from the other room, then materialized on the opposite side of the foyer. He was the perfect complement to Olivia, Mary decided. Just a few inches taller than his wife, he was distinguished looking—probably late forties judging by the slight graying at the temples of his auburn hair.

"Richard, this is Mary Godwin. I've hired her to help Matilda," Olivia said.

His brow creased as he looked at Mary and Jack—then turned an expectant look on his wife. "They're from the agency?"

"I didn't hire her through the . . . the usual channels," Olivia explained.

Richard studied the two rather forlorn-looking figures in front of him.

"Might I have a moment, Olivia?" Richard asked. He took her arm and moved across the foyer through double glass doors. Olivia held up a finger toward Mary. "I'll be right back. Anna, upstairs with you and get ready for bed," she said, then followed him into a book-lined study.

Anna wrinkled up her face in obvious annoyance but must have decided her mother was in no mood for an argument. Mary watched the girl trudge upstairs while Olivia and Richard Edmunds closed the study door behind them.

"You stay here," Matilda instructed. "I'll be back in a moment."

Mary kept her eyes on the person behind the glass door of the study who was probably holding her future in his hands. He was standing in the center of the room, arms crossed and head slightly tipped. Olivia, just a few feet in front of him, was nodding her head and using her hands as if she were telling a story. Mary couldn't hear the words—could only surmise the passionate nature of the conversation by watching Olivia. She laid her hand on her son's shoulder. *This is just a glimpse into how you observe the world, Jack.*

# Chapter Nine

OLIVIA STEPPED OUT OF THE STUDY and glanced around.

"Matilda?"

"Right here, ma'am," Matilda said as she returned to the foyer.

"Please introduce Mary and Jack to Miss Bea. Make sure she gets them something to eat. While she's getting that ready, you may show them to their room and acquaint Mary with the layout of the house," she said with a smile for them all.

Matilda sighed and gestured for Mary and Jack to follow her. "C'mon, then."

Mary held Jack's hand and followed Matilda.

Her relief was enormous, even though she couldn't be sure Mr. Edmunds hadn't just agreed to something temporary.

"I've been with the Edmundses since Douglas was a toddler—before Anna was even born," Matilda announced as they headed down the hall.

"That's a long time."

"I'm practically a member of the family."

"You're awful lucky, then."

"Mrs. Edmunds gets me a real nice bathrobe every Christmas and chocolates for my birthdays," Matilda continued.

"She sounds like a generous employer." Mary hurried to keep up with the older woman as she led them toward the back of the house. They entered a spacious room with floor-to-ceiling cabinets, state-of-the-art appliances, and an island in the center big enough to seat at least a dozen people. A delicious aroma, probably from dinner, still lingered and made her mouth water.

"Guess you can figure out this is the kitchen."

"It's . . . so big," Mary commented, looking around.

"Mr. and Mrs. Edmunds do a lot of entertaining," Matilda said. "You and the boy will take your meals in here. The dining room—that's for the family only. Understood?"

"Yes—yes, I understand," Mary answered quickly.

A dark-skinned woman entered the kitchen from

the side pantry. "That's Miss Bea," Matilda said with a wave of her hand. "She's queen of this kitchen, and she won't let you forget it, will you, Miss Bea?"

"Who'll I be remindin'?" the middle-aged woman asked. Mary noticed she was wearing the same uniform as Matilda—right down to the pink handkerchief. The gray dress was filled out even more amply than Matilda's.

"The new maid and her boy," Matilda said abruptly.

"I'm Mary and this is Jack," Mary told the woman.

"Now, how's come you get help and I don't?" Miss Bea groused. "Seems to me I'm the one on my feet all day. And now I'll be cookin' for two more." Miss Bea shook her head and looked the two figures over. "Seems like ya could use some meat on them bones. The help eats on the half hour. Six-thirty for breakfast, eleven-thirty for lunch, and four-thirty for supper. And I don't want—what's his name?—Jack under my feet, hear?"

Mary nodded and couldn't help but smile. *Regular meals—cooked in a kitchen—eaten with Jack.* "That sounds fine."

"Mrs. Edmunds wants you to fix 'em something to eat," Matilda said.

"Does she, now? Well, come on back after Tildy shows you round, and I'll have somethin' ready to feed ya."

"Thanks," Mary said.

Matilda led them on a tour of the rest of the first floor—a library, Olivia's office, the living room, dining room, *two* bathrooms, and a sunroom with floor-to-ceiling windows. Mary was admiring them when she heard Matilda at her elbow say in a low but intense voice, "Just don't get any ideas 'bout stealing my job, you hear? I'll make your life miserable if you so much as hint you can handle all the jobs in this house alone."

"I'm not looking to take away your job," Mary protested. "Mrs. Edmunds is wanting help for *you*—"

"'Cause when it comes right down to brass tacks, *I'm* the one who helped corral little Anna when she was toddling around, and I'm the one who served at their anniversary party, and I'm the one who'll be staying if someone has to go."

Mary thought she heard just a tinge of doubt in the older woman's tone. "I'm not after your job," Mary repeated. "I'm just grateful to have one at all. Besides, you're like part of the family."

Matilda nodded, then abruptly started moving again. "You make your way through this breezeway to the servants' quarters," the woman said as they passed through the interior door into a long room with an end wall of floor-to-ceiling windows. Mary looked out through the glass to the back of the house—and stared. It was dark, but the full moon illuminated an astonishing view.

Stars glittered over a lawn that seemed to disappear over a black body of water reflecting the moonlight.

She felt the world stop for just a moment, felt her heart tumble with gratitude. Tears of joy filled her eyes, and she stiffened with the effort of holding back sobs. *Thank you, God . . . thank you, thank you, thank you. . . .*

Matilda cleared her throat, and Mary realized the woman was watching her. "I'm guessing you've been living somewhere a little less . . . grand?"

Mary swallowed the lump in her throat. "You might say that." Her smile was wobbly and she felt a bit self-conscious. "And with the cold weather, I was pretty worried about Jack and where . . . you know . . . how . . ."

For a moment Matilda's face softened. "I don't know, and I guess I don't wanna know 'bout that kind of worry," she said as she started moving again. "Tomorrow I'll show you where the carpet sweeper is and the rest of the cleaning supplies. Mrs. Edmunds is real particular about the woodwork in the house, and the mister won't tolerate a speck of dust in his study. . . ."

Mary nodded as Matilda talked on, trying to focus on the instructions she was being given, but mostly giddy with the thought that her luck seemed to have finally changed.

# Chapter Ten

THE SUN WAS HIGH in an unclouded sky, and Mary could actually feel the heat of it through the transparent wall in the breezeway as she polished the glass. Jack, sitting at her feet, had his eyes fixed on the lake, which looked as if it rose up to meet the bluff at the end of the yard.

She moved her hand back and forth with the window chamois, creating a kind of metronome as she hummed. The tune reflected her mood. She was happy, and for the first time in a very long time, she felt as though she belonged. She even loved the gray uniform she was wearing. It was the newest thing she owned. Or at least she owned as long as she worked for the Edmundses, she amended.

The job was such a gift—something she thought of every time she woke up in the comfortable room she shared with Jack. She vowed she would never take any of it for granted. She worked hard, finishing each task as thoroughly as she knew how, so Olivia Edmunds would never have a reason to regret having invited her into her car, then offering her this job that was so perfect in so many ways.

Mary finished the window cleaning by forming a giant square with the chamois as she wiped off the last of the cleaner, the streaks staying only long enough to look like a picture frame. She peered through her makeshift frame at the same view that was holding Jack spellbound.

"It's like there's nothing else in the world besides you and me when we look out at the beauty," she said. "We're in a cocoon here, Jack. Safe and sound."

The kitchen smelled wonderful—as always. Mary and Jack entered to the aroma of freshly baked oatmeal cookies and something with cinnamon. Miss Bea bustled back and forth from the center island to the large stove, where a teakettle started to whistle.

"Mary, you seen Tildy?" Miss Bea asked as she deftly lifted the brass pot from the burner and set it on a wooden tray on the island.

"I think she said she was going to clean the library," Mary answered, opening a supply closet built into a wall near the door. "Do you want me to find her for you?" she asked as she put away the window cleaner.

Miss Bea shook her head impatiently. "No. When Tildy wants to disappear for a nap, it's hard to say where she'll curl up. You'll just have to serve this tea for Mr. Edmunds and his guest yourself. They're in his study."

"Oh. Well. Maybe you should—"

"I can't. It ain't my place." Bea lifted the wooden tray from the island and carried it toward

Mary. "You take it in, pour the tea, and put in any cream or sugars they might want."

She handed Mary the tray. "Jack can stay here with me."

"Oh no . . ."

Miss Bea put a hand on Jack's shoulder and leaned down so he could see her broad smile—which widened when he smiled back for a brief moment.

"You been here two weeks now, and Jack's been your shadow. Douglas used to sit in here and eat cookies fresh from the oven. Let 'im stay and have cookies like a regular little boy," Miss Bea said as she straightened up. "He *do* like cookies, don't he?"

"Oh, sure," Mary said. "It's just that—"

"Get on, now, 'fore the water gets cold and I gotta heat it up all over again." Bea waved Mary away and took Jack's hand. "We be right here when you're done."

Mary watched as Miss Bea offered Jack a cookie, which he accepted without even a glance in her direction. She turned from the room with a half smile. *He's going to eat cookies with Miss Bea like a regular little boy.*

The study door was open, and Mary stopped at the threshold. Richard Edmunds sat behind the large regency desk, hands tented together as he listened to a man seated across from him.

"So what are you trying to tell me, Howard?" Richard asked impatiently.

"I'm saying that your insurance policy is over ten years old, Richard. Since then the cost of living index has risen by thirty-seven percent." Howard leaned forward in his chair. "The last significant change we made was adding Anna when she was born."

Uncertain about interrupting, Mary remained near the door. She didn't think she'd been noticed, but Richard glanced at her and raised his eyebrows.

"Excuse me. I have your tea," she said quietly, and he motioned her forward.

The study was one of her favorite rooms in the house. The oriental carpet sank under her feet as she made her way across the room. Rich brown wainscoting met subtle olive green walls. The shelves lining three of the walls contained volumes and volumes of leather-bound books with gold leaf printed on the spines. *I'll bet just one of those books is worth as much as three days' wages for me.* She walked past the window with a beautiful view of Lake Michigan. Ambient light suffused the whole room in a soft golden glow.

"You don't need to take my word that you're underinsured, Richard. The numbers on these pages don't lie." Howard pushed a bound document across the desk.

Mary stopped at the desk, uncertain about where to put the tea, but once again Richard gestured. As she set the tray down on the leather inlay of the desk, the man called Howard looked at her with barely veiled admiration. "Well, this certainly isn't Matilda, is it?"

"No, this is Mary. She's been with us a couple of weeks," Richard said as he perused the documents. "Are you sure these figures on page two are accurate? I thought—"

"What happened to Matilda—you finally put her out to pasture?" Howard chuckled, his eyes still on Mary.

Richard flicked his eyes from the paper to Howard. He sounded annoyed as he said, "No, Matilda's practically one of the family by now. Olivia just thought she could use some help."

"Most attractive help," Howard said under his breath.

Mary felt a hot blush crawl up her neck. Richard looked up at her and raised an expectant eyebrow. "You will pour?"

"Yes, sir." She fumbled at first with the teapot but managed to fill the cups, trying to ignore Howard's gaze.

"Aren't we fancy? White gloves to serve tea," Howard observed. "I take two sugars and cream."

Richard reached for his own cup and dropped in a sugar cube.

*Remember that—he takes one sugar. . . .*

"So what's my bottom line here?" Richard asked, looking once more at the page.

"It boils down to Olivia, Douglas, and Anna." Howard finally took his eyes off Mary. "If something were to happen to you—the question is: Do you want them to continue to have the same kind of life they're accustomed to now? Money that will take care of them for the rest of their lives if you're not here? Knowing *they'll* have security and peace of mind when you're gone should give *you* peace of mind while you're still here," Howard said easily.

"Of course that's what I want."

"Then you'll need to add significant dollars to your life insurance policy. I know it's painful, and death is an ugly subject, but we're all going to die someday. Some of us will just leave our loved ones more prepared than others."

*We're all going to die someday . . . leave our loved ones more prepared . . .* The words whirled through Mary's mind as she placed Howard's cup on a napkin in front of him and turned to walk quickly from the room.

*Money that will take care of them . . . of Jack . . . for the rest of his life if I'm not here . . . if I'm not here . . .*

# Chapter Eleven

ANNA EDMUNDS'S BEDROOM WAS DECIDEDLY feminine—pink dotted swiss wallpaper, pink brocade skirt around the four-poster canopy bed, ornate crown molding around the ceiling, and pink milk glass sconces on the walls. What wasn't pink was a brilliant white. Mary felt as if she were cleaning a page out of a princess fairytale book. Jack was sitting on the cushioned window seat watching Anna practice her flute. She stood in front of a large cherry armoire, where a pink satin dress hung in front of its doors. Anna finished the lilting melody with accomplished ease, and Mary put down her duster to clap for her, though the sound was muffled by her gloves.

"That was really pretty, Anna," she said. "What's it called?"

"'Canon in D,'" Anna answered. "I'm performing it tonight at my recital, and Tommy Breton is going to accompany me on the piano."

"I'm guessing you'll be the best one there," Mary said. "I'm going to clean your bathroom now. Will that be all right with you?"

Anna shrugged. "Sure."

Mary walked across to Jack, holding out her hand for him to come with her.

"Jack can stay in here with me," Anna offered.

Mary took a moment to think about it. "Well, all right, if you're sure you don't mind," she said. "The bathroom won't take me long."

The colors in the bathroom echoed the bedroom. Everything that could be pink *was* pink except for the white tub and toilet. She pulled on rubber gloves over the white ones and poured scouring powder into the sink. She could hear Anna chattering away to Jack in the other room.

"Here, Jack. I've got an idea. Stand right here. . . ."

Mary peeked out the door to see Anna ushering Jack toward the armoire and turning him to stand next to it. He lifted his hand to stroke the pink satin. Anna followed his gesture, saying, "Oh yes, Jack, isn't it smooth and silky?"

Mary smiled and turned back to her work. She rinsed out the sink, the sound of the water momentarily drowning out Anna's voice.

"Oh, that's perfect for you," she heard Anna saying, sounding amused, when Mary turned off the brass-handled faucet. "Wait—I've got something in my closet. . . . Don't you just love my dress for the recital, Jack? Isn't it the most beautiful thing you've ever seen? Mother took me to every dress shop in Chicago to find it! Here, now . . . oh, that looks good. Pink's my favorite color, but I think you must like blue—right? I think all boys like blue. My brother has blue walls in his room. Do you know why I'm home from school today? It's 'cause they closed the school to get ready for the recital tonight—I get to wear an orchid corsage."

Mary smiled at the happy chatter. She liked the way Anna talked to Jack as if he could hear her. *Just like I do.* Mary ran a cloth over the mirror above the vanity and then removed her rubber gloves and gathered up her cleaning supplies. She heard Anna giggle. "There—that's the perfect touch!"

"Mary," Anna called. "Come and see."

Mary snapped off the light in the bathroom and walked into the bedroom. There was Jack wearing a long blue dress over his clothes, a feather boa, and a big floppy hat tilted down over one eye. Anna held a bottle of pink nail polish in her hand.

"Ta-dah!" Anna said. "Doesn't he look great?"

"Uh, yeah. He looks great." Mary smiled. "But I bet your mom wouldn't appreciate you messing up your good clothes like that."

"Oh, these are just old clothes I play dress-up in," Anna scoffed. "The only new thing is my nail polish. I tried to paint his nails, but he keeps curling up his fingers."

Jack was staring stoically forward, not seeming to mind his mannequin role.

Mary smiled again and moved to lift the brim of the hat so she could see his face. "Yes, I'm thinking blue was the best choice, little man," she said softly.

"I've got dress-up clothes you can use, Mary," Anna offered. "I'll bet they'd look really pretty on you."

"Oh, I've got to get back to work, Anna. Let's just take these things off Jack—"

"At least let me do *your* nails?" Anna begged.

"No, thank you. I really mustn't take the time."

"Oh, please. I'm bored and it's so long till the recital," she said in her best pleading tones.

"I don't wear polish," Mary said with a firm shake of her head.

"Why? Because of your gloves?"

"Well, yes . . ."

"My mom says your hands are scarred," Anna said with a little shiver. "Is that right? Do they hurt?"

"No, they don't—"

"Can I see them?"

Mary quickly shook her head. "No. I never take my gloves off."

"Not even for Jack?"

"Not even for Jack. He's never seen my hands."

"Do they look scary?"

"Yes, I'm afraid they do."

"I don't get scared very easy," Anna said earnestly. "I'm braver than most boys even— braver than Jack, probably. I wouldn't get scared if you showed me your hands."

Mary shook her head and began to remove the clothing on Jack.

"How about just a small peek under your glove? You know—just by your wrist?"

"No, Anna. Your mother wouldn't like that, and like I said, I never take off my gloves in front of anyone."

"I'm not just anyone," Anna said, her lips pulling down at the corners. "I'm the daughter of the woman you work for—and I'm asking you nicely."

Mary slipped the hat from Jack's head and removed the feather boa from around his neck. "I'm sorry, Anna, but I can't."

Anxious now to get out of the bedroom, Mary unbuttoned the back of the blue dress and let it fall from his shoulders to his feet.

"C'mon, Mary. I'm not a baby. I just want to see your hands." She pouted.

Mary took a deep breath and stepped away from Jack. She turned and peeled back an inch of fabric from her wrist, revealing a patch of crimson red skin.

Anna's eyes widened, and before Mary could pull the glove back in place, the girl's finger had touched the damaged skin.

# Chapter Twelve

OLIVIA ARRIVED HOME LATE in the afternoon and swept into the foyer, a bitter winter wind nipping at her heels. Mary had been pacing for over an hour, and she felt like a nervous wreck as she met her employer at the door.

"Mrs. Edmunds . . ."

Olivia barely glanced at Mary before handing her a small shopping bag and moving on to the table in the foyer. "Take this upstairs to Anna, please, Mary."

Mary, holding a Bible in her hand, shifted it to the crook of her arm and took the bag. "Please, may I speak to you?"

"After you run it upstairs, Mary," Olivia said briskly, putting her pocketbook down on the table along with a small corsage box.

"Yes, I will, Mrs. Edmunds, but—"

"How did the day get away from me?" Olivia muttered with a cursory look at the grandfather clock. "Where's Matilda?"

"I don't know, but if you'll just listen—"

"Remind Bea that dinner's to be half an hour earlier tonight and that Mr. Edmunds won't be home," Olivia said, starting across the foyer toward Richard's study. "He's meeting us at the recital—"

"I don't think Mr. Edmunds should go to the recital," Mary blurted out.

Olivia stopped and turned. "Excuse me?"

Mary watched as Olivia's frown deepened, nearly forcing Mary into silence. "I don't think *anyone* should go to the recital," Mary said cautiously as she moved toward Olivia. Then she hurried on. "Remember the day we met and I started to tell you about Jack's—his gift? That he can sometimes touch someone and see things?"

The grandfather clock in the foyer chimed the half hour. An uneasy look crossed Olivia's face as she glanced again that way. Jack stood next to it, staring at her. "I'm not sure where you're going with this, but I don't think I'm going to like it. You'd better get to it, Mary."

"He sees numbers," Mary said quickly, "and with my help, he can write them down. This is what he wrote after we left Anna's room today." With shaking hands, Mary opened her Bible and removed a slip of paper, handing it to Olivia.

Olivia looked at Jack, then down at the paper. " 'Forty, thirteen, forty-two'?"

"The numbers are, first, the books in order as they appear in the Bible, then the chapter and the verse." Mary all but shoved the Bible into Olivia's hands. "I have it underlined. Please . . . please read it."

Olivia shook her head, but turned her attention to the open pages and read aloud. " 'And shall cast them into a furnace of fire: there shall be wailing and gnashing of teeth.' "

"Jack saw *those* numbers, *that* verse, when he touched Anna earlier today," Mary said. "That's a warning—you can't let her go to the recital, and we have to warn people there's going to be a fire!"

Olivia's eyebrows lifted in disbelief. "You can't honestly believe that this—this verse about God's wrath against humanity has anything to do with my sweet Anna! That's just insane!"

"I'm not saying the Scripture Jack saw was made for this particular moment in time—but I am saying that this is how the warning was shown to him. It's unique. It's the way the gift was given."

"It's absolutely *absurd* to think God would be communicating through a deaf-mute boy by using numbers."

Mary shook her head. "In the book of Numbers, God uses a donkey to tell the donkey's master, Balaam—"

"I know that story, but still . . ." Olivia interrupted.

"If God can use a donkey to warn someone, why not Jack? He's offering the only information he has—the only way he can. I believe with all my heart that this verse is telling us that Anna—and others—could be badly hurt or even *killed* by a fire from a furnace."

"We have a furnace right here in this house," Olivia argued. "What about that?"

"Phillip must turn it off right away. That way

we'll know she'll be safe when you keep her home."

Olivia thrust the Bible back into Mary's hands. "Anna has been practicing for this recital for weeks, and I won't disappoint her based on some wild story about a donkey and numbers and—"

"Please, Mrs. Edmunds, I'm begging you not to let her go."

Olivia grabbed the shopping bag from Mary's hand. "I don't want you going anywhere near my daughter—"

"The recital isn't worth it, Mrs. Edmunds! You'll never forgive yourself if you let her go."

"I'm letting *you* go, Mary. Consider yourself relieved of your duties." Olivia's voice trembled and tears started to well up in her eyes. She turned away toward the stairs.

"I'd rather be on the streets than safe in this beautiful house," Mary said to the woman's back, "knowing I didn't do everything I could to make you see, make you understand, that the threat to Anna is real."

Olivia started up the stairs. Mary tried one more time. "Please, Mrs. Edmunds, if there's even a tiny part of you that believes any of this, you can't let Anna go—and you have to call the school and warn them!"

Mary watched as Olivia climbed the stairs, never once looking back.

# Chapter Thirteen

RICHARD EDMUNDS SLIPPED THE KEY into the ignition, anticipating the familiar easing of tension that accompanied the hum of the engine. The day had been filled with problems—from the moment he stepped foot in the facility until he'd put out the last looming fire just fifteen minutes earlier. He now attempted to push the problems of work from his mind and focus on the road, but he was irritated to find that the bizarre conversation he'd had with Olivia that afternoon kept intruding on his thoughts. He'd not had a moment to himself since the call—no time to decipher the cryptic things she had been saying. But now bits and pieces of the conversation came rushing back to him.

*"He says there's going to be a fire at the school, Richard!"*

*"Who says?"*

*"Jack! Mary's son—"*

*"Jack—the deaf-kid Jack?"*

*"She showed me a Bible verse that was horrible—"*

*"Bible verse? You're not making any—"*

*"Fires and furnaces and gnashing of teeth! Mary's adamant that I don't let Anna attend the recital."*

*"Since when do you let the hired help tell you*

*what to do? I've got two hundred employees I have to keep in line, Liv. You've got three. Tell her to—"*

"She's put me in an untenable position!"

"Listen, I've got an angry shipbuilder in Maine looking for a shipment of a thousand—"

"Who cares about that right now, Richard! I'm talking about our daughter! Anna will never forgive me if I keep her home. All the practicing . . . the dress . . . she's excited to play for us. . . ."

"I trust your judgment. Do what you think is best."

"I don't know what's best," she'd shouted into the phone. "But she's left me no choice but to heed her warning. . . ."

"I don't have time for this, Olivia. Am I meeting you at the recital or not?"

"You haven't heard a word I've said!"

Richard had shaken his head when he heard the hard click of the phone in his ear, and he shook it again now. He still couldn't believe she'd hung up on him. *I work like a dog six days a week for my family—and she hangs up on me?*

"Who cares . . . who cares?" he sputtered aloud in the confines of the car. "You'd *better* care, Olivia! Those shipments keep a roof over your head—a very *nice* roof—and food on the table. Diamonds, furs! Nobody wants for anything— nobody does without. How 'bout a little appreciation for dear old dad? I work, I give! I've even made sure there won't be so much as a hiccup in everyone's life if I die! *Who cares?!*"

Preoccupied with his impassioned soliloquy, Richard didn't immediately hear the sound of sirens roaring up behind him, but when he did, he reacted quickly and pulled to the side of the road to allow several emergency vehicles to pass. It was a rare sight in quiet Highland Park, and he wondered what poor soul was in need of so much help. Realizing the cold had crept into the car, he reached for the knob on the dashboard to crank up the heat. Just as the warm blast of air filled the car, he saw smoke rising in the distance.

*"There's going to be a fire at the school . . . a fire at the school."*

The heat in the car couldn't take away the chill that shot up his spine as he grabbed for the gear shift, slammed his foot on the gas pedal, and sped toward Anna's school.

Flames danced against the black sky, leaping in and out of the smoke that billowed into gray clouds even in the darkness. Lights from fire trucks, police cars, and ambulances lit up the scene with red strobes and reflected off the hood of Richard's dark sedan as he braked to a quick stop. As he got out of his car, he became a witness to the chaos—yelling, panic, flames devouring the south wing of Anna's school. *The wing where her recital . . .*

The acrid smell in the air made Richard pull out his handkerchief and put it over his nose and mouth as orange ash shimmered down in front of him—an ember came to rest just inches from his shoe. Suddenly Olivia's ranting and raving became much more gripping—she'd said she would heed Mary's warning. *Didn't she?* Since he'd been going straight home, he assumed she wasn't taking Anna to the recital. *Olivia's stubborn—and I goaded her. Told her not to take orders from servants . . . Please, God . . . don't let them be in there because of something stupid I said.*

He rushed toward a fireman pulling a hose from a pumper truck, and even from a distance he could feel the heat from the inferno.

"My wife and daughter might be in there!" he shouted at the fireman. But his words were lost in an earsplitting explosion of shattering glass. Richard reflexively ducked as the fireman manhandling the hose shouted to another fireman just arriving on the scene. "Start a red line from the booster tank—we're gonna need it!"

The jaw-dropping scene spread out in front of Richard was surreal. He struggled to get his incoherent thoughts together and tried again to get the fireman's attention as he dragged the feeder hose toward the flames.

"My family! I don't know . . ."

But a policeman had him by the arm and was

pulling him backward. "Look out, fella! Let 'im do his job."

Richard jerked his arm away from the cop. "I've got to—"

"Just stay back. We don't need more casualties!" the cop yelled over the din of sirens and the roar of the fire.

"Casualties? I could have people in there. . . ." But the sentence died on his lips as two medics came toward him with a gurney carrying a man badly burned, his features barely distinguishable. Richard cringed, swallowing down the bile that rose in his throat. As they moved past him, the man suddenly opened his mouth in an agonizing scream, his lips pulled back over clenched teeth. *"There will be gnashing of teeth . . . gnashing of teeth."* Richard stumbled backward, reeling from the horrific sights and the pungent smells.

*Olivia . . . Anna . . . no . . . no,* he wept, his voice crackling like the flames from the fire. *Please, oh-God, oh-God, oh-God . . .*

Richard burst through the front door of the house into the empty foyer. The lights were on, but the house was quiet. Too quiet.

"Olivia!" he shouted, surprising even himself with the volume of his voice. "Olivia!"

He was halfway to the staircase when he called out again, "Olivia! Anna!"

"Richard! Keep your voice down!" He heard

Olivia's hiss from the top of the stairs. "Anna has finally calmed down enough to sleep, and I don't want you to wake—"

"She's fine, then? She's okay?" He almost ran to the bottom of the staircase.

"No, of course she's not okay," Olivia said as she started down the stairs. "She's devastated that I kept her home from her own recital."

Richard lowered himself onto the bottom step, his legs suddenly too weak to support him.

"You don't have to tell me how crazy I am," she said wearily. "I don't have the energy to hear it. But Richard . . . Richard, if you'd heard the things she told me . . . and with such conviction! Then maybe you'd have done the same thing." She stepped past him and turned. "If there could be the slightest . . . the tiniest bit of truth to her warning," she continued her defense, "well, then . . . I had to keep her home and have Phillip turn off the furnace, which is why it's so cold. . . ." She looked down into his face as he wiped tears from his eyes.

"Richard? What is it? What's wrong?" she asked. He wasn't ready for words, so he reached out, barely moving his fingers in an effort to summon her to sit beside him. As she lowered herself to the stair beside him, he instantly pulled her into his arms. She buried her face in his coat as he hugged her tightly.

Then she pulled back enough to look up into his eyes. "Is that . . . smoke I smell?"

He nodded, trying to get his emotions in check by clearing his throat. But there was still a catch in his voice when he spoke. "It happened, Liv. Just like they told you it would."

She shook her head. "No. Not really," she whispered. "It couldn't have really happened—"

"The school is in flames."

In their room, Jack sat tapping the fingers of his right hand against his left palm with Mary's trembling arms wrapped tightly around him. It was as if holding her son and keeping him safe would make the horror a little easier to bear. *The people—the poor people who had been hurt . . . who had died.* It made her tear up for the umpteenth time since she had delivered Jack's numbers to Olivia. She knew from Matilda that Olivia had kept Anna home and was grateful. But she also knew the scope of the fire would be felt long after this night.

A knock on her bedroom door startled her out of the moment. "Come in," she called in a shaky voice.

As soon as she saw Richard's and Olivia's faces, Mary knew. She released her grip on Jack and got to her feet. Richard was as white as a sheet, and she could see he was doing his best to keep his composure. Olivia wasn't even attempting to stop the tears that ran down her cheeks.

"You saved Anna's life," Richard began in a

voice husky with emotion. "I don't even know how to begin to thank you."

"Richard was there . . . saw the fire at the school," Olivia said. "He saw people . . . burned."

"It was horrible," he said with a shake of his head, as if trying to clear away the vision. "Beyond horrible."

"I called people after I decided to keep Anna home . . . they thought I was crazy." Olivia hiccupped out a clipped laugh. "*I* thought I was crazy . . . but I told them I wasn't letting Anna go. I don't know who listened . . . and who didn't. . . ."

"You tried," Mary said, then admitted, "and so did I. I called the school myself and told them what was going to happen. They thought I was making a crank call." A tear slipped down Mary's cheek, and she quickly brushed it away.

Richard couldn't seem to take his eyes off Jack. "How did he know? How does he do that?"

Mary shook her head. "It's a gift . . . and we don't always understand how gifts like this work."

"His gift is extraordinary," Richard said. Mary could hear the reverence and respect in his voice. She nodded.

Olivia lifted a handkerchief to her nose. "I need to make some calls. Check on friends . . . their families." Impulsively, she reached out and wrapped her arms around Mary, hugging her close. "Thank you for making me listen! Thank you a thousand times for not giving up!"

Richard moved toward Jack and put a hand on the little boy's shoulder. He cleared his throat. "I know you can't hear me, son, but someday I hope you can understand how grateful we are."

Mary closed the door behind them and looked back at her son. She noticed he was still tapping. She moved to kneel in front of him and reached out to cover his hands with her own.

"Things are going to change again, Jack, and I don't know where the gift is going to take us."

# Chapter Fourteen

THE FACT THAT THIS WAS NOT HER WORLD was painfully obvious to Mary. She felt as if she stood with one foot in her past and another in her present, and neither felt real. Both a spectator and a participant, she observed the hustle and bustle for the dinner party in honor of the governor that evening along with being thoroughly involved herself in all the preparations. She was polishing silver that was already shining and replacing arrangements of flowers that were simply the wrong color. She tucked lemon zest and sprigs of mint discreetly in all corners of the house—*It smells like an early spring*—as she watched deliverymen bring in beautiful linens pressed to perfection. She answered the door to let in a photographer with his equipment, on site in time to get familiar with the lighting in the dining room, the foyer, and the staircase, where photographs would be taken throughout the evening. A brand-new maid's uniform—this one a white blouse with gold handkerchief in the pocket and a black skirt, along with a white pleated cap—hung in her room. She would help serve dinner to the twenty hand-selected guests the Edmundses had invited by engraved invitation.

She couldn't help but attempt a guess at the amount being spent on this one dinner alone. Money had always represented to her a lack or a need—the rent was due; the cupboard was bare; shoes were worn; Jack had outgrown his pants. Her next paycheck was spent before she ever held it in her hand. She was witnessing firsthand the beautiful things that money could buy, but it wasn't those valuables that interested her; it was peace of mind and security. *That* was something to think about, to strive for. Peace of mind . . . about Jack and his future.

"That looks good—except you're putting the salad fork just a little too close to the dinner fork," Matilda instructed Mary from the other side of the dining room table, already sparkling with crystal goblets and three beautiful fresh-flower arrangements with gold candlesticks down the center.

Mary adjusted the small fork just a fraction and Matilda smiled her approval. "Good. Do it just like that for all twenty-two settings. I'm going to gussy up a little, and then when you're done you should do the same. Make sure the gold hankie is folded so the three points show an inch above your pocket."

Matilda started to shuffle out of the room, then turned back to Mary. "Did Miss Bea show you the special dessert she made for our little hero?"

*Our little hero . . .*

Mary nodded. "Yes, Jack's in the kitchen with her right now eating a piece. Last time I saw him he had a chocolate mustache."

"It was my idea to add the whipping cream to the top." Tildy beamed proudly. "I figured it would look more like a celebration with whipping cream and a cherry on top."

"It was so sweet of you and Miss Bea to do that for Jack," Mary said with a smile.

"I'm thinking he should have a hero's cake once a week forever," the woman proclaimed loudly as she moved into the hall. She stopped again to wag a friendly finger at Mary. "Don't forget 'bout that hankie."

"I won't," Mary promised, then turned to the massive sideboard against a wall painted with a rural scene of Tuscany. She carefully picked up a stack of gold-rimmed china selected to coordinate perfectly with the gold-colored linen tablecloth. Matching covers had been draped over the chairs and tied with ropes of brown silk. Place cards had been strategically placed earlier by Mrs. Edmunds herself.

Two floor-to-ceiling cathedral-style windows on the opposite wall from the mural each framed a copse of trees perfectly. The light in the room darkened as the late afternoon sun disappeared behind a cloud. Mary reached for a switch on the wall, illuminating two crystal chandeliers hanging over each end of the long table. Prisms of light spilled across the river of gold silk stretching down the center, creating tiny rainbows of color.

Olivia entered the dining room wearing a gray silk A-line skirt and cashmere sweater set scattered with seed pearls. She looked carefully over the table where Mary had already completed half the place settings.

"It's looking lovely," Olivia said as she adjusted the angle of a place card.

Mary moved back to the sideboard. "I, uh, wanted to thank you," she said to Olivia.

"Thank *me?*" Olivia asked with surprise.

Mary nodded. "I couldn't help but overhear a few of the phone calls you've been getting. I know it must be hard not to answer directly the questions about . . . about how you knew to warn people about the fire."

"Richard and I—and several others—owe you and Jack so much, Mary. The least everyone in the house can do is to try our best to keep your secret."

"Pretty soon people will forget, and all the curiosity will die down." Mary set down another plate, this one below a place card that read *Governor John Flynn.*

"Maybe," Olivia said skeptically. "But things like this do fascinate people. Things they don't under-stand—things they can't do themselves. There are people who would love to have Jack's gift."

"What about his silence?" Mary asked without thinking.

Olivia paused, then replied with a wry smile, "I know there are times Richard wishes *I* had that gift." They both laughed, then Olivia was back to business. "Matilda has explained to you about how dinner will go tonight?"

Mary nodded. "She did. And I'll make sure Jack stays in the kitchen with Miss Bea so he won't be in the way."

"It's entirely possible we owe Anna's life to Jack, Mary. He is *never* in the way."

Pockets of conversation passed back and forth across the beautiful table, where candles flickered and silverware scraped softly over china plates. Light ripples of laughter floated over the entire group whenever an amusing response or anecdote was heard. Mary and Matilda were clearing away dinner plates, moving quietly and discreetly between guests, their presence mostly unobserved.

Olivia had placed Governor John Flynn at the

middle of the table on the side where he'd have a view of the windows and the fire in the fireplace, with every ear accessible. Handsome, in his early fifties, Flynn wore the celebrity of his office with ease. His air of confidence was impossible to ignore but actually served to highlight the surprisingly unremarkable qualities of his wife. Constance Flynn, a mousy little woman who rarely contributed anything to a conversation, was from a very wealthy family. Rumor had it that John had married the daughter to get to the checkbook of the father. As first lady of the state of Illinois, Constance had neither presence nor political clout, but she seemed content to stand dutifully by her husband's side in photographs, cut ribbons at openings, and attend the functions and fund-raisers John deemed worthy—case in point, the Edmundses' dinner party.

The governor was speaking to the woman seated to his left—Emily Torrent, an attractive woman who smiled at anything and everything he said. But when Mary started to serve on the opposite side of the table, she found herself feeling uncomfortable when he seemed to be staring at her. Emily, a woman who obviously didn't appreciate being ignored, put a proprietary hand on the governor's arm as she tried to reclaim his attention. "John, we do so appreciate all of the resources you've used to help us start rebuilding our school so quickly."

"Not at all, Emily. That was such a tragedy," he said, shaking his head. "Thank goodness more people weren't hurt."

Mary continued on with her duties, collecting plates, clearing the table.

"All I know is—I owe a great debt to Olivia," Emily said sweetly as she looked across the table to their hostess. "She's the one who warned me not to attend the recital, you know."

Mary moved a bit faster, catching Matilda's eye to hurry her along. Matilda gave a nearly imperceptible nod and stepped up the pace.

"No debt is owed, Emily," Olivia said with an easy smile. She turned to a woman seated on the other side of Governor Flynn. "Amanda? How are the plans for the new wing at the Gad's Hill Library coming along?"

"Stalled, I'm afraid," Amanda answered.

"Excuse my interruption, ladies," the governor said with a charming smile. "But I think Emily has brought up a little bit of a mystery—and I love mysteries."

Olivia saw Mary's back as she moved out of the room with a stack of dishes. Matilda stood behind the governor, and Olivia gave her a slight nod, sending her out of the dining room as well.

"Yes, Liv, you've ducked my question before, so now I'll be droll and ask you again in front of everyone," Emily said, her cheek dimpling playfully. "How is it that you knew about the fire before it happened?"

"I've been dying to ask you that too, Olivia," another woman piped up from the other end of the table.

"I . . . didn't exactly *know*. . . ." Olivia looked quickly to Richard for help.

"I don't know about everyone else, but that fire isn't my idea of appealing dinner conversation," Richard told the group. "Does anyone need anything? How about coffee? Tea?"

"Don't be fractious, Richard. We're not talking about the grisly details of the fire," Emily's husband, Stanley, put in. "We're asking Olivia how she came to be able to call and warn us not to attend with our Susan. Something we're so thankful for—"

"Yes, Olivia—tell us." The clamor for information began.

"C'mon, Liv—everyone is grateful for the warnings. We just want to know *how you knew* to make those calls!"

"I heard it was because of a . . . *maid*." Emily Torrent looked directly across the table at Olivia. "Is that true?"

Olivia's heart sank as Mary and Matilda reentered the dining room with a dessert cart between them.

"We have Bea's famous chocolate mousse for dessert," Olivia announced.

"Actually—I heard it wasn't exactly a maid who knew something terrible was going to happen. It was her son," Emily said with a look of satisfaction.

"I'd really rather not talk about this, if you all don't mind." Olivia tried to soften the statement with a smile and nodded to the two women with the cart.

Mary placed a crystal cup of chocolate mousse in front of each of the guests as Matilda pushed the cart forward.

"Don't be coy, Olivia," the governor chuckled jovially. "The more mysterious you make this, the more we'll insist on answers."

"Oh, this is silly," Emily huffed as Mary moved behind her and slid her dessert into place. The woman reached out to put her hand on Mary's arm.

"You have to be so incredibly proud of your son." She turned so she could look up into Mary's eyes. "You're Mary—and his name is Jack, isn't it?"

Olivia, wishing there was something she could do, watched Mary hesitate. "Yes, my son's name is Jack."

"And he's the one—isn't he? I mean *the one* who predicted the fire."

"Emily, really . . ." Olivia pleaded.

"Anna told Susie," Emily went on, lifting her shoulders in an exaggerated shrug. "It's ridiculous to keep it a secret. The boy is a hero."

"Understandably, Mary would like to protect her son from any . . . publicity about this," Olivia answered. "Jack is a special child. He's a deaf-mute, so obviously he can't answer any questions about . . . about what he does. . . ." Olivia's voice trailed off as she looked apologetically at Mary.

"Then the plot thickens!" the governor declared. "The mystery of how he does what he does is as fascinating as the fact that he can do it at all!"

Mary's heart was pounding in her chest as she continued to move between the dessert cart and the table. It wasn't that familiar, fearful clutch of her heart . . . more of a tripping into uncharted territory. They were talking about Jack. *The governor thinks Jack is fascinating. My son . . . special. Fascinating . . .*

"Mary?" Governor Flynn addressed her directly.

Mary stopped and looked at him. "Yes, sir?"

"Might we have the honor of meeting your son? Is he here with you?"

*Will seeing him turn fascination to pity because he can't hear?* Her natural instincts as a mother to protect her child made her feel very wary.

"He's in the kitchen, but if you don't mind, I'd rather not bring him in," she finally said. "He's shy and not used to attention. I'd . . ." She glanced at Olivia but knew her kind benefactor had done all she could in the circumstances.

The governor tented his fingers together and

pressed them against his mouth before offering her his kindest smile. "Anyone can see what a wonderful, protective mother you are, Mary. But surely you know how valuable someone with Jack's gift could be to the world."

*Valuable . . . to the world . . .*

"Personally, I'd like to shake the hand of the young man who helped several people in this room, as well as others in our community, avoid a terrible heartbreak," he said.

She heard other guests around the table murmuring agreement, and she looked into faces of people who seemed to sincerely want to meet her son.

Mary finally nodded at the governor. "All right. I'll go get him."

"Excellent." Governor Flynn beamed a smile around the table. A ripple of conversation followed Mary out of the room. She heard Emily Torrent say smugly, "There now—the secret's out, and the roof didn't come crashing down."

"It wasn't my secret to tell, Emily," Olivia answered quietly.

Matilda was just placing the last cup of chocolate mousse in front of the last guest at the table when Mary reentered the dining room, holding Jack's hand.

A collective intake of breath as they saw him took her by surprise. She looked at the faces all turned toward her son. *They're looking at him with wonder—respectfully . . . admiringly. . . .* The realization filled her with tenderness, with pride.

"This is Jack," she said as she led him toward John Flynn, all the while conscious of the whispered speculation and observations from the people at the table.

"So handsome!"

"What a beautiful boy. . . ."

"He looks wise—doesn't he?"

"I think he looks like her. . . ."

"Ah, young Jack, the man of the hour," Governor Flynn said, turning his chair so that he could look right into Jack's face when Mary stopped next to him at the table. He smiled at the boy, but Jack stared back impassively. The governor looked up at Mary. "He is indeed a fine-looking lad."

"Thank you."

"Does he perhaps read lips—or communicate in some other fashion—sign language maybe?"

Mary shook her head.

"Oh, well, that's . . ."

*Please don't say "too bad"—or "that's terrible"—or "I'm sorry" . . .*

". . . even more impressive, then," the governor finished. "I have an idea. Why don't you let Jack show us what he can do?"

Mary drew him into her arms, wrapping them across his chest. "I'm sorry, sir, but I don't think that's a good idea."

"Oh, come on. What's the harm?"

"It's not like that," she explained. "It's not something he can just turn on and off at will. There isn't always a . . . a prophecy, a special word, when he touches someone."

The governor smiled broadly. "Well, then—I repeat. What's the harm in giving it a whirl?"

She wasn't prepared for this. She and Jack had no experience with a room filled with people who would all be watching—and judging—and leaving the room with ideas about her boy that would be formed in the space of just a few minutes. She shook her head again.

"Like I said, he's shy, and I just don't think it's . . . it's wise to put him on the spot like this. . . ."

Olivia started to say something, but the governor waved her off. "Pardon me for saying this, Mary, but when Jack was born . . . the way he is, you were obviously given a great responsibility as his mother to see that he fulfills his potential. I think Shakespeare said it best: 'Be not afraid of greatness: some are born great, some achieve greatness and some have greatness thrust upon them.' Let Jack be great," he finished with a politician's authority and confidence.

Mary let her gaze sweep around the table at the rapt expressions on the faces of the guests. *Let Jack be great. . . .*

"Would you mind if . . . if we turned off the lights?" Mary asked.

The governor looked surprised but shrugged. "All right by me if it makes him feel less self-conscious." He looked across the table. "Olivia? Lights?"

Olivia looked at Richard, who got up from the table and went to the switch for the chandeliers. The only lights now left in the room were the candles glowing over the table.

"Are we good?" the governor asked Mary, but she shook her head.

"Please. The candles too," she insisted.

"You heard the lady," the governor said. "Out they go."

Guests leaned forward to extinguish the candles, leaving only the sheen of moonlight coming through the windows.

"This is like a séance."

"Did you know Mary Todd Lincoln, President Lincoln's wife, held séances in the White House?" someone chuckled.

"Awful rumors—"

"Don't you need crystal balls or something?"

"How would you know, Emily?"

"No, it's nothing like that," Mary interjected, keeping her voice as steady as she could. "There is absolutely no attempt to communicate with spirits or mediums. *Never.*"

The room went silent.

"Please hold still when I put Jack's hand over yours, sir," Mary said softly in the dark room.

"Okay, ready when you are," Flynn said.

Mary was sure she detected a note of amusement in his voice, but she ignored it as she took Jack's hand in hers and placed it on the governor's hand. She thought she felt Flynn stiffen for a moment, and then in seconds she slipped Jack's hand from the governor's. After a moment she said, "The lights can come back on."

The guests blinked as the chandeliers blazed back to life. Mary stood with her hands on Jack's shoulders.

"Well, that was painless, wasn't it?" The governor smiled broadly. "Now—how do we find out what Jack is predicting for me?"

"We need a pencil and a piece of paper," Mary said quietly. "Unless you've changed your mind . . . ?"

The governor reached into the inside pocket of his tuxedo and withdrew a pen and a business card. "A good public servant is always prepared."

Mary felt every eye on them as the governor pushed back from the table and guided her into his chair. She pulled Jack onto her lap and placed the card facedown on the table. She placed Jack's fingers into position around the pen, and everyone's eyes were glued to their hands moving slowly and carefully across the back of the card. In less than a minute, she put Jack back on his feet, stood and smoothed out her skirt, and handed the card to Governor Flynn.

"Thank you for sharing your son with us tonight, Mary," he said warmly, but his eye was on the small rectangle of white in his hand.

"You're welcome," she replied.

"I'd love to have Jack tell *me* what's in store," Emily Torrent said, obviously attempting to be humorous.

"Me too," another woman added from the end of the table.

"I don't think we should impose on Jack again tonight," Richard said in a tone that brooked no argument.

Mary took Jack's hand and turned toward the doorway.

"Mary, once you get Jack settled with Bea, I think we're ready for our coffee," Olivia called.

"I'll be right back with it," she said, hurrying Jack from the room.

The guests turned their attention back to John Flynn, who was studying the card, a frown on his face.

"Well? What does it say?" Emily demanded.

The governor looked at Olivia. "Numbers? The boy wrote some numbers—what's *that* supposed to mean?"

"How well do you know your Bible, John?" Olivia asked.

"What? My . . . Bible?"

She nodded. "As I understand it, it's kind of a

code. Mary explained that the first number is the sequential book of the Bible. The second number is the chapter of that book, and the third is the verse."

"He uses the *Bible* to convey what he sees happening?"

"Actually, according to Mary, what he sees are the numbers . . . the words—and meaning—are found by following this code."

John Flynn looked down the length of the table at Richard and grinned. "Richard, my man—we need a Bible."

Richard pushed back from the table. "I have one in my study. I'll be right back."

He hurried from the room, but before Olivia could say anything, the guests were all following suit—pushing back chairs, dropping napkins beside empty dessert cups, all talking at once as they moved out of the dining room.

They gathered around Richard's desk while he opened the Bible to the index. Richard made brief eye contact with Olivia and then looked at Governor Flynn.

"What's the first number, please?"

John held up the card—a showman enjoying the attention. He adjusted a pair of reading glasses from his pocket and announced, "It's nineteen!"

"Olivia—where on earth did you find them—

Mary and her son?" Emily asked as she stood next to her husband.

"I happened upon them several weeks ago. She and Jack were actually . . . in rather dire straits. No one would allow her to keep Jack with her while she worked. I just wanted to help, and I hired her."

"Most generous . . ." someone murmured.

"Not at all," Olivia deferred. "We're just so grateful—she's a wonderful worker, but now we're even more grateful to both of them."

"Here it is," Richard said, finger in place on the index. "The nineteenth book is the book of Psalms."

People were immediately attentive. The governor looked back at the card in his hand. "The next number is one hundred and nine."

Richard flipped pages and looked up again. "All right. That's the chapter—what's the verse? What's the next number?"

"Eight," the governor said with a grin. "Eight— guess that's the number that tells my fate!" A ripple of laughter ran through the room as Richard ran his finger down the page. His eyes slid over the words, but he didn't look up.

"Well? Are you going to read it or not?" Stanley Torrent said. "Come on, now, Richard. Don't keep us in the dark."

"Yes, Rich—tell me. What does the boy predict?" Flynn's voice boomed out like an announcer at a carnival.

Richard looked up at the assembled group, his eyes stopping briefly on Olivia—and then back on the page. His reluctance to read it aloud was clearly evident. He cleared his throat. " 'Let his days be few; and let another take his office,' " Richard read slowly.

The room was filled with grave silence. Finally the governor was able to force a chuckle. His wife moved closer. "Well—guess I'd better dust off my law degree," he quipped. "My days in the governor's mansion seem numbered."

A rumble of supportive comments surged out of the group, but none sounded sincere in their reassurances that it was all an enormous mistake.

Richard started to close the Bible, but Governor Flynn stepped up and put his hand between the pages. "Mind if I take a look?" Though he had tried to keep his voice light, there was an edge to the question.

Richard wordlessly handed him the book. "Sorry about the chapter and verse, but November is months away—things can change for the better. . . ."

"He's just a kid. A deaf-mute kid, at that," the governor tossed out.

Constance came up beside him and looked down at the open pages of the Bible, and then put her hand on his arm. He shrugged it off and slammed the Bible closed.

"John, I have a photographer here waiting to

take some pictures for the society page. Could we impose on you and Constance?" Olivia asked skillfully.

"Impose away," John said as he put on a smile and ushered his wife from the room. The other guests left the study in small groups, heads together—talking in subdued tones.

Olivia tucked her arm through Richard's as they trailed behind their guests into the formal living room. "What do you think?" she whispered.

"I think we should tell Tildy not to serve the Dom Perignon with dessert," Richard said in a voice meant only for Olivia.

"But it's the twenty-one vintage—the best we have in the cellar."

"I know," he said wryly. "Tell her to switch to the Taittinger—no use wasting the good stuff on the losing candidate."

# Chapter Fifteen

WHEN SHE LOOKED BACK ON IT, Mary realized it was one of those times when she should have clearly seen what was happening. But in the middle of it—the exciting, flattering, satisfying, gratifying middle of it—she had no idea the world, once more, was shifting beneath her feet.

It began the day after the governor's dinner when Olivia answered another phone call about Jack, this time from a newspaper reporter. Mary was passing through the foyer with Jack as Olivia lifted her eyebrows at her and cupped her hand over the mouthpiece.

"It's a reporter from the *Chicago Daily Times*. He wants to come over with a photographer and do a story on Jack for the morning edition. What do you want me to tell him?"

*A reporter to do a story about Jack? Everyone will know about his gift! They will know he's far more than a deaf-mute.* The thought was thrilling, but in the next instant she remembered. *Jerry.* Mary had a sudden mental image of Jerry sitting at the kitchen table, the newspaper spread in front of him on a Saturday morning. *Only the local paper—he'd probably never see a paper from Chicago. But still, to be on the safe side . . .*

Mary shook her head. "I don't think so."

"Are you sure? They'll probably run a story anyway. At least this way you'd have some control over the content," Olivia said quietly, her hand still over the phone.

She hesitated. "I'll think about it."

Mary listened as Olivia handled the reporter with the composure of someone who was used to giving interviews, who had sat for photographers, read about herself in the society pages on more than a few occasions.

Olivia hung up the phone and sighed. "My best guess is it's just the first of many. I asked our guests last night not to say anything about Jack—

but that request no doubt fell on deaf ears." Olivia immediately blushed at her thoughtlessness. She hurried on, "But now that the word's leaked out about who provided the warning, and that he's a deaf-mute child . . ." She shook her head. "Well, I don't have to tell you how newsworthy that is. Anyway, I'll field any calls for you until you decide if you want to cooperate with the press or not."

*A servant's master is answering the calls. . . .* Mary smiled. "Thank you, Mrs. Edmunds. I really appreciate that."

"Well, why wouldn't a reporter wanna do a story 'bout our Jack?" Miss Bea muttered as she put a sandwich in front of him. "He's like a little . . . a little prophet. Who wouldn't wanna know more 'bout a real-live prophet?"

Mary tucked a napkin in Jack's collar, looking at the food on the plate. "You're spoiling him, Miss Bea. I don't know how a prophet eats," she quipped with a little smile, "but Jack's been eating like a small king lately."

"And that's how he's gonna keep eatin' long as I'm workin' in this kitchen," Bea declared.

"Maybe you should ask Jack to see if he knows how long you're going to be working here, Bea," Matilda suggested archly from her perch at the counter.

But Miss Bea shook her head. "Once ya know

what tomorrow's bringin', ya might not wanna wake up."

Matilda bobbed her head in agreement. "That's how I see it." She reached for the tuner on the radio. "Time for my program."

The announcer's voice filled the kitchen. "*The Goldbergs* radio drama is brought to you today by Procter and Gamble's Oxydol: the soap that cuts grease twenty-five percent faster than other soaps. In today's episode we join Molly, Jake, and their friends as they try to find a way to come up with the money. . . ." And the voice droned on.

Mary couldn't help herself—she also had become a fan of the radio serial that played every day while they were having their lunch. She hung on every word, just like Tildy and Bea.

When they cut away from the drama for local news fifteen minutes later, Matilda sighed. "I hope those Goldbergs get enough money to buy those flower seeds," she said over the beginning of the news report. "That Mildred Holt needs to turn loose a few coins." The weatherman called for low clouds and a few days of mild temperatures.

"And now the newsworthy items from our own backyard," the announcer said. "Katharine Hepburn and Cary Grant star in *Bringing Up Baby,* still playing at the Chicago Theater for the fourth straight week in a row. Governor and Mrs. Flynn visited the children's ward at the hospital today. The governor brought licorice and comic books for the kids. And speaking of kids—word has it that a child was the one responsible for warning so many out in Highland Park about the fire that gutted one wing of the Keller Academy two weeks ago."

"Jack! He's talking about Jack!" Tildy exclaimed. Mary, stunned, leaned toward the radio. "Reliable sources, close friends of socialites Richard and Olivia Edmunds, say that a deaf-mute boy prophesied the event in an unusual way. The boy's mother is in the Edmundses' employ."

"That's you, Mary!" Miss Bea put in, finger pointed toward Mary. "You're 'the boy's mother in the Edmundses' employ'!"

"And to think they're talking about our Jack on the same station that *The Goldbergs* are on!" Tildy said, genuine awe in her voice. "Just think how many people know about Jack now!"

Mary shook her head in amazement. "I can't believe it," she said, thrilled at the mention of Jack on the radio.

"He's like a famous person," Miss Bea offered with a grin. "Everybody gonna know our Jack."

*Jack—famous?* "How many people do you suppose listen to the news after *The Goldbergs* are on?" Mary wondered.

"Enough," Miss Bea said.

"Enough for what?"

"Enough to change things around here." Her words proved to be as prophetic as Jack's numbers.

· · ·

The chaos wore a calm disguise in the beginning. Mary, unsure of her ability to handle an interview, was happy to let Olivia field the questions.

"Mrs. Edmunds! Did you know Jack was special when you hired his mother to be your maid?" a reporter, among a handful of others gathered on the edge of the lawn, called out to Olivia.

"I think of Jack and his mother as part of the family," Olivia said, climbing into the Rolls in the driveway. She paused to add, "She's not just our maid. And, yes—though I didn't know exactly what Jack could do, I did sense that he was special. My own sixth sense, if you will."

Olivia was adept at giving out just enough information to make the reporter feel as if he was getting an exclusive—but not enough to give away any personal details about Jack or Mary. Olivia told Mary that when being interviewed, less is always more. Never volunteer information—only allude to what you want the reporter to glean from your statement. So, as far as the greater Chicago metro area was concerned, Mary and Jack were born and bred in Illinois. Their last name was never in print, and Jack's appearance remained a mystery, since no one was allowed to photograph the boy. Olivia found herself rather enjoying the spotlight—as was Richard at work and Anna at school. At least at first.

• • •

The current of speculation and curiosity running through succeeding days, though, turned from a meandering stream to a gushing river. It started to push its way into even the menial tasks of the household and upset the balance of life at the Edmundses. The initial phone calls gave way to more reporters and photographers camped out near the driveway, all hoping to get a glimpse of the boy. It was impossible for Phillip to back the car out of the drive without worrying he might hit a photographer or reporter skulking along the bushes. Matilda had her photo taken one morning by a man crouching beside the front steps when she stepped outside to get the newspaper. Olivia, though initially pleased by the attention when she attended a fund-raiser for her special Gad's Hill Library project, was soon annoyed by the censure she was hearing for not allowing people into her home to be touched by the boy who seemed to have all the answers.

Prestige and reverence for Jack had been alluring, even intoxicating, for Mary. People were finally realizing that her boy had something to say—even without a voice. But the intrusiveness of the press, as well as those who had started showing up at the front door looking for an audience "with the little prophet," was becoming more than tiresome. She couldn't take Jack outside for fear of a photographer capturing his image, and even though Richard hired a security guard to keep people away from the house, Mary always rushed Jack through the glass breezeway when they made their way from their quarters to the main house. No more stopping to gaze at the beautiful view or enjoying quiet, uninterrupted moments while she polished the glass. If someone took Jack's picture and put it in the paper . . . She trembled at the possible consequences.

"Been hearin' that tickle in your throat for two days now, Mary," Miss Bea said. "I'm gonna brew you some tea and honey. Maybe it'll soothe your cough."

Bea put the kettle on while Mary, Jack, and Tildy had their lunch. The drone of the voices on the radio from *The Goldbergs* almost masked the knock on the kitchen delivery door. They all glanced through the window at a familiar face, and Miss Bea made her way over to open the door for Wally, their deliveryman from the market. Tildy turned up the volume on the radio.

"Got everything you ordered," Wally said as he walked into the kitchen and set a box of food down on the large center island. "Ticket's in the box." Miss Bea started to pull the contents from the box, checking the order against the list in her hand.

Wally looked in Mary and Jack's direction and lifted his chin in a small acknowledgment. "Afternoon."

"Good afternoon," Mary answered.

"Nice day, but I smell a change in the air. Supposed to be a front coming through tonight and tomorrow," he said conversationally.

"I guess we could use the rain," Mary answered, even as Tildy shushed them both and leaned closer to the radio.

"What's this?" Miss Bea asked, pulling a Brownie camera out from under a sack of rice.

Wally casually plucked the camera from her hand. "Oh, that's mine," he said. "Didn't mean to leave it in there."

It happened very quickly. Mary reached for Jack, who was sitting on a stool near the counter. Snagging him around the waist, she pulled him back against her just as Wally snapped a picture. The sudden flash from the camera startled them all into attention.

"Wally! You can't be doin' that!" Miss Bea exclaimed, advancing toward him. Mary turned Jack's face into her uniform to prevent another photograph.

But Wally was already hustling to the kitchen door, camera in hand, and threw a look of apology over his shoulder. "Sorry, but I need the money," he said, yanking the door open. It slammed behind him.

Now there would be a face to put with articles about Jack. The whole city of Chicago would get to see her boy's handsome face in the paper—not something she had gone looking for, but there it was anyway. Jack's fame had just increased.

When the photo of Jack was published the next morning, the people of Chicago saw a dark-haired, wide-eyed little boy looking back at them. Mary shook her head at the irony of the whole thing. She had wanted people to recognize Jack as a special human being in his own right—someone different but no less valuable than any other person. And now . . . her wish had come true. Jack was famous in Chicago. Without uttering a word, he was being revered and admired and respected. She thought about the posters of the movie stars in the theater lobby where she'd once worked—and how in awe she was of them. Their fame made them seem untouchable. *Maybe people are thinking about Jack like that now. And that I'm lucky to be his mother . . . no more "Poor Mary with the mute child." Blessed Mary with the prophet child!*

Mary carefully folded the newspaper so the picture of Jack wouldn't crease, then turned back to Jack, who was watching her. She smiled. "Just like always, we're in this together, little man. Now we'll just have to see where it takes us."

It was night and close to eleven o'clock when a terrified scream came from upstairs. Olivia sprang to her feet from the living room sofa, her needlepoint falling to the floor. "What was that?"

Richard also jumped out of his chair, throwing aside the newspaper. "Anna!" He bolted across the room with Olivia close behind. Another loud cry assaulted them as they ran into the foyer toward the staircase.

"Daddy! Daddy!" Anna was flying down the stairs toward them, her face white with fear. And groping his way behind her—a bedraggled-looking man in a tattered army coat and wool hat pulled down over his ears, his eyes dark and wild.

Olivia screamed.

"Call the police! Call them now!" Richard was shouting. Olivia looked frantically between her daughter and the telephone, hesitating only long enough to see Anna stumble into her father's arms at the bottom step.

On seeing Richard, the intruder stopped short and threw his hands in the air. "I don't mean no harm to the girl," he mumbled. "It's just the boy I'm needin' to see."

"He came . . . in . . . my . . . window!" Anna gasped out between sobs.

"They're on their way," Olivia said in a shaky voice, hanging up the telephone. "The police will be here soon."

"Take Anna into the other room," Richard ordered, his eyes firmly on the intruder. He released his hold on his daughter only when Olivia folded her arms around the terrified little girl.

"Listen, I ain't got no gun or nothin'. I just wanna talk to the boy." The man started down the stairs again.

"Stop right there!" Richard commanded as Olivia hurried Anna out.

But the intruder kept descending. "I got a bet to place—a horse race I *can't* lose. Just need the kid to tell me the winner—"

"I said stay right there! You're not talking to anyone, you hear me?"

"Jus' like a rich man to keep somethin' good all to hisself," the man grumbled.

The whine of distant sirens drew both men's attention to the door.

Richard looked back at the intruder. "You're going to jail."

The man suddenly leaped down the last few steps, landing with a thud. "Not again I'm not!" With surprising alacrity, he ran past Richard, turned the lock on the door, and bolted outside—right into the glare of flashing red lights.

Late the following day Mary and Jack were waiting as requested in Mr. Edmunds's study. Mary hadn't slept at all after the household's pandemonium of the previous night. She'd seen how terrified Anna was, along with the disbelief and outrage on Olivia's and Richard's faces. Anna had clung first to her mother, then her father, her haunted-looking eyes darting around the room.

"I'm so sorry, Anna! So sorry . . ." Mary had said, but she knew her words were of little comfort.

"It's not your fault, Mary," Richard had told her. "Not yours or Jack's—there are lunatics out there, and you don't have any control over that," he'd added in a low voice as Olivia had walked Anna back up the stairs, assuring the little girl that she would stay with her for the night.

The morning edition had run a front-page story about the break-in, and reporters and photographers had been out in force all day, anxious for a follow-up to the previous night's drama. Mary had heard little from Olivia, other than further reassurances that the Edmundses didn't blame her at all.

But Mary knew what was coming—why they'd been summoned. The only way the Edmundses could ensure no other intruders were tempted to force their way in to see Jack was to remove the temptation. . . .

Mary looked up as Richard entered the study, a white envelope in his hand. *Like the one I lost . . .* momentarily flitted through her mind. She stood, Jack by her side.

"I'm sorry, Mary." There was genuine regret in his voice. "But it's come down to the safety of my family."

Mary tried to answer but coughed into her hand. Her throat had gotten worse in the last few days.

"I know you don't have a choice," she finally managed.

"If you decide to stay in town, I'll be more than happy to find a place for you. . . . I have some contacts—"

"No, thank you. I think leaving Chicago is the best for us. We'll find someplace where no one knows about Jack."

Olivia and Anna appeared in the doorway, looking strained, uncomfortable. "We just wanted to . . . to say . . ." But Olivia couldn't continue and shook her head, her eyes filled with tears. Anna walked quickly to Mary and Jack, giving him a quick peck on the cheek and standing on tiptoe to do the same for Mary. Quickly she returned to her mother's side.

The two women looked a long moment at each other, conveying a silent understanding that their children came first above any other considerations. A tiny ghost of a smile from Mary was met with a nearly imperceptible nod from Olivia.

Richard gently placed the envelope in Mary's hand. "There's enough here to see you through several weeks."

Mary nodded her thanks.

"Once you've packed, Phillip will discreetly get your things to the car. He has a blanket to throw over you and Jack until you're past all the crazies at the gate. They'll never know you're there."

Mary nodded again.

"We'll always be . . . grateful to you and Jack," he said with a little break in his voice. "We can't ever tell you how much . . ."

Mary waited a moment, then said, "And I'll always be grateful that you gave me a job—a home—when no one else would." Her voice sounded gravelly in her ears, and her head was aching—even her skin hurt. *A fever . . . ?* She thought about sitting down but was afraid she wouldn't be able to stand again.

Richard was saying, "You'll be all right . . . you'll do fine, Mary," though his tone was skeptical.

"Yes, we'll be fine," she echoed faintly.

Richard and Olivia stood at the rain-swept window with Anna and watched the glow of the taillights as Phillip maneuvered the car past the reporters and photographers, all jockeying to snap the prize picture to run in the next edition. One by one they turned away when they realized they'd only captured the driver.

"I'll make a statement to the press tomorrow morning, informing them that Mary and her son are no longer in our employ, therefore no longer living in our home. Maybe then life will get back to normal."

"Maybe for us." Olivia's voice sounded ragged and tired. "I'm not sure 'normal' is something that can ever happen for Mary and Jack. . . ."

# Chapter Sixteen

STANDING IN THE LOBBY of the damp bus station, Mary didn't know if the aches she was feeling were from actual illness or from fear and loss. Had it really only been a couple of hours since her life had unraveled—again? She looked down at Jack, standing patiently, always patiently. Resisting the urge to cough, she gazed slowly about the station without moving her head. *I'm fine! Just need a warm bus out of town. Two seats side by side so I can rest . . .*

She saw a long green board behind the counter. Moving closer, Mary had to concentrate on the posted schedule to make the words come into focus.

The man behind the counter cleared his throat. "May I help you?"

"When does the next bus leave?"

"What city?" he demanded, shaking his head. She again searched the listings, trying to make sense of the jumble of numbers and destinations.

"There's one *scheduled* to leave at eleven for Milwaukee," he informed her, impatience coloring his tone, "but right now nothing's on time because of the storm."

"I'll take two tickets anyway," she said in a husky voice, fumbling with the clasp on her pocketbook.

"I'd wait on buying 'em"—he looked at her more closely—"in case we cancel."

She had no other plan. *A bus ticket to some other town* was her only idea as she'd left the Edmundses. Her wet coat felt like a hundred-pound weight, and she pulled her arms from the sleeves, suddenly so hot she felt suffocated. Using the back of her glove, she drew a trembling hand across her perspiring forehead just as a woman came rushing up.

"I know him!" she called out as she pointed at Jack. "He's the boy in the paper—the one who predicted the fire!"

Mary shook her head, pulling Jack with her as she backed away. But the woman kept advancing. "It *is* him—right?"

Mary tried to find her voice but started to cough. She pulled Jack away, but the woman had begun drawing attention to all three of them. "Just stay put a second, will ya?" she persisted. "I only want to talk to the boy prophet . . . Jack! His name is Jack. I saw his picture in the paper—"

"No, no . . ." Mary finally croaked out. The room around her seemed to swim. "You're mistaken."

The woman would not be put off and pulled a few bills from her pocketbook. She waved them at Mary. "I need to find out something—something important about my future," she insisted, practically stepping on Mary's toes. "I've got some money here. You can have it. Please? Just let the boy—"

"We don't want your money," Mary said, feeling trapped by her relentless badgering. She turned to find a way out and saw an older woman heading straight for her. *Oh no. Not another one . . .*

"Well, *finally!* I was beginning to give up on you, Sally!" the woman said with a broad smile. "And, Bobby! Look how much you've grown!" She wagged a finger at Jack. "I was afraid the storm had kept you home."

Mary swallowed, wincing from the pain in her throat. "I'm sorry . . . ?"

The first woman frowned. *"Bobby?* This kid's name is Bobby?" She looked between the boy and the stranger, who stood with a smile on her face. "Are you sure? I could have sworn he's the kid who could tell the future!"

"I think I'd know my own granddaughter and great-grandson, wouldn't I?" the second woman insisted. She looked at Mary and raised her brows. "Right, Sally?"

Mary hesitated, then found the presence of mind to nod. "Right. Yes—"

"Fine, then," the annoying woman grumped, "but just so's you know—your Bobby's got a double right here in Chicago." She gave Jack one more searching look and shook her head as she turned away. "Coulda sworn it was him. . . ."

The older woman looked at Mary apologetically. "I hope I didn't overstep, my dear, but she looked like she was becoming quite a pest."

"She was. Thank you."

"You're welcome," she said, gazing at Mary with concern in her eyes. "You're not well."

Mary shook her head and coughed again.

"I've got some seats over there." She pointed to a row against the wall. "Would you like to come and sit by me?"

Mary felt uncertain. She whispered, "You know who he is . . . don't you?"

The old woman nodded. "I admit I too recognized him from the picture in the newspaper."

"You . . . you want something from him too?" Mary asked guardedly.

"No, dear. Nothing at all," she replied. "I'm Agnes Meriwether—and I believe you're Jack's mother."

"Yes . . . yes, I'm Mary." She still wasn't sure she could trust . . . Agnes, was it?

"It's a pleasure to meet you, Mary. Now—come over here and sit down before you fall down. You look weak as a kitten." Without waiting for a response, Agnes picked up Mary's suitcase and started across the floor.

Mary couldn't help but feel relief that someone had made a decision for her. She was beyond tired as she fumbled for Jack's hand, holding it tight while they followed Agnes. She tried to focus on the silver in Agnes's hair, the turquoise of the knit cardigan swaying back and forth in front of her.

"Please, sit." Agnes gestured to the row of chairs she'd obviously staked out as her own. "I've been here awhile, and from the looks of it, I don't think any of us'll be leaving anytime soon."

Mary helped Jack into a chair and then eased into the one next to him, leaning her head back against the wall. The reprieve almost made her cry.

Before Agnes sat down too, she looked closely at Jack. "You're a very handsome boy," she said. "Beautiful brown eyes. You know they say the eyes are the windows of the soul." She paused, then smiled. "Jack must have a beautiful soul."

Agnes started to chat, and Mary tried to concentrate on the words. But her body was now giving in to chills sweeping over her skin in waves, followed by a candlewick of heat up and down her arms. She vaguely understood she was doing a poor job of holding up her end of the conversation, but Agnes plunged valiantly on, talking of warm weather and sunshine, "out of this awful Chicago rain and sleet and snow. . . ."

Somehow, Mary eventually let the woman know that she was unemployed and planning to board a bus to a new city, ". . . maybe Milwaukee, a city where people haven't read the *Chicago Daily Times* and wouldn't be recognizing . . ." The room grew dark and started to spin.

"Mary? Are you all right?" Agnes's voice came from some faraway place. "You're sick, dear.

Even if the bus does leave tonight, I don't think you can be on it."

When the floor started to rise, Mary thought it would feel so good to let go . . . turn loose . . . slip right out of her chair and lie down. So she did.

## Chapter Seventeen

*"MOMMY?"*

*"I'm here, buddy."*

*"Where?"*

*"Right in here. Come and find me."*

*"I made this for you. It's called a mobile."*

*"That's beautiful, Jack. Let's hang it from the ceiling. . . ."*

The ceiling looked unfamiliar, swirls in white plaster that made her dizzy as she tried to focus on it. *That . . . that isn't right.*

"Fever's still high . . . just something cool on your head, dear." *Someone's putting out the fire.* A drop of water ran down the side of her face—like a tear trailing from her eye. *Nice and cool.*

*"Mommy?"*

*"Yes, Jack?"*

*"Snow angels today?"*

*"Not today, little man."* He looked so small walking away that it broke her heart. *"Wait, Jack—don't go without me. Stay here, and we'll play in the snow tomorrow. Jack?"*

* * *

*"Are you feeling any better, Mary?"*
 *"No. Yes. I don't know. Mother?"*
 *"Yes?"*
 *"Where's Jack?"*
 *"Jack who?"*
 *"Jack! My son. Your grandson!"*
 *"There is no Jack, Mary."*
 *"Don't say that! I have a child. A boy. Jack!"*
 *"You're doing it again. Telling lies. That makes*
*me sad, Mary."*
 *"Go find him. Please—bring him to me."*
 *"Such an imagination will get you into trouble."*
 *"I'm not imagining, Mother. I'm not!"*
 *"You're imagining . . . me."*

The waking was gradual, like coming up from under water to the surface. Hazy and lazy and close enough to touch. Finally Mary slowly opened her eyes, squinting at the sunlight through the window, with no idea where she was. The bed was comfortable, the room felt homey. There was a glass of water on the bedside table, and she reached for it to soothe the dryness of her throat.

Her body felt sore—stiff—foreign. She flexed her fingers, still encased in her gloves, and she saw she was wearing her own cotton nightgown. She struggled to raise herself up on an elbow and took a sip from the glass.

A gauzy memory flitted past—the woman at the bus station. *Agnes.* That was real—wasn't it? Arriving at a house someplace, barely managing to walk inside while someone supported her firmly around her waist. *Is that what happened?* Memory intertwined with the residue of her dreams, and then it solidified into one panic-stricken thought.

*Jack.*

She saw her robe at the bottom of the bed. Moving stiffly but as quickly as she could manage, Mary staggered out of the bedroom.

The living room of the house was empty, the space so quiet Mary heard the ticking of a clock on the fireplace mantel.

"Hello?" Her voice sounded husky, and her heart hammered in her chest. *I'm in a stranger's house and can't find my son.*

"Agnes?" The name felt strange on her tongue—as if it were the first time she'd said it.

*Please, please, please . . .*

"You're up, dear!"

Mary turned and saw Agnes—with Jack right by her side. Mary clutched at the wall. "Jack," she breathed.

Agnes put her hand on his back and gave him a little push. "Go see Mommy."

As if he'd heard her, Jack crossed to Mary and stopped right in front of her. She leaned down and touched his nose, then drew the familiar heart around his face. And for a long moment he stood, focused and smiling, in front of her.

"What day is this?" Mary finally rasped out as she knelt to put her arms around her son.

"Friday."

Mary felt her mouth drop open. "But we met on—"

"Tuesday evening," Agnes supplied. "I've seen my share of influenza over the years, and you sure had yourself a good dose of it."

"Oh, you've been exposed—and your house. . . . I'm so sorry."

Agnes waved a dismissive hand. "Oh, posh. I've never caught the flu and don't plan to now. Guess I'm too old or too ornery."

"I don't know how to begin to thank you," Mary started. "There are no words . . ."

Agnes clucked her tongue. "You just did."

"I don't know what we would have done. . . ." Mary tried to reach back in her memory to the bus station.

Agnes smiled. "People who *need* each other— *find* each other, Mary. That's all that happened. Now—can you eat a little something?"

Mary put a hand on her stomach and grimaced. "I don't think so. Not yet."

"Then—at the very least some tea?"

"I think I could . . . yes, I could drink some tea."

Agnes nodded. "Good. And I've learned that

Jack has a taste for hot cocoa," she said. "You curl up on the sofa, and we'll have a nice little chat."

The afghan tucked around Mary's legs was beautifully crafted, multicolored with tiny stitches speaking volumes about the maker's skill with a crochet hook. As she looked around the room, she noted it was neat as a pin, nearly devoid of clutter or personal "dust catchers," as her foster mother would say about knickknacks and photos on shelves or tabletops. Mary sat in a haze of contentment, sipping tea on the overstuffed floral sofa with Jack tucked in beside her. She watched the amber-orange flames that curled around a log burning in the fireplace.

"I feel terrible that you put off your trip because of me." Mary looked at the way Agnes's nimble hands worked a pair of knitting needles.

"Don't be silly. I can go anytime I want," Agnes insisted. "I was just looking to get out of the cold for a while, is all."

"So a vacation someplace warm—?"

"Like I said, I can do that anytime." Agnes smiled comfortably. "Options for someone my age are wide open."

"I guess my options are open too." Mary laid her hand on Jack's knee.

"Tell me about the gloves, dear," Agnes said. "I have to confess I started to take them off after the cab driver helped me get you into the house. I just assumed they were for warmth—"

"You saw my hands?" Mary asked with a quick look at Jack. "Was Jack—did he see—?"

"No, I didn't *see* them. Nor did Jack. I only meant that when I started to remove your gloves, I saw a little bit of the scarring. But Jack was already fast asleep on the couch while I was trying to get you more comfortable."

Mary sighed her relief. "I can't explain my hands to him, and I don't know what he'd think if he saw them. I just decided to never remove my gloves in front of him."

"I see. . . ." Agnes nodded.

Mary finally answered the unspoken question. "Both my hands were burned when I was a little girl."

"That's awful." Agnes shook her head. "How did it happen, dear?"

"An accident in the kitchen. Some boiling water . . ." Mary's voice trailed off.

"What a shame. A tragedy for such a beautiful woman."

Mary didn't know how to respond, so she said nothing.

"And what of Jack's father, may I ask?"

"He's . . . not in our lives anymore."

"My Henry's been gone for ten years. He was a wonderful man, and to this day I still miss him."

"I'm sorry for your loss."

"And I'm sorry for yours," Agnes said quietly.

"Don't be," Mary answered shortly. Then, "It sounds like Henry was a good man."

"He was," Agnes agreed. "I was blessed to find him."

"And we were lucky to find you at the bus station." Mary smiled.

"I don't think it was luck at all," Agnes replied. "I think it was . . . Providence."

"Well, whatever you want to call it, I'm grateful," Mary said. "And we'll get on our way as quickly as we can."

Agnes gazed at Mary with an unreadable expression in her eyes. "Providence isn't something you rush, Mary. Let's just wait and see what happens—shall we?"

# Chapter Eighteen

MARY FELT POSITIVELY *LIGHT* AS she knelt beside Agnes to help turn over the soil in flower beds bordering the small, sunny yellow house. The early spring day was warm enough that they could work without winter jackets—the first time since she'd left Minnesota that they weren't burdened with extra layers. Jack sat on his heels, his attention fixed on some fat worms squirming their way in and out of the loose soil.

"I wish I had extra gardening gloves for you,"

Agnes commented, looking at Mary's gloves now the color of the dirt.

"Don't worry. I have several pairs," Mary said as she dug up some weeds. She looked up at Agnes, who sat on a small gardening stool, and smiled. "I'm enjoying this."

"Me too. Feeling the warmth of the sun, fresh air, anticipating God's beauty to spiff up things around here—"

"I was wondering about that, Agnes. Why are you going to all this trouble when you might not be here to see the lilies come up?"

Agnes contemplated for a moment. "You know, I might have been too hasty about leaving Chicago when I was at the bus station the night we met," she admitted. "Days like this make me realize winter always ends, and it's beautiful right here. Besides, now I have you and Jack to consider."

The comment surprised Mary but also touched her more than she could say. "Oh, Agnes—that's so sweet, but Jack and I aren't your responsibility," she argued. "We'll be moving on soon, and then you'll—"

"But you said you have no family, no specific destination." With a helping hand from Mary, Agnes rose slowly up off her stool, groaning with the effort.

Mary looked at her, shielding her eyes from the sun. "Yes, that's true, but that has nothing to do with your plans."

"Let's take a break," Agnes suggested as she rubbed a spot on her lower back. "The sunshine hasn't caught up to my arthritis yet." She moved to the front porch next to the flower beds and lowered herself onto the top step.

Mary noticed that Jack had changed position to sit cross-legged on the grass. His gaze now was on the horizon—and Mary was content to let him stay there. She sat down on the step next to Agnes.

"When I was a little girl, I used to help my folks in our garden," Mary said after a companionable moment. "It's one of the happiest memories of my childhood."

"What happened to them? To your parents?"

Mary took a while to answer. "My mother found out that Dad was cheating on her. There was lots of yelling . . . name-calling. Drinking. No more flowers to plant." She looked at Agnes and forced a smile.

"That must have been so hard for you."

Mary nodded and wove her fingers together around her knees. "My father eventually left us—left town—left me. I've always felt like the whole thing was my fault. That he hated me."

"I'm sure he let you know it was ridiculous for you to blame yourself," Agnes hurried to say.

"He stayed in touch for a few months after he left—and then I quit hearing from him. My mother gradually quit functioning. She lived on the couch with a bottle. My grandparents were dead. . . ." She followed Jack's gaze to the horizon. "My teacher intervened, and when the school found out how I was living, I was sent to a foster family—and before a year was out, my mother died. They said she died from acute alcoholism—but I think it was more like she just gave up on living."

"And eventually you met Jack's father?"

A small, sad smile. "I met Jerry when I was sixteen. I was living with my third set of foster parents by then. Jerry was ready to give me the world on a silver platter. When he proposed I was thrilled. He didn't care about my hands . . . he told me I was beautiful."

"And he was right," Agnes said. "About that, anyway." The two women shared a rueful smile as Jack climbed up the steps to settle between them.

"Somehow, in the beginning, Jerry made me believe all those things he told me. I fell in love with him—with the life he was offering me. Our own house, our own family. Children I could love. I set out to be the best mother in the world."

"Sounds like a good plan."

"You know what they say—the best-laid plans . . ." Mary sighed. "Anyway, it wasn't quite what I'd envisioned. I spent most of my marriage worried I'd say the wrong thing, make a wrong move, wear the wrong clothes. We had a roof over our heads and food on the table, but Jerry was growing more impatient with me—with Jack." Mary looked away for a moment, then back at Agnes. "I worried that his temper was escalating. . . ." She gave a small shrug. "Then, well . . . let's just say that an opportunity presented itself, a possibility for us to get away with a chance to survive, so I took it."

"You took control of your own life."

"I guess I did."

"Maybe it's time to do that again."

"What do you mean?"

Agnes pushed up the sleeves of her cardigan. "I've been thinking a lot about this, Mary, and I think you and Jack should stay here—with me."

Mary's mouth dropped in surprise.

"Stay here in the house with me—indefinitely," the woman added.

"We can't do that—"

"And why not?"

*Why not?* "Well, for one thing, the offer is way too generous."

"It's not generous—it's practical," Agnes said with a firm shake of her head. "We can split the rent," she explained. "Henry's life-insurance money is going to run out, and, frankly, I could use the help."

"I'd be happy to split the rent with you, but my money will last only a few months. I have to find a job. And there are too many people here who recognize Jack from the paper."

"And that's bad?"

"Yes, Agnes! You saw how that woman practically chased us around the bus station. That was nothing compared to what was going on at the Edmundses' house." Mary felt herself stiffen at the memory. "Remember, I told you about it? Reporters and photographers out on the lawn, people calling—coming to the door. A drifter even broke into the house to try to get to Jack. It's why we had to leave, why I was trying to escape this city the night we met."

"In the newspaper, they called Jack a prophet," Agnes mused, looking down at the boy between them. "Is that what he is?"

Mary also looked at her son, his focus now trained on a tree whose branches were just beginning to bud. "The only thing I know for sure is that he's special. I see it . . . as a divine gift."

"A gift from God?"

Mary nodded. "Yes, I believe it is."

"So Jack touches someone and can see the future?"

"No . . . not like that." Mary paused to look over Jack's head at Agnes. "I believe when he touches someone, he somehow sees numbers . . . maybe even words. I've figured out that—that the numbers match a chapter and verse in the Bible, and the passage means something to the person he touches."

"So he writes the numbers he sees?"

Mary nodded. "With my help."

"That's such a blessing, Mary. For both of you. I really don't think it's something to hide."

"I'm happy that because of the gift some were spared from that tragic fire," Mary said. "I'm glad that people finally see how special Jack is. Something that I've always known." She looked away again. "But the gift can also be a burden."

"How do you mean?"

"The verse won't always be good news." Mary turned away from Agnes's questioning gaze.

Agnes leaned toward Mary. "If God would allow Jack to live in his own world of silence, then surely God knows he's strong enough to live with the burden of the gift."

"Jack won't live with it anymore," Mary said, "because I'm going to make sure he won't be in a position to see the numbers—the chapter and verse—again."

"Pardon me for saying so, dear, but I think you're looking at this the wrong way," Agnes said. "You're afraid of the gift because of what's happened. The situation got out of control. It seems to me that you need to take charge—"

"I don't understand what you mean." Mary frowned.

"That woman in the bus station," Agnes said. "The one who was so desperate to get her 'chapter and verse,' as you call it, was willing to chase you across the room waving money in your face."

"*That's* the kind of craziness I'm talking about!"

Agnes raised her eyebrows. "The woman wouldn't have chased you if you'd given her what she wanted."

"You mean right there in the bus station?" Mary shook her head. "It wouldn't have been possible."

"I was only using that woman as an example, dear. I'm suggesting that you make appointments—one at a time. If people think they'll be given a chance for a word, they'll be patient. They want some hope, some insight. They want to believe in something more than what they can see with their eyes. They want to *touch* the divine. If you took charge of the gift, there wouldn't be the craziness. Because everyone would have their chance."

"It sounds like you're suggesting a . . . a business," Mary said.

"I'm suggesting that you allow Jack to use the spiritual gift God gave him and in return receive money."

"You want us to *profit* from a spiritual gift?"

"A pastor profits from his spiritual gift of preaching, a gospel singer profits from his or her spiritual gift of singing, a Christian author profits from the inspirational words he writes, does he not?" Agnes sounded as if she was just warming up to the subject. "Jack has a gift—a divine gift— that has a purpose."

Mary mulled that over, finally giving a brief nod.

"In fact the evangelist D. L. Moody, who preached right here in Chicago, founded the Moody Bible Institute, which is still going to this day. Should he not have received financial help from his supporters for all the good things he did?"

Mary did not answer, but she remembered the statement she'd overheard in Richard Edmunds's study . . . *"We're all going to die someday. Some of us will just leave our loved ones more prepared. . . ."*

She slipped her arm around Jack's shoulders.

"Don't you think God wants you to keep a roof over his head and food on the table? Give him some kind of security?"

Agnes's words echoed those running through her own mind, and Mary nodded slowly. "I do worry about what will happen to him when I'm gone," she said, her voice nearly inaudible even to herself.

"Things happen all the time that we don't expect," Agnes said. "Like a bad case of influenza that knocks you out in a bus station. You could have died from that, Mary—and then what would have happened to Jack?"

Mary shuddered. "My worst nightmare is that . . . that he could end up in a state hospital."

"If you save up enough, that would never happen. You could make arrangements in advance for his care."

"I know I need to provide some kind of insurance for his future." Mary hesitated, then, "But I still wonder if God really would want him to be paid for his gift."

"Maybe God has given Jack this gift, this ability, for that very reason, Mary. As a way to help you . . . help Jack. A way to save enough to provide for him when you are not able to. I just don't see how you can turn your back on that. . . ." Agnes was silent.

"Your home will become a revolving door for people looking for answers," Mary argued. "And there is no guarantee that Jack—that he will always have a verse for someone who is wanting direction." She rushed on, "And sometimes it wouldn't be what the person wanted to hear—that could get unpleasant."

"Let me worry about all that, Mary. I can be a bulldog when I need to be. I think together we can figure it all out—make it all work. And Jack will be using his gift—just like God intended when He blessed him with it."

"You'll probably get tired of it all," Mary murmured.

"Even if things get difficult, I will not ask you to leave, Mary. Not unless you want to. I think you might possibly be the daughter I never had . . . but always wanted," she concluded, her tone full of warmth.

"That's an amazing thing to say, Agnes." Mary

looked at her with tears in her eyes. "Thank you."
"You and I and Jack can be a family. We can help each other the way families do. I'm too old to hold down a steady job, and you can't find a job where you can bring Jack. I think we were meant to meet, Mary. I think it really *was* Providence." Agnes got up from the porch step and smiled. "I'm going in to start some stew," she said. "I'll leave you here to think it over."

Before Mary could respond, Agnes had slipped through the front door, leaving her alone on the porch with her thoughts.

She glanced at Jack, who was lying back on the porch, hands behind his head, staring at the wispy clouds floating by.

*We could stay. Stay in this house, Jack. Stay with Agnes, and she'll make our supper and bake cookies and be our bulldog if people get too pushy. Preparation for your future, little buddy . . .*

Mary watched as two boys rode past on their Schwinns. A mother pushing a baby buggy smiled at them as she passed. The trees in the yard were beginning to bud in the spring temperatures, and the grass would be dark green in only a few weeks.

Mary spotted something she hadn't seen in nearly a year. She got Jack's attention and led him from the porch to a wispy, round white puff on a stem—a dandelion that had sprouted up overnight. *A wish stick.* Mary grasped the hollow stem and pulled it out of the lawn. *How many of these did I find when I was a little girl? How many wishes did I make?*

Mary looked down at Jack and held the dandelion out for him to see. She felt the warm spring sun on her face, heard the radio wafting out of the front door. Somewhere in the neighborhood a dog was barking and a child laughed. *Make a wish. Wish for normal. Wish for safe. Wish for Jack to live happily ever after even if . . . even when I'm not with him.*

Mary put the wish stick right next to her lips and blew.

# Chapter Nineteen

THE OUTLINE OF A SLIGHT WOMAN was silhouetted on the other side of the screen door. Agnes leaned a little closer to the mesh and peered through. "Yes?" she asked.

"Yes. Yes, hello, I'm Trudy Childress. I'm here to see the boy . . . Jack."

Agnes opened the screen door. "I'm Agnes." She smiled. "Please—come in." She held the door open, and Trudy entered the house and looked around nervously.

The young woman attempted a smile. "I need some help."

"Well, you may have come to just the right place." Agnes beckoned her into the room. "That's a lovely dress," she noted. "Perfect for a spring day."

"Thank you," Trudy answered, her hand fluttering briefly at the neckline.

"And it is a beautiful day," Agnes continued. "Isn't it? I think summer is just around the corner."

"Uh-huh . . ."

Agnes put a reassuring hand on Trudy's arm. "There's nothing to be nervous about, my dear. I promise."

Trudy nodded—but didn't seem convinced. She gazed around the living room. "Is *he* in here?" she asked timidly.

"Jack is with his mother in the other room," Agnes replied. "I'll take you to them if you wish."

Agnes moved across the living room, but when she glanced back, Trudy was standing as if glued to the floor.

"Miss Childress?"

"I . . . I just need a minute," Trudy stammered. "Is that okay? Only a . . . a minute?"

Mary entered the room from the opposite side and approached the young woman. "Hello—I'm Jack's mother, Mary," she said warmly, reaching out her hand.

"Trudy. Nice to meet you," she mumbled, shaking her hand but looking past her to the hallway beyond.

"Jack's waiting in the other room," Mary told her.

• • •

Mary watched the young woman, obviously debating if she wanted to go through with this or not, and wondered if this moment was as surreal to her as it was to Mary. She followed Trudy's gaze as she looked around at the floral-print couch and the chairs and the braided rug—*everything looks normal, but the normalness of everything actually accentuates the strangeness of the situation.* Benny Goodman's band on the radio playing "Sometimes I'm Happy" gave way to Bing Crosby's smooth voice singing a love song. Seconds seemed to actually slow down as Mary waited and Trudy avoided eye contact.

Agnes cleared her throat. "Trudy? Are you sure you want to do this?" she asked quietly. "Because if you don't—"

"I'm sure!" she answered quickly. "Really, I am. It's just that what Jack writes for me today will impact the rest of my life."

Mary had to strain to hear the last phrase. She glanced at Agnes, but she looked unperturbed and was nodding sympathetically.

"Well, yes, I suppose that could be true," Agnes said calmly.

"He could write down something that will make me so happy . . . or . . . or it can be the end of everything. . . ."

Mary cut her gaze to Agnes again, filled with

new doubts about this undertaking. *No amount of money is worth this fear, this uncertainty.* But she reminded herself that the gift wasn't hers or Jack's, but God's. Then Jack walked into the room.

He looked completely innocent, peaceful. His hair was longer since they'd left the Edmundses, and it brushed his eyebrows and framed his chestnut-colored eyes. For a moment Mary saw that lucid look—that *aware look* she couldn't predict.

"That's him," Trudy said with an awe that made Mary both proud and uncomfortable. But Agnes smiled encouragingly.

"I've been carrying around his picture from the newspaper ever since I saw it, but it really doesn't do him justice," Trudy said, staring at Jack.

"Why don't you follow Mary and Jack into the other room," Agnes suggested. "I'll wait right here. All right?"

At Trudy's nod, Mary took Jack's hand to lead him down the hall, and Trudy moved slowly to follow. "I'm scared," she whispered. Mary heard her and paused, glancing back over her shoulder as Agnes gave Trudy a reassuring pat and smile. "True courage is not the absence of fear—but the willingness to proceed anyway."

The room was quiet and dark enough so they all seemed like silhouettes.

"It's best for Jack if the room is darkened,"

Mary began when they were all seated at a small table near the wall. "And now I'm going to place your hand on Jack's. Okay?"

Mary could hear Trudy take a deep breath.

"Okay, I'm ready."

Using just the tips of her fingers, Mary guided Trudy's hand onto Jack's small one.

Trudy blinked and squinted against the light when Agnes appeared quietly to open the curtains. The girl watched in amazement as Jack, with his mother's help, began to form numbers on a piece of paper.

"I feel like my heart might beat out of my chest, I'm so worried," Trudy said with a nervous little laugh.

Completing the last number, Mary handed the paper to Trudy. "These numbers represent, first, the sequential book of the Bible," she explained, pointing to each one, "then the chapter and the verse."

Trudy looked at the paper, then at Mary and Jack, her eyes full of questions.

"Agnes will bring a Bible if you'd like her to. . . ."

Trudy nodded slowly, laying the sheet on the coffee table.

Agnes was already moving toward them with a Bible in her hand. She looked at the sheet. "One, two, and twenty-four," Agnes murmured, opening to the book of Genesis and turning to the second chapter. "Here it is. Should I read it, or do you want—?"

"No. No, please. You read it," Trudy begged her.

" 'Therefore shall a man leave his father and his mother, and shall cleave unto his wife: and they shall be one flesh,' " Agnes read aloud. She looked up from the page to Trudy. "What do you think, my dear? Does this have meaning for you?"

Trudy half laughed, half sobbed. "I've been engaged for three years to a man I never thought would leave his mother—but now . . . now I know he's going to do it. Lyle's really going to get up the courage to cut those apron strings his mother has knotted around him! I was wondering if I should break off the engagement or what . . ."

The young woman's eyes were filled with tears as Mary came up beside her and placed a hand on her arm. "It's easier to be patient when you know your patience will be rewarded."

Trudy smiled. "Thank you! Thank you so much!"

"You're welcome," Mary said.

"Please . . ." Trudy pressed a bill into Mary's palm. "It's a donation—for Jack."

"This is a lot of money, Trudy," Mary protested, looking at the five dollars lying on her glove.

"You can't put a price on peace of mind," Trudy said. "I'd give him ten times that if I had it!"

Mary looked over at Jack, who had moved to

look out the window as Agnes led Trudy from the room. Maybe Agnes was right—maybe this gift was intended to be a blessing to those who were looking for help. And a blessing to Jack.

# Chapter Twenty

AS SPRING MOVED INTO EARLY SUMMER, the number of people coming to meet the "boy prophet" grew each day. Mary and Agnes were amazed at the quick-spreading news of the gift—and never turned anyone away, no matter what time of day or night it was. As Agnes had pointed out, they had no idea how long the gift would remain. They must "let his gift shine, dear, while he has it."

But Mary worried aloud. "I wish Jack could understand why we're doing this, Agnes—why we're spending hours each day in the company of complete strangers. I wish there was a way for me to help him realize this gift is to help people—and to help him . . . to ensure his future—"

"He'll know someday, dear," Agnes said confidently. "Someday it will all become clear to him. Until then you'll keep saving enough money to make sure he has that secure future, whatever happens."

It wasn't long before they had fine-tuned how it all worked. Agnes met the clients at the door and led them to a room to meet Mary and Jack.

"The prophecy, the verse you receive," Mary would say, "is usually about what is most pressing on your heart and life."

Though Mary saw the reverence that each client had for Jack, she did not want to hear the passage being read to them. She knew that some might experience pain when they looked up the numbers Jack wrote, so Agnes took on the role of leading their guests to the front room and helping them find their chapter and verse. Agnes received any donations they felt they wanted to give—a jar of jam or a nickel and, occasionally, an amount unfathomably generous to the two women, particularly during such hard times.

"I still can't help but feel uncomfortable, Agnes, that we're using a gift from God to make money," Mary said one night after Jack was tucked into bed.

"God wouldn't have given Jack the gift if He hadn't wanted the boy to use it somehow. You can't turn your back on this amazing ability Jack has to help people."

So, instead, Mary turned her back on the financial end of things, preferring to leave the handling of the donations to Agnes. She made weekly deposits into their account at the bank.

Jack had never provided Agnes with her own chapter and verse. "I get my answers directly from the Lord, Mary," she explained. "I've no need for any other source of comfort."

Mary watched Jack carefully to make sure he was doing well physically, but he was her same little boy in spite of the stream of people wanting his gift. He still loved hot chocolate, but he had developed a new passion over the summer: cold bottles of sarsaparilla. Agnes made sure to keep them stocked in the icebox. He also showed a propensity for puzzles when Mary could get him to focus on the colorful pieces.

There were many affirmations that Jack's numbers and the Scriptures they identified were indeed prophetic. Trudy had been the first to return, beaming with the news she was planning a January wedding—with her future mother-in-law's help. Others came with small tokens of appreciation—bouquets of flowers, a handwritten card, cakes and brownies and other items given in thanks for Jack's insight. Those were moments when Mary felt good about her decision to allow Jack to use the gift. But sometimes she lay awake thinking about the sorrow some people bore because of the knowledge their message had brought them.

So word circulated, and those continuing to come for their own answers made the formerly quiet street something else entirely. Neighbors on either side of the yellow house began to complain. Mr. Merkel, on the east side, posted a No Trespassing sign in his yard. Mr. and Mrs. Hawkins on the west threatened to turn their dog loose on the next person who parked in their driveway.

Mary watched in amazement as Agnes dealt with the complaints of the neighbors as efficiently as she seemed to do everything else, striking a deal to pay them each a few dollars a week for their inconvenience. Both neighbors seemed happy to get the extra money.

It was the first week in November. The three were at breakfast, and Agnes was sipping coffee while she read the Chicago morning newspaper.

"Well, we have a new governor," Agnes announced, laying the paper on the table.

"Oh, right . . ." Mary glanced at the headline splashed across the front page: "Westerly Defeats Flynn!"

"What do you mean? You already knew this?"

"The Edmundses gave a dinner party for Governor Flynn when I was working there, and he insisted on getting a chapter and verse from Jack," Mary said.

"*Really?* Do you remember what it was?" Agnes asked.

Mary nodded somberly. "I remember. It was Psalm one hundred nine, verse eight. 'Let his days be few; and let another take his office.'"

Agnes's eyes grew wide, and then she laughed. "Oh, I don't think Governor Flynn was very happy with his chapter and verse! I wonder if he thought about Jack yesterday when he lost the race to Charles Westerly."

"I sure hope not," Mary said, feeling uncomfortable. "Actually, I don't think Governor Flynn believed in Jack's gift."

Agnes got up to pour herself another cup of coffee and chuckled again. "Well, I'll bet he believes now!"

"Maybe you're right."

Agnes sat down at the table and looked squarely at Mary. "You rarely mention your time at the Edmundses. Do you think about it much?"

Mary smiled. "I'll always be thankful to Mrs. Edmunds for giving me that job, but I'm happy right here with you."

"It was a big fancy house. You must miss that, don't you?"

"It was large and lovely, but I don't miss that part. What I really loved was the view of the lake. It didn't matter if it was cloudy or sunny or raining or snowing. Looking out at that water was just so . . . peaceful."

"Peaceful is good." Agnes nodded.

Mary smiled. "Yes, Agnes. Peaceful is *really* good. Isn't it, little buddy?" she said as she leaned toward Jack.

It was a week before Thanksgiving when Agnes led a man into the back room where Mary and Jack were sitting.

"Mary, this is Eldon Smith." Agnes introduced a rumpled, frail-looking figure. The stoop-shouldered man was chewing nervously on a thumbnail while his eyes roamed over the room. When they came to rest on Mary, she could see a blush rising from the neck of his white shirt and over his pale cheeks. He looked away.

"Hello, Mr. Smith," Mary said with a smile she hoped would put him at ease. "Should I call you Eldon?"

"Uh-huh," he murmured, using his free hand to smooth down strands of hair that had been carefully combed to cover a balding spot.

"Would you like to sit down?" she asked, gesturing to the table and chairs.

"Is that how it's done, then?" he asked in a thin voice filled with uncertainty.

Mary nodded.

Eldon flicked his eyes back to Jack. "That him?"

Mary nodded again. "Yes. This is Jack."

He moved toward a chair, sliding his hands over wrinkled gray flannel trousers as he sat down on the other side of Jack.

Mary caught Agnes's eye and lifted her eyebrows, just as the older woman flashed a quick grin and went to close the curtains as usual before departing. Mary, Jack, and Eldon were now dark shadows.

"I don't much like dark places," Eldon managed nervously.

"It won't be dark for long," Mary assured him. "But this is how the gift works for Jack. Agnes was supposed to tell you—"

"She did." He swallowed loud enough to hear it. "She explained how it works. I just—you know—don't like the dark."

"If you'd prefer not to continue—"

"No, no. I'm okay," he said quickly.

Mary said patiently, "Jack is ready." She reached over and took Eldon's hand to place it on Jack's.

It was only moments later when Mary was at the windows and quickly sweeping back the curtains. In the sunshine now illuminating the room, she looked at Eldon Smith. He was staring directly at Jack with an expression that sent a wave of goose bumps across her skin.

She hurried back to the table and sat down.

Eldon shifted his gaze to her. "So do I get my numbers now?"

Mary put the pencil into Jack's hand and helped him write the series of numbers on the paper. They were legible in spite of her shaking hand. She shoved the paper toward Eldon and pulled Jack to his feet.

"Is something wrong?" The man stared up at her, his eyes like dark pools.

"You have your chapter and verse. Now you must go," she said as firmly as she could.

"So what about my numbers?" His tone sounded menacing, mocking. "What do they mean?"

The door opened and Agnes put her head around it with a bright smile. "All right then, Mr. Smith—"

This time Mary did not wait for Agnes to look up the passage. " 'And Jesus asked him, saying, What is thy name? And he said, Legion: because many devils were entered into him.' " Her voice shook with every word.

Eldon rose slowly, and suddenly he seemed much more physically imposing than when he'd entered—the stooped shoulders had squared, his chest thrust out, and his neck was so tense Mary could see muscled cords where before she'd noticed only the pink blush.

"You must get out!" Mary repeated, working hard to keep her voice steady.

"What happened to your hands, Mary?"

"Nothing of any matter to you. You will go *now*."

"Did you burn yourself as a little girl? Dunk them in boiling water because Mommy called you a little demon?"

"Mary?" Agnes was moving quickly toward them.

"Shut up, crone!" His head swiveled to fix his eyes on Agnes. The man's voice was more animal than human. "You wretched old hag! Stealing money." He turned from Agnes, his black eyes once more on Mary. "Don't let a few wrinkles and gray hair fool you, Mary." He moved closer.

"Don't come near my son!"

Eldon's lips peeled back in a sneer. "We're talking to him right now. All of us—Legion, you know—"

"Leave my son alone. Get out of our house now!"

He ignored her and advanced again. A string of what sounded like gibberish spilled from his mouth.

"In Jesus' name, I command you to leave!" Mary said with conviction.

"Yes, in Jesus' name!" Agnes echoed loudly.

Eldon growled and spewed a stream of blasphemous words into the room. He sounded like an animal about to attack, and Agnes whimpered as she backed herself against the doorframe.

But a wave of boldness filled Mary, and she straightened to her full height as she pinned Eldon in her sight. "In Jesus' name, I command you to leave! By the power of the Holy Spirit I command you to leave now!" She kept one arm securely around Jack and raised her other hand in the air with her palm toward Eldon as she repeated the command.

It was as if he suddenly collapsed into himself. Eldon covered his ears with both hands and began to scream. He turned and ran from the room, knocking Agnes to the floor as he passed through the door.

# Chapter Twenty-one

SNOW FELL FROM A STEEL GRAY SKY and dusted the slate roof of the two-story white brick colonial. Trees surrounding the house had shed their leaves, and the bare branches had ribbons of white snow icing running from trunk to tip. The neighborhood was quiet at midafternoon—children in school, fathers at work, wives busy with the details of running their households. A green 1938 Buick Coupe rolled up the cobblestone drive in front of the house, stopping midway. The car's exhaust blew silvery puffs into the air, making a foglike effect.

"Thanks for the ride home, Burton. Enjoy the holidays with your family," Charles Westerly said to his driver as he reached for the door handle on the passenger side. "That's what I plan to do."

"Thanks, I will. Haven't been seeing too much of them in the last few weeks, what with all your meetings at the statehouse and all. But," he quickly added, "don't give it a thought, sir—it's my job, and I'm glad to have one!" Burton lifted his hat as he nodded toward the front window sporting a colorful hand-drawn turkey. "Happy Thanksgiving, sir."

For the moment, the two weren't the governor-elect of Illinois and his driver, just two fathers looking forward to the traditional holiday. Charles said, "Tell your wife to give little Jessie a teaspoon of honey before bed—might help that cough of hers. I know it works for my daughter when she's feeling under the weather."

Charles paused in front of his house as the snow fell, marveling at the quiet. He heard the motor of the Buick fade as it rounded a corner—and then the ensuing hush. Life was good. He had been campaigning hard for the last nine months and promising the voters of Illinois things he knew he could deliver as governor.

When he was a state representative for the district that included Chicago, he'd loved serving the people, loved seeing actual changes that helped improve the lives of those who had given up on ever getting out of the economic depression. He was tired of the self-serving way John Flynn had run the state, and apparently the people of Illinois were too.

He couldn't help his smile as he thought about election day. He'd entered the polling place with his family and seen his name on the ballot for the highest office in the state. He knew his story was the American dream, and it made great press. His grin spread when he thought about the teasing he'd heard from his wife, Lila. *"Are you sure you don't want to follow me behind the little curtain at the polling place, darling,"* she'd said, *"and make sure I don't vote for John Flynn? Maybe I don't want all these Illinois women swooning over my handsome husband!"* They had laughed together before he turned serious and assured Lila that when he took the oath of office in January, she would be the loveliest first lady the state had ever seen.

The smile stayed on his face as he walked toward the front door, his footprints leaving a path through the pristine snow.

Lila Westerly was sitting in the stiff Queen Anne chair in the corner of the master bedroom. She hadn't moved in over an hour. She heard the front door open and close, but it was too early for her daughter, Stephanie. The school bus wouldn't be dropping her off for another two hours.

Lila knew it was Charles. He'd promised he'd be home early, and he was. He'd kept his promise— *that* promise anyway. Still, she didn't move— didn't even blink. She heard him call out for the maid, but Lila had given Genevieve the day off. As Lila listened to her husband move around on the floor below, she could picture exactly what he was doing—hanging his coat and hat on the tree in the foyer, carrying his leather briefcase to his study, slipping out of his shoes at the foot of the stairs so he wouldn't scuff the hardwood that Genevieve polished every week, treading up the stairs in his stocking feet as he made his way to their second-floor bedroom, where she waited.

"Lila?" he called out, but she didn't answer. She

heard the beating of her own heart; felt the clamminess of her hands, but didn't move them from her lap. She wondered idly if the moisture from her hands would stain her green silk dress. She shifted slightly to accommodate the book that rested between her leg and the inside of the chair.

"Lila? You up here?" His voice sounded as it always had, yet somehow this time it was more like fingernails down a chalkboard. She shuddered—then went still again. He came around the corner and entered the room—a smile lighting his face when he saw her.

"Hey, there, sweetheart. I was calling you," he said, moving toward her as he loosened his necktie. "I said I'd be home early. I'm not even going to the office until Monday. We can have some real time together as a family."

He pulled the tie off and unfastened the cuff links from his shirtsleeves, dropping them into a velvet-lined box on the bureau. He glanced into the mirror on the wall over the piece of dark cherry furniture. He could see her reflected in the glass. "Where's Genevieve?"

"Her mother went into the hospital this morning. I gave her the day off," Lila answered in a monotone.

"Oh, I'm sorry about that. Is it serious?" She could see him looking at her in the mirror.

"Her mother is ninety-three. Everything at her age is serious."

"Poor Gen. She's not going to do well if something happens to her mom," he said. "From all appearances, they seem very close."

"Appearances can be deceiving," Lila said. He finally turned to face her, and she noted the small wrinkle on his forehead.

"Are you all right, Lila?"

Of their own accord her lips arranged themselves into a thin smile that lasted only a second. She chose to ignore the question and instead asked one of her own.

"How was *your* day?" *Can't he hear it in my voice?*

"Great. More than great. It's finally hitting me, Lila—that in less than two months I'll be sworn in as governor of Illinois!"

"I highly doubt that."

The wrinkle in his forehead deepened into a frown as he crossed the room toward her. "What—I don't know what you mean."

"Ask me about *my* day, Charles. Ask me what kind of day *I* had," she said.

"Okay, of course. I'm sorry. Something is obviously wrong," he said. "I can see that now."

"Then ask me," she insisted.

"How was your day, Lila?" She heard the worry in his voice, and it gave her the tiniest hint of satisfaction.

"It turns out," she began, "that this has been the worst day of my life."

She could see he wasn't prepared for that. Her statement was shocking. *Good. There's a lot of "shocking" going around.*

He hurried toward her and knelt by the chair. "Is it Stephanie? Is she—?"

"Stephanie is fine. Safe and sound in school."

"Oh, thank God," he said. "You had me scared to death."

"That's little consolation."

"What is going on, Lila? What's wrong? Just say it!" His voice always deepened when he was upset or worried. It had been something she'd always found endearing. But not this time.

"I signed for a special-delivery letter for you today," she said. "Normally, of course, Genevieve would have done that and put it in your study, but—"

"She wasn't here."

"That's right. Do you think that might have been fate?"

"I have no idea what you're talking about." He stared intently into her face.

"I thought the letter might be important, so I opened it." She lifted her chin boldly. "I'm not in the habit of opening your mail, but as I said, I thought with your election and all, it might be something you'd need to know right away."

"I don't care that you opened it, Lila. I've never cared if you opened my mail," he said.

"Let me assure you that I'll never do it again."

"I just told you that I don't mind."

"Your mail won't be coming here anymore, so you see, the opportunity won't present itself."

"Lila—this is crazy. I don't know what's got you so upset, but I want to make it right—whatever it is." His voice grew deeper with each word.

She reached for the book beside her, and Charles saw it was a Bible. She opened it and pulled out a single piece of paper and a newspaper photograph. "Let me read you a little of the letter I opened— while you look at this." She handed him a newsprint photograph of a little boy.

He studied the picture, and she again saw the furrow in his brow deepen. " 'Boy prophet predicts fire,' " he said, reading the caption aloud. "I remember this article. He's the kid who warned people about the school fire the night of the recital—"

" 'Dear Mr. Westerly,' " Lila interrupted as she began to read aloud, " 'I'm writing to you because I feel duty-bound before God to inform you that my son saw something important about you when someone you know came looking for direction from a chapter and verse. The truth is, a man with a past like yours has no right to hold the office of governor of our state. Unless you withdraw your name immediately, it's my responsibility to take the information from the verse we found after meeting your sister-in-law to the newspaper.' "

Lila stopped reading and looked at his face. She was gratified to see some confusion along with a flash of fear in his eyes.

"A verse?" Lila heard the slight tremor in his voice.

"Yes, a verse from the Bible, Charles." She thrust the paper at him. "The boy wrote out 'three, eighteen, eighteen.'"

He lifted his eyes from the paper and shook his head. "This is crazy. This whole thing is crazy. Who listens to a little boy who writes out numbers?"

"Half of Chicago right now," Lila said thinly.

Charles crumpled the page in his hand. "I certainly won't respond to some crackpot attempt at blackmail."

Lila opened the Bible. "Three is Leviticus, chapter eighteen, verse eighteen." She turned to a marked page. "'Neither shalt thou take a wife to her sister, to vex her, to uncover her nakedness, beside the other in her life time.'"

"I don't know what—"

"I'm no theologian, Charles, but even I know what this verse means," she said in a tone that chilled the air between them.

"Lila," he whispered hoarsely, the color sliding from his face. "Please—"

"Don't insult me with another lie."

"Lila, I can make this right—"

"You *can't* make it right, Charles. When a

man—a husband *and* a father—sleeps with his wife's sister, you can *never* make that right."

His past collided with his present with such force that Charles felt himself physically reeling from the blow. What scared him more than anything was that he couldn't see pain in his wife's eyes. Instead her expression was devoid of *any* emotion. Hurt, anger, tears, confusion—all would have been better than this flat, glazed stare.

"Lila, you have to believe me when I tell you—"

"I've already spoken to Rebecca, and she has admitted the affair to me. She doesn't know how I found out—and I'm not giving her the satisfaction of knowing."

"It was a long time ago—a lifetime ago!"

"Yes. *Stephanie's* lifetime if I'm not mistaken," she said through gritted teeth.

"You were different then. *We* were different. After Stephanie's birth you completely changed. You all but said you didn't love me anymore. You didn't think we had a future . . . and I was lonely. I went to talk to Rebecca, to ask her advice. She knows you so well, and I was at a loss . . ."

Charles knew how hollow his words—his *excuses*—were. He knew there was nothing in the world that could justify the betrayal of his wife.

"I was clinically depressed, Charles. You know that. You *knew* that back then. And there is no way you can remotely believe this was my fault."

He watched Lila finally move from the chair—stiffly at first—then with the fluid grace he'd always admired. She made her way toward the bureau, put the Bible on top, then leaned with her back against the drawers, staring out the window.

"I know, I know, Lila," he said. "It was totally my fault. And it was just once, Lila! I swear to you, it only happened the one time."

"How chivalrous of you to take all the blame. Are you saying you *raped* my sister?"

He didn't think the conversation could get any worse. He felt like he'd been kicked in the gut. "No—of course not!" *This can't be happening. This can't be the discussion we're having. . . .*

"Then the blame belongs to Rebecca too. You're equally culpable. Equally despicable," she said calmly. "Equally dead to me."

"You don't mean that. You're angry. Hurt. As you should be—have every right to be."

"How generous of you to be so supportive of my emotions, Charles. I find out through some pint-sized clairvoyant's mother that the two people I trusted more than any others in the world betrayed me during the darkest days of my life! I find out that you're not the person I thought you were! I find out that my only sister has been lying to my face for years, coming to Christmas dinners and birthday parties and giving her brother-in-law—*my husband*—chaste kisses on the cheek when she arrives and leaves!"

"We—neither she nor I wanted to hurt you, Lila, by telling you. You were so fragile then, and as you got better and happier . . . I couldn't bear to shatter your newfound enthusiasm for life."

"Were you ever going to tell me the truth?" She stared right into his soul, and he knew he couldn't lie anymore.

"No," he said, his voice low, "I was not." But he rushed on quickly, "I'll make this up to you, Lila—I will! I don't dare hope that you'll forgive me right now—but in time maybe you can find it in your heart to put this behind us. I will forfeit the governor's office tomorrow—the scandal will never hit the papers. I love you and Stephanie more than anything in the world. Please don't leave me. I can't live without you both!"

"I don't expect you to," she said. As he watched, she calmly reached behind her into the top bureau drawer and withdrew a small pistol. "Because I don't expect you to live at all."

"Lila! Think about what you're doing." He took a step backward. She raised the gun and pointed it at him.

"Did you think about what *you* were doing? Did you and Rebecca have a good laugh at my expense?! Poor little Lila with her little post-partum depression, her tears—"

"No! It wasn't like that!" Charles felt nearly beside himself with fear, desperation for them both. "I told you it was a terrible, terrible mistake.

One I've wished I could take back every day since!"

"A 'mistake' is an error in the checkbook, Charles. What you did can never be fixed. Never be forgotten. *Never* be forgiven!"

He could see her hand trembling from the weight of the gun—or the weight of the conversation. Either way he was staring at the small derringer pistol he'd bought for her own protection. *I even taught her how to use it. . . .*

"Think about Stephanie—think about her." He was pleading now. "If you do this—if you shoot me—they'll put you in jail, Lila."

"Stephanie deserves the most perfect world I can give her—and that world doesn't include you!"

His last thought as the gun went off was that he deserved the bullet that slammed into his chest.

# Chapter Twenty-two

MARY AND JACK HAD NOT SEEN another client since the incident with Eldon Smith. Neither was she sure they'd ever be able to again. She had seen evil before, experienced it firsthand even—but it had never actually come knocking on the door for an audience with her son.

"I'm taking Jack to church Sunday, Agnes," Mary said.

"Church?"

Mary nodded. "Would you come with us?"

Agnes shook her head. "Oh no. No thanks. Too many rules, too much hypocrisy." Agnes poured a cup of coffee and carried it over to Mary. "Time is what you need. What you both need. That's why I've kept turning people away. But, Mary, you still have Jack's future to consider."

*Jack's future*, Mary thought. *Hope or despair. Gift or no gift. Worth or worthless . . .*

The walk wasn't far—only a few blocks through modest neighborhoods where people were already starting to hang Christmas wreaths on their doors. Mary saw the white steeple of the church, and suddenly memories made a quick montage in her head—sitting between her parents as a child, her feet far from the floor, shiny black shoes dangling in the air, her dad's strong hands holding the hymnal, her mom slipping a stick of Black Jack gum out of her purse when Mary got restless. She hadn't been to church for many years—maybe since she was Jack's age. . . . She felt a quick flip of nerves in her stomach as they got close enough to the building to hear organ music as the front door opened and closed. What if someone recognized Jack? And if they did, how would they react?

Mary took a deep breath before pulling the door open and leading Jack into the sanctuary. She found a place for them on a pew in the back just as the organist started another beautiful prelude. *It sounds familiar*, she thought as she settled Jack beside her. *Yes, I think it's a hymn . . . Amazing grace, how sweet . . . something.* She couldn't remember any more of it.

The air was redolent with beeswax polish and a familiar blend of women's powder and perfumes that took her right back to her childhood again. She held Jack's hand, looking around as discreetly as she could. She suddenly felt so . . . so visible, so exposed. *This is a mistake—*

"Good morning!" An usher was heading her way with a smile and an outstretched bulletin. "Welcome to you both!"

Her nerves stilled enough to take the bulletin and greet the friendly man before she turned toward the front. A song leader walked behind the pulpit and led them in some hymns. Many of them seemed familiar, and Mary found herself singing with the congregation, following along in the hymnbook.

The pastor had a comforting, reassuring presence. His unassuming clergy robes didn't draw attention away from the man or what he was saying. She tried to listen to his words, but her own confused thoughts kept getting in the way. She glanced around at the other faces in the pews. Almost everyone was focused on the sermon, but her gaze met the eyes of someone who'd come to see Jack at the house once. The man quickly looked away. She sighed and turned her attention back to the pastor. His warmth and sincerity had a quality that made her wonder . . . *Maybe I could talk with this pastor, tell him, explain it all—share my fears. Is he someone who can help us?*

The service ended; the sanctuary emptied. But Mary and Jack stayed seated. Mary wasn't exactly sure why she waited, *but maybe* . . .

"Hope I'm not disturbing you." The pastor came toward them and stood in the aisle beside their pew. He smiled. "Just didn't know if you wanted to be alone . . . or maybe talk."

Up close, the man exuded the same warmth Mary had felt during his sermon. With his gray, thinning hair and a fan of wrinkles around his eyes, Mary guessed him to be close to sixty. His blue eyes were clear, not clouded with age. He bent a leg to kneel on the pew ahead of theirs and reached over the back for her hand.

"I'm Pastor Martz." His hand was firm, but he placed his other one on top of hers, and that felt gentle.

"I'm Mary . . . and this is my son, Jack," she answered.

He looked at Jack, who stared straight ahead as if neither of them were there. "May I ask if he was born deaf?"

Surprised, she nodded. "He's never spoken a

word either," she said. "If you don't mind—if you have time, I would like to talk."

He smiled and sat down in the pew, still facing them over the back and groaning slightly as he straightened out his knee. "This time of year, the cold weather takes up residence in my arthritic knees."

"I'm sorry to hear that," she offered.

"It's another reminder that I'm getting up there in years and need to get as much done as possible."

Mary nodded, suddenly not sure what to say or where to start, or if she should say anything at all.

"Do you want to tell me what's causing your confusion, Mary?" His tone was more inviting than probing.

She knit her fingers together, her gloves overlapping each other in her lap. "I do," she said. "But I feel a little strange. I mean, we've only just met. . . ."

When she did not continue, he went on, "Sometimes a need can be so great we can't afford the luxury of getting acquainted."

That made sense—she certainly had a great need, and luxury wasn't part of her life. She plunged on. "My son, Jack—maybe you've heard of him? He has a . . . gift. A spiritual gift that involves . . ."

Pastor Martz's brows rose as he looked at Jack. "Numbers?"

Mary nodded.

"When I read the article in the paper about the fire at the school and how Jack was able to warn people, I remember thinking it was a miracle," he said. "A gift like that is truly amazing."

Her eyes welled with tears, and she tried to swallow down the lump in her throat. It seemed like this man did understand. "Hundreds of people—and I do mean hundreds—have been to see Jack. They've come for a passage of Scripture that he provides with a series of numbers. They are looking for divine insight into their lives from a little boy who can't hear their questions and who can't voice the answer any other way than through numbers written on a piece of paper. And . . . they also give gifts . . . of money and other things." She looked away, then faced him squarely, though her heart was pounding. "Do you . . . do you believe what we're doing is wrong?"

"Do you?"

Mary thought for a while. "I'm not sure. It all really started when I became worried about Jack's future—you know, about what would happen to him when I'm no longer able to care for him. Where would he live? Who would watch out for him? Would he be put into one of those institutions? But it seems like no matter what I do, it turns out I put my son in harm's way."

"How is that, Mary?"

"The other day, a strange man came to us. Because I've allowed Jack to use his gift, I opened a door that evil walked right through. Right into the house. The man seemed to be . . . well, possessed with a demon."

She looked for some shock, disbelief, or judgment on the pastor's face, but all she saw was compassion.

"What did the man say or do that makes you believe he was possessed?"

"He brought up things," she said softly. "Things that no one could have known. About me. About my past. Agnes saw it too. She agreed the man was possessed."

"Who is Agnes?"

"She took us in when I was sick and has taken care of us ever since. She's become a dear friend."

"If I may ask, what did the man say about you?"

Her shoulders moved with the breath she exhaled. "He mentioned an accident that happened to me when I was a child—my hands were badly burned." She glanced down at her gloves, then back at his face. "And he said the thing that frightened me the most. He said *demons* were talking to my son!"

"I can see why that would frighten you," he said. "What did you do?"

"I felt a kind of . . . of power rush over me, and I kept my arm around Jack and commanded the man to leave in Jesus' name."

The pastor nodded ever so slightly. "And that made him leave."

She nodded also. "It did."

"And your friend Agnes? What did she do?"

"She was terrified. She had never experienced anything like it."

"So the man's . . . comments. Were they only about you and Jack, or did he say anything about Agnes?"

"He said she was a swindler—stealing money."

"From whom?"

"He didn't say."

The pastor pondered just a moment, and she saw a furrow crease his brow. "Could it be from you?"

Mary shook her head quickly. "No. That's not possible. What he said was a lie."

"But what he said about you was accurate?"

"Yes."

"Then why wouldn't it be true about Agnes?"

"If you knew Agnes, you would know. She's a sweet, gentle old woman—"

"Don't let a few wrinkles and gray hair fool you, Mary."

She stared at him, her mouth open in surprise. "I can't believe you just said that."

"Why?"

"Because he—that man used the exact same words."

The pastor looked past her for a moment, his gaze unfocused for a few seconds. Then, "Would Jack give me a Scripture?"

Mary stared. "You mean now? Are you sure?"

"Yes, please, now would be fine."

Her mouth went dry. "I don't think so. No, I mean, it only works—he must have a darkened room." *Take Jack's hand and get up.* "Actually, we should get going. I've taken up enough of your time, Pastor Martz, and Agnes will be looking for us." She kept her voice as even as she could.

"Mary, if you truly believe Jack has been given a divine gift, then evil has no claim on that gift. But even gifts from God can be distorted. Christians can be duped into believing that what they're doing is right as long as it's in the name of God—and things of the occult can sometimes be very hard to discern. The line between actual prophecy and fortune-telling can become so blurred we can barely even see it."

"This is—it's not what you think," she said quickly. "I'm just scared now. I don't want to do anything else that God would hate me for. I don't want Him to take Jack away from me—"

"I think that most of our sin comes from not trusting God's goodness," he said earnestly. "In our humanness, we hold tightly on to the reins of our destiny, acting as our own god, not trusting that where He leads us will be good. And in doing so, we make a mess of our own lives."

She shook her head. "I don't think you're understanding *my* problem—what I'm asking—"

"I believe the questions we ask are rarely the

true issues of our hearts. There is usually something else—something deep down that's troubling us. Waiting to be brought out into the light of day, where it can be dealt with and healed."

"I have no idea what that would be, Pastor—but I do know I'm facing a true dilemma. Do I continue to use the gift to secure a future for my son when I'm no longer able to care for him—or do I stop because it's not right and just hope he doesn't end up institutionalized when I'm gone?"

"You know what I think, Mary? What I *sense?*"

She shook her head.

"I sense the truth is being covered up like your hands—because you trust no one, including God." He leaned toward her. "Most people don't want to trust God because they're afraid He'll ask them to sacrifice—and they don't want to do that. But that's not you. You know too well what it means to sacrifice. Jack has made sure of that. Your stumbling block to trust comes from somewhere deep down—a *hurt so deep* it stops you from allowing that trust to blossom and grow."

"How do you know that?" she asked quietly.

"Because you are here, talking with me. Which says to me you have no one in your life you can turn to—no one you can trust."

She knew he was right—hated the fact that he was right. But she hadn't come here to wrestle with her own issues. She had come to find someone who would tell her that what she was doing was all right. She tried to smile as she stood and reached for Jack's hand.

"Thank you for your time, Pastor," she said, already moving toward the end of the pew and the aisle.

"Mary?"

She stopped and turned.

"The gift. It's much bigger than anything you've ever dreamed. You simply need to trust the One that gave it."

Charles Westerly sat at a small table pushed against the wall of his shabby studio apartment. His elbow was propped on the table, a glass cradled in the palm of his hand. By rotating his wrist he caught the dim light coming through the tiny window into the glass and watched the topaz-colored liquid as he swirled it around. A quote from Shakespeare had been popping into his head and irritating him no end for the last couple of weeks. *Time is the justice that examines all offenders.* It had taken six years for his offense to come to light, to be "examined," but it wouldn't take much time at all for the woman who'd ruined his life to be served with *his* justice. He thought about the irony of what the doctor had said to him the day he was released from the hospital—and he almost smiled.

"You're one lucky man, Mr. Westerly. If that bullet had entered just an inch to the left, it would have killed you. Your shoulder will heal in time—but it'll bother you some when it's cold." *He was right about the cold*, Charles thought as his shoulder throbbed, but the doc had been wrong about the lucky part. He wished more than anything that Lila's bullet had found his heart and killed him. Death would be preferable to the desolate existence he was barely enduring now. He lowered the drink to the table, then rotated his left shoulder—again and again—welcoming the stinging from the bullet wound. The physical pain was a tangible punishment he could deal himself for the demise of his family, for the shambles his life had become. He stretched out his feet and connected with a pile of newspapers lying on the floor. He once more found the headline stating that Charles Westerly had given up his governorship.

He raised his glass over the paper. "Here's to ya, Ex-Governor Westerly," he said caustically before tilting his head back and swallowing the whiskey in one gulp. He brought the glass down next to an open Bible where a worn picture of Mary and Jack lay. As usual the sight of the two of them gave him a place to focus his anger, and that was good. The anger gave him a reason to get up each day. The emotion gave him something to think about besides the living hell of the days he'd been slogging through.

He refilled his glass with the liquid breakfast

and impulsively kicked at the pile of newspapers at his feet, further scattering them across the floor. He caught sight of another headline, the one that had been splashed across the paper the day after he was shot. *Well, at least I'm not making the papers anymore.* He recalled how hard Sam, his campaign manager, had worked before the election to get his name in the papers. "Any publicity in an election year is good publicity," according to Sam. But Sam hadn't known then that his star candidate would win, get shot in his own home by his own wife, then withdraw as governor through a statement issued from a hospital bed. Oh, the stuff and fodder of scandals.

With a flash of searing shame and remorse, Charles thought about the terrible fallout with all those he knew and loved—family, friends, campaign workers, those who had believed in him, even loved him. *Well, take a number, ladies and gentlemen. You'll never hate me more than I hate myself.* He threw back another swallow, and it registered that the alcohol didn't burn going down his throat anymore. He kept waiting for the endless drinks to numb him, but, ironically, they were having the opposite effect. The more he drank, the clearer—and agonizingly painful—his memories were. Could grief actually kill a person? Could his anguish over losing his wife and daughter do what Lila's bullet had not? How many times had he asked someone to call Lila when he had been in the hospital? How many times had he begged to see his daughter? What had Lila told Stephanie—surely not the truth, had she? How could a six-year-old understand that the father she looked up to—the man she adored more than anyone in the world—was a lying, cheating, no-account shell of a human being.

*Please, God, don't let Stephanie find out the truth about me* was the one prayer he prayed night and day. He thought he'd eventually be able to bear the rest, but he was sure he could never bear that. He remembered the look on the detectives' faces when they came to the hospital to question him about "the incident." Overnight he'd gotten pretty good at lying. "I got the gun for my wife for protection, Officers," he told them, holding steady eye contact with them. "There are a lot of nut cases out there gunning for you when you're in politics, you know. Anyway, I was showing her how to aim it and didn't realize it was loaded. It was completely my fault. Lila is absolutely blameless in this. It was just a crazy accident. . . ."

Lila and Stephanie had never come to the hospital to see him. A lawyer served him with divorce papers on December second, the day after he publicly withdrew from the governor's office citing "personal reasons related to the welfare of my family."

Picking up the tattered picture of Mary and Jack once again, he began to think about calling in some favors. He might be out of politics, but he still had a few friends in high places. He carefully folded the newspaper photo and put it back in the Bible, in the book of Leviticus, eighteenth chapter, eighteenth verse.

## Chapter Twenty-three

THE TEMPERATURE WAS FLIRTING WITH the freezing mark when Mary and Jack stepped through the double doors into the First National Bank of Chicago. Close to noon on Monday, it was only the third time Mary had set foot in the bank, the other two times being with Agnes. Opening an account last spring, then making a substantial deposit with their first month's donations—and now.

Her conversation with the pastor along with the accusations Eldon Smith had made had planted a tiny seed of doubt about Agnes that wouldn't go away. Mary spent the rest of her Sunday trying to ignore the nagging thoughts—through Agnes's polite questions about church, through the meatloaf they had for supper, and even through *The Jack Benny Program* on the radio. But after tossing and turning much of the night, she had finally decided there was only one way to put the doubts to rest.

Agnes had looked a little confused when Mary had told the woman she had some errands to run, but hadn't asked any questions other than if she wanted some company.

"No thanks," Mary told her. "We'll be fine."

"All right, dear," Agnes said. "Maybe I'll use the time to catch up on my knitting. I'm thinking of chicken and dumplings for dinner—sound good?"

Mary was feeling guilty and more than a little foolish by the time she and Jack had entered the bank, passed the security guard, and got in line at the teller's window. *She's making chicken and dumplings for dinner! She's not a swindler. She's Agnes!*

When it was her turn at the teller's window, Mary produced the bank book that Agnes kept in the drawer in the kitchen.

"I'd like to check the balance in my account, please," she said. "This is the account number." She pushed the bank book into the small dip in the counter below the barred window and into the teller's hands.

The woman smiled at her. "Certainly, ma'am. One moment, please."

It only took a minute, maybe less, for the teller to look at the ledger and write a figure down on a slip of paper. She tucked it inside the passbook and slid it back under the bars. "Is there anything else I can do for you, Mrs. Meriwether?"

"Oh no—sorry. I'm Miss Godwin. Mrs. Meriwether's name is on the account also because we needed for her to be able to make deposits—"

"Oh, my mistake, Miss Godwin. Is there anything else?"

"No," Mary said as she opened the passbook and looked at the figure. Her eyes were wide when she looked up again at the teller. "There's been some mistake," she said. "I don't know exactly how much money I have in my account—but I know it's considerably more than this!"

The teller shook her head. "That's the correct balance, ma'am."

"But how can that be? I know I had a lot more money than this! Where's the rest of it?"

"I can assure you, Miss Godwin, that we keep detailed records—" The teller took another look at the ledger, running her finger slowly down the column. "And there is not a mistake here."

"But I haven't made any withdrawals," Mary protested.

The teller hesitated. "Well, as we've already discussed, there is another person on your account. Maybe you should check with Mrs. Meriwether."

"Frankly, I'm shocked and hurt that you'd be questioning me like this, Mary," Agnes said, indignation coloring her voice.

Mary paced back and forth. "I don't *want* to question you, Agnes, but I knew the things that man said about *me* were true—and then when he said things about you . . ."

"Do I look like a swindler?"

"Well, no, of course not, but—"

"Do I look like someone who has an ounce of guilt?"

"No, you don't, but—"

"I mean I *am* guilty of caring too much . . . opening myself up to people I barely know and trying to help them," Agnes said softly, dabbing at her eyes. "I guess we're calling compassion a crime now."

"Agnes—"

"I mean, dear, have I been anything but supportive since I met you and Jack? I just don't understand why you'd take something some lunatic said over me—"

"I was at the bank today, Agnes," Mary said.

"Oh," Agnes replied. "I guess that was your errand?"

Mary nodded and pulled the bank book from the pocket of her sweater. "Where did all the money go?"

Agnes sighed. "I really didn't want to have to explain that to you yet."

"Did you take the money from this account?"

Agnes looked at her for what seemed like a very long minute, then nodded. "Yes. I did."

Even with her suspicions, Mary hadn't been prepared for the admission. She dropped into a chair and looked at Agnes, feeling deep hurt and disappointment. "I can't believe you'd do that—"

"You shouldn't make assumptions until you have all the facts, dear," Agnes responded quietly.

"It's not an 'assumption' that the money is gone—and you just admitted to me that you took it! You knew that was the only reason I agreed to use Jack's gift like we've been doing—"

"Yes, of course I know all that!" Agnes interrupted. "And that's why you need to give me some credit here." She raised her hand, palm upright. "I'm not going to explain further—I'm going to show you," Agnes said. "You'd better get your coats. It's freezing outside."

Mary was in the passenger seat and Jack in the back as Agnes maneuvered her old Ford northeast away from the city. Downtown buildings were replaced by large, old homes, and the shoreline of Lake Michigan came into view.

Mary sighed. "Won't you just tell me where we're going?"

"You'll see soon enough," Agnes said. She slowed to turn a corner and then rolled the car to a stop at the edge of a sweeping yard covered with a fine layer of snow. Agnes turned off the engine and looked at Mary. "Here we are," she said.

"Where's 'here'?" Mary asked, looking out her window. Agnes did not answer but motioned for her to get out of the car.

"The house is vacant," Agnes said abruptly, pointing toward a large wood-and-stone house sitting impressively in a copse of tall oak and maple trees. Mary could smell the lake water, that earthy, slightly metallic scent that reminded her of the Minnesota lakes of her childhood.

Agnes was already following Jack up the driveway. "Come, take a closer look."

A wide porch ran the length of the house. Tall wooden timbers held it in place and a stone turret at one end went up three stories like an old lighthouse. Mary watched Agnes climb the timbered steps to the porch and reach her hand up beside a windowsill.

"Let's look inside," Agnes said as she plucked a key from a nail beside the window and fit it neatly into the lock on the front door. The door swung open.

Mary hesitated. "How did you know the key was there?"

"I've been here before. My real estate agent brought me and gave me the grand tour a few weeks ago. Come on," Agnes said, motioning. "It can't hurt to have a look around."

Jack crossed the threshold first with Mary right behind him. She stopped and stared at the huge room boasting a stone fireplace with long windows on either side. Mary crossed the oak plank floor and took in the staircase, the built-in bookcases, and a massive picture window offering a lake view that was nothing short of spectacular. The water looked like a piece of blue glass shimmering under the winter sun. A long dock jutted out from the rocky shoreline. In spite of her lingering irritation and confusion over Agnes and the missing money, Mary couldn't help but be impressed by her surroundings.

"Beautiful, isn't it?" Agnes said as she came to stand beside her at the window.

"Yes, it is."

"Can't you just picture Jack fishing off that dock?" Agnes asked. "Give him a bamboo pole and some worms and he could probably catch your dinner. While you sit and read a favorite book—"

"That would be something," Mary agreed.

"And this fireplace mantel over here," Agnes said as she turned, "just begs for Christmas stockings, don't you think?"

"I suppose so," Mary said slowly.

"Why, I'll bet you could fit fifteen stockings across that mantel." Agnes chuckled. "That would keep Santa busy."

Mary automatically smiled at the word picture Agnes was painting.

"This place is grand," Agnes said, "but it's been vacant for a while, and the owners fell on hard times when the market crashed in twenty-nine. So they didn't keep up with the maintenance like they should have. It needs a lot of work—new paint, cracked plaster to be repaired, the floors need to be sanded and buffed. But after a few months of elbow grease, this place could be magnificent again."

Mary walked to the center of the room and turned in a slow circle. "I can't begin to imagine how it would feel to live in a house like this."

"You don't have to imagine it, dear," Agnes said.

"What on earth do you mean?"

"I *did* take the money from your account, Mary. I took it to put a down payment on this place. The house is yours—if you want it."

While Agnes explained about the house, Mary stared at the deed Agnes now handed to her. *Mary Godwin, property owner, property owner, me! Property owner!*

"I already told you the owners lost it when the market crashed," Agnes was saying, "but what I didn't tell you was that the bank had to foreclose on the house. I was able to get it for a song!"

"But I don't have enough for something like this," Mary said.

"You had the money for a sizeable down payment, and the payments on the mortgage are next to nothing," Agnes said. "I worked it all out with the bank on your behalf. There are lots of permits to get for the work to be done before you can move in," she went on. "Contractors say a minimum of nine months, depending on how quickly the work goes."

Mary, speechless, stood wide-eyed as she looked around at all the possibilities. *Their own home—their own place in the world forever and ever . . .*

"You told me you wanted security for Jack," Agnes said with a sweep of her arm.

"Oh, but Agnes—"

"And you told me what you missed about the Edmundses' house was the view of the lake. You said it was peaceful. It's what I wanted to give you. Peace."

Mary shook her head. "The pastor yesterday told me he thought I had some . . . difficulty with trust. I guess he's right."

Agnes raised her brows. "I may not agree with church rules, but I have to say I agree with that pastor."

"I'm sorry about what I said, Agnes. . . ."

She waved a dismissive hand. "No, no. It's my fault. I should have discussed all of this with you, but you're so reluctant to do anything for yourself I was afraid you'd take too long to make up your mind. We'd lose it to someone willing to make the commitment immediately."

Agnes paused, then continued, "This is a home where Jack can live his life with beautiful views out the windows, with enough space that he can have one special room—just to put together puzzles! You can have a library and a study, a refuge for the two of you when you are *really* ready to stop meeting with clients. This is a stone-and-wood version of all your dreams come true, Mary. You deserve this; Jack deserves this. You have to dig in your heels and believe in your heart that what you're doing is right—no matter what anyone else says to you. You have to focus on what you want for Jack and never lose that focus. Really, all you have to do is continue the important work the two of you started."

Mary pressed the deed to her chest. "I'm—well, I'm not sure I'm strong enough to say no."

"Then say yes," Agnes persisted.

"Will you live here with us when it's finished?"

Agnes's answering smile was immediate. "I think I could do that."

Mary smiled back. "Then—yes."

"Good! Wonderful! And in the meantime, I just happen to know someone who can knit three matching Christmas stockings for that mantel!"

# Chapter Twenty-four

MARY AND JACK CAME AROUND the corner of the block that put them back on their neighborhood street. Their last-minute trip to the market for Agnes had taken longer than Mary had planned, and the sun had all but disappeared in the swath of clouds above. Crosby's "Pennies From Heaven" had been playing on the grocer's radio, and now the song was stuck in her head, taking her thoughts back to the last afternoon she'd been with Jack in their little kitchen in Minnesota. She had a moment of pure gratitude that they weren't there anymore.

Mary shifted the bag of groceries to her other arm and smiled when she thought of the bag of chocolates she'd managed to sneak into the grocery bag as a surprise for Jack. But her smile faded when she saw two cars parked in front of Agnes's house. *Who is that? We didn't have any appointments. . . .* As they drew closer, she could see the first car was a nondescript blue sedan, but the car parked in front of it—*It can't be!*—was a black squad car. She picked up her pace as she snagged Jack's hand with her free hand.

"Something's happened . . . something bad!" she said, nearly running. A ball of fear had formed inside, and she ran up the steps, pulling Jack along with her. They went through the storm door at the side of the house and ran through the mudroom with Mary calling out, "Agnes! Agnes—is everything okay?"

Hurrying into the living room, she saw right away that everything was *not* okay. Agnes was sitting on the couch, face pale and strained looking, and two uniformed police officers and another man stood near the fireplace. But the sight that made her heart leap in her chest was her husband standing only four feet away. Her worst nightmare had come true.

*Jerry has found us. . . . Help me God, help me God, help me God. . . .*

The officers moved toward her, and she pulled Jack against her. Somewhere in the periphery of her awareness she heard the voices of Agnes and Jerry.

"I'm sorry, Mary, I had to let them in. . . ."

"There he is! That's my son!"

"Mary Sinclair, we have a warrant here for your arrest—"

"What—what do you mean?" She didn't recognize the voice as her own.

"—for violating Statute 565–153: parental kidnapping, which is a class D felony offense," the officer said, holding out a piece of paper as the other officer pulled a pair of handcuffs from his belt.

"You don't understand . . . I can explain—"

"You can tell it to a judge, lady," the same officer said. "Put your hands behind your back."

Mary felt the world tilting underneath her feet. The man by the fireplace looked familiar, but who he was didn't matter. *They're going to take me away from Jack!* Agnes was saying something, but the ringing fear in Mary's ears made her unaware of anything but Jerry's hard eyes and the sneer she knew was meant only for her.

"I hope you get a good lawyer," Jerry was saying. "You'll sure need one."

"Wait! You can't just arrest me on something Jerry said! You can't—"

"You took my son and you took our life savings, Mary. Those are facts I didn't make up," Jerry shot back.

Mary grabbed at one of the police officer's shirts. "I only took the money and Jack away because I found out he was leaving us. He had plans with another woman! He was going to divorce me and leave us homeless—"

"Which, of course, is a lie," Jerry said, sounding smooth and reasonable.

"And if you'd caught us—you might have beaten us!" she choked out.

"Now, Mary, there's another lie. You know I've never lifted a hand toward you. This comes down to you and your lying, thieving ways." He was obviously picking up steam, and his voice now had an angry edge that chilled Mary to the bone. "You're the one living hundreds of miles from home with a stranger. You're the one who took my son without so much as a good-bye, leaving me to worry myself sick about him for all these months!"

"No, really, officers, that's not how it was," Mary said, trying to keep her shaky voice even. "He hates Jack. He's always hated Jack!"

"Let's have your hands, ma'am," the cop said.

Mary stepped back again, dragging Jack with her, shaking her head, pleading for her freedom. "Please don't do this. Please—I'm begging you— don't do this. My son needs me!"

"His father is perfectly capable of caring for him until we get this sorted out," the man near the fireplace said.

"Who—who are you? What do you know about me—about my son?"

"Charles Westerly," he said confidently, staring directly into her face.

Mary did not pause to figure it out. She cried, "You can't let Jerry take my son. Please! Leave him here with Agnes—"

"I'll keep him, Mary," Agnes put in quickly. "He'll stay with me until they see this is all a big mistake."

"I'm afraid not, ma'am," the cop said.

"He's coming with me." Jerry waved Agnes off.

"Your hands, Mrs. Sinclair," the officer said impatiently.

Oblivious to the tears sliding down her face, Mary gulped for air. "Please. Don't do this. . . ."

The officer dropped his voice. "You're making this harder on your son. Put your hands behind your back, and we'll get this over with."

Jerry stepped forward, put a hand on Jack's shoulder, and drew him away from Mary. She watched as Jack rapidly tapped the fingers of his right hand against the palm of his left in a nervous tic. Sobs tore from her throat and everything in her world fell apart as the officer forced her hands behind her back. She felt her knees buckle and her legs betray her as she crumpled to the floor. Both officers flanked her, lifting her firmly under the arms as they started toward the door.

"I'll find you a lawyer, Mary! I'll do whatever I can to fix this!" Agnes shouted as the officers pulled Mary out the door.

Charles watched the door close behind Mary and the officers. Jerry kept his hand on Jack's shoulder, and the boy's fingers continued to tap against his other palm. Agnes looked stunned as she started to move toward Jack—but Jerry stopped her with merely a look.

"Maybe you'll be good enough to get some of the kid's things together." His tone brooked no argument. "Just what he needs for a couple a' nights. I'll be back for the rest in a few days."

Agnes glared. "You don't fool me. I know what kind of man you are."

"Just get his things," Jerry snapped.

Resigned, she left the room.

Jerry turned to Charles. "Thank you for giving me back my son."

Charles gave a brief nod. "You have temporary custody until the trial," he explained, "which I'll push to occur as quickly as possible so you can get back to your life."

"Got it, thanks." Jerry gave Jack's shoulder another firm squeeze. "She cleaned me out when she left—any chance I could get any of that back?"

"You're still married—so technically you're entitled to half," Charles said.

"Great. Just hope she didn't burn through it all."

Agnes came back with the battered suitcase. "Here are some of his things," she said stiffly. "I put his pajamas, underwear, a toothbrush, some socks and—"

"Yeah. Fine." Jerry grabbed it. "C'mon, kid."

"Wait!" Agnes said. She hurried to the closet and pulled out Jack's green scarf and knelt in front of him to wrap it around his neck.

When she put her arms around the boy, now standing as still as a statue, Jerry abruptly said, "Let's go, son." He again placed his large hand on Jack's shoulder and pushed him toward the door.

Agnes looked at Charles as he started after them. "You've made a terrible mistake, Mr. Westerly."

"It wouldn't be the first one." Charles nodded. "Good afternoon."

Charles stepped outside and walked through the falling snow to the car, where Jerry and Jack were already waiting.

# Chapter Twenty-five

IT WAS LATE EVENING by the time Jerry's growling stomach reminded him that he and Jack hadn't had dinner. They went into Lou's Steak Den, a modest restaurant next door to the cheap hotel Westerly had booked for them until Mary's case went to trial.

The hostess standing behind the cash register looked up wearily as the bell over the door signaled their entrance. Her gray hair was a close-knit cap of curls, and her pink cardigan stayed in place around her shoulders with a chain of faux pearls between the opening. She grabbed a couple of menus from the counter and held them out toward Jerry.

"Here ya go. Pick out a booth, an' Marianne'll be right with you to take your order," she told him with a sigh.

Jerry took the menus and cupped his hand around Jack's neck to get him to move toward a booth next to a row of windows. Two other tables in the place were occupied. Jack moved across the room slowly, but Jerry exerted just enough pressure behind him to keep him going.

The kid had already proven to be a pain in the neck—just like he remembered. Jerry had never understood why Mary hadn't just parked him in one of those state places the minute they'd found out he was deaf and dumb. But she wouldn't hear of it, and had given him the impression she thought he was a monster for even suggesting it.

Jerry, fingers laced on the scarred wood-grain table, looked at the boy staring back at him. He cracked his knuckles, then dropping his hands flat on the surface, leaned toward Jack.

"So—guess you must be pretty ticked about now, huh? Yeah, well join the club." He shook his head and propped his chin in his hand while he studied Jack. "I had plans for us, kid. Playing ball, fishing together . . . I was gonna teach you the fine art of sales. Figured you'd grow up, and we'd have our own agency—Sinclair and Son. Has a nice ring to it." The slight melancholy tone to his voice faded and he narrowed his eyes at Jack. "And then I had a new plan—which you and your mom ruined again when you disappeared into thin air with my dough. I spend months getting a classy dame like Alice Jean to take an interest in me—and then, *wham!* She dumps me when she finds out I got nothing but lint in my pockets! Lost my job when I was out looking for you for two stinkin' months, lost my new Caddy, and nearly ended up on the street. You know what it's like doin' maintenance like a janitor, Jack? Your old man is sittin' at the bottom of the barrel all because of you and your idiot mom!"

Jerry sat back against the booth and cocked his head to the side. "Got anything to say about that, kiddo? Any kinda defense? Just one word that makes sense, and I'll forget about the whole thing. Forgive and forget."

Jack didn't move a muscle, didn't even blink.

"That's what I thought. Stubborn till the end," Jerry growled. "And since you didn't ask me to forgive you—I'm not. We *all* have to pay the price when we do somethin' wrong, kid—even you. Once they throw your mom in the can, we'll see about someplace for you. Maybe a room with a window and three squares a day. But there's no way I'm taking you home with me. You can be the state's problem like you shoulda been eight years ago."

Jerry smiled and once more splayed his hands flat on the table, leaning even further toward Jack. "Life's about to change for you, bud—and this time, there's not a thing your mamma can do about it."

Jerry blew out a breath and looked around the room. A young woman in a white blouse and black skirt was heading their way with two glasses of water.

"Hi, sorry about the wait," she chirped. "Welcome to Lou's. I'm Marianne, your waitress." She put the glasses in front of each of them. "We have two specials tonight: chipped beef on toast or chopped steak on a bun with cottage fries," she offered, pad and pencil at the ready.

"Which one would you recommend, Marianne?" Jerry offered her his best smile—the one he knew produced a small dimple in his left cheek. She smiled right back.

"Probably the chopped steak. It's a nickel more than the chipped beef, but you get more food," she said, smiling again.

"So I'll splurge tonight," he said. "Make it the chopped steak."

"Anything else?"

"Nope. That'll do it."

She looked at Jack, his face reflected in the dark window. "Nothing for your son?"

"Oh . . . yeah."

"What about it, sweetie? What can I bring you?"

"Bring him a toasted cheese," Jerry said.

"Is that what you want, cutie?" Marianne asked Jack.

Jerry hated the way Jack just sat there like a lump, hated that his own son was so flawed. He lifted himself up, leaned across the booth, and tapped Jack's arm. "Yeah, he's not being rude—he's deaf."

"Oh, I'm sorry," Marianne said as Jack turned big brown eyes to her. "Do—you—read—lips?"

"No, he doesn't," Jerry said curtly, forgetting all about flirting. Now she was just irritating him. "Like I told you—a cheese sandwich."

"Okay," she said, still studying Jack. "You know—he looks real familiar to me. Have you been in here with him before?"

"Nope."

"Hmm. Maybe somewhere else, then . . ."

"They say everybody's got a twin," Jerry said. "And I'm fading away from hunger here."

Marianne pulled her eyes away from Jack and flashed a quick smile at Jerry. "Gotcha." She scribbled on her order pad. "Chopped steak, cheese sandwich comin' right up."

"Waitress! Miss!" An older man at a nearby table had his hand in the air, and she hurried away.

Jerry gulped down his glass of water and reached for Jack's. "Revenge is thirsty business, kid," he said. He had the second glass midway to his mouth when he noticed the waitress and the older couple casting quick glances in Jack's direction as they talked.

He downed the glass of water and slid it back toward Jack. Dropping an elbow to the table, he propped his chin against his hand and let his eyes meander back to the threesome, still gabbing. *Incompetent broad*, he thought as he watched them continue to cast furtive looks at him and Jack. *She'll sure be surprised at her tip tonight.*

He swore under his breath and muttered, "It's like being an exhibit at the zoo—come and feed a peanut to the deaf an' dumb kid."

Suddenly all three of them were on their way over, the waitress and the older couple. Jerry shook his head. "About my order," he said loudly as Marianne got closer.

"I know, and I'm so sorry . . . but we have a question," she said.

*"What?"*

The older woman motioned toward Jack. "That's Jack—am I right? *The* Jack?"

Jerry frowned. "Yeah," he said slowly. "That's his name."

The couple beamed at each other and then at

Marianne. "I knew it—I knew it was him! We're the Kowalskis," the woman said, talking rapidly. "We recognized him the second you walked in. When we went to the house for our chapter and verse, the room was kinda dark, but we'd know that sweet face and those beautiful eyes anywhere!"

"I told you I'd seen him somewheres!" Marianne inserted triumphantly. "As soon as Patsy and Jim here asked if that was him, I figured it out." She grinned at Jerry as if they were sharing some wonderful secret, and took a playful swipe at his shoulder. "But you must get this all the time."

Jerry shook his head. "I don't know—"

"I mean, when you've got a son like Jack, who's practically a celebrity, you must have people saying they recognize him all the time!" Marianne squatted down next to the Jack. "You look just like that picture in the newspaper—only more handsome in person."

"Where's his mother—Mary, if I remember correctly?" Jim asked. "She's not with you tonight?"

"No . . . she's not," Jerry said.

"She's a wonderful woman," Patsy said. "You're both so generous to allow your son to share his gift with people."

Jerry frowned now, trying to remember what Charles Westerly had mentioned. Something about Mary and Jack making a few bucks.

"The Scripture Jack gave us helped so much,"

Jim was saying. "I only wish we could have given a bigger donation. Six dollars seems so little for the peace of mind we got."

Jerry's brows shot up.

"I got three-ninety in tips so far tonight," Marianne put in. "Would you be willing to let Jack give me a chapter and verse right here?"

Jerry shook his head. "No, we couldn't do that right now." He scrambled through his vague memory of the conversation with Westerly. *What is this all about?*

"Sorry," he said, wishing he knew how the scam worked—it could pay for their supper. "His mother and I have a . . . policy . . . about not letting him, uh, do it, in public."

"The other woman told us they only see clients at the house."

*That must mean that Agnes woman knows. . . .*
"Uh, yes, that's right," Jerry said. "Now—if you don't mind, do you think you might put in our order? Jack is awfully hungry."

Jerry sat back against the booth and looked at Jack with new eyes as the three smiled and made their departures.

"Just exactly how many six-dollar 'donations' have you collected, son? A better question—where's all that money?"

Jerry tented his fingers together over the table and looked out the window. "Mary, Mary, Mary—you are just full of surprises. . . ."

# Chapter Twenty-six

MARY HAD NOT SLEPT ALL NIGHT—her twitching, nervous muscles would not let her be still. She'd been pacing back and forth in the small holding cell since the sun had come up. Her bare hands were knotted into fists at her side, and she couldn't shake the feeling that she was naked somehow. They had taken her gloves along with everything else when they booked her.

"Nothing extra in the cell, ma'am. No belts, jewelry, heeled shoes—gloves. Sorry." This officer had indeed looked sorry, especially when she pulled her gloves off, weeping as she stood under the glaring light in the small office where she'd been "processed." At the sight of her scarred hands, he had hesitated, almost as if he were going to give her gloves back to her. But then he tucked them into a box with the rest of her things.

During that long, terrible night, images of Jack's face stayed firmly in front of her, whether or not her eyes were closed. His expression when he'd seen Jerry, those poor little fingers tapping furiously against his palm that told her he was worried. *He's never been away from me. Please, let it be that Jerry changed his mind and left Jack with Agnes. Maybe that's why she hasn't been here yet—maybe she can't come because she's at home taking care of him.*

Mary had been hoping, praying, pleading all night long that this would all turn out to be a huge mistake. That Agnes would get in touch with a sympathetic lawyer who might have a better outlook than the court-appointed attorney who had paid her a visit right after she'd been booked. Young, inexperienced, and more than a little pessimistic, she quickly realized. The conversation had gone so badly she hated to even think about it, but in the small confines of the cell, her mind kept going there anyway.

She could still hear his flat, no-nonsense voice: *"Bail's been denied because you're considered a flight risk—there are interstate laws in place, and you took your son from Minnesota to Illinois without his father's knowledge or consent—Illinois officials have discretionary authority to assist in the case because this is where they found the child and arrested you . . . Trial will be here in Chicago . . . Father has physical custody—he can legally take your son back to Minnesota during your incarceration if you're found guilty . . . What the heck happened to your hands?"* And it didn't get better from there.

After pacing what seemed like miles and miles, Mary still remained on her feet but finally could not lift them anymore. Leaning her aching forehead against the cold steel bars of her cell, she closed her eyes and prayed once more that when she opened them, she would be lying in her own bed with Jack breathing evenly in his sleep right beside her. Her mind needed the fantasy that everything was all right—if only for a few seconds. She took some deep breaths, willing her heart to beat normally instead of at the terrified gallop that had been pounding in her chest all night long.

"Mary—you've got visitors." A man's voice interrupted her reverie, and she opened her eyes. *Jack!* Her arms reached out to him through the bars. She couldn't believe her son was right in front of her—and at the same time she hated that he was seeing her in a cell. *Maybe I am asleep— maybe he's not really here, and I'm dreaming.* That's when she saw Jerry right behind him. *No! It's a nightmare. . . .*

"You got ten minutes," the police officer said. "That's it." He turned and left.

"Jack!" she cried. She saw on his face when it registered who he was seeing—but in a place he didn't, *couldn't* understand. He moved toward her, and she tried to keep her tears in check. She reached out again, then remembered her hands were bare. The fingers of his right hand were tapping against his left palm. *Tapping, tapping, tapping.*

Jerry took a menacing step closer to the bars. "Where's my money? The money you stole from me—the money I worked my tail off for!"

"Someone stole it," she said, her voice shaking, "right after we got to the city. Is he eating—is Jack okay?"

"Stolen? Stolen! You're lyin' to me."

She shook her head. "I swear before God. Someone took the envelope from my purse."

"So it's gone? *All* of it?"

She nodded, and a strand of hair fell across her face. Without thinking she reached up to tuck it behind her ear. She saw Jerry's eyes move to the scars—and his grimace.

He swore at her. "You better figure out how to get me my money back, or I'm gonna make sure you rot in jail."

"I'm sorry, Jerry. I'll get you the money. Just, please, talk to someone! Tell them it wasn't kidnapping," she pleaded. "You know you don't want to take care of Jack!"

"Let's talk about the money you and Jack have been making while you've been living with the old lady," he said. "We're still married, so I figure it's *all* mine."

"You can have it," she said quickly. "I don't care. Just tell the judge this is all a huge mistake."

He pursed his lips and drew his brows together. "I might be able to talk your way out of this mess," he said. "But first I need to know how you're working the scam."

"Scam? What do you mean?"

His smile was mocking. "I mean the—what is

it?—this 'chapter and verse' scam you and Jack are pulling."

"But it's not a scam," she argued. "The Scripture references Jack writes are real—they're true. They are accurate—"

"Okay, fine." Jerry was rolling his eyes. "Then tell me the *scheme*—how does the deal work? Is there a crystal ball or flickering candles or maybe you look at tea leaves—?"

"No, nothing like that. I told you it's real," she insisted. "Jack touches the person's hand, and then with my help he writes out three numbers. The number of the book of the Bible, the number of the chapter, and the number of the verse."

"That's it?" He smiled. "There's gotta be more suckers in this world than lollipops."

Mary looked into Jack's face. Those brown eyes were asking so many questions, and it tore her apart inside that she couldn't make him understand what was happening. *I don't understand what's happening myself....* "How did you find us?" she asked Jerry. "Did you read about Jack in the paper?"

"Better luck than that. Charles Westerly. He came knockin' on my door."

*Charles Westerly?* "Why? Did he say?" Mary could hear the new tremble in her voice.

"Not really. He's a strange bird," Jerry answered nonchalantly. "You musta really ticked him off somehow. You're good at that—an' nobody knows it better'n me."

"I'm so sorry, Jerry. I'd take it all back if I could, but right now I'm telling you the truth. If you want, I can prove it," she rushed on. "Just let me place your hand in Jack's, and we can find out where all of this will lead." Mary cautiously reached out to take Jerry's hand, but he instantly put his out of reach.

"Let's just say I believe you. Okay, talk to me about the money you've made with the kid. How much?"

*The money is all he cares about—it's all he's ever cared about. . . .*

"I think there could be . . . quite a lot," she said slowly.

"You *think?*"

"Agnes handles all the money," she said. "Her name's on the account with mine."

Jerry's jaw dropped. "Are you *kidding* me?"

She heard the change in tone, saw the flash of irritation and anger in his eyes. *No, no, no—don't get mad. . . .*

"What kind of an idiot lets somebody she hardly knows have access to all her money? You might as well've let Jack control the finances! Of all the stupid—"

"This will make it easier for you to get the money!" Mary said quickly. "She can take you to the bank and withdraw it, using her signature!"

Jerry stared hard at her for a while. "You better hope it works like that," he finally said. " 'Cause if it doesn't, I will be more'n happy to stand in front of the judge and tell him all about my broken heart and how badly my son has been damaged by his mother's cruel and criminal actions."

"Agnes will give you the money," Mary assured him, "and you can tell the judge it was all a mistake. He'll let me out, and . . . and then you can see for yourself how Jack's gift works."

"That's how it'd go if we lived in a perfect world," Jerry said with a thin-lipped smile. "But let's face it—this world is far from perfect."

"Time's up," the police officer said as he stepped into view.

Jerry grabbed Jack and pulled him back from the cell bars. Mary had to bite her lip to keep from crying out at the look of confusion and fear on Jack's face. "Go see Agnes," she said as convincingly as she could manage. "She'll give you the money. Tell her I said to give all of it to you!"

"Let's just hope she's home," Jerry said. "I'm not too good at waiting."

As Jerry led Jack away, Mary had to remind herself to breathe.

# Chapter Twenty-seven

IT WAS TEN FORTY-FIVE in the morning by the time Agnes returned home and pulled her car up in front of her house. An early riser—it wasn't unusual for her to have had two cups of coffee before six o'clock—it irritated her that the rest of her world, especially the bank, insisted on mid-morning openings.

Hurrying now to make up for lost time, Agnes took quick measure of the house and yard, specifically the *not marked snow* in the front, as she drove slowly along the side of her house to the garage. The light snow that had fallen the night before was pristine, untouched by footprints on the sidewalk, steps, or front porch.

Inside the back door that led into the kitchen, Agnes dropped her handbag on the counter so she could peel off her coat, pausing only long enough to wonder what she could have forgotten. She ran through a mental checklist as she walked quickly into her bedroom. *Let's see, Mother's recipe box from the pantry and the silver spoon I got at Niagara Falls . . .*

Agnes heard her knees creak as she bent to grab the two suitcases, all ready to go. One more quick glance around the room. She turned to lug the cases through the living room and kitchen, out the back door—she'd soon be on her way.

She rounded the corner of the hallway, and one of the cases banged into her leg. "Ouch!"

But the pain was quickly forgotten when she moved into the living room. Jack was standing by the window, looking straight at her. Her free hand flew to her chest. "Jack?"

"And Jack's daddy" came Jerry's voice from the

right. She whirled to see him standing on the threshold between the kitchen and the living room, his hands behind his back. He looked pointedly at the suitcases, and Agnes felt a clutch of fear. She willed herself to keep a calm look on her face.

"Going somewhere, Agnes?"

"I didn't hear you knock," she said evenly as she put the cases on the floor.

"No? Maybe age is creepin' up on you," he said. "They say hearing is one of the first things to go."

Agnes moved toward Jack, working at a smile on her face. "How are you, dear? Are you well?" She put a hand on his shoulder.

"He's fine. And I asked you a question," Jerry said. "Where are you off to with the suitcases?"

Agnes turned to face him. "Not that it's any of your business, but I'm taking some things over to Mary at the jail."

His brows shot up. "Really? They'll let her have personal things in her cell? Two suitcases full?"

Agnes tilted her head slightly to the side. "I wouldn't know for sure, having never been to a jail before. Now if you'll excuse me, I really need to get going." Agnes turned back toward the suitcases, but Jerry swung his hand out from behind his back to reveal Agnes's handbag.

She started toward him. "Where did you get that? Give that to me!"

"Sure thing," he said with a grin as he tossed it

toward her. But Jerry swung his other arm out from behind his back, where his hand grasped a thick cotton zippered bag. "I think *this* is what you're really looking for—isn't it?" He unzipped the bag. "I guess when you're as good a customer as my wife, the First National Bank even supplies one of their own teller bags when you make a hefty withdrawal."

Agnes clutched her purse against her pounding heart. "That money belongs to me—it's not yours. You have no claim on it."

"Wrong. We both know this is Jack's money. And since I'm Jack's dad and have custody of him, the money goes with me." Jerry cut his glance back and forth between Agnes and the bag as he quickly thumbed through the bills. He issued a low whistle. "Man, oh, man. Must be some scam you two've been running. There's gotta be a few thousand in here."

"I'm telling you, that money is mine—from my late husband's estate," Agnes insisted.

"You got this much money from your dead husband, and you live in a place like this?" Jerry gestured around the humble living room. "I don't think so, you conniving—"

"I don't care what you think," Agnes snapped. "Now put that money down and get out of my house before I call the police."

"Go ahead," Jerry said. "We can both point fingers at each other, but at the end of the day,

Mary's gonna be the tie breaker, Agnes. She'll tell the cops she wanted you to give all the money in her account to me—just like she already said to me."

"Mary will regret that impulsive decision," Agnes said. "I was just trying to protect her."

Jerry smiled. "That's most caring of you, Agnes, but Mary's a big girl and she knows her own mind."

Agnes felt imminent defeat in every bone of her body. She could barely stand on her shaky legs and leaned against the brick of the fireplace for support when she saw the look of pure victory on Jerry's face.

He shrugged. "So I'm guessing you'll want to unpack your things, Agnes. You're not going any-where—but I'll be happy to tell Mary how you were trying to *protect* her," he said, crossing toward Jack. "C'mon, kid. We're leaving."

But he never made it all the way to his son. His legs crumpled underneath him as a fireplace poker slammed into the back of his head. Jerry never saw what hit him, never saw Agnes standing over him with the poker, didn't feel it when she deftly plucked the bag of money from his hand. She quickly felt for his pulse on the side of his neck— not dead. Just out cold. She turned and looked into Jack's eyes.

"Your mommy should have done it years ago," she said. "But even harder."

As always, it was impossible to tell what the boy was thinking. But one thing for sure—he could never tell anyone about what had just transpired. Agnes took Jack's arm and led him to the couch. A half-finished puzzle was scattered over the coffee table.

"Here, Jack. Work on the puzzle like a good boy, and when Daddy wakes up, he'll probably take you right back to your mother." Agnes leaned down and looked into his eyes.

"My, my, my, Jack. This isn't the way I thought this day would end," she said. "And I'm sorry, dear heart, I really am, but you have to stay here. I can't bring you with me. You understand, don't you? I'm old, and you have your whole life ahead of you. I'm sure your mamma is going to be back with you real soon."

Jack didn't move—didn't so much as blink— and, she noted with a quick look at the man out cold on the floor, neither did Jerry. Agnes stuffed the teller's bag into her purse, picked up the suitcases, and without another look back, walked out.

Jerry slowly became aware of a dull, low sound. His head was throbbing, and he realized his own moaning was what he was hearing—well, at least he wasn't dead. He winced as he gradually sat up, his fingers automatically probing the lump the size of an egg on the back of his head. His mouth was desert dry, he felt very cold, and the room swam in front of him.

After a few moments, he carefully moved his eyes without moving his head and looked around the room. He was alone. No Agnes, no Jack—no suitcases and certainly no bag of money. The ticking of the clock above the mantel drew his attention. *It's four o'clock.* It had been barely after ten-thirty when he'd slipped into the house with Jack right after the old woman.

"Jack?" He realized immediately that was pointless. When he saw the iron fireplace poker on the floor, he went back over the last few things he remembered—Jack near the window, the bag of money in his hand, the argument, and then nothing.

He used the couch to leverage himself up, pleased that he could stand at all. The pain in the back of his head was still bad, but he could feel some strength returning. He shivered—the room felt as if there was a window open. After a few tentative steps, he chased the draft, following the cold air through the living room into the kitchen. The back door stood wide open.

The snow from the previous night had iced over into tiny diamond crystals sparkling in the late afternoon sun. Jerry looked down and saw two sets of footprints—both small, but one set definitely smaller than the other. They led away from the house toward the garage. It wasn't a very big leap for Jerry to assume Agnes took Jack. After all, she knew how the scam worked. In fact, Jerry was sure that Agnes had come up with the whole concept in the first place.

He followed the footprints for a few feet, but suddenly the tracks split. The larger footprints kept on to the garage. The smaller set turned abruptly and went out toward the street. Jerry followed the smaller footprints clearly visible in the otherwise unmarked snow. They led across the yard, and he then lost them at the street's edge—but he found something else. A green mitten, Jack's green mitten lying in the gutter.

He stuffed the mitten into his pants pocket, fuming that he'd been bested by an old lady and his own kid. So maybe Jack wasn't with Agnes after all. But no matter. That's not what the police would hear. Jerry started to work out the details he'd tell the police. He'd keep it simple—that was the secret of a good lie.

But then it dawned on Jerry that the police shouldn't be his first call. *I'll call Charles Westerly, the man who came looking for me in the first place—the one who started this whole thing. . . .*

# Chapter Twenty-eight

## *Madison, Wisconsin*

THE BLOOMER CHOCOLATE DELIVERY TRUCK moved down Madison's quiet, nearly deserted State Street. The driver yawned, shifting behind the wheel to stretch sore muscles as he motored past businesses, still dark and locked up tight. Pete Albert knew from his run just two weeks ago, though, that someone would be at the Kopper Kettle Sweet Shoppe to take his delivery. The owner was a spitfire of a woman—stubborn, trying desperately to hang on to the shop she'd started just before the Depression sucked the air right out of the country.

Pete made Bloomer deliveries twice a month to Helen Gaines. "My customers might come in to buy a Bloomer candy bar, but by the time they leave I've sold them some of my homemade cookies," Helen had told him proudly. "So you just keep those deliveries coming."

Pete parked in front of the Kopper Kettle, pulling on heavy gloves and wool hat before stepping out of the warm cab. At the back of the truck he nearly lost his footing on the ice on the pavement and had to grab the bumper to keep his balance. The temperature hovered around ten degrees—*too cold for man or beast*, he grumbled silently. This was his fourth and last stop since leaving Chicago. He was hungry and thirsty and hoping Helen would wrap up some of her fluffy divinity and chocolate cookies for the return trip.

Pete rolled up the wooden door of the truck, and the grating noise brought Helen to the door of the shop. She waved through the glass, and Pete waved back before climbing into the back. The boxes had shifted during the hundred-seventy-mile drive. The largest box, filled to the brim with chocolate products for Helen, had moved to the corner. Pete felt the truck rock beneath his weight as he worked his way toward the box. He started to reach for it—then yelled out when the box actually moved *toward* him.

"Who's there? Show yourself! C'mon out right now!"

Pete cautiously leaned forward to peer over the top of the box—and he saw a green cap skimming above some dark hair and large brown eyes. The little boy was crouched behind the box, his arms wrapped tightly around his knees.

"Holy cow! What'cha doing in here, kid?" Pete reached down and hauled Jack up by his armpits. "You're frozen like a hare in the headlights."

The boy stared back at him.

"Where in the wide world did you come from?"

"C'mon, now—the jig's up. Let's at least have a name."

*Nothing.* Pete sighed and gripped the boy's arm

to walk him to the edge of the truck. When Pete jumped out the back, he offered the small hitch-hiker a hand, but the boy ignored it as he jumped down and immediately started to walk away.

Pete snagged his arm again. "Oh, no you don't. You're not going anywheres till I get some answers."

Helen must have seen what was happening and came out the door. "Let's get inside, where it's warmer," she said after Pete started to give her the story.

"You're cold as an icicle, honey." Helen laid a hand on the child's red cheek as she led them both to a small dinette. Pete finished his account, and the woman turned again to the boy. "Won't you please tell me your name? I'm Helen—and that's Pete."

"He's sure not talkin'," Pete said. "Probably better call the police."

After Helen returned, she asked, "How long do you s'pose he was in the back of the truck?" Then, directing her attention back to the boy, "Where are you from, sweetie?"

Pete shook his head at the silence. "I sure got no idea. I didn't see him when I made my stop at Evanston—and I coulda swore he weren't in there when I unloaded at Waukegan and Milwaukee." He looked at Jack. "But he had to climb in some-where, and I know it wasn't here."

"Let's get you warmed up, then maybe you'll

feel more like talking." Helen hurried around a counter, its glass front filled with chocolate candy bars and all kinds of other delectable treats.

Pete called, "*I'll* feel more like talking if you can dredge up a cookie or two—maybe some hot cocoa? Made with Bloomer chocolate?" he added with a grin.

Helen nodded absently, her eye on the mysterious visitor. "I'd guess he's a runaway. Seems awful young, though. Are you running away from something, hon?"

"I ran away once," Pete commented. "Caught a ride in the back of a sugar beet truck, but the smell had me leaping out at the first stop!" He looked at the small boy, still sitting stoically with his eyes taking in Helen's every move. "At least this kid picked a better load to travel with—a truck filled with chocolate!"

Helen returned with a tray holding a plate of cookies and two mugs. "This'll help thaw you out." She placed the mugs in front of her two guests. "Here—do you like hot chocolate?" she asked the boy, pushing his mug closer.

Helen sat down at the table and watched the little boy bring it to his lips and carefully take a sip. She propped her elbows on the table. "I guess he does," she said, then pushed the plate of cookies toward him. "Have a cookie. Have two." She shook her head. "Your mamma must be worried half to death about you. We need to let her know you're all right. Won't you *please* tell us your name?" She lowered her face to look directly into his.

Pete finished off another cookie, staring at the boy. "I'd be out of my mind if one of my kids went missing." He looked out the front window of the shop to the dark street. "Shouldn't somebody be here by now?"

Helen nodded, picked up another cookie, and held it out to the boy. "It's been—what?—twenty minutes since I called the station," she said, adding wryly, "Makes me hope I'm never robbed."

They heard the sound of a police siren in the distance. Pete's brows arched. "Did you tell 'em you were being robbed?"

She chuckled and shook her head. Both Pete and Helen looked toward the front window and the scream of the siren. The flashing light on the police cruiser lit the shop as it pulled up.

"Oh, that's loud," she said with a shake of her head as the siren suddenly went silent. Pete turned back and glanced at the boy.

"He didn't look." Pete frowned, watching the boy quietly chewing his cookie.

"What do you mean?"

"He didn't look when we heard the siren. What little boy doesn't look when he hears a police car coming?"

Helen's eyes grew wide. "It's not that he won't talk to us—it's that he *can't*. He's deaf."

• • •

Officer Sheldon Leonard hated working nights—not so much about the hours, but because his pretty little wife was at home alone. She'd been clear that being alone wasn't something she relished. Bottom line—Sheldon was worried. He loved her, and he knew he'd married up when he'd tied the knot with Diane. He was pretty sure their union had left her disappointed, and Sheldon felt in his gut that she'd walk out on him given the right circumstances. And working nights was making that a lot easier.

He entered the Kopper Kettle and inhaled the sweet scents permeating the air.

"Hello, Helen." He moved toward the table where the boy sat with Helen and a man dressed in a delivery uniform. "I'm Officer Leonard," he told the man. "You called about a boy?" stating the obvious.

Helen nodded and pointed at the child, who had yet to turn and look at Sheldon. "This is him. We don't know his name or where he's from—nothing at all about him. Well, except we think he might be deaf."

Sheldon came up beside the boy and slapped his hands together loudly, but he didn't even flinch. "Deaf, huh?" He took a knee, and the boy's eyes grew large. "What's—your—name—son?" Sheldon asked loudly.

The man and Helen exchanged a glance. "Uh,

he can't hear you. He's not talking," the man said.

Sheldon sighed and got to his feet, pulling a pad from his back pocket. "I need your name," he said.

"Why? I didn't do nothin'."

"Just for my report," the officer replied. "Tell me your name and what happened."

When Pete finished his two-minute account, Sheldon shook his head at the scant details he had. Helen had added a few comments, but basically . . . he had nothing. "Anybody want to volunteer to keep him until we find his parents?" Sheldon asked.

Pete quickly shook his head. "Don't look at me. I'm in the middle of a shift. . . ."

Sheldon glanced at Helen, who looked down at the floor. "I wish I could . . . I really do . . . but . . ." She hesitated, then brought her eyes up to meet his. "I'm living in the back of my shop right now. I've only got a cot back there, and there's no place for a little boy."

"Helen, you never said anything," Pete said, honest surprise in his tone.

"It's fine." She forced a little smile. "At least I'm always here for deliveries."

Sheldon sighed. "Okay, I guess the kid's coming with me."

"Do you think you'll find his parents?" Helen asked anxiously. "I just hate that he's all alone—"

"I dunno. That'll depend on if anybody's filed a

report about a missing kid," he said. "If not . . . well . . . I dunno."

"Somebody's got to be worrying about him," Pete said.

"Or somebody cut him loose because he's too much trouble," Sheldon replied in a low voice.

"I can't believe anyone would do that," Helen exclaimed. "I just can't believe it! Especially somebody so defenseless—"

"You'd be amazed at what people will do," Sheldon said cryptically. "It would flat-out floor you."

The three stood there contemplating the nameless little stowaway.

Sheldon sighed again and looked across the front seat of the squad car. His little passenger meant he'd be facing mountains of paper work. He'd need to fill out reports, make phone calls, check the Teletype for bulletins about missing kids. This was going to take him hours, probably the rest of his shift. Which meant if he was going to take a drive past his house, check on things, he'd better do it now. It wasn't as if the kid was going to voice any objections.

Sheldon cautiously made the turn onto his street and cut the headlights of the car. He motored slowly down the shadowy block, keeping the engine just above idle, until he was only a house away from his own driveway. He turned the key and the engine silenced completely while he rolled to a stop at the curb.

The porch light was off, and Sheldon frowned. He always told his wife that a lighted entry was a good deterrent to crime. Burglars weren't going to stand under a light and pry open a locked front door. He made a mental note to be patient when he reminded Diane *again* to be more careful. The curtains were pulled across the front window, some lacy things that Diane had insisted on but Sheldon had argued didn't provide enough privacy from the street. In the end she'd gotten her way, and even now Sheldon knew he'd been right as he watched her silhouette pass behind the curtains. *At least she's home*, he thought with satisfaction—until he noticed she wasn't alone. Another form—this one definitely male, leaned over and their shadows met for a kiss. Stunned, Sheldon stared as the two broke apart and stepped out of view.

Fury replaced his surprise as Sheldon fumbled for the car door handle and yanked it open—just as the interloper in his house slipped outside to the front porch. The man kept close to the porch wall, moving silently, until Sheldon's angry yell punctuated the quiet night. Cursing a blue streak, Sheldon broke into a run, and the man leaped off the porch and darted into the dark shadows around the house. Sheldon veered toward the side yard in time to hear an engine start, realizing too late that the man's car had been parked in the rear out of sight. He changed direction and ran back toward the street just as the car careened around the house, missing him by only a few feet. Sheldon made a valiant attempt to chase down the car, logic and reason a distant second to the adrenaline-fueled anger that kept him moving until the taillights of the car disappeared at the end of the block.

*Diane! You lying, cheating floozy—and in my own house!*

He stomped his way back toward the house, intent on confronting Diane, but his own rage actually worried him. *I could kill her. . . . I'm so mad right now I could actually kill her. . . .*

His hand went to his holstered gun as he looked at the front window. No sign of his wife behind the curtains now. He started toward the door but then stopped, acutely aware that he didn't trust himself right then. Better to take a drive and cool off before he went inside. *She woulda heard me— better still, let Diane stew in her own betrayal.*

Sheldon arrived back at his car. The door stood open, and he slid inside and slammed the steering wheel with the heel of his hand. He looked across the seat at the kid he'd totally forgotten.

"What are you lookin' at?" he demanded.

He couldn't go back to the station now—he couldn't take any of the joking and sarcastic asides that he normally shrugged off. Tonight he'd snap if anyone dared to bring up Diane's name. And by now maybe they already knew about his tart of a wife. Knew that he'd not been man enough for her. Maybe that rat who ran out of his house was at the local bar right now shooting off his mouth about his little dalliance with the good cop's wife, then slipping right past him at his own door.

Sheldon could feel his blood pressure rising with every new thought. *They'll all figure they were right.* The Sheldon Leonards of the world didn't end up with women like Diane. At least not for long.

"Officer Leonard?" the voice of the dispatcher scratched out into the air.

Sheldon picked up the radio mike. "Leonard."

"You make that call to the Kopper Kettle?" the dispatcher asked.

"Yeah." He looked across the seat at the kid. "A false alarm. They found the kids' parents."

"Roger."

That would be the story he'd feed Helen Gaines the next morning when he made a quick run to the Kopper Kettle. The kid's folks had been found in—maybe Evanston, he'd say—and no one would be the wiser.

"Life ain't perfect, kid. Fact is, it downright stinks. There's a place I know where you'll fit right in," Sheldon said out loud, reaching for the ignition. "I can't promise you'll love it . . . but since you ran away from the last place you were, it's probably not any worse."

He shook his head at the quiet voice nagging him from the inside. "Actually, kid," he said as he put the car in gear, "what would they do with you back at the station? Probably the same thing."

Less than an hour later, after mentally running through more scenarios than he could count about what to do when he got home, Sheldon coasted the last few yards to stop in front of a large brick building with two wings jutting out on either side. In the gray light just before dawn, the building presented a façade that seemed stately—until one looked closer at the bars on every window and the high fence running the perimeter of the place.

The wind moaned through a copse of tall pines behind the building and gave Sheldon just the sound cover he needed to get out of the car, open the boy's door, and hustle him to the front of the building. Looking around under the small umbrella of light provided by two sconces on either side of the door, Sheldon found what he was looking for.

"Don't move, kid," he said. "Someone will be right with you." Sheldon pressed the buzzer, holding his finger on the button for a count of ten—then dashed back to the squad car. The engine caught, and he was rolling away from the building within thirty seconds.

. . .

Moments later the door to the Rock River Poorhouse opened, and a woman in a white uniform looked down at a little boy standing alone in the cold. She saw the glow of red taillights at the end of the long driveway. Shivering, she reached out to grab his arm and draw him inside.

# Chapter Twenty-nine

### *Chicago, Illinois*

CHARLES AND JERRY STOOD ON ONE SIDE of a dusty glass window and peered into a room holding a table and two chairs. The light cast an unnatural yellow haze on the tiled floor and white brick walls. A door on the right wall was closed.

"What's takin' so blasted long?" Jerry was more than irritated. "That old woman could be halfway to Timbuktu by now! *With* my son."

A uniformed officer came into the room carrying two cups of coffee. He handed one to Charles. "Here ya go, one sugar, no cream." The other went to Jerry. "Two sugars."

The door in the small room was opening. "They're bringing her in now," the cop said.

Charles nodded. "Her attorney here?"

"Yeah. Just arrived."

As if on cue, a man in a dark suit entered the small room and looked straight at the glass—or from his side, the *mirror*—and arched an eyebrow.

"Okay, we get you're a genius and know we're here," the cop said with a shake of his head. "Lawyers. They're all the same. All flash and show—you know? This one's named Patrick something or other. O'Sullivan, I think."

Charles cast a sidelong glance at the cop. "I'm a lawyer," he said with a glance at the man's badge, "Officer Roark."

The policeman choked on his coffee. Charles hid a smile, noting the man had the good grace to look embarrassed.

"Right, sorry, Mr. Westerly. I guess I just think of you as governor—or, you know, almost governor."

Jerry scowled through the glass. "What kind of a lawyer defends someone who's kidnapped her own son? Doesn't he have a *conscience?*"

Charles gave Jerry a quick glance. He had to ask himself why he was sticking around. He didn't really need to hear the interrogation—but even as he told himself that, he knew he wouldn't leave. When all was said and done, Mary Godwin Sinclair hadn't really been what he'd expected—and it bothered him.

"It's about time," Jerry said. Charles turned his attention back to the interrogation room as the door once again opened. He watched as Patrick O'Sullivan stood while another uniformed officer led Mary inside. The cop with Charles pressed a button near the glass, allowing them to hear the conversation in the room. Charles heard O'Sullivan greet his client.

"Hello, Mrs. Sinclair," he said. "How are you?"

"Sneaky—that's how," Jerry muttered under his breath, fogging the glass in front of his mouth.

Watching as Mary looked around the small room, Charles took note that though her hands were bare, she kept her fingers curled into her palms and pressed close to her sides.

"I'm wondering what's going on," she said, her voice sounding shaky even through the metallic hum of the microphone.

Charles was struck once again by how pretty she was, even in the washed-out artificial light.

"There are some questions they want you to answer," Patrick said. "Someone should be along shortly."

A man in a three-piece suit entered the room with a leather briefcase. He nodded curtly to Patrick and Mary. "I'm Robert Nevins from the district attorney's office," he said importantly, putting his briefcase down on the table and flipping the latch. "Why don't you have a seat, Mrs. Sinclair."

Patrick pulled out a chair, and Mary lowered herself into it, carefully crossing her hands palms up in her lap. "Can you please tell me what this is about?" she asked, leaning forward slightly. "Is it about Jack? About my son? Did . . . did Jerry decide not to keep him?"

"That's right, sweetheart," Charles heard Jerry grumble. "Blame me right away."

"Now that you've brought him up—let's start with Jerry," Nevins said smoothly. "Why wouldn't Jack's father *want* to keep him?"

Mary shook her head. Tears were pooling in her eyes. "I keep telling everybody that Jerry doesn't *want* Jack. He's never wanted Jack. He was . . . cruel. To me, to my son. He doesn't love Jack, and he's got him now only to punish me. . . ."

Charles angled his perspective so he could see Jerry in the periphery of his vision as he continued to watch Mary. He saw Jerry's jaw tighten. "She's a liar. He's my kid, and none of her lies change that one speck!"

"Define *cruel*," Nevins was saying.

Charles saw Mary catch her lower lip in her teeth.

"You know, *mean*. Nasty and . . . and bad tempered, scary," she said. Then tears spilled from her eyes. "Is Jack . . . okay?"

Jerry muttered again from his vantage point behind the glass. "No, he's not okay. You've got him gallivanting off with an old broad who coulda killed me with that poker!"

Charles ignored Jerry and sipped his coffee, watching as Nevins pulled some notes from his briefcase. He flipped up a piece of paper and scanned it—likely purposely ignoring her and her question. Charles knew he had his next question at the ready and was simply extending her anxiety.

Patrick now cleared his throat. "Nevins?"

The man cut his eyes from the paper back to Mary. He put the sheet down and slipped his hands into his pockets. "How well do you know Agnes Meriwether?"

Charles saw Mary frown. "Why are you—what do you mean?"

"I'm asking the questions," Nevins said. "How well do you know her?"

"We live with her," Mary said. "Jack and I do."

"In her house on Moreland Street?"

Mary nodded slowly. "She took us in when . . . when we didn't have any place else to go." Her voice was barely audible.

"You could've come home!" Jerry spat out with his mouth just inches from the glass. "You shouldn't have run out. . . ."

"Quiet," Charles hissed.

"Okay, let's start again. How did you happen to meet Agnes?" Nevins continued.

"We met in Chicago at the bus station," Mary said. "There was a storm, and the buses weren't going to run. She offered us a place to stay that night."

"So you were trying to leave town?" Nevins asked.

"You don't have to answer that, Mary," O'Sullivan cut in. "It's not pertinent right now."

"Fine. We'll leave that for the trial," Nevins responded with a thin smile. "Let's get back to Agnes. How long ago did you meet her?"

"I don't understand why you need to know—"

"Just answer the question."

"Several months ago."

"Did you ever meet any of her relatives or close friends?"

"Why? I don't understand—"

Charles could hear Nevins expel a loud, irritated breath. "This'll go much quicker if you'll stop answering *my* questions *with a question* and tell me what I want to know."

"She's always been irritating like that," Jerry muttered.

"I never met any of her friends . . . or family," Mary said.

"Do you know what Mrs. Meriwether's financial situation is?" Nevins asked.

"No, I don't." Charles could hear the impatience in her voice. "What about my son?"

"What about him?"

"I want to know if he's all right, if . . ." She paused.

Charles saw Nevins and O'Sullivan exchange a glance—and he could see that Mary had noticed too.

"What is it? What's going on? Is *Agnes* okay?"

The concern in her voice rose with every word.

"He's really gettin' to her," Officer Roark said. Charles had forgotten the cop was still in the room.

Nevins rubbed a hand over his jaw before leaning on the table toward her. "I don't know, Mary. She's missing."

Mary looked from Nevins to Patrick—and back again. She shook her head. "Missing? Missing from where?"

"Do you trust Agnes with your son?" Nevins asked.

"Of course. She loves him."

"I hope you're right—and I hope she treats Jack better than she treated your husband," Nevins said.

Mary sat up straight and looked at Patrick. "What . . . what does he mean?"

It was Nevins who answered. "*I mean* that Jerry was knocked unconscious when he went to your house to pick up some of Jack's things. He and Agnes had a dispute, and she hit him with an iron poker. When he came to, they both were gone."

*"Gone?"*

Charles could barely hear her. All the color had drained from her face, and she raised a trembling hand to her mouth.

"He's missing," Nevins said abruptly. "And so is Agnes Meriwether. We have every reason to believe Agnes took the boy and left town."

Charles didn't realize he was leaning so close to the glass he too was fogging it with his breath. He watched the emotions playing across Mary's face. She pressed her lips with her fingers, then wiped her eyes.

"He's not with Jerry anymore?" she finally asked.

"You know darn good and well he isn't," Jerry growled.

Nevins said, "No. Jerry doesn't know where Jack is—other than he believes him to be with Agnes."

Mary shuddered as more tears rolled down her cheeks. "He's with Agnes. He's okay. . . ."

"Why would she take the boy, Mary? Do you have any idea about that?"

Mary sniffed, shook her head. "No."

"Maybe—just maybe—this really turns out to be good news for you, Mary. How about that?" Nevins continued.

"The only thing I care about is Jack," Mary said. "I want him safe—with someone who'll take good care of him until I can be with him again."

"So you're telling me you had no knowledge of Agnes's plan—and you have no knowledge of where they might be?"

Mary shook her head.

*If she's acting, she's good.* Charles watched her search for composure—wiping a red, scarred hand quickly over her cheek to brush away new tears.

"The day you met Agnes—at the bus station, you say—where was she going? To a friend's or to some relatives, maybe?"

"I . . . don't know . . ." Mary shook her head.

"Think about it," Nevins pressed. "She must have said, 'I'm on my way to . . . '?"

Mary didn't hesitate and shook her head again. "No—she didn't say anything like that. I have no idea where she was planning to go."

"And if you think real hard, you can't come up with where Agnes might have run off to?"

"No."

"Liar, liar, liar," Jerry was chanting under his breath, then, "Make her talk!"

Charles watched Mary tilt her chin up and look Nevins in the eye, but he could also see her trembling as Nevins leaned toward her.

"If you *are* withholding information and are complicit in this, we'll bring another kidnapping charge against you, Mary," Nevins said firmly. "If you've got something to tell me, now would be the time."

"She said she doesn't know anything," Patrick insisted. Mary held her hands together in the folds of her dress and looked past Nevins to some point on the wall.

Charles could tell she was done talking, but there was something different about her expression than when she'd first walked into the room. Something had changed.

# Chapter Thirty

## *Rock River, Wisconsin*

A HEAVY WOODEN DOOR OVERGROWN with lichen slowly closed, causing it to blend into the eight-foot hedge that grew around it. To the casual passerby, the door would be nearly undetectable, but to those employed by the Rock River Poorhouse it provided passage from the sane world to the insane—and back again. The covered labyrinth inside didn't discriminate between day and night—in that sense it was timeless. But in every other way the silent tunnel magnified the loneliness, exacerbated the faint of heart, and mocked those with the fortitude to enter at all.

Felix Stanhope wasn't thinking of fortitude as he walked down the twelve steps and made his way along the concrete tunnel. He was planning his next turn in the maze—watching for the now-familiar graffiti scrawled across the wall: *Despair breeds here*—his landmark to veer left in another thirty steps. He moved through the catacomb, the only speck of movement or color in what seemed like a grainy photograph faded to gray with time.

At six foot five, Felix had to duck when he came to one of the dimly lit bulbs hanging every fifty feet or so from the ceiling. A homely man by all accounts, Felix was not troubled at the sparse light down below the buildings of the Rock River Poorhouse. He preferred it to the harsh light of day, where his craggy complexion and nearly bald head drew catcalls and insults from the inmates— the ones who loosely called the facility home. Those who could form a sentence at all.

Felix knew his shift had officially started when he entered the adolescent ward and the stale smell of vomit assaulted him. He pushed his wheeled metal bucket into the large room, windows barred, and automatically leaned to the left when a flat tray sailed right at him. It crashed into the wall behind him and clattered to the floor. He didn't have to look for the small perpetrator—she stood in the center of the room, performing a little jig in her green hospital-issue pajamas—which she wore backward.

"That was me! All me! Claps and whistles for me!" Eleven-year-old Louise grinned wickedly at Felix. "I'll getcha next time."

"You can't hit the broad side of a barn, Louise," Felix said mildly as he scanned the room. Fourteen unmade beds, two large tables, someone's breakfast overturned under a window. Children ranging from eight to sixteen were in various stages of dress, whether pajamas or day uniform consisting of gray pants and shirt—actually the day and night uniforms not all that different except for the color. An undercurrent of moaning, crying, and talking blended together in a cacophony that Felix had come to think of as normal. The staffers referred to the adolescent ward as the *kids' zoo*—which meant he was the zoo's janitor.

He looked at the last bed on the ward—the one under the biggest window—where a dark-haired boy sat, arms wrapped around knees drawn to his chest, eyes staring up at the blue sky beyond the flat bars. Felix couldn't help but be impressed. The new kid was in the same position he'd been in when Felix's shift had ended the day before.

"It's medication time." The steely voice of attendant Geoffrey filled the room. The big man entered with a tray full of small paper cups holding various pills. He breezed right past Felix as if he weren't there.

"Line up," Geoffrey called over the racket as he put his tray on one of the tables. A few of the kids did as he asked—but most did not. Felix looked over at the boy at the window. He didn't move— didn't so much as turn his head at the instruction from the attendant.

While Geoffrey tackled the job of getting the medication into, first, the cooperative, then the uncooperative kids, Felix dipped his cotton mop into the bucket of water, pulled it as dry as pos- sible through the attached roller, and painted figure eights on the yellow linoleum. His mopping pattern would eventually render the floor clean for another twenty-four hours—or twenty-four seconds, depending on when the next accident occurred.

"You're a mean kinda ugly, Felix," Louise taunted from the vicinity of his kneecaps. He looked down to see her scooting backward over the damp floor on her rear end.

"Get up, Louise," he said.

"I'm drying the floor with my butt," she announced, continuing her progress over the floor, "and you're welcome. Ugly people don't usually get any help—so you should be happy. Not happy that you're ugly. Happy that I'm helping."

"Did you get your pills yet from Geoffrey?"

She kept scooting. "He gave 'em to the other me."

Felix turned to see Laura, the mirror image of Louise, dutifully swallowing some pills while Geoffrey watched her.

"It's her today, not me. Tomorrow it'll be me, not her," Louise chanted as she braced her bare heel on the floor and spun herself around to head the other way. She scooted past a fourteen-year-old boy who sat on the edge of his bed, repeating the same mantra over and over: "I don't belong here. I don't—"

"Yeah you do, Johnny," Louise corrected loudly. "You're nuts—wacko—crazier 'n a loon."

Louise jumped to her feet and grabbed Felix's mop. He tried to hold on to it, but Louise was quicker and threw the dripping mop between her legs. Straddling the handle, she rode it over to Laura, and her twin climbed on behind her.

"I don't belong here," Johnny continued in a monotone.

Louise and Laura slid past Johnny on the mop, leaving water streaking on the floor behind them.

"Yupper, you do," Louise chortled. "You do, you do, you do!"

"You surely do do do!" Laura joined in. And then Louise let out a scream, loud and long and at the top of her lungs.

*Never can get used to that. . . .* Felix felt his heart rate returning to normal. He started after the twins. They were making a circuit of the room on the horse mop.

"I don't belong here," Johnny said, hands folded together in his lap.

"So I've heard," Felix said, lunging for the mop as the girls came within reach. He snagged the handle, and the girls abruptly stopped, climbed off, and headed toward the bed in the corner.

"I think that boy should be my new husband," Louise said.

Felix watched Louise and Laura link arms as they approached the boy, still hugging his knees and staring at the sky. "My old husband is dead. Deader than dead dead dead."

The two climbed onto the bed and took up spaces on either side of him. He remained absolutely still—as if completely unaware of their presence. Louise put a hand on his shoulder and pushed him toward Laura. He swayed away, and Laura mirrored her sister's movement and pushed him back.

Felix dipped his mop into the bucket and started to figure-eight his way toward that corner of the room.

"I'm picking you to love me best," Louise said loudly into the boy's ear. "I'm pretty, not ugly, so it's all right if you love me best."

The rule in the zoo was that Felix wasn't to interfere with the inmates—he had neither the experience nor the desire to get in the middle of the frequent altercations. But for some reason, he couldn't take watching the sisters push the boy back and forth.

"Leave 'im alone!" Felix grabbed Louise under the armpits. She issued another loud scream, followed by her sister. The boy didn't even flinch.

"Stop it this instant!" The woman's voice did little to end the screams from the twins. But when they looked toward the door and saw that the voice had reinforcements, they broke off the awful noise at the exact same moment.

Felix hustled back to his mop, ducking his head but watching as Nurse Bess, with a handful of charts in her arms, walked into the ward with Dr. Horace Tanner at her side. The twins seemed to shrink into themselves, once more linking arms.

"Good morning, Johnny," Dr. Tanner said in a calm, soothing tone. "How are you today?"

Felix had once attempted approaching a wounded deer in the woods, something he was always reminded of when Dr. Tanner pasted on his smile and so gently approached his ward charges. But like the wounded deer, they usually ran. Johnny was no exception as he scrambled back into his bed, pulling the covers up and over his head. His muffled voice came from underneath the blanket.

"I don't belong here. . . ."

If Dr. Tanner ever took offense at the rebukes he generally received, Felix had never seen it.

"Who do we have here?" Dr. Tanner asked Bess, standing at his side like a general's aide.

She flipped open one of the charts in her hand. "Patient number four-twenty-four—we found a name tag sewn onto his shirt. It says he's Jack."

Dr. Tanner reached for Jack's shoulder and turned the boy to face him.

"Diagnosis?"

Nurse Bess scanned the chart. "A quick evaluation yesterday revealed profound deafness. And the boy's apparently also mute."

"Any family?"

Felix watched the nurse shake her head. "An anonymous party left him on the doorstep. No note—no nothing."

Dr. Tanner studied Jack for a few more seconds,

then abruptly moved away toward the center of the room.

The kids all watched with wary eyes. Felix knew the drill—knew that Dr. Tanner wasn't leaving the room without one of them. He just didn't know which one—none of them did, except the doctor.

"And how might Anastasia be today?" Dr. Tanner asked, looking in the direction of a girl with bandaged hands and feet. She kept her eyes on the rubber ball on the floor. Dr. Tanner stepped closer.

"I'd like you to come with me, Anastasia. Can you do that, please?"

She shook her head. Dr. Tanner moved even closer as Nurse Bess suddenly appeared by his side with a wheelchair.

"Come now, Anastasia. Be a good girl. You know what good girls get, don't you?"

She looked up—directly at the big white pocket on the doctor's lab coat. Felix could see a half-moon of red above the top. Dr. Tanner reached in and withdrew the prize—a huge red-striped lollipop on a stick.

"Good girls get the lolly—don't they?"

Anastasia nodded slowly. He held the lollipop out toward her as Nurse Bess pushed the chair in close. She put a hand under Anastasia's elbow and helped the girl up.

"Into the chair with you and off for a ride," Dr.

Tanner said in his hypnotically gentle voice. "And, of course—the lolly is yours."

Anastasia was guided into the wheelchair and held out a tentative hand for the sucker, which Dr. Tanner handed over with a smile.

*Eleven*, thought Felix as he watched them wheel the girl out of the zoo. Eleven times he'd seen—they'd all seen—the lollypop come out of that deep pocket in Dr. Tanner's coat. Felix turned to look at the boy in the corner, see if there was any reaction at all. But he—"Jack," it was—had never moved from his post at the window.

# Chapter Thirty-one

## *Oakdale Reformatory*
### JANUARY 1939

AS FAR AS MARY WAS CONCERNED, she was on a ride into limbo. The engine of the prison bus droned on, its constant, unvarying rumble grating on every nerve in her body. The ride made her think of her marriage to Jerry—something to endure, something to tune out, something to get through as best she could. But at least when she'd been living with Jerry, she'd had a single bright spot in every day. *Jack.* For a tiny moment she let herself wonder how she would have carried on if Jerry still had Jack—and knew it would have been impossible. She shuddered—then quickly pushed the thought out of her head. *No! Don't even think about it. Agnes has him. That's why she never came to see me. She knew she had to take him away from Jerry. She'll take good care of him for me. And somehow, she'll figure out a way to get in touch with me and let me know where they are.* These sentences were well rehearsed, a litany she constantly replayed whenever her imagination betrayed her.

Mary knew Agnes to be a smart, informed woman. She felt sure that if her friend was still anywhere close to Chicago—merely anywhere inside the state lines—Agnes would have seen the newspaper articles about the trial and Mary's sentencing. Patrick O'Sullivan had said the story was in all the papers—right after he'd apologized for the guilty verdict the jury had returned. "I'm so sorry, Mary." He'd sounded genuinely regretful. "I'll file an appeal, but to tell you the truth . . ."

He didn't have to finish his sentence. Mary knew that the jury had been against her from the moment Robert Nevins had painted her as a self-absorbed woman who had nothing but selfish motives for taking her son away from his father. "She wanted her son all to herself for one reason and one reason only, ladies and gentlemen of the jury," he'd told them in his closing arguments. "She didn't want to share the cash cow. She wanted to exploit Jack's handicap without his father standing in the way. And even now—well,

I believe she's involved in her son's disappearance. I believe Mary Sinclair knows exactly where her boy is, who he's with, and she's not talking! I believe you need to send a clear message to parents everywhere that says we won't tolerate this kind of behavior—especially when a handicapped child is involved!"

They had sent a message all right, Mary thought as she watched sleet hit the glass of the bus windows and roll down, settling on the gunmetal gray frame of the vehicle. *They sent a message that will last eighteen months.* But as horrible as her situation was, she had convinced herself she could tolerate anything as long as she knew Jack was safe with Agnes and someday they'd be back together again. Agnes had been a godsend—of that Mary had no doubt, despite the efforts of the prosecuting attorney to paint her in a bad light. Mary knew the truth—Agnes would take care of her boy.

The bus driver slowed down, then made a sharp turn, and suddenly through the windshield Mary and the other passengers had their first view of the Oakdale State Reformatory for Women. Mary knew they were someplace south of Chicago, and they'd been traveling for a couple of hours.

The building looked more like an exclusive country manor than a facility for society's female criminals. Pine trees stretched halfway up round turrets on the front and sides of the brick building.

Shrubs formed a winding fence around the structure, now glistening with shiny ice from the current sleet storm. Mary could hear the other women muttering.

"Doesn't look half bad. . . ."

"Kinda pretty, really."

"Never seed a hotel lookin' that fancy."

The driver pulled the bus around back to another large rectangular brick building. The windows were all barred, and a wire fence ran behind it. The women's chatter stopped at once, and Mary was sure there wasn't a doubt among them that *this* building was to be their new home. The driver cut the engine, and almost immediately a uniformed woman hurried out into the weather and onto the bus. Water dripping from her billed hat and coat, she gave each of them a long, appraising look.

"The state of Illinois welcomes you to Oakdale, ladies. And in all honesty, we hope you have an *unpleasant* stay," she finished with a grim smile.

The new inmates filed into the processing room and stood with their backs against a beige wall. The guard who had led them inside introduced herself as Hannah Jorgenson—"Sergeant Jorgenson to you." A substantial woman who looked even more impatient than she sounded, she paced back and forth in front of them while she recited the rules of the place. "It doesn't matter to me what you did to earn your stint in here," the sergeant said. "What matters is that you behave better here at Oakdale than you did out there in the world. Everyone here works. Everyone here cooperates. Everyone here wants to be anywhere *but* here. Your prison matrons are the final authority on everything that happens, and they aren't looking to be your friend. They're paid to keep you in line and make sure you obey the rules." As if on cue, two other female guards entered the room. Sergeant Jorgenson pointed at each woman as she introduced them. "That's Bonnie—she'll give you your uniform. And that's Ruth—she'll take care of your personal effects."

Ruth and Bonnie stepped forward. Bonnie, short, gray-haired, and stocky, passed out plain gray muslin dresses to each woman, along with a pair of black stockings and shoes. Ruth, wearing a no-nonsense, no-sympathy expression above her khaki uniform, followed behind with four baskets.

"Your clothes, shoes, jewelry—anything we *don't give you* goes into the basket," she instructed by rote.

None of the women moved.

"Let's get to it," she barked. "Strip off your street clothes—except for brassieres and underpants—and yank on those dresses."

A young woman on Mary's left, who she thought was named Shirley, cleared her throat nervously. "You want us to change right here?"

"That's right, sweet pea. This ain't Bloomingdale's, where you get your own private fitting room."

Under the watchful eyes of Hannah, Ruth, and Bonnie, the women set about the humiliating task of undressing in a room full of strangers. Mary put her pocketbook in the basket and stepped out of her shoes. After unbuttoning her dress, she let it pool at her feet while she hurried to tug the long-sleeved gray muslin uniform over her head. Dressed in under a minute, Mary dropped her clothes into the basket with her pocketbook. The muslin dress buttoned up the front, and she made quick work fastening the buttons while the others finished their own metamorphosis from free women to incarcerated members of the Oakdale population.

"Pick up your baskets," Bonnie told them, "and follow me."

Mary held her own basket in her arms and started to follow Shirley, but Ruth put her arm in front to stop her.

"We ain't having high tea," she said to Mary, looking pointedly at her gloves. "Take 'em off an' put 'em in the basket."

"I . . . I always wear them," Mary stammered. "My hands are . . . were . . . burned and they are ugly to look at . . ."

"Yeah? Well, cry me a river, but it don't matter," Ruth said. "Let's take 'em off."

Mary handed Ruth her basket while she peeled the glove from her right hand. Shirley, standing next to Mary, sucked in her breath. Ruth drew her brows together, then looked at Mary. "I'll let the other guards know we're making an exception," Ruth said. "Put it back on."

Mary nodded and slipped her hand back into the glove. Ruth shoved the basket back into her arms. "Let's go. Lunch in ten minutes, you got thirty minutes to eat—and after that you'll hear a bell. When it rings, go to the west side of the food hall, and I'll be there with your job assignments," she said. "Any questions?"

The women all shook their heads, then followed Ruth toward their new lives.


The air in the dim corridor seemed to grow thicker with every step Mary took. She tried to match her pace to Ruth's as the guard led her away from the food hall toward the job that would be hers for the duration of her stay at Oakdale.

"Feel that?" Ruth asked over her shoulder.

"Feel what?"

"The wet air that we're headin' into," Ruth said with a touch of impatience. "Do ya feel it?"

Mary nodded as she took a double step to keep up. "Yes, ma'am."

"That's where you'll be working," Ruth said. "We call it the swamp." Mary waited for her to say something else, but the guard said nothing further for the rest of the trip down the humid corridor. Mary saw a large open door at the end of the hall, and as they got closer she read the simple sign posted overhead: Laundry. She followed Ruth over the threshold.

It wasn't hard for Mary to figure out how the prison laundry had earned its nickname. The air was hot and moist, and already she could feel the material of her rough-woven muslin dress starting to cling to her skin.

The large room had institutional washing and drying machines along one wall, shelves and bins along another, and a long table in the center where four women were engaged in the doubtlessly endless task of folding clean laundry into stacks of linens, towels, and the muslin uniforms.

"You start right after breakfast each morning, Monday through Saturday. There's a service for believers on Sunday mornings," Ruth said, then finished under her breath, "if you can still believe in anything in this place."

Ruth glanced around the room. "Dottie! Over here," she called out when her eyes fell on a black woman. The woman, maybe in her mid-thirties, lowered the top of a large press, and steam enveloped her—then dissipated. After she raised the lid of the press, Dottie came toward Mary and Ruth.

"This is Mary," Ruth said to Dottie. "She's been assigned here."

Dottie raised an eyebrow at Mary's gloves. "Goin' to a cotillion?"

"I said she could keep the gloves on," Ruth said firmly, "so lay off."

Dottie raised both brows. "You make the rules. Guess that means you get to change 'em."

"Just show her what to do." Ruth turned and stalked away.

Dottie looked again at Mary's hands. "Must be somethin' bad under that white cloth."

Mary nodded. "There is."

"You do it—or was it done to you?" Dottie asked.

The question took Mary by surprise. She studied the woman in front of her. Everything about Dottie seemed to mirror the bluntness of her question. Her hair was pulled back in a no-nonsense braid; her large eyes were framed by deep lines that told more about a hard life than about age. The sleeves of her dress were pushed to her elbows, and she propped a hand on her hip.

"Nobody's ever asked me that before," Mary finally said.

Dottie shrugged. "So which is it?"

"I did it."

"Huh," Dottie replied. "How 'bout that."

Dottie turned away and Mary followed. The other women in the room barely glanced at her, continuing at their tasks. "All a' the prison laundry's done in here, and there's never a shortage. Inmates are responsible for gettin' their stuff to us." She gestured to the bins on the wall, where black net bags were rolled and stuffed into small cubbies. "Everything's marked with a prisoner's number—when it's clean, goes inside the bag."

"All right," Mary said, nodding. They walked past two large washing machines. One woman was loading dirty clothes, and the other was taking clean ones out, giving each wet piece a good shake.

"Irene shakes off the wet 'fore it goes in ta dry," Dottie said. "I guess for obvious reasons we ain't gonna put you on the washer. You'd spend your whole time wringing out those lady gloves of yours.

"We got jobs in receiving, sorting, flatwork, marking, bundling," Dottie continued with another glance at Mary, "but those the better jobs, an' they go by seniority. Let's see," she said, looking around, "you be on the steam press. It's back-breakin' work 'cause you's on your feet from the time you start till you quit for the day. If the temperature don't kill you, the humidity'll make ya wish you were dead." She grinned. "I'm thinkin' it's got to be a little like being in the devil's kitchen."

"How long have you been doing this?" Mary ventured.

Dottie grinned again, but the smile didn't reach her eyes. "You mean how long I been locked up?"

Embarrassed, Mary swallowed, and Dottie laughed. "No need to look all uncomfortable. We *both* locked up and away from all the 'good' people out there. Fact is, in here you no better'n me."

"I didn't mean—"

"Twelve years," Dottie said as they stopped at the steam-press table—the same one the woman had been working at when Ruth called her over.

Mary couldn't keep the incredulity out of her voice. *"Twelve years?"*

Dottie lifted the top of the large steam press. "That's right."

"And you're still working *here—on this?*"

Dottie pulled a wrinkled dress from a pile next to the press. "I work the press 'cause I *choose* to," she said with an edge. "Turns out I like being in the devil's kitchen."

Dottie spread the dress out flat on the press, careful not to touch any of the hot surfaces. "You mess this part up, an' the whole thing gots to be done over again," she said. "A piece of fabric folded 'fore the top comes down, and it's in there permanent like. Understand?"

Mary nodded. "Yes, it must be smooth."

"Right. Smooth," Dottie agreed. "So how long you here for?"

"Eighteen months."

Dottie stopped and looked at her. "That's it? What'd you do?"

"They say I kidnapped my son away from his father," Mary said quietly, "but that's not the truth of it. The reasons we ran had been building for a while—I finally just had a chance to get away."

"Mean son of a gun, huh?"

"Yes, he sure could be."

Dottie took a moment, then nodded. "I know something 'bout that."

"You were married to a man like that?"

Dottie drew dark brows together and scoffed. "No—never had the 'displeasure' of bein' married. It was my *daddy* was the mean one. Man didn't have a shred of a conscience 'bout what he did to me—or to my baby sister."

"So you took your sister and ran away from home?"

Dottie lowered the press so the steam billowed out from the sides and swirled around both of them. "Nope. Shot 'im instead. A dead man can't chase you."

Her cell was small, but thankfully she was alone during the night. She hadn't ever spent this much time around so many people. The constant noise was grating—someone always talking, complaining, machines in the laundry whirring, and, finally, the cell doors clanking shut. Though Jack was always someplace in her awareness, she welcomed the time to sit on the hard cot in her nine-by-five space and let her mind create elaborate settings for what he might be doing right at that very moment. Maybe Agnes was sitting with Jack in a cozy room, and he'd be wearing his plaid flannels and slippers, working on a puzzle. Then the two of them finishing some hot cocoa and his favorite sugar cookies . . .

A woman's voice suddenly filled the air. " 'I hope she'll be a fool—that's the best thing a girl can be in this world, a beautiful little fool. . . .' " she said, sounding as if she was quoting from something.

Mary watched a woman pushing a metal cart filled with books come into view, stopping right in front of Mary's cell. Her glasses, a black-framed pair with white surgical tape holding them together across her nose, made her eyes appear owlish behind the thick lenses.

" 'You see, I think everything's terrible anyhow!' " She almost yelled the words at Mary.

"Excuse me?" Mary said, frowning.

"*The Great Gatsby*, F. Scott Fitzgerald, chapter one . . . great book. Great, great novel. Would you like it? Got it right here—"

"No, I don't think so. . . ." Mary shook her head.

"I'm Jenny, by the way," the little woman said. "I heard about you."

"I'm Mary."

From down the way came a shout. "Jenny, quit yer gabbing and get on down here! I been waiting for that Pearl Buck story for a month now!"

"Hold your water," Jenny yelled back, then turned to Mary and lowered her voice. "I got other books . . . if you're interested. Nothing quite like reading to help pass the time—make you feel connected to something outside this place. . . ."

"Do you have a Bible?" Mary suddenly asked.

Jenny nodded and started to rummage through the stacks of books. She ducked down and pulled a Bible off the bottom of the cart. She passed it through the bars to Mary.

"I come around once a week," Jenny said. "You can switch it out or keep it as long as you think you need it."

"You move slower'n molasses, Jenny!" The same woman's voice from down the cell block yelled, "I want *East Wind: West Wind,* and I know you got it in!"

"Sorry! Just gave it away!" Jenny hollered back.

Jenny plucked the novel by Pearl Buck off the cart and thrust it toward Mary. Lowering her voice, she said, "Here—I don't like to lie." She offered a sardonic smile as Mary reluctantly accepted the second volume. "Some people never learn that impatience gets you nowhere but frustrated in here. See ya round."

Jenny started to move on down the line, continuing her recitation from Gatsby. " 'I know! I've been everywhere and seen everything and done everything!' "

Mary went to the cot and sat down. "Another

day's behind us, Jack," she whispered. "Tomorrow brings us closer to the day we're together again." She opened the Bible in her lap and pointed her index finger to the page. "And until then I'm missing you. Always missing you." Softly she began to read aloud, her finger tracing under each word as she read.

# Chapter Thirty-two

## *Rock River, Wisconsin*

BETWEEN ONE O'CLOCK AND FIVE O'CLOCK on the third Tuesday of every month, the outside world was granted admission to the zoo. Felix hated Visitors' Day for a myriad of reasons, not the least of which was the false atmosphere—literal and philosophical—about the place for a few hours. The overpowering scent of pine cleaner hung in the air, never quite masking the odors that were a permanent presence in the children's ward. On many of those Tuesdays he had watched visitors enter, sniff, wrinkle their noses—then part their lips as most made the decision to breathe through their mouths. Every janitor in the place had a checklist of things to be done prior to Visitors' Day: clean linens, clean floor, nothing sticky on the tables, no old food lurking in corners or hidden under the cots. The bottom line was that the poorhouse needed to be clean enough to continue receiving money from the state—but anything else was overkill. Felix always made the effort to do everything he was required to do—including dousing the place with a healthy dose of the pine cleaner—but in reality he knew that the smells of the zoo were as much a part of it as the faded linoleum floor and the bars on the windows. He couldn't change out the stale air any more than he could muffle the sounds—the *yelps*, *helps*, and *stops* that could be heard on any given day just by walking along the corridors.

Even worse were the artificially friendly faces and voices put on by the medical staff for those few hours.

"Oh yes, Johnny is doing so well. . . ."

"She is eating again, I'm glad to say. . . ."

"Oh, my dear little Louise, you mustn't throw . . ."

And so on. When the clock struck one on Visitors' Day, Felix usually tried to be out of the ward. But more often than not he had some last-minute duties that held him in the confines of the room. This day was no exception. A young patient, Oliver, had provided a last-minute entry into the "How can I make your job more difficult?" category, and Felix was trying to scour a four-letter word off the wall next to the door.

*Little monster—I bet it's the only word he can spell. Where on earth did he get a red crayon?* Felix found it ironic that it was the janitors who got blamed for those words scrawled on the walls.

*If they could really help these poor souls they're warehousing, the kids wouldn't be writing obscenities on the walls in the first place.*

He was still on his knees by the door when Dr. Tanner escorted Louise and Laura's parents into the ward. Mr. and Mrs. Carnine wore the worry of hard times draped like cloaks around their shoulders. They stopped to sign a check-in sheet hanging on a clipboard by the door. The twins were chanting and spinning together in the center of the room, but when they saw Dr. Tanner with their parents, they stopped and stared.

Felix glanced at Mrs. Carnine and found she was looking anywhere but into her children's fearful faces. *It's not you they're afraid of . . . it's him.*

Oliver's mother walked into the ward, but Oliver had his back to the door. She picked up the clipboard, and Felix noticed she took an exorbitant amount of time to sign her name. Finally she let the clipboard fall back against the wall and stood in the doorway, looking toward her son.

It was always a kind of dance at first. Parents finding their way with children they saw once a month—children they didn't understand, couldn't cope with, and of whom, more often than not, they were afraid. Oliver's mother was a regular visitor, but everyone in the room had to steel themselves against the tirade of profanity he'd throw at her whenever he saw her. Felix had to give the woman credit for showing up at all. He figured by the time she recovered from one visit, it was time to turn around and do it all over again.

Dr. Tanner disappeared from the ward, and Oliver's mother put a hand on Felix's arm. She nodded toward the bed where Anastasia was lying on her back—a veritable study in bandages. Her neck was in a brace, her right arm in a cast, and her ribs wrapped tightly with white tape.

"What happened to her?" she whispered.

"I can't say for sure," Felix said. "I suppose sometimes patients need extra . . . traction."

Oliver's mom nodded as if this made perfect sense. "Oh."

Felix stood and walked to the back of the room. He glanced again at Anastasia as he passed. *Patient three-ninety-seven. Good girls get the lolly.* He knew no one would question the girl's new misery. No one knew—or cared—that she spent her days looking at a water spot on the ceiling. *Does she even know what she's looking at? Is she in pain? She most certainly is in an earthbound version of hell . . . but can that actually be the case if she's unaware? Did she slip into la-la land—or has she been pushed?*

Felix had spent sleepless nights wondering about the various occupants of the poorhouse. *Where's the point of no return? The place in the mind that suddenly—or not so suddenly—snaps and says, "I can't be like the rest of them. I want to belong—but I can't think or feel or be. . . ."*

Was it possible for a person to be treading in the world of "normal," and the next moment pass through some kind of gate and slip into a madness that held you captive until someone could find the key and let you out of your own lunacy? *Is it contagious—the insanity? What if I'm exposing myself to all the strange workings of their minds, and one day I say something that's just a little off-kilter. The next day it grows worse, until finally I'm not cleaning the floors anymore—someone else is cleaning them around me. Would I know that I'm one of them? Would I even realize I'd traded spaces in the world?* He tamped down the thought he'd wrestled with more than once.

Felix gathered some rags from the back closet to clean up a mess one of the kids had left on the floor. From the corner of his eye he saw Johnny's grandfather shuffle into the room as he did every month and write with a shaky hand on the sign-in sheet. Then the old man made his way to his grandson, sat down next to him on top of the table, and put his hand on the boy's knee. Neither of them said a word, but the ritual always touched Felix. *Someone who really cares.* From his vantage point he could also see Jack—alone on his cot, his gaze fixed on some point out the window—and wondered if there was *someone, somewhere,* who cared about him. Who might even visit. For the boy's sake he sure hoped so.

Visitors' Day had officially come to an end, put away for another month so life in the zoo could go back to its own normal. Dr. Tanner and Nurse Bess came into the ward. Felix—after one wet mattress, two overturned dinner trays, and one can of DDT to chase away a line of ants—was ready to clock out for the day. He heard the hush that fell over the ward when Dr. Tanner went over and lifted the visitors' sign-in sheet. "As we expected, no visitors for four-twenty-four today," the doctor said, sounding rather satisfied.

He dropped the clipboard and it banged against the wall. He motioned to the nurse and walked toward Jack. Felix quietly picked up a mop and moved closer.

Dr. Tanner squatted down next to the boy and snapped his fingers right in front of his eyes. "That's encouraging. He blinked. He has the capacity to respond on some level."

"Geoffrey has reported cooperation during restroom breaks," Nurse Bess told him. "The boy handles the process without any help. But he's not eating—and only sleeps when he can't hold out at the window any longer."

"No effort at communication at all?" Dr. Tanner frowned into Jack's face. "Maybe someone has taught him some rudimentary signing."

"Not that I've seen," the nurse said.

Dr. Tanner turned the boy away from the

window and looked closely into his eyes. "Is anyone home in there?" he quipped, then released him. The boy immediately resumed his position at the window.

"No potential here," he said with a shake of his head. He rose and sniffed at the air. "It smells in here," he said. "Too much Pine-Sol?"

Felix was about to slip out the door, but Bess motioned him over. "Open a window and air it out for a while," she ordered tersely.

Felix nodded and went to the closest window, the one by Jack's bed, and cranked it open as far as it would go. Fresh air came into the room through the restricted two-inch space—and Jack suddenly leaned forward and pressed his nose against the screen, inhaling deeply. Dr. Tanner didn't say anything, but Felix saw the flicker of interest in his eyes as he stared at patient four-twenty-four.

Felix wished that someone had come to visit the boy.

# Chapter Thirty-three

MARY MOVED INTO THE FOOD HALL and fell in line for breakfast. Her mind, as always, was filled with thoughts of Jack. As she picked up her bowl, she pictured him having a bowl of oatmeal, imagined the time they'd be back together, having breakfast at their own little table. And afterward she'd help him with a puzzle. . . .

She crossed the room to join a group of women already seated around a long table. She thought about those moments when she'd looked into his eyes and *had known* he was seeing her, really connecting with her. She'd give up a year of her life for a moment like that today, but she'd have to wait. *What if the wait is so long we never have a moment like that again?*

Mary slipped into a seat beside Dottie, nodding to a few other women she recognized. One of them offered a smile. "Hey," she said. "Remember me? We were processed together."

*What if Jack doesn't remember me?*

"Yes, hi," Mary said. *What if I look into those big brown eyes and there's nothing there—not even a flicker of recognition. What if he forgets I'm his mother?*

"Are you surviving?"

Mary managed a nod. "You?" *I won't be able to stand that. . . .*

Shirley held up a bandaged index finger. "They got me sewing uniforms. I've already been to the infirmary for putting a needle through my finger."

Mary grimaced. "I'm sorry. I hope it doesn't hurt you much. I'm in the laundry," she added with a quick glance at Dottie. "It's not so bad."

Mary lowered her face and stared down at her oatmeal. *He'll remember me . . . won't he? Eighteen months isn't forever. It just feels like it. . . . Now, stop it! Quit thinking about it!* She shook herself out of her own thoughts and looked up to find several staring at her.

Dottie smirked over her own bowl. "Does praying over it make it taste better?"

Mary took a spoonful of the oatmeal, then smacked her lips and licked them. "Ummm," she murmured.

The women laughed—even Dottie. A woman named Irene picked up a forkful of eggs and shoved them into her mouth. She grimaced. "Shoulda prayed."

They chuckled again, and Mary forced a small smile.

"What're you in for?" Shirley asked around her bite.

"Kidnapping my son away from his father," she said quietly.

"I didn't know you had a kid," Verla said, leaning around Dottie to look at Mary.

"His name is Jack, and he's eight years old—and I miss him every minute of every day."

"Where's your boy now—with his dad?" Shirley asked.

"No. Thankfully, Jack's not with him. I'm hoping he's with someone else, a woman I know and trust."

"Jack know you're in the slammer?" Dottie wondered.

"Jack's a deaf-mute," Mary said. "He doesn't

know where I am. And I don't know for sure where he is."

Verla frowned. "Hey—I read about a deaf-mute kid who tells the future. He ain't that kid, is he?"

Mary hesitated, then nodded. "Yes, he is."

"So we got the mother of a celebrity with us— how about that? You make some money off your kid, Mary?"

"Any donations people gave to Jack were for his future," Mary said. "To take care of him when I'm gone."

"You're gone now," Shirley observed, still shoveling in her breakfast.

Dottie chuckled. "You got yourself a kid who tells the future an' didn't know the cops is comin' to get you so's you could run?"

"Jack's—his gift doesn't work for me," she said. "Only for others."

"That's not so handy," Irene commented. "You're getting gypped on that deal."

Verla raised a brow. "Well, I'd sure like a chance to spend some time with him. I got a probation hearing coming up, and it'd be good to know how it's gonna go."

"They's gonna tell you no—jes' like the last time," Dottie said. "Don't need no boy prophet to tell you *your* future."

Shirley shoved her plate away. "Good grief, if I eat like this every day, I'm gonna get wide as a house."

"Go ahead and beef up if ya want to—ain't no men around to tell you your middle's spreading or your rear end's wide as a truck," Irene said with a smile.

Color crept up Shirley's neck to her cheeks, but she tentatively reached for the last piece of bacon on her plate.

"What'd you do to earn your stint in here, princess?" Irene asked Shirley.

Shirley hesitated. "I ran over my husband with the car."

The women exchanged glances. Shirley stuffed the bacon into her mouth.

"Hell's bells—what'd he *do?*"

"He called me fat," Shirley said, chewing the bacon. The women around Mary laughed.

But Mary's attention was suddenly caught by a woman getting up from her place two tables away. She was heading away from Mary toward the counter where trays were stacked and trash thrown away. But something about her seemed awfully familiar—silvery hair moving in concert with rounded hips across which the muslin dress stretched. Mary frowned and watched as the woman dropped her utensils into a bucket of water and plopped her tray down on top of several others. Just as she turned, another inmate stepped into Mary's view. *Move, move . . . move . . .*

She stood and pushed back her chair. *It can't be . . . it can't be her. . . .*

"Hey, Mary," Shirley said. "You okay?"

The familiar-looking woman now was clearly in view, and Mary felt the strength leave her legs. She grasped the table for support.

"She looks like she's seen a ghost," Verla observed, snapping her fingers in front of Mary's face. "Yoo-hoo! Mary—"

Mary stumbled her way around the end of the table, maneuvering through the food hall past chairs and tables and people who were looking at her as if she were crazy. Now the woman with the silvery hair was headed back to her seat.

*Please don't let it be her, please, please, God— let me be wrong!* But as Mary got closer, her heart nearly stopped. The woman looked straight at her.

"Agnes . . ." Mary could hardly speak.

"Hello, dear. I wondered if you were here. How are you?"

"What . . . what are you doing here, Agnes? Where's *Jack?*"

Agnes wrapped her arms around her middle. "I think the expression is 'locked up.' I'm locked up, just like you."

"But . . . but *where's Jack?*" Mary repeated, her voice strangled in her throat.

"I don't know," Agnes said, "which is exactly what I told the police when they tried to arrest me for kidnapping him!"

Mary saw curious faces around them watching the little drama. *She doesn't want to give it away*

*. . . doesn't want anyone to hear where he is. . . . She's still protecting him.*

Mary moved closer, lowering her voice. "I'm grateful that you took and hid him, Agnes. I really am. I'm sorry you ended up in here, but now I just need to know where Jack is and that he's all right."

Agnes sighed and shook her head, looking almost sympathetic. "I think the pastor was wrong about you, dear. You do know how to trust. It's just that you trust the wrong people."

Mary stared at Agnes. The woman said, "I don't have Jack, and I don't know where he is." There was no mistaking the certainty in her voice. "The last time I saw him was in our little living room with—well, with Jerry laid out on the floor. When I left, Jack was working a puzzle. You know, the one with the puppies in the field—"

"Jerry said *you* took him," Mary gasped out.

Agnes's expression hardened. "Jerry is a liar," she spat. "You certainly were right to leave that no-good son of a gun."

Mary was stunned at the hard glint in the woman's eyes and her acid tone. She couldn't reconcile her with the Agnes she'd known for months. "When they told me you hit Jerry over the head," Mary said, her lips trembling, "I thought it was so you could get Jack away from him. I thought you'd taken him away to protect him until

I could get out of here, and we'd all be together again."

Agnes arched a brow at Mary. "Jerry wanted the money, Mary. All of it. And I couldn't let that happen, could I? I worked just as hard for that money as you and Jack did."

Mary grabbed the back of a chair. "He would have left Jack alone if he'd simply gotten the money!"

"You're far too gullible, dear. It's a character flaw of yours," Agnes said.

Mary's eyes swam with tears. "All this time I thought you had Jack. I thought—I hoped he was safe with you. That you were taking care of him for me . . . It's the only thing that's kept me sane—"

"The police know I didn't have Jack," Agnes said sharply.

"Then what happened? Why are you here?" *This can't be happening . . . this can't be real—*

"Because of Jerry, the cops started digging around," Agnes muttered. "They came up with something else, pinned me with an inheritance racket. . . ." But Mary didn't hear anything else as she stared at this stranger, this woman with Agnes's name whose face and expression and tone were totally unfamiliar and frightening.

Agnes stepped back and smiled, but even that was hard edged and evil looking. "There's one good thing about this place," she said. "I never have to cook."

The woman turned abruptly, moving with the others making their way to the door.

*Jack. Jack. Jack. He really is missing. He's alone and scared, sick, confused, cold, hungry. . . .*

"Mary."

*Jerry lied to me. . . . Does he have Jack? He wouldn't want him . . . maybe to use him . . . ?*

"Mary!"

*I have to get out of here—have to find him—I can't breathe. . . .*

"*Mary!* Let's go!" Someone had a hold on her arm and was pulling her forward. Her feet were moving, but she didn't know how.

"Don't know what jes' happened," Dottie was whispering fiercely in her ear, "but them guards are watchin' an' ya need to get on back to work."

They passed a large trash receptacle near the door, and Mary veered toward it, leaned over, and lost her breakfast. Shaking, she straightened, and with Dottie's arm around her for support, Mary moved slowly from the food hall. *I knew I couldn't trust you, God. . . .*

# Chapter Thirty-four

## *Rock River, Wisconsin*

THE TWO ORDERLIES STANDING TOGETHER at the end of the hall didn't look twice at Felix as he gathered some items from the maintenance closet. Felix may as well have been invisible—but he was used to it. Used to the fact that people only saw him when it suited their purposes. *Got a family thing going on Sunday, Felix. Take my shift for me? The wife and I are headed to the lake for the day, Felix—trade me shifts? You send the rest of your hair out for cleaning, Stanhope? Does Ichabod Crane know he has a twin? Maybe you could be the janitor in Sleepy Hollow. . . .*

Otherwise Felix was *persona non grata*. He worked hard at his job, saved the little money he made, and thought about a day when he wouldn't be surrounded by the saddest of humanity. He pulled clean sheets and pillowcases from the closet, easily overhearing the orderlies' conversation.

"You put your money in the pool yet?"

"You betcha. Ten bucks on one-eighty-three."

"*One-eighty-three* . . . you're nuts! One-eighty-three's been here two years," the first orderly argued.

"Wife just died." Felix heard the confidence in the voice of the man who'd just bet ten bucks.

"Well, the winning number is already on his way to ride the white lightning, and it ain't one-eighty-three." This from Number Two.

"How do you know?"

"'Cause I walked by them on the way here, heading the kid toward the C wing. Doggone it! What's *that* kid's number?"

"Not the one I picked."

"Did he have a lollipop in his hand?"

"Not this time."

"Who's the fool now? No sucker, no lightning—"

"Yeah? Well, we'll see who's the sucker, sucker."

Felix quietly closed the door as the men walked away without a glance in his direction.

Carrying an armload of fresh linens, Felix hurried into the zoo and immediately looked toward Jack's cot. The boy was not there. He crossed the room, all the while his head swiveling. *The white lightning. But no sucker, no lightning . . .* The boy wasn't his problem—so what if it was the first time since his arrival Jack wasn't sitting at the window. Maybe they'd taken him for an exam. Felix started to strip the boy's cot. Or maybe someone finally came to claim him. *Someone who cares about him . . . someone who'll take good care of him.* But a wave of unease swept over him.

*"You put your money in the pool yet?"*

*"It ain't one-eighty-three."*

"Where's Jack, Louise?" Felix asked as calmly as he could manage. He was looking at just her feet sticking out from under the table.

"Jack's gone, gone, gone," Louise chanted.

"Who took Jack, Louise?" Felix asked, a sick feeling in the pit of his stomach.

*"Did he have a lollipop in his hand?"*

*"Not this time."*

Felix looked back at the cot. He didn't see a tell-tale lollipop. There was always the bribe—always the lolly. He bent down low enough to look under the table at the twins. Laura stuck her tongue out at him, and it was bright red. He cut his eyes to Louise and saw it—Dr. Tanner's calling card. Louise was sucking on the big red lollipop.

The C wing of the poorhouse was off-limits to visitors. The paint on the walls was blistered like peeling sunburn, and the ceiling was stained with rusty yellow watermarks that spread in circles from the corners. This was the wing where the medical side of things occurred—for the staffs' eyes and ears only. A place where treatments varied and stories stayed behind when those who worked in unmentionable jobs went home and tried to forget what they did to earn enough to feed their family.

Jack lay on a thin white mattress covering a stainless steel table in the middle of room 7C. The little boy offered no resistance at all. His expression was blank—eyes unfocused and heavy lidded thanks to the medication.

"Make sure the restraint is tight," Nurse Bess instructed. The orderlies fastened a leather strap over Jack's midsection while Nurse Bess herself applied petroleum jelly to both sides of the boy's temples. Dr. Tanner entered from an anteroom and moved to the table to put a hand on Jack's limp arm.

"I want to help you, Jack," he said soothingly. "I want to help you into the light of this life. I want to release you from the prison of your own mind. I'm doing this for you."

He nodded to Nurse Bess, who proceeded to put a metal headband with cotton pads on the ends across Jack's head. One of the orderlies pushed a rubber block between his teeth.

"Document this as Electroshock Case Number Twelve, patient four-twenty-four," Dr. Tanner said. Nurse Bess dutifully recorded every word. Then he looked at her. "All right. Step into the other room."

Without another look at Jack, Nurse Bess disappeared into the anteroom. The orderlies, familiar with procedure, stood on both sides of patient four-twenty-four. Several wires led from the metal headband to a gray metal junction box on a small table nearby. Dr. Tanner stepped over to the junction box and grasped its red handle.

"I'll count to three—then flip the switch. Hold

him as still as you can for a count of fifteen." The men on either side of Jack each braced themselves, hands on his shoulders and legs.

"One, two, three . . ."

The static sound of electricity surged through the room and through Jack's small body. He strained against the restraints, bit down hard on the rubber block between his teeth as the doctor counted. "Fifteen, fourteen, thirteen, twelve . . ."

Suddenly the ECT machine silenced and the room went black. Dr. Tanner cursed in the instant quiet. "Find out what happened! Immediately!"

"It's a power outage," one of the orderlies offered.

"I know what it is, thank you. Find the source and fix it!"

"What about the boy?"

"Leave him. Hurry up."

"Doctor?" Bess's voice came out of the darkness. "Is there anything I can do?"

"It's best to stay put," he said. The orderlies felt their way around in the dark, bumping into Bess as they went out.

It was less than two minutes later when the lights came on in room 7C. Dr. Tanner stood just as he'd been, holding on to the handle of the metal junction box. Nurse Bess stood in the doorway of the anteroom, and the orderlies stared from behind her. The only difference from two minutes before was the location of patient number four-twenty-four. He was gone.

• • •

In his panic he had taken a wrong turn—he was sure of it. Or was he? Had he passed the graffiti on the wall? Made the turn that would lead him out of the web and into the sunshine? He rushed through the eerie half-light of the tunnel and nearly passed out when he heard thundering footsteps racing up behind him. Someone close was breathing hard, so close he was afraid to turn. The running dialogue in his head was relentless—*turn and look! Check and see! The devil you know is better than the devil you don't know. . . .*

He whipped his head around, but the gloom behind him was empty except for the speck of light hanging from the low ceiling. The sound of the thundering, the erratic breathing, still filled his ears. Then he realized with a start that the thundering was his own heart, the breathing his own attempts to calm himself. He kept moving through the shadowed passageway and finally saw the graffiti on the wall that told him he was on the right path—*"Despair breeds here." Ain't that the truth?*

A sudden scream punched through the air, and he stepped up his pace—but the laundry cart was impeding his progress. The wheels weren't cooperating, spinning off in different directions that made a straight path nearly impossible. Another scream. *Someone's moving patients . . . must be raining outside, and me without an umbrella.* He laughed aloud at his own warped worry. *I'm running away from my job—probably will become a fugitive for my actions, and I'm worried about an umbrella?!*

The tunnel's ceiling was sloping lower, and he ducked to miss one of the single bulbs. The labyrinth grew narrower and darker as he struggled to get the laundry cart to turn left. *Almost there, almost, almost . . .* He reached the end of the tunnel and pushed against the heavy door—and felt stinging raindrops on his cheeks.

He yanked wadded sheets from the top of the laundry cart and then lifted his bundle and placed it carefully on the ground. *What have I done? What am I going to do? I'm as crazy as some of the patients in the wards I clean. They'll miss him, but it'll be a while until someone misses me. Maybe being invisible is a good thing. . . .*

Felix Stanhope looked at Jack, pale and still on the ground, and laid his head on the little boy's chest. He felt instant relief when he heard the steady heartbeat.

"It's just the two of us now, Jack. Just the two of us—but I promise, no one is going to hurt you again."

As the rain let up and the sun slipped out of the clouds, Felix lifted the boy into his arms and walked away. He would never set foot inside that door again.

# Chapter Thirty-five

## SUMMERTIME 1939

MARY DIDN'T MIND THE DARK. Didn't mind that she hadn't spoken to another person in a week—or that the tasteless food was passed through a small opening in the windowless door, and the well water to drink smelled of iron. She didn't mind that she had spent seven days in solitary confinement as punishment for the scene she caused the last time she'd seen Agnes in the food hall. A snide comment from Agnes had been the match that finally lit the dry timber of her rage into an inferno of frustration and anger and betrayal. She'd thrown her food tray, chair, utensils—anything she could get her hands on. When Bonnie grabbed her arm to stop her, Mary had sealed her fate by lashing out at the guard. But truly she didn't mind having the time alone in the dark—she didn't have to see Agnes.

What Mary *did* mind were the constant nightmare scenarios running through her thoughts. She imagined Jack in every possible place, feeling every possible emotion. She felt guilty for being in a room with a roof and a floor and food—not knowing if Jack at least had that much. Her mind went places she begged it not to go. *Jack sick, Jack lost, or Jack . . .* she could hardly bear to think the word, *dead*. To preserve her sanity, she forced herself to remember the good things. Jack's smile, the joy in his eyes at seeing her. And then their reunion, the celebration at being together again. *I'll never let anyone else into our lives ever again. I'll never trust another deceiver like Jerry—or Agnes . . . never ever. I only need Jack, and he only needs me, and the rest of the world can go to hell. . . .*

A flood of light shot across the floor when the door to her cell opened. She had to close her eyes for a moment against the brightness.

"If you're ready to play nice, Mary, you can come out now." Mary squinted in Ruth's direction and slowly unfolded herself from the hard cot.

The guard stepped out of the way as Mary stumbled toward the door.

"You're going to the showers first," Ruth said, wrinkling her nose. They headed down a dingy hall in the prison's basement. "And then you'll have a few minutes in your cell to change before you get back to work."

Mary's muscles were stiff, and she walked slowly behind Ruth, pushing her hair out of her face and trying to focus on what Ruth was saying.

"You know all those letters you been sending out into the world? Well, one of 'em mighta hooked a response while you was thinking over your sins," Ruth said over her shoulder.

It took her a moment, but Mary finally raised

her eyes to look up at the guard. She had to clear her throat before she could croak out a word. "I . . . got some mail?"

"Yeah."

Mary picked up her pace, suddenly anxious. "Could I get it now? Before my shower?"

Ruth sighed. "You still don't get it, do you? This ain't about what *you* want. It's about what you *have to do.* You're taking a shower now 'cause you sure need one. *Then* I'll give you a few minutes with your letter. And, Mary—don't even think about going near Agnes Meriwether, or you'll find yourself coming out of solitary confinement looking older than that old lady. But, listen to me, she ain't your problem anymore. Stay outta trouble and you just might cut a couple a' months off your time. You get me?"

Mary stopped midstep.

Ruth turned. "What now?"

"Are you saying I could shorten my sentence—?"

"Yeah, lots a' times good behavior is rewarded by shaving time off the end. Now, let's go rinse the week off of you."

Mary's gloves were damp from the shower, and she knotted her hands into fists at her sides while she waited impatiently outside her cell for Ruth to open the door. Her wet hair hung loosely down her back, and she felt a chill race down her spine—whether from cold or nerves, she couldn't tell. The key clanked and the door slid open. Mary hurried toward the single white envelope lying in the middle of the floor. The door slammed shut behind her.

"I'll be back in ten. Lunch is nearly over, and you need to get back to the laundry," Ruth said through the bars.

Mary had already forgotten Ruth's presence as she picked up the envelope and sat down on the cot. She started to rip it open, thinking of all the letters she'd written since learning Agnes didn't have Jack, all the pleas to the police and the state's attorney and even the judge who had sentenced her. She'd even written to Jerry, begging for any information about Jack, any shred of knowledge about where he might be and who he might be with. And then praying over and over that he was alive, and hoping someone, somewhere, might have the decency to tell her.

*All those letters and not a single answer from anyone—until now.* Her hands shook as she looked at the return address, then realized the dampness from her gloves had made some of the ink run in the corner. She quickly pulled off both gloves and dropped them on the cot beside her. Looking again at the return address, she saw it was from the tenth precinct police station in Chicago.

*If I don't look, I still have hope. . . . If I don't look, I can still pretend he's okay. . . . Look inside!*

*It might be good. It might have the news that Jack is fine and in foster care with some nice family with lots of children and . . .*

She tore open the envelope and pulled out the letter. "Dear Mrs. Sinclair, Regarding the whereabouts of your son, Jack Godwin Sinclair . . ." She sucked in a sharp breath and her mouth was instantly dry. "We have contacted your husband, who still maintains the position that the boy is not with him. . . ." Her heartbeat was loud in her own ears. "We have contacted hospitals and morgues in a fifty-mile radius, and no one matching Jack's unique description has been found. We are, unfortunately, at a loss at this time as to where he is or who he might be with. Without a single lead to go on, the investigation has been suspended at this time. . . ."

The letter slipped from her trembling hands just as a bell rang. *They are giving up. They aren't even looking for him anymore. How could an eight—* he's nine now—*nine-year-old boy survive on his own for this long, and no one see him?*

"Mary."

She closed her eyes and felt the despair seep into every part of her body. She was responsible for this tragic situation. She had failed her son on every level, and now she wouldn't have another chance to make it up to him.

"Mary . . ." Ruth's voice cut through her thoughts. "I've got a situation in the garment room that I need to see to. Can I trust that you'll go to the laundry right now?"

Mary lifted her head slowly and looked at her—then nodded.

Ruth nodded back. "Then come. Right now." Ruth unlocked the cell door as Mary slowly rose from the cot. The woman hesitated just a second before saying, "I'm sorry 'bout the letter."

Mary woodenly stepped over the envelope and sheet of paper on the floor and moved out into the hall.

# Chapter Thirty-six

## *Lincoln, Nebraska*

IT WAS WANDERLUST. The moving trains beckoned hoboes from all walks of life with a train whistle, an "all aboard," and a promise of faraway places and conversations that lasted long into the night with strangers who became fast friends. They compared adventures around campfires, spoke of escaping dangers with bravado tempered with respect for their fellow travelers. Racing through dark nights under a smattering of stars and a full moon, the boxcars clattered noisily while the air rushing into the open doors told tales of the places they'd passed—orange blossoms and pine trees, stockyards and factories. The rocking of the train soothed them into deep sleep, and the brakes from the engineers jolted them to jump off into new places where odd jobs and kind people would be discovered. There was infinite freedom, unfettered from the usual anchors of life. No permanent job, no time clock or gas bill or boss to tell you what to do and how to do it. Unique talents on the road provided a coin or two here and there—an onion or a carrot or a potato for shining some shoes, fixing a cupboard, picking cotton, or harvesting grapes.

Self-made identities could be reinvented with every new group of travelers joined at a campfire. It was one of the many things Felix loved about the new life he'd embarked on with Jack right after they'd made their break from the Rock River Poorhouse.

"I go by Fleet Foot Felix," he'd say when he met a new set of fellow travelers. "And this here's Lucky Jack."

The first time they'd chased a freighter had been both exhilarating and terrifying. Catching on to a car on a steep incline as the train slowed, Felix had all but thrown Jack into the clattering space, then had pulled himself up the iron ladder into a world of shaking boxcars smelling of pine tar and creosote.

Jack's skin had become browned by the summer sun; his hair had grown longer, and shaggy bangs fell across his eyes when he dipped his head. He was an ideal traveling companion—he didn't talk, didn't make demands, didn't make trouble, never had an opinion on where they should go next. Felix found he actually enjoyed the boy's company—and liked that he was never alone. He'd been with Jack long enough now to recognize when the boy slipped into his own world—he would stare into space for minutes or sometimes hours. There were times when Felix envied Jack that escape—envied the fact that he could actually disappear into his own head. Felix had found a freedom in a hobo's life, but sometimes he thought Jack's world was even freer.

It was early one morning when Felix and Jack hopped off a freighter just before it pulled into the yards at Lincoln, Nebraska. They picked their way along the outskirts of town, paralleling the tracks at a distance and following signs Felix had learned to read, markings that were a code unique to the hobo community. The signs could turn up anywhere—fences, posts, sidewalks, trestles, railroad-line side equipment. These coded signals could warn fellow knights of the road of possible trouble, law enforcement, helpful homes that would gladly provide a meal—and even if there was a mean dog in the yard.

Felix's stomach growled, and he heard Jack's doing the same thing. It had been a long time since their last meal. "I s'pose we could break down and use some of our cash for lunch," he said aloud, "but I'm hoping that money lasts us until fall, and we can hire ourselves on with a harvesting outfit." He'd grown used to these one-sided conversations. In their first days together, Felix had felt somewhat foolish carrying on a dialogue with someone who couldn't hear him, but gradually he'd learned to relax and say whatever was on his mind.

Jack was watching a pair of crows performing showy maneuvers and racing each other down to the ground to fight over the carcass of a rabbit.

"That's one way to get lunch," Felix observed. He spotted a large circle with a line drawn through the center painted on the corner of a road sign. He raised an eyebrow.

"Sign says we're on a good road," he said with some satisfaction and a pat on Jack's shoulder. "Maybe there's something to eat up ahead."

It was only a short thirty minutes later that Felix saw another hobo message. Tacked to a tree on the edge of a yard enclosed with a half-painted white picket fence, a stick figure cat was drawn next to four long straight lines. *A kindhearted lady who feeds for chores.* Felix led Jack to the back door and didn't hesitate to knock.

The lady was seventy-five if she was a day, but spry of spirit and generous of heart. She paced off a portion of her picket fence. "If the two of you can find the energy to do ten slats each, I can find the energy to make up a couple of fried eggs sandwiches and some cherry pie," she said in a voice that sounded years younger than her face looked.

"Just ten apiece you say?" Felix asked as she handed him a wide brush and a bucket of white paint. "We could do more."

She shook her head with a knowing smile. "I get four or five of you every week at my door. Most leave feeling full in the belly and a little happier with themselves if they lend a hand for the food they get. I'm about out of things to keep folks busy until fall, when I can get help raking the leaves."

Felix studied the old woman—name of Luanne Purvis, she'd told them. "Don't you ever worry about opening your door to strangers, ma'am?"

"I never was much of a worrier." She swatted at a mosquito looking to grow fatter on the nape of her neck. "I give it all to the Lord and let Him sort it out for me." She looked at Jack. "Do you want cheese on your egg sandwich?" Jack looked at her while he brushed at his own mosquito.

"He can't hear a word you're saying," Felix explained. "So he never utters a word in reply."

Luanne nodded her acceptance of the facts about Jack. "All boys like cheese," she concluded and turned back toward her house. Felix felt grateful there were people like Luanne Purvis in the world.

"Headed someplace in particular—or just putting distance between this place and another?" The man's face was etched with wrinkles, and Felix had to squint to make out the lines radiating from his eyes that said he was friendly.

"Just looking for a place to stop for the night," Felix said as he put his hand on Jack's shoulder. The gesture had come to be second nature when he felt protective of the boy. The man had come out of nowhere and fallen into step beside them. The brown pack on his back left little doubt that he was a fellow traveler.

"We're of like minds, then," the man said. "I'm headed to the jungle on the far side of Lincoln."

Felix raised his brows. "A good stopover?"

"It was last year when I was through here," he said. "I'm Ray Dawson."

"I'm Felix and this here is Jack," Felix told him. "I'll tell you right off that Jack's a deaf-mute, so there's no point in asking him anything."

Felix could see he'd piqued Ray's interest when the man's eyes cut to Jack and stayed there. "No point in staring at him either." Felix pulled the boy a little closer. "It's not like he's got two heads or anything."

"No," Ray said without apology. "But I imagine he's got a pretty unique perspective."

"I guess that's probably true, but it doesn't do any good to speculate. He can't *say* what his perspective is."

"We can imagine, can't we? Imagine what it's like for him?" Ray took another look at Jack.

"What for?"

Ray grinned. "Because I'm a writer and that's what writers do. They imagine. They look for perspective. They try and see the world through the eyes of someone else, then paint a picture with words. I've met lots and lots of people riding the rails—but I have to admit, Jack's a first for me."

"What do you write?"

"Mostly poetry," Ray said. "Someday you go and visit the New York Public Library and look up the name Ray Dawson in their card catalog. I'll have a book or two there—that's a promise."

It was already dark when they arrived at a clearing close enough to hear the distant whistle of the train. Felix took in the scene as they approached and knew he'd found a Mecca for road-weary bums. Hoboes of every age filled the large camp that had grown up along the banks of a running creek. A campfire blazed in the center, and a large kettle was suspended from an iron rod. A wizened old woman stood over it stirring so hard the liquid was spilling over the sides. The sparks from the fire shot high into the night sky. Bedrolls littered the ground, and there were even some mattresses underneath the canopy of mature trees, now dark shadows against the sky. Tired, dirty, ragged, and whiskered, people sat on crates and boxes, close enough to the fire to keep the mosquitoes at bay but far enough away not to feel the heat.

"I smell mulligan stew." Ray Dawson lifted the

pack from his back and dropped it near an unoccupied box. He fished around in his bundle and finally withdrew an ear of corn and a potato.

Felix sniffed appreciatively and pushed down on Jack's shoulder so the boy would take a seat on a crate. "I've got a few pieces of Swiss chard and a strip of jerky," Felix said, opening his worn satchel. He took his offerings and followed Ray Dawson to the kettle. They both tossed in their contributions to the broth, whose ingredients were as varied as the people surrounding the flames.

There was the inevitable talk about bad experiences with the bulls—hobo talk for railroad guards patrolling the train yards. Their assignment was to keep the boxcars clear of those looking for a free ride, people like them. Felix had listened to stories of bulls with guns, with bats and clubs and fingers just itching to find a hobo they could shake down. Any money they found never made it into the hands of the railroad owners. No matter what Felix heard about the big, bad, mean bulls, he always silently concluded, *Don't get caught.*

Later, eating the stew from their own tins, Felix and Jack sat in a circle of people swapping stories of the road.

A young woman in overalls, seated on the ground in front of a young man on a crate behind her, put her hand on his knee and smiled shyly. "Me and Billy got hitched last week on the Union Pacific somewheres crossing Kansas. The preacher what tied the knot was ridin' the blinds with nothin' but his Bible and an extra pair a' shoes."

A man and woman across the campfire were surrounded by five children. The youngest stretched across both their laps, sleeping as if she were on the best mattress in the finest hotel. "We been south croppin' cotton off the Frisco line," the man told the group. "Pay is fifty cents ever' hundred pounds, but not one a' us can pick another lick till we get the cotton burrs outta our fingers. I'm figuring we'll head to the Pacific and give berries a try."

Felix took another bite of stew but stopped chewing when the man next to him said, "I made it all the way through the big war without a scratch, but a run-in with a bull took my arm." Felix looked at the man's empty sleeve pinned at the shoulder. "Meanest son of a gun ya ever saw."

Talk gradually turned to the next stop on the adventure highway, and Felix decided he and Jack would throw in with the group planning to hop a freighter headed out of state before dawn. His fellow road knights assured him there were no bulls in the yards only a stone's throw away, that it was one of the easiest places in the country to climb into an empty boxcar. They'd stay up all night and then sleep to the click of the rails all the way to Chicago.

Ray Dawson suddenly pulled a harmonica from

his pocket and pointed it at the newlyweds seated across from him. "This one's for you," he said. "May you have many years of happiness together."

He started to play a melody that soon had everyone tapping their toes.

*Music's universal,* Felix thought. *Everyone enjoys a good tune.* He looked at Jack, whose eyes were heavy lidded. *Almost everyone, that is.* He put his arm around the boy as he brought a mason jar to his own lips for a swig of white lightning someone was passing around the circle. He felt the slow burn in his throat as the liquid traveled down and settled with a wallop in the pit of his belly. He tapped his foot to the music and felt Jack's head settle against his arm. He passed the jar on, and before he knew it, a cup of bay rum had found its way into his hand. Between the liquor, the music, and the company, Felix couldn't think of a better way to pass a summer night.

## Chapter Thirty-seven

### *Barrington, Illinois*

HE WAS HAVING A TERRIBLY NOISY DREAM that made the pounding in his head more excruciating by the second. Felix worked to open his eyes, but he wished he could drop back into the slumber that had claimed him only minutes after he and

Jack had staked out their spot in the spacious Burlington Railroad boxcar. He vaguely remembered the admonition from Ray Dawson that they needed to jump off the car before they hit the Western Avenue yard—but that was all. He couldn't even dredge up the memory of the train leaving Lincoln behind. *I'm done with moonshine and bay rum—*

"On your feet, freeloaders!" *Not a dream—a nightmare . . .*

Felix struggled to his feet and felt Jack pressing against him. The huge man stood just in front of him and slapped a sawed-off bat across his palm with a strength that made Felix's knees weak. The bull wore a blue shirt with CB&Q Railroad stitched across the pocket. Felix took a quick inventory of his fellow passengers and recognized only two faces from the night before. Ray Dawson was nowhere to be found. *He's missing another perspective,* Felix thought illogically. One of the men in the car with Felix made a break for the open door, but a gunshot stopped him from jumping. Another bull appeared in the doorway with a grin. "What'cha got to pay your fare?"

"Everything I got is in this here knapsack. Take it all," the man pleaded as he held up his worn-out sack. The bull in the boxcar with him grabbed his small knapsack and dumped out the contents. He scooped up a pack of cigarettes and a pocket watch.

"This all you got, you sorry—?" The bull spit as he took a swing, hitting the man on his left kneecap. The man cried out in pain and stumbled to the back of the car.

"Please, no . . . don't hit me!"

The bull grabbed him by the scruff of the neck, and Felix winced with the sound of the man's leather shoes squeaking across the metal floor. The bull tossed the man out of the car like a rag doll. Felix looked around for his own satchel and spotted it at Jack's feet.

The bull smiled. "Next."

"I don't have anything worth anything," Felix said.

"You better hope you do." The bull jerked open the satchel and turned out the meager belongings that Felix carted from one place to another.

"Don't hurt the boy. He just goes where I tell him to," Felix said as the clothes hit the ground along with a brown leather softball that rolled across the car toward the door. The guard outside the car caught it and tossed it back to the bull near Felix. "Game of catch?"

"The ball's worth nothing, but I can clean and scrub boxcars if you want," Felix suggested.

The bull held the worn ball in the palm of his hand and studied it. "Worth nothing, huh? You sure about that?"

Felix took a tentative step toward the bull and held out his hand. "You don't want that."

The bull tugged at the stitching, a slow smile

spreading across his face. "Oh, I think I do." He pulled hard at the opening he'd made, and Felix felt his heart sink.

"You get a prize for the best stash hiding I've seen so far." The bull shook the ball, and coins clattered and paper bills spilled out onto the hard deck of the boxcar. The other guard clambered up and inside.

"Whoa, now—ain't this just your lucky day!" The two bulls gathered up the money, forgetting all about Felix and Jack. Felix looked down at the boy and could see him furiously tapping the fingers of his right hand against the palm of his left. *I'm scared too, kid.* . . . Felix didn't even bother to collect his satchel. He grabbed Jack's arm and they leapt out of the boxcar.

The Western Avenue railroad yard was bustling with activity as Felix and Jack started away from the tracks.

"Hey, 'bo! Catch!"

Felix looked back over his shoulder at the bull standing in the open doorway of the boxcar. He threw the softball, but instead of arcing into the air toward Felix, the empty shell dropped lifelessly to the ground. Felix stared at the torn-up ball. *Guess no place is safe.*

As they walked away from the train yards, Felix remembered the dollar bill he had stashed in his sock. At least they could pay for a meal if they couldn't work for one.

"No more white lightning for me, Jack," Felix said as he massaged his left temple. "And I think we'll walk for a while," he mused aloud. "I'm in no hurry to hop another freighter—are you?"

He looked down at the boy, but Jack had stopped walking and was standing near a telephone pole looking at a colorful flyer nailed to the wood. Curious, Felix backtracked, more taken with the look on the boy's face than the advertisement. Jack was grinning from ear to ear at a clown with his own exaggerated smile plastered in the middle of the page. It was the Bixby Brothers' circus— "Come one! Come all! Fifteen cents to get in the big top!"

Felix cut his glance between Jack and the picture of the clown—and then smiled to himself. "C'mon, Lucky Jack—we're going to a circus."

Felix sensed that the Bixby Brothers' Spectacular Show under the ninety-foot big top was about to end. He saw performers slipping through a back flap in the tent, horses being led right out the main door, clowns gathering up their props even as the aerialists—the Flying DeBeniditos—performed high above the ground in their red sequined outfits. The crowd gathered below them gasped and clapped with each flip of their flawless routine. Seated in the nosebleed section of the bleachers beside Jack, Felix glanced over a sea of straw boater hats, white hankies moving air around flushed faces, bobbing balloons and stiff pennants on sticks popping up and down enthusiastically. He could smell cotton candy and roasted peanuts, hot dogs and fried onions, animal sweat and sawdust.

Having never been to a circus before, Felix was watching the show with unabashed pleasure. They'd seen Boris the Lion Tamer put his lions through their paces, monkeys and zebras, an elephant and jugglers. Tatiana, a beautiful woman in a flowing blue gown, rode bareback on a snow-white horse, and the ringmaster had introduced the crowd to Three-Pete, a man with three arms who could wave in all directions at the same time—and the audience had applauded like crazy. *They love that he's different. Celebrating that he's odd!* Felix had a fine time, and he could tell Jack had enjoyed it too by his reaction to the clowns—his widemouthed smile and bright eyes.

He gave a tug on Jack's arm and gestured for the boy to follow him as he slipped off the back of the bleachers and began to climb down. Jack had no trouble following his lead, and they landed on their feet just as the calliope heaved one last sweet high-pitched note signaling the end of the Flying DeBeniditos act. He grabbed Jack's hand and pulled the boy with him toward the back flap of the tent he'd noticed from his high vantage point.

They stepped through the flap of the tent into the choreographed chaos behind the scenes, past a sign that warned: Off Limits to the Public. Though the music had just ended inside the big top, Felix could see preparations were already being made to move on. Animals were being fed and watered, clowns were in a state of half dress, with suspenders hanging off their shoulders, hats askew, as they collected whatever props they'd used in the big show.

A couple of men in dungarees and white T-shirts hurried past Felix and Jack, shooting them a curious look but heading toward a roll of canvas on the ground. Six other men were doubled over at the waist, trying to roll the material like a long, fat sausage.

"I got no time for this!" a raspy voice bellowed twenty feet to Felix's right. He turned and watched a portly middle-aged man wearing an old derby hat and a moth-eaten blue sweater poke his finger repeatedly into the chest of a much younger and obviously inebriated man. With every poke in his chest, the man leaned back, then came forward again like a dummy with sandbag feet.

"Easy there, Angelo," the man slurred. "S'no big thing."

"Yeah, it is too, Eddie. The professor's on a tear, and it's your fault! He stepped in three fresh piles of poop on his way out the back door. You know how he feels about them shiny boots of his."

Felix glanced at the ground and could see he'd just missed some big road apples himself.

"Yep. He loves his boots," the man said, blowing out an exasperated breath that had Angelo stepping back.

"And he hates your bony butt," Angelo told him. "We've been through this before, Eddie. The professor wants you *gone*."

Eddie barely blinked, then threw his arm up in the air. "Who needs ya? Who needs this stinkin' job—and I do mean *stinkin'!*"

*I do,* Felix thought as he grabbed a square-headed shovel that had been dropped in the dirt. He set about scooping up the trail of droppings, disturbing the flies that had already begun to congregate. Eddie staggered past, and his shoe slipped in the pungent dung.

"Somebody should clean up this mess!" he yelled loudly, then laughed at his own joke. He shook his leg to clear off the muck and weaved a path away from the big top. Felix put some muscle into his chore, realizing that the man called Angelo was coming toward him.

"Whadd'ya think you're doing in my backyard?" He released a brown stream of tobacco juice in an impressive arc from between his teeth.

"Cleaning up." Felix stopped and leaned on the shovel.

"You just get a yen to scoop poop?" Angelo raised an eyebrow at him and tipped back the brim of his hat.

"I'm looking for a job—and it looks like you just got an opening," Felix said boldly.

"You been a roustabout before?"

"Roustabout?"

Angelo smirked. "That's a no."

"I've been a janitor since I was old enough to employ," Felix said. "This doesn't seem like much of a mess to me."

"Oh, we get worse. Stuff that'll curl your nose hairs," Angelo retorted as he tipped his head to the side, giving Felix the once-over. "You're ugly—not ugly enough to be billed as a freak, but ugly enough to be part of this group of misfits."

*Part of this group . . . part of something!*

"Pay ain't much, but food is part of the deal." Angelo held out his hand toward Felix. "Name is Angelo Martinetti. General manager of the show."

"Felix Stanhope." He pumped Angelo's hand and hoped he could match the strength in the older man's hand. "And that's Jack."

Angelo frowned and looked over at the boy, who was standing just outside the back door of the tent. "Why do I care about him?"

"He's with me," Felix said. "He's a good kid. He's deaf as a post and doesn't make a peep."

"He's your kid?" Angelo asked.

"Uh, yeah. Jack Stanhope. Can't sign on without him."

Angelo looked again at the boy. "Musta got his looks from his ma." He pulled off his derby, scratched his head, and spit again. "Lucky for you I'm shorthanded—was even before I gave Eddie the boot. Your kid gets hurt, we won't be responsible. You'll have to sign papers that say so."

Felix nodded. "I'll keep a good eye on him."

"All right, then." He gestured to all the activity. The lot, the "backyard," as Angelo had called it, was filled with about seventy people engaged in breaking down the large big top and the smaller tents set up around the perimeter.

"We're not any bigger than you see right here," he said. " 'Course we were bigger before the crash in twenty-nine. Had twenty train cars and rode the tracks from town to town, but now . . . we're rolling with our lumber trucks and any wagon that'll make the journey. We drive at night, set up at dawn, and try for a three-day turnout if the town's big enough. You and the boy will bunk with the rest of the clean-up crew. Roustabouts can get a little territorial, so watch how much space you take at first."

A man Felix recognized as the ringmaster from the show made his way toward them in his licorice red coat and tan jodhpurs. His shiny black boots went to his knees, and Felix could have sworn the sky was reflected in them when the man stopped next to Angelo.

"The situation is under control?" The ringmaster addressed the question to Angelo but studied

Felix. Felix couldn't identify the man's accent—or even if it was real.

"Yeah. I canned Eddie," Angelo said. "Just like you wanted."

"That's excellent news," the ringmaster said. "Other than being able to drink his own weight every day, he was worthless."

"Yeah, well, lucky for us, we got a First of May here who just happened to be looking for a job and has lots of experience in the clean-up department," Angelo said.

"Ah, a rookie, eh?" He turned to Felix. "I am Professor Pygmalion," the man said without offering his hand. "I am the ringmaster of this great show. Keep the animal poop out from under my boots, and we'll get along famously." Then with a curt nod to Felix and Angelo, the professor moved on.

Felix raised his eyebrows. "What's he a professor of?"

Angelo rolled his eyes. "He taught school in another life, but now he's a professor of all things that irritate me."

A loud shouting match suddenly broke out between two workers heaving the heavy roll of canvas onto the back of a flatbed truck. Angelo looked over his shoulder with a curse. He threw a glance back at Felix.

"Welcome to the show," Angelo said. "Keep the kid out of my way, and keep up with the manure.

Teardown takes about forty minutes, and then we hit the road—and we don't leave no droppings behind—got it?"

Felix kept his expression stoic. "Got it."

As soon as Angelo rushed over to a shouting match that had dissolved into a fistfight, Felix let himself grin. He had loved riding the blinds, but he knew it was too dangerous for Jack. Now they'd get to keep living like hoboes, but with a legitimate ride from place to place, food in their bellies, and a place to sleep at night. No more railroad bulls to worry about.

Felix could see the boy was occupied watching all the activity going on around him. He turned back to his task and thought how much he preferred cleaning up animal messes than the ones in the children's ward. It looked like he'd traded one "zoo" for another, but he'd found a place where ugly didn't matter—ugly was, in fact, an asset. He was officially part of a group. He and Jack.

He slid the shovel under a pile of manure and smiled. *Life doesn't get any better than this. . . .*

# Chapter Thirty-eight

## *Chicago, Illinois*
## MAY 1940

IT WAS A MOMENT SHE'D IMAGINED so many times, dreamed of both waking and sleeping, that Mary couldn't believe it was real. She heard the gate lock behind her, and she lifted her face toward a flock of birds flying in tight formation. They settled on the branches of a tall oak stretching skyward toward the spring sun. The birds chattered noisily, sounding like the women of Oakdale Reformatory gathered around the tables in the food hall, Mary noted wryly. Her coat hung over her arm, and she smoothed out the wrinkles of her dress, the one that had been taken away with her few belongings a year and four months ago. She stared at the tiny flowers on the blue background of the fabric—strange but familiar. The waist of her dress moved freely, and she felt it hanging loosely from her shoulders. *Must be a couple of sizes too big.*

A breeze blew strands of hair across her face, and she found a ribbon in her purse and tied it back. She inhaled deeply, smelling the dew-laden grass under her feet. It amazed her that she had made it to this point, that her heart had continued to beat after she'd read the letter about Jack—the letter that said they couldn't find him and weren't going to look anymore. That was the day she'd given up. She had given the Bible back to Jenny when the book cart rolled past Mary's cell.

*"Want a good book to take your mind off your troubles?"*

*"Thought I had one—turns out I was wrong."*

There were no bright spots in her life. A dark cloud constantly lay over her like a shroud. She wanted to die, but her body became a traitor. Her lungs still filled with air; her heart continued to pump—and all without her willing participation. She moved by rote through her days.

And Dottie wasn't standing for it. *"You ain't doin' your boy nothin' good by having this pity party! You gonna be weak as a baby kitten if you don't buck up and change your attitude! You ain't gonna be strong enough to find him when you get out of here."*

Mary had tried to ignore her, told her to mind her own business—even asked for a transfer to some other job in the prison. But the truth of the matter was that Dottie was impossible to ignore, and they denied her request to change jobs. After months of hearing Dottie cajole, lecture, berate, and coax, something finally sank in.

*"Okay, let's go over this one more time. Why are you in here, Mary?"*

*"Because someone who didn't know me or my ex-husband or my son said I had kidnapped Jack."*

*"That's right. And who was that?"*

*"Charles Westerly."*

*Dottie had nodded approvingly. "He took away your son—he took away your life—he took it all away because he was important enough to do it. Don't seem fair—does it? He gets to go on with his life even though he ruined yours."*

Her days had gradually taken on a new purpose. As she had once imagined Jack with Agnes, Mary now started to imagine something very different. With every passing day she pictured Charles Westerly in his daily routine—going to work, going home, eating his supper . . . and playing with his child. And as her rage grew, her strength of purpose increased. As long as she focused on how she was going to take all the things Charles Westerly loved away from him, she would survive long enough to get out of prison and find her son. Dottie's order replayed in her head morning, noon, and night: *"Remember why you're here, and remember who did this to you."*

She remembered. And now it was time to do something about it. The birds grew quiet and then lifted off the branches of the tree. She watched them scatter again—flying free. *Free.*

With sixteen dollars in her pocketbook—*the state of Illinois offers you a dollar for every month of your incarceration*—and wearing the same clothes she'd arrived in, Mary Godwin walked away from the Oakdale State Reformatory for Women and never looked back.

Charles Westerly had chosen this place to live for two reasons: one was the cheap rent—all he could afford since he had given everything to Lila in the divorce—and, two, it was all he felt he deserved. *Be it ever so humble . . .* he thought grimly as he headed to the south side of Chicago around six-thirty in the evening. He parked his car in front of the dilapidated brick building he now called home and tried not to think about how he'd been living less than two years ago—the beautiful home, the loving wife and daughter. *Stop. Don't!*

He was tired, hungry, and discouraged as he fit his key in the lock of his door. He opened the door to his small, dingy apartment tucked into a row of ten others just like it in the questionable part of town. The room was dark, and he stepped carefully, knowing—or at least hoping—a week's worth of mail would be scattered on the floor where the mail carrier had dropped it through a slot in the door. But as he moved his foot back and forth over the floor, it didn't connect with a single letter. There was a familiar twinge of disappointment mixed with a bright spot—*at least there are no bills.* Turning slightly, he thrust his arm out in front of him like a blindman and ran his hand over the wall. On connecting with the switch, an overhead light blinked on and illuminated the true shabbiness of the place. He dropped a scratched leather briefcase on the floor and lifted his shoulders to roll the soreness out of tight muscles.

"Hello, Mr. Westerly."

He spun in the direction of a woman's voice. She was sitting in the corner of the tiny living room. Her hair was longer, her face thinner. Even though there was a hard edge to her expression, and her dark brown eyes held anger, Mary Godwin Sinclair was just as lovely as Charles remembered.

"Hello, Miss Godwin."

She stared at him for a moment. "You took my son from me and ruined my life," she said. "You might as well call me Mary."

Charles shook his head, his shoulders slumping from months and months of regret. "I'm so sorry about everything," he said, a choked sound. "So sorry . . ."

"Why would you be sorry now? I've spent the last sixteen months and three days agonizing over Jack. Where is he? Hungry? Cold, thirsty, sick, scared, hurt—?"

"Mary, I—"

"Is he even still alive?"

"Please, let me tell you what I've been—"

"Lights-out at night was the worst," Mary continued as if he'd not responded. Her eyes were fixed on some point on the wall. "Lying there worrying that Jack thinks I abandoned him. He doesn't understand—can't hear. No one can explain things to him like they can explain to another little boy. The only time I wasn't thinking about Jack, I was hating you"—she moved her eyes to his face—"and wondering how to get even with you for what you've done."

"I don't blame you," Charles said, still standing in the spot from which he'd first seen her.

"Even though according to the state of Illinois I'm a free woman now, my head is still in prison until I find my son. . . ."

Charles could barely hear the last phrase. He saw her trembling, a slight shaking of her shoulders, heard the tremor in her voice. He had so hoped that when they finally had this encounter, he would be giving her back her son. *One more colossal failure on my part.*

"How did you find me?" he asked.

"Phone book."

"How did you get in?"

"I told the landlord I was your sister from Kenosha here for a surprise visit. He said you travel a lot, and he let me in."

"Pretty resourceful."

"I've lived with liars my whole life," she said. "I guess I've learned how it's done."

"I'm so sorry, Mary," Charles said again.

She shook her head. "I walked around your house and tried to think of a plan. I went through your mail—your gas bill is past due—and then I found something that made everything clear. I found this."

Mary stood and raised a gun that had been hidden in her lap. "My so-called friend Agnes—she would say that my finding this gun was Providence."

She raised the weapon and pointed it at him. "I've racked my brain trying to figure out what I did to you—"

"A blackmail letter intended for me that my wife accidentally read," Charles said. "It was signed by you."

He watched her digest the information and saw the flicker of surprise in her eyes.

"I didn't write any letter. . . ."

"I know that . . . now. The letter reported that my sister-in-law Rebecca had come to see you and your son for a Scripture—and from the information in that verse, you demanded I resign as governor, or you were going to go public with an incident that proved to be the worst mistake I've ever made."

"I would never have done something like that." She was shaking her head back and forth.

"I didn't know you—didn't know that," he said, noting that the gun was back in her lap.

"You didn't think about coming and asking?"

"When my wife left me and took my daughter, I wasn't thinking straight. All I wanted was revenge."

"I do know how *that* feels."

"After I met you and watched you through the trial, I realized you weren't the person I thought you were. I started questioning the origins of that letter, and I was able eventually to trace it back to my adversary, Governor Flynn. Really, Mary, I am *so* sorry." He could see the devastation in her eyes. "I know that words can never *ever* repay you for what you have lost—"

"You took Jack and gave him to the one person in the world I was trying to protect him from!"

Charles slowly shook his head. "I convinced myself that you had wrongly stolen Jack from his father and were purposely keeping him from him—and I let Jerry take me for a fool when he played the role of grieving dad. I believed it . . . because I wanted to believe it."

"It doesn't matter." She raised the gun again, and it trembled in her hand. "Because of you, Jack is lost in the world somewhere, and it's all because of you."

"That's how I felt when I lost Stephanie, my daughter. I thought it was your fault, and I wanted you to pay."

"Then at least you understand why I'm going to shoot you," she said, her tone frighteningly calm. She pulled back the hammer.

"I've been shot with that same gun once before—deservedly so. I can't argue that I don't deserve it again," he said quietly.

Mary stared at him, then slowly shook her head and started to cry—silent, heart-wrenching tears that rolled down her cheeks. Charles felt a strong impulse to go and dry her tears. He actually took a step toward her in spite of the gun still trained on his chest.

"Don't," she said. The gun, trembling, lowered an inch.

"I'm sorry, Mary. I know what I've done is unforgivable—"

"Be quiet!" Her arm was slowly sinking.

"I can't undo what I put into motion," he said, his own eyes welling with tears. "If there was any way I could go back, undo—"

"You can't."

"I've been looking for him, Mary. I've been looking all over for Jack!"

She stared at him with those large brown eyes. "I don't believe you."

"It's true," he said. "I've been looking for Jack ever since I found out he wasn't with Agnes. That's where I've been—it's why my landlord told you I travel. I go out for a week at a time, come home and do some legal work to make some money, then go back on the road again." He watched as she wiped her cheek with the back of her gloved hand. He could feel a tear on his own cheek. "I came home to clean up and shower. I'm packing some clean clothes and leaving again early in the morning. If you need a place to stay, you can have the bed, and I'll sleep on the couch. But with or without you, I'm going to keep looking."

"Why?"

"Because I need to find him almost as much as you do," he said, his voice sounding ragged. He gave her one last look, walked into the tiny bathroom, and closed the door.

Mary kept her eyes moving back and forth as they motored through Chicago in the 1932 Ford that Charles drove. By this point in her life, nothing really surprised her any longer. Sitting in the front seat next to the man she'd wished to hell and back . . . well, it almost made sense. She didn't know how much ground he'd covered looking for Jack, but she knew he'd been able to do a lot more than she had. And for that, she'd use every bit of willpower she had to swallow her pride, her anger, and her mistrust if it meant finding her son faster than she would if she were searching alone.

She'd spent a sleepless night in the apartment, wondering if she was making the right decision, worrying that Charles Westerly would slip out in the morning without her. She had been ready and waiting when he knocked on the bedroom door that morning just after dawn. They left together, strangers who had a single purpose.

"Are we looking in the city?" she asked, finally breaking the silence that had lingered between them since leaving his place twenty minutes before.

"I've already covered it," he said.

"The *whole* city?" She was skeptical.

"More or less," he said. "I've got contacts in most of the police precincts. I check in every week to see about any reports involving children."

"So where are we going?"

"Moline," he answered.

"Moline? That's south?"

He nodded. "Southwest—about a hundred and fifty miles or so."

"What about Rockford?"

"Been there."

"Elgin?"

"Done it."

"Well, then, what about—?" But she didn't finish when Charles hooked an arm over the back of the seat and half turned to look at her.

"It'd probably be easier if you just look at the maps I've got in the backseat," he said. "Open the briefcase. It'll give you a pretty good idea of where I've already looked."

She turned and looked over the seat at the brown case.

"I have to stop to fill up with gas." Charles turned into a Texaco filling station, rolling the Ford across the driveway air hose, dinging it twice, and triggering the appearance of a station attendant from the white enameled building. His crisp tan uniform had a gold star on the shirt pocket with *Elmer* embroidered above it.

"Morning, Mr. Westerly," Elmer said to Charles through the open window. "Fill 'er up?"

"Yeah, thanks, Elmer. How's the coffee this morning?"

"Not bad," he said. "Will's inside. He'll get it for you."

Charles opened the driver's door and looked at Mary. "Cup of coffee? I won't be stopping again for about fifty miles."

She nodded. "Thanks."

When Charles went into the station, Mary reached behind the seat and pulled the briefcase onto her lap. Releasing the clasps, she opened it and discovered dozens of maps inside. Besides one of Illinois, there were maps of Iowa, Michigan, and Wisconsin. Several of them were obviously well used, with corners dog-eared, folds creased so some of the printing had worn off. The top one was of Indiana, and she opened it. She traced her finger along a trail of red x's—state highways, cities, and even major streets. Handwritten notes in a sharp, concise penmanship along the margins included dates, names of hotels, hospitals, diners . . . someone's name here and there. *All the places he's been looking . . . really looking for Jack.*

Elmer slammed the hood down, and she turned from the maps toward the plate-glass window. Charles was standing in front of a cash register, talking to a man in a uniform identical to Elmer's.

*"I've been looking for Jack. I need to find him almost as much as you do"* echoed in her mind as she watched him.

Charles took a step, and she lost sight of him when he moved behind some tires on display, saw him appear briefly, and then he was gone again behind a poster taped to the window advertising Texaco's Golden Motor Oil. She looked more closely and saw another flyer, not as big as the ad for oil, but it was a decent size on white card stock. *Missing Child! Reward if Found!*

Mary's heart stuttered in her chest as she hurried to slip the briefcase from her lap and open the door. She was across the space in a few steps, staring at a picture of her son.

*Jack!* The flyer gave pertinent information, including his handicap, approximate size, age, date he was last seen. And a phone number to call with any information. The photo was the one that had appeared in the *Chicago Daily Times*. She reached out to lay her hand on Jack's image.

Mary felt Charles approach and stand a few feet away. She tore her gaze away from Jack's picture to look at him. "You? You did this?"

He nodded, holding a cardboard tray with two cups of coffee and two doughnuts. "Ready?" he asked.

She looked at the window again, then turned to follow him back to the car. *I believe him. . . .*

• • •

Wind rushed in the driver's-side window as they sped down the highway. Mary subconsciously counted the telephone poles along the road as they passed. *Twenty, twenty-one, twenty-two, twenty-three . . . all the places he's been, and he still hasn't given up. . . .*

"How many flyers have you put up?" she asked, capturing her hair whipping around her face with her gloved hand and holding it against her shoulder. At another time and place she would have enjoyed the ride—it had been a long time since she'd sat in the front seat of a car with the spring air flowing around her.

Charles had crooked his elbow out the window and his right wrist was hooked over the top of the steering wheel. "I had a hundred made, and I've circulated almost all of them. There are a few left in the trunk."

"How did you get the picture of Jack?"

"You probably recognize it from the Chicago paper," he explained. "I went to the newspaper office, and they had an archived copy of the photograph."

Mary looked at Charles's profile for a moment. *He probably would have made a good governor.* He looked like a man who could command authority, even though he seemed satisfied with his morning coffee from Texaco in a waxed cup. He glanced at her, and she turned her gaze to the windshield.

"There was a phone number on the flyer," she said.

"It's an answering service," he said. "I check in with them every other day to see if anyone has called."

"Has anyone? Called, I mean?"

"I'd say a couple dozen phone calls have come in, and I've checked out every one of the leads, but . . ."

Mary just nodded.

"Some of them were from people trying to be helpful, and some of the tips come from crackpots who get their kicks from messing around with something like that."

"I wrote letters from Oakdale," she said. "Dozens of letters to anyone I thought might be able to tell me about Jack. I don't know if I can ever explain how painful it is to send those hopeful letters out there in the world—and *never* get anything in return."

His expression darkened. "No need to explain. The pain must have been unbearable for you."

"It never occurred to me to write to *you*," she confessed. "Especially not . . ." But she didn't finish.

A moment passed before he glanced at her. "I thought of telling you about my search, but I'd already caused you so much pain, I couldn't bear to be the one to give you false hope as well."

"You wanted to find him and then tell me."

"That was the plan," he said with a rueful smile. "Guess I shouldn't have kept it a secret."

"We all have our secrets, I suppose," she said, her words almost lost in the rush of air through the window.

He murmured his agreement, and Mary turned to look out the window, her hand still gripping her hair. "But have you ever kept a secret that you wouldn't tell anyone because of what could happen if the truth came out? The kind of secret you'll even lie about for the sake of helping or protecting someone you love?"

When he didn't immediately answer, she looked back at him, at the tense set of his jaw.

He finally nodded. "I should have done a lot of things differently," he said.

Mary's answer was heavy with regret. "That sums up my life."

The road sign announced *Moline 45 miles.*

"How do you go about it?" Mary asked, changing the subject. "How do you start looking once you're in a city?"

"It varies with the size of the place," he began. "I usually start at the police station, check the hospitals, the local morgue . . ." He flinched and glanced at her with a look of apology. "I'm sorry, that was—"

"Don't be sorry," she said. "I asked." She turned back to the scenery out the window.

"Tell me about Jack," he suggested after a few more miles.

She contemplated for a moment, then, "He likes puzzles. And anything chocolate. His smile always starts in his eyes, and then kind of meanders down to his mouth—like he's giving me a bonus by letting me see his teeth." She couldn't help but smile at the mental image, and she caught Charles staring at her and shrugged self-consciously. "It's funny the things you notice about your own child," she said. "He's been special since he was born, but I've always had an uphill battle to get anyone else to see it."

"You're talking about the . . . gift? The prophecy?"

She hesitated, holding her right hand out the window against the wind. "That's part of it," she finally said, "but he's so much more than that. He's a self-contained miracle, even though he's filled with a bundle of emotions that can't come out, words that can't be expressed, sounds that I don't even know if he can imagine. But—it *is* the gift that makes him a valuable person in the eyes of the world. I finally realized that."

"So the gift is real?"

She closed her eyes for a moment at the implication, then forced herself to answer calmly. "It's as real as the maps in your briefcase, as accurate as the red lines you've drawn along those highways."

"Seems like a big burden for such a little boy," Charles said.

Mary felt the truth of the words, the weight of his statement, the regret that she'd allowed Jack to be caught up in all the gift entailed. She tugged the cuff of one glove a little higher on her wrist, then clasped her hands together in her lap. The wind went back to swirling her hair around her face.

"I asked Jerry about your gloves," Charles said, a hint of apology in his voice. "He told me you were burned as a child."

"Is that all he said?" she asked warily.

"Pretty much," he admitted. "If you have a choice, he said you never take them off."

"Well, for once Jerry wasn't lying," she said mockingly.

"How old were you when it happened?"

"Eight. Same as Jack's age when . . . when we were separated." She cast a quick glance at him. "My mother was canning . . . there was boiling water, and . . ." Her voice faded with the memory. "And I've been wearing my gloves ever since."

"Can I ask you something else?"

"Okay."

"How did you wind up with a man like Jerry?" He kept his eyes on the road.

Mary sighed. "I was young—only sixteen when we met. And I was living with a foster family."

"What happened to your parents?"

She allowed herself a small smile. "They were

so in love when I was little. I remember lots of whispers and kisses and quiet dinners that didn't include me. But then my dad made a terrible mistake. My mother . . . well, she found out he was having an affair." She looked over at Charles and could see his hands gripping the steering wheel. "Am I saying too much?"

He shook his head.

"Anyway, she couldn't stay with him after that. Couldn't forgive him—couldn't forgive herself for not being enough for him, I guess. She started to drink. My dad moved away, not wanting to have anything to do with me—with us." Her voice softened. "She literally drank herself to death."

"And your dad? Do you see him?"

"Never. I don't know where he is or anything about his life."

"So you met Jerry . . ." he prompted.

She nodded. "I wasn't getting along too well with my foster parents. Jerry proposed, and I said yes. It didn't take long for me to see I'd made a terrible mistake, but by then I was pregnant with Jack. . . ."

"I remember when my daughter was born," Charles said softly. "The best day of my life."

"And that's how it should be, isn't it?" Mary asked, her voice also low. "The best day."

Amazed at herself for all she'd said, all she'd revealed, Mary turned her face back toward the passenger's window.

# Chapter Thirty-nine

MOLINE, ILLINOIS, LOOKED LIKE MANY of the other towns Charles had visited in his search for Jack, the difference this time being the company he had. Mary Godwin was a mystery to him. How she could bear to be in such proximity to him, the one who had ruined her life, was beyond him. But she was doing it, and with a fair amount of grace. He saw the wariness, moments when even anger flashed in her eyes when she looked at him. But for the most part, he felt as though they were becoming allies in the battle to find Jack. For that he was grateful and more than a little humbled.

They made stops at both the Moline police station and the hospital with their picture of Jack; but it was the same story as every other place he'd been. No one had seen the boy. He knew it was hard on Mary, and though he didn't want to repress her hopes, he tried to keep a realistic tone to the search. Any information would be welcome, but she needed to understand it was like looking for the proverbial needle in a haystack.

"Hope tempered with caution," he said to her when they arrived in the center of town. They each took opposite sides of the main drag, entering all the biggest diners with Jack's picture to ask employees and patrons if they recognized the little boy. Occasionally Charles would get permission to post one of the flyers in a storefront window. Now, standing at the corner of Fourth and Main, he looked across the street and could see another person shaking his head as Mary held up a flyer.

He saw her shoulders round in discouragement, watched her steps slow as she made her way toward another person on the block. He crossed the street.

"Let's take a break," he suggested as Mary watched a young woman pushing a baby buggy past them.

"No, thanks, I don't need a break."

"Surely you could use something to eat?"

She shook her head. "I'm not hungry."

"Thirsty, then?"

"Not really."

"Come on. Not even a hot dog or a hamburger or a club sandwich?"

"No," she insisted.

"Look, Mary. We could be at this for a day, a week, another month. You need to keep up your strength, and if you don't eat, you'll get sick. You won't be worth anything to Jack if you are not taking care of yourself now."

"You make a good argument," she said with a shadow of a smile. "Must be a lawyer."

He grinned. "Comes with the territory. You may not be hungry, but I am. I saw they have an A&W Root Beer stand here. Ever had a root-beer float?"

• • •

The A&W was on the other side of Moline, the well-traveled side with a frontage road spilling onto the highway that ran north and south. Several barstools were placed along an outside counter running the length of the building. Charles pulled out a stool and motioned for Mary to have a seat.

She perched on the stool in front of a screened window, and he sat down next to her. A teenage boy spoke through the screen before they had even gotten settled. "WhatcanIgetcha?"

"Two floats, please," Charles said. "And take your time and make sure they're really good, because I've been bragging on them."

"Coming right up in mugs so cold they'll freeze your hands," the boy said, a bit slower this time. "You might be glad you're wearing gloves, lady."

Mary smiled. "That's good to know."

The shadow behind the screen disappeared.

When the screen on the window slid up, the boy pushed two frosty glass mugs toward them. "Here ya go," he said. "That'll be thirty cents."

After Charles dug out the change and passed it across the counter, Mary wrapped her hand around the cold mug and smiled. "I *am* glad to be wearing my gloves." She took a tentative sip through the fat straw.

Charles watched her eyes widen. "What'd I tell you?" he said with a grin. "You like it. I can tell."

Mary *did* like it, but she wasn't ready to give

him the satisfaction of knowing that. Wasn't ready to like the man as much as she was starting to. It felt wrong to have a light moment, wrong to smile when Jack was still missing.

"It's not bad," she finally conceded with another sip.

"Not bad! My daughter calls it heaven in a glass."

Mary saw a light in his eyes, followed by a flicker of longing when he mentioned his daughter.

"How old is she?"

"She turned eight last month."

"Almost Jack's age," she mused. "Do you ever see her?"

His face was really all the answer she needed. "No. My ex-wife moved away right after . . . after the whole mess with that letter."

"She shouldn't keep your daughter from you," Mary said. "It's not right."

"In Lila's eyes, I'm not a good man anymore," he said. "You kept Jack from Jerry because you believe he's not a good man."

"It's not the same thing at all." She frowned. "Jerry doesn't love Jack—he never has. He views him as worthless—a weight around his neck. I can see you truly love your daughter. I know you ache to see her."

"I write her letters," he said quietly. "Two or three times a week. And I wait . . . wait for her to write back." He stirred what was left of his float with the straw. "I'm still waiting."

"Don't give up," she urged. "Never give up."

"Quitting isn't in my nature," he said with a small smile.

"I'm coming to see that," she said with an answering smile.

They both heard it at the same time—a hint of a melody floating on the spring breeze. Mary twirled on her stool and looked at the frontage road paralleling the A&W. Coming into view was a convoy of big trucks of every shape and size. The first truck in the procession was painted white with bright blue lettering: *The Bixby Brothers' Spectacular Show!* The music was emanating from a bright red calliope on the bed of the second truck in line.

"Look—a traveling circus," Mary said. "I loved the circus when I was little."

"Guess traveling by rail is too expensive anymore," Charles said. "Have to truck the stuff around now."

They watched the livestock trucks roll past, one holding an enormous roll of blue-striped canvas, a horse trailer followed by enclosed trucks beeping their horns to get the news out. A gold-edged wagon with *Boris the Lion Tamer* written in fancy script on the side came next, along with several cars and pickups filled with an assortment of people, some even small enough to be children.

Finally, at the tail end of the line, an oversized truck hauling a silver Airstream trailer pulled up in front of the A&W, and a tall man in a stovepipe hat jumped out and ran toward the stand.

"Hello!" he called to Charles and Mary with a jaunty tip of his hat before knocking on the screened window. The teenager appeared.

"I got a poster for the circus here," he said. "Mind if I put it up? We're doing three shows in Rockford—might catch people passing through."

"Be my guest," the teenager said, motioning toward the wall.

"Come on out and see the show—we got something for everybody!"

Mary and Charles watched as the man pulled some putty from his pocket and tacked up his poster: "Bixby Brothers' Spectacular Show—Equestrian Delights, The Flying DeBeniditos, Rarities and Oddities!"

"Good day to you now," he said with another tip of his hat before returning to the truck. It roared off to catch the circus convoy, the driver tapping the horn over and over.

"I'll bet you could get your hot dog there," Mary quipped.

"Food *was* always my favorite part of the circus," he acknowledged. He glanced at the poster and then knocked on the window. The boy's shadow appeared.

"We've got a flyer to put up alongside the circus

poster," he said. "A missing boy. Okay with you?"

"Sure. Stick it up there," he said. "And I'll take a look at it and keep my eye out. Kids love root-beer floats, you know."

Mary looked at Jack's face staring at her from the flyer pinned up next to the Bixby Brothers' circus poster. She knew she'd never get used to posting pictures of her son—and then driving away. It was like leaving him all over again.

"We can make it to Burlington, Iowa, today if you're okay with that."

She merely nodded.

Back in the Ford, they headed in the opposite direction from the Bixby Brothers' traveling circus.

# Chapter Forty

### *Rockford, Illinois*

IT WAS AN AMAZING THING to behold. The roustabouts swarmed over a vacant piece of flat, unadorned land, and just two hours later a tent city sprang up like mushrooms, beckoning the townies to come and witness wonders like they'd never seen. Entertainment promising to lift them out of the doldrums of lost jobs, lost savings, and lost hope, and transport them to a magical place where clowns ruled and elephants danced.

When the tickets had been sold and the candy butchers prepared to comb through the bleachers hawking their wares, the performers lined up at the back door of the big top, waiting for their cue. The first few times Felix witnessed the spectacle, he had been amazed at the order that could come from the seeming chaos. The minutes leading up to the opening parade of the show—*the spec,* when all the performers and animals trooped past the appreciative crowd—were plagued with anxious moments, hasty costume repairs, surly horses impatient with standing in line, and a camel with a talent for spitting as far as Timbuktu. But any bickering, nerves, or impatience all disappeared the minute the music started under the white canvas big top.

"Now, go wow 'em!" Angelo would call out in his unique style, and Professor Pygmalion would high-step in his shiny boots, pushing through the flap of the door and into the makeshift arena.

Walking in discreetly behind the last animal, Felix and Jack stood and watched the spec with two other clean-up men. Freckles's moniker was self-evident, and Jugs was a wizened old geezer who looked way too arthritic to wield a broom or shovel. He moved slowly behind the animals but could be the first in line when the flag on top of the Pie House signaled chow time.

As the performers came full circle, Tatiana, the bareback rider, deftly leapt off the back of her horse, Blanca, and raised an eyebrow at Felix. "Present for you outside center ring, First of May," she told him before disappearing through the back flap of canvas. Felix turned and looked after her, but Freckles gave him a rough shove. "Pipe dream, buddy boy. Tatiana is off-limits—especially to a workingman. We don't mix with performers," he growled.

Felix swiveled his head and hoped Freckles wouldn't notice the red he felt creeping up his neck. "I wasn't . . . it's not . . . I just wonder how long people are going to call me First of May. I have an actual name, you know."

"Quit your whinin'. At least she calls you somethin'," Freckles retorted as the circle of performers all filed back through the door and the music changed to signal the professor. He stepped into the center ring in his long-tailed red coat and, this time, a pair of striped jodhpurs.

"Ladieeeezzz and gentlemennnnnn, and children of all ages! I am your ringmaster, Professor Pygmalion, and I welcome you to the Bixby Brothers' Spectacular Show!" As the crowd hooted and hollered and clapped, Felix gave Jack a nudge, and they moved with Freckles and Jugs to make a discreet circle of the ring, removing all evidence of an animal's possible indiscretion.

Under a five-o'clock sun, with the strains of the calliope in the background, Angelo spread the word in the backyard after the last scheduled show.

"Straw house today, folks! We're staying over," he shouted at the roustabouts who were already positioned to tear down the big top the minute the last spectator left.

Felix had already mucked out the menagerie tent when he caught the happy ripple of conversations across the lot. He found Freckles sitting against the sidewall of the Pie House, hands locked behind his head and a smile on his face.

"What's going on?" Felix asked him.

"Greed," he grinned. "Sold-out shows today. We're staying over to try to get in another crowd tomorrow."

"So that means . . . ?"

"Means we're ahead of the alley apples and can actually take a break tonight," Freckles told him.

Jugs came limping past them, trademark brown jug hanging from his crooked index finger. "Got a spot for you boys once we get a fire burning to keep away the danged bugs," he said, moving faster than Felix thought possible. Freckles scrambled to his feet and brushed the sawdust from his pants before he dug into his pocket.

"Hey! I got matches!" he yelled as he went after Jugs.

Acceptance was a funny thing. Having never had it, Felix thought just a piece of it would satisfy—but was astonished to discover he wanted more. He liked his job and was happy to be part of the cleanup crew. For the first time he didn't stand out because of his homely appearance, living as he was in the land of the odd, the freaks, the nomads. But still, he found himself wishing for acceptance by the likes of Tatiana, the professor, and Boris the lion tamer.

He looked down at Jack, who was staring up at him. Felix smiled—Jack smiled back. "You and me, kid—there's always you and me," he said affectionately as he pushed Jack's hair out of his eyes.

Felix accepted the jug from the clown seated to his right and took a long swig—and fought the urge to spit it out. It burned his throat as it went down and settled in his gut like a spark from the campfire. Jack, who had somehow picked up a dry, hacking cough, was curled on his side next to Felix.

"Poor little guy. I've got something for him if you want it." Wanda, one of the clowns who'd actually removed her makeup, knelt behind Felix with a tin cup. Jack coughed again.

"What is it?" he asked Wanda.

"Just a little whiskey and honey. It'll soothe his throat and stop the cough long enough for him to get some sleep. Used to give it to my nephew all the time," she explained.

*That jug works like a charm*, Felix thought as a

pleasant fogginess settled over him. He chuckled as he listened to clown stories while Jack actually snored beside him on a horse blanket after downing some of Wanda's concoction. They passed the bottle around the circle more times than he could count. He remembered thinking how nice it was to fit in, even it if wasn't with the muckety-mucks.

The lot slowly came to life. Felix cracked an eye and quickly closed it again. It was past dawn, people were moving around him, and the smell of coffee filled the air. It was the combination that roused Felix. He didn't move at first, convinced that if he did, his head would explode along with his bladder. He was vaguely aware of the scratchy surface of the horsehair blanket beneath his left cheek, and this time he opened both eyes, expecting to be face-to-face with Jack.

But Jack wasn't there. Gingerly, Felix turned his head and looked on the other side, but all he saw was Go-Go curled on his side, head cradled on the hat he wore for his act.

Felix sat up and steadied himself with a hand in the dirt. Bleary-eyed, he looked around the circle—but still didn't see Jack. A ripple of unease got him up on his feet.

It was the first time Felix could remember that Jack had left his side. He looked around the imme-diate area, started asking those around him if they'd seen the boy. But no one could recall seeing him since the campfire the night before. Fifteen minutes later Felix was in a full-blown panic. He moved from tent to tent, calling Jack's name even while realizing how ridiculous it was for him to call for a child who couldn't hear.

Wanda came out of the Pie House. "What is it? What's wrong?"

"It's Jack," Felix said. "He was gone when I woke up, and I can't find him."

"We'll find him," she said confidently. She cupped her hand on the side of her mouth and yelled, "Hey, Rube!"

The circus's universal cry for help was passed from tent to tent until the word had spread among the entire show that Jack was missing. Suddenly there were no "classes" of people. No workingmen or performers—no candy butchers or cleaning men. The circus was a family searching for one of their own. They spread out along the midway, behind the big top, and along the periphery of the field. Felix suddenly realized how much he'd grown to care about the little boy with the captivating eyes and smile. *"It's just the two of us now, Jack,"* he remembered telling Jack. *"Just the two of us—but I promise, no one is going to hurt you again."*

The crowd watched, sick with horror, as the little boy stood up, rubbing his eyes. He was inside the lions' cage, and they could see the male's tail swish onto the back of Jack's leg. Jack brushed it away before looking behind him at the giant cat, staring right into his eyes.

Felix, hands gripping the cage's bars, knew the moment Jack realized he was inside with three lions, and so did the circus historian, who captured the moment with his camera. The boy looked out at the crowd just as a trainer raised a rifle to his shoulder and put his eye on the gunsight. Those who told the story later swore that Jack couldn't bear the thought of the cats being shot, and in one calm movement he started toward the door.

As Jack approached, Boris carefully opened it just a crack, then wider, holding his hand out to the boy and motioning with his finger for him to come forward. Jack never looked back, but the crowd gasped when the huge male suddenly stood and shook his mane—then yawned as if to show everyone how big his teeth really were. The two females kept their yellow eyes on Jack, but they didn't move a muscle as Boris got ahold of Jack's arm and slowly guided him through the opening.

Jack stood outside on the wooden ramp leading from the cage, and a reverent hush fell over the group. As Boris moved Jack down the ramp, Go-Go the clown took off his hat and held it over his chest. The professor bent at the waist in a bow, and Freckles reached out and touched Jack's arm as Wanda started to cry. Low murmurs from the likes of Tatiana and Flash, Bertie and Three-Pete started to ripple through the circus family, and Felix heard comments like: ". . . must be somethin' special in that boy—animals recognize a particular spirit," and ". . . I knew he was more than just another kid. . . ."

Boris kept his hand on Jack's shoulder until they stood right in front of Felix, who dropped to his knees and pulled him into a long hug while everyone cheered.

# Chapter Forty-one

## *Madison, Wisconsin*

*HE'S ALIVE . . . HE'S ALIVE! Someone actually saw him, talked to him, gave him cookies and hot chocolate!* Mary willed herself to remain still in the front seat of Charles's car, but it was so hard to sit there and watch the scenery rush past— knowing that she might find out where Jack was that very day!

"Did you see that? Only fifteen more miles!" She grabbed the map between them on the seat. "Where are the directions to the place? You have them—don't you?" She scattered the other maps on the seat. "Did we lose it? Where is it?"

Charles unexpectedly reached over and took her gloved hand. "I have the directions and the address in my pocket—and in my memory. We'll find the place—I promise."

Mary felt him gently squeeze her hand and, for a moment, let herself believe that everything might be all right. "Okay." She nodded. "We'll find it."

"We'll find Jack," Charles said.

She smiled. "We'll find Jack—*today*," she added. "I can't believe it's a real tip. I can't believe the truck driver saw your flyer! I can't believe you called the answering service at the exact right time! I can't believe it's—*Jack!*"

He grinned at her excitement. "Everything he said checks out—and he's positive the picture he saw on the flyer is the same little boy who hitched a ride in the back of his truck. It's Jack."

"He—Jack must have been thinking about the night we left Jerry," Mary said slowly.

"What do you mean?" Charles asked, turning with a curious glance.

"We climbed into the back of a furniture delivery truck to get out of town. I'm never sure what he remembers and what he doesn't—"

"At least he must have recalled that," Charles said.

Mary smiled again and pulled her hand free to turn the knob on the car radio. Static filled the interior of the car as she searched for a station, and then they heard Duke Ellington's voice, "It don't mean a thing if it ain't got that swing. . . ."

Mary glanced over at Charles in time to see his jaw tighten. "Too loud?"

He shook his head. "No, it's fine."

"Maybe you don't like Duke Ellington?"

He tried for a nonchalant shrug, but Mary could see he was bothered.

"The song reminds me of Stephanie," he finally said. "She loved it—used to sing the silly lyrics until it drove me nuts."

Mary grinned and chanted, "Wadadado, wadadadodadoh."

"Whup de dittle ittle up," Charles finished with a sheepish smile. "I'd listen to those lyrics all day long now if I could hear her singing them."

"We must be nearly there—aren't we nearly there?" Mary asked, her mind back to Jack.

"We're getting closer," he said patiently.

"The woman will know something. She has to know something. But what if she doesn't remember? What if she won't say for some reason? What if Pete Albert was wrong, and it wasn't Jack at all?"

They passed another sign along the highway: *Madison 3 miles*.

"What if you don't think about 'what if's' anymore . . . and we'll answer all those questions in about three miles?"

Mary looked straight ahead and gripped her hands tightly. "What if I told you I'm scared?"

"It's okay," Charles said quietly. "I'm scared too."

Mary and Charles walked toward the entrance of the Kopper Kettle Sweet Shoppe and, without saying a word, paused at the same time.

"You ready?" he asked.

A slight nod from her, and he put his hand on the small of her back and the other on the doorknob. They heard the soft tinkle of a bell when the door opened and they stepped into the shop. It smelled of chocolate and cinnamon.

The proprietor stood behind the counter and smiled. "Welcome to the Kopper Kettle," she said. "Are you here for lunch?"

Charles smiled. "Actually, we're hoping for some information." He reached inside his coat pocket and withdrew the picture of Jack.

"We spoke to Pete Albert, a deliveryman from Bloomer Chocolates," Charles said. "And he told us to ask for Helen."

"I'm Helen." She smiled. "You know Pete? How is he? I haven't seen him in a while." Her smile faded. "I don't order from Bloomer's anymore."

"He's doing fine," Charles said. "The reason we're here is that he told us about a boy he brought into your place a while back—a stowaway on his truck. Do you remember?"

"Oh, sure, I remember. Sweet little kid," Helen said. "I gave him some hot chocolate and cookies."

Mary took the paper from Charles and moved it

across the counter toward Helen. "This is Jack. Is he—is he the boy who was in your shop?"

Helen plucked the glasses from the chain around her neck and slid them onto her nose. She peered at the picture of Jack. "That's him, all right. Poor little guy never said a word. We finally figured out he couldn't hear us."

Mary reached for Charles's arm and gripped it tightly. "Pete told us you called the local police?"

Helen nodded. "That's right."

"Pete couldn't remember the officer's name," Charles said.

"No, I s'pose he wouldn't. He only met him the one time," Helen said. "But he's in here every couple of weeks or so. His name is Sheldon Leonard—he used to work the night shift."

"I don't suppose Officer Leonard told you what happened with Jack?" Charles asked carefully. Mary reached for Charles's hand and held it tightly while Helen frowned.

"He did come back and tell me. He knew I was worried about the little tyke," she said. "I woulda taken him in myself if I could have. Sheldon asked me to, but I told him I live here in the back and couldn't do it . . . then I got to worrying about what happened to him—those brown eyes nearly melted my soul—"

"Helen? What happened to Jack?"

"Oh. Sheldon came right back in to see me the morning after he'd taken the boy—*Jack*, is it?—to tell me that he'd located some relatives in Evanston, and they'd had a joyous reunion." She offered them a satisfied smile and handed them back the picture.

"Relatives?" Mary's voice sounded hoarse in her own ears. "There are no relatives."

Charles put his arm around Mary's shoulders and spoke into Mary's ear. "We knew we'd have to talk to the cop who took him. Now we know his name," he said quietly. "We're still okay here."

"The little fella hasn't run off again, has he?" Helen asked with concern. "He's awful young to be hopping into the back of delivery trucks. Not that I should be poking my nose into this, but if he's running away, he must be unhappy at home."

"He can't find home!" Mary said shakily. "He can't find me—I'm his mother!"

"His *mother?* Oh my—" Helen waved a hand and stared at Mary sympathetically. "You know, it's entirely possible I got it wrong about your son. At my age I do my share of scrambling details."

"We'll need to talk to Officer Leonard," Charles said. "Can you direct us to the police station?"

"Take State Street west until you hit Second Avenue. The station is on the corner," Helen answered.

"Thanks for your time." Charles nodded. "And thanks for what you did for Jack."

Charles and Mary turned to leave, but Helen

stopped them. "Hold on a minute." She hurried into the back, reappearing a moment later with a green cap and a single green mitten in her hand. She passed them over the counter to Mary. "He forgot these that night."

Mary put the cap to her nose, closed her eyes, and inhaled. *Oh, Jack* . . .

Charles slipped his hand under her elbow. "Time to talk to Officer Leonard."

An air of joviality in the Second Precinct took Mary and Charles by surprise. Hearty laughter from several uniformed cops standing around a small desk in the middle of the room was incongruous with the official city seal of Madison on the dingy white wall behind them.

The two stopped at the counter dividing the desks from the entrance and waited. But the officers were focused on a small radio. It took only a few seconds to recognize the familiar voices of Amos and Andy.

"Excuse me?" Charles called. A couple of the men looked over, and one held up an index finger.

"Hang on a second, buddy." Amos delivered a punch line, and the men all laughed again.

"We're looking for Officer Sheldon Leonard," Charles said.

A man poked his head around a fellow officer and eyed them. Charles cocked his head to one side. "Officer Leonard?"

One of the men nudged Sheldon. "Go on—see what they want."

Sheldon sighed and walked over to the counter. "I'm Officer Leonard."

"I'm Charles Westerly and this is Mary Godwin," Charles said. "We're here about a little boy who was turned over to you."

Mary watched quick frown lines crease Officer Leonard's forehead before he neutralized his expression and shook his head. "Little boy? Afraid I don't know what you're—"

"This little boy." Charles was already sliding Jack's picture across the counter. Laughter from behind as the radio program ended tensed Mary's nerves further while she waited for Sheldon's answer.

Sheldon picked up the picture and studied it, then handed it back to Charles. "Cute kid—but I've never seen him before."

"That's strange, because we just left Helen at the Kopper Kettle, and she tells us the last time she saw this boy he was riding off in a patrol car with you."

Mary grabbed the edge of the counter. "Please—please, just tell us what happened to him—"

"Look, Helen is a sweet lady and all, but her memory isn't as sharp as it might be, you know what I mean? Just last week she called and had me check out a possible burglary at her place. She heard noises coming from the back room, and it turned out to be a squirrel with a sweet tooth," he said with a half grin.

"Helen's not the only one who saw you drive off with him," Charles said in a clear voice, loud enough to be heard by the cops now at their desks. "Pete Albert, a delivery truck driver from Chicago, was also there that night. He'd swear in court that the boy was given over to your protective custody."

A couple of the other officers lifted their heads to look at the little group by the counter. Sheldon reached for the picture again. "Lemme have another look at the kid. Maybe it'll jog some kind of memory."

"Just make sure the memory is fact—not fiction," Charles said firmly as he handed him Jack's picture. "I may have forgotten to mention that I'm an attorney, and I'd hate to file a dereliction of duty report about you with your chief."

"Just hang on a minute," Sheldon said nervously. "I see all kinds of people when I'm on duty. Sometimes they all run together. . . ." He looked down at Jack's picture. "But now that I look a little longer, I think I do remember this kid. Yeah, yeah, I remember him now."

"Where is he?"

"It took a little doin' on my part, on account of the kid being deaf and dumb and all, but I was able to track down his relatives in Waukegan and left him with them," Sheldon said.

"You told Helen that you left him in Evanston with relatives," Charles countered.

"Oh, right. Evanston. I had another case in Waukegan and . . ."

"We'd like to see your report," Charles said.

Sheldon shook his head. "Are you from Social Services?" he asked, lowering his voice and directing his question at Mary. "Is that what this is about?"

"*This* is about my son! My son who has no relatives in Waukegan or Evanston or anywhere else!" The timbre of her voice rose with her increasing panic and frustration. She carefully enunciated each word. "Where—is—my—son?!"

All heads were turned in their direction. Sheldon swallowed hard and grimaced. "Keep it down, all right? This doesn't concern anyone else in here."

"Where is he?"

"Look . . . a kid like that who can't say a word, can't hear a word, doesn't have a parent around to look after him"—he cast a meaningful look at Mary—"a kid like that is gonna eventually end up exactly where I took him."

"And where it that?" she asked in a strained voice.

"It's a place a little over an hour from here," Sheldon said, eyes on the counter.

"*Where?*" Charles hissed.

"The Rock River Poorhouse," Sheldon said hurriedly. "They know what to do with . . . people like him."

*"You just left him there?!"* Mary nearly shrieked.

Sheldon shrugged. "If you see a dog running loose on the streets, you know the animal's better off in the pound, where it can't get hurt—right? It's the same thing."

Mary's hand shot out and slapped Sheldon across the face. Two officers yelled and started toward them, but Sheldon held up his hand. He gave Mary a wry look. "No good deed goes unpunished."

"How do we get there?" From Charles.

"Head northeast on Highway 151. You'll find it."

Charles started to take Mary's arm, but she was already ahead of him—striding on shaky legs toward the door.

# Chapter Forty-two

## *Rock River, Wisconsin*

"I'M MARY GODWIN—UH, MARY *Sinclair,* and I'm here for my son," Mary said breathlessly to a woman at a registration desk. "His name is Jack, and he's eight—no, nine years old . . ."

Charles put a steadying hand on Mary's arm. "You probably wouldn't have his name," he said to the attendant whose badge pinned to her white uniform read *Hazel.* "He was brought in—dropped off—with no paper work."

Hazel shook her head with a frown. "We haven't had anyone recently. . . ."

"It would have been well over a year ago now. . . ."

*Over a year! Jack, I'm here! I'm right here to get you!* Mary felt as if her heart were going to leap out of her chest. "Please, he's a little boy with dark hair and brown eyes . . . and he's very sweet and no trouble," she said in a rush of words.

"I still don't know of anyone like—"

"He's a deaf-mute," Charles added.

"Oh, I should have told you that," Mary said. "I just need—want to see him so much—"

"We know Jack is here because a police officer in Madison told us this is where he brought him."

Mary pulled the well-worn picture of Jack from her pocketbook and spread it on the desk. "This is Jack. Now, please, tell me where he is."

Hazel looked at the picture, and Mary saw a flicker of recognition in her eyes, and a flash of something that made her stomach clutch.

"I'll just need to call someone." The woman hit a buzzer on the counter next to a telephone. "If you'll have a seat over there . . ." She indicated some chairs in a waiting area.

Mary shook her head. "No. I don't want to sit. I just want to be taken to my son. *Now.*"

A man suddenly appeared in the reception area and walked toward Mary and Charles.

"That's Mr. Stevenson. He's the director of the facility," Hazel said quickly.

Mary watched Mr. Stevenson throw an irritated glance at the receptionist. "What is it, Hazel?"

Hazel motioned for him to come closer, and he frowned as he joined her behind the desk. She lowered her voice as she pushed Jack's picture toward him. "They're here about—*him*. She's his mother."

Mr. Stevenson cleared his throat and studied the picture before he handed it back to Mary.

*Say something! His room number! He's a model patient! He eats all his dinner. . . . Say something—anything! Jack—I'm here! I'm so close now. . . .*

"There are certain procedures to follow in a case like this," he finally said. "I'm going to need to take a few minutes to get some paper work together for you to sign."

"She'll fill out whatever you need," Charles said calmly, "but I'm sure you can understand that she wants to see her son immediately. He should never have been here—it was all a tragic mistake. . . ."

"You are the boy's father?" Mr. Stevenson asked.

"No. The family . . . attorney," he answered.

"Attorney?"

"Can we talk *after* I see Jack?" Mary asked urgently.

Mr. Stevenson looked at Hazel and raised a concerned brow. "Locate *Horace* for me."

"If you don't mind, I'll have the two of you wait

in my office," Stevenson said, "while I see to a few things."

"*I do mind!* Someone take me to Jack!" Mary shouted.

Hazel turned her back while she spoke into a phone.

"Please," Stevenson said. "My office first."

Mary and Charles sat in chairs close together— her hand holding tightly to his large, reassuring grip.

"Where *are* they?" she said tensely.

"I don't know. Maybe they're bringing him to you," he suggested.

She sat up a little taller. "Maybe you're right. Maybe they don't want me to see where he's been." She shuddered. "Oh, please, God, I hope you're right because I don't think I can stand another minute knowing he's right here in the same building with me. . . ."

The door opened and Mr. Stevenson stepped inside with another man in a white coat. A doctor's coat.

"Mrs. Sinclair, this is Dr. Horace Tanner." Mr. Stevenson sounded relieved as he took a seat behind his large desk.

"I don't understand," she exclaimed. "What's wrong? Is Jack sick? Is that it? Have you been treating him for something?"

Dr. Tanner cleared his throat and looked down at

the floor. "I'm afraid I have some rather distressing news for you."

She pulled her hand away from Charles and pushed to her feet. "I don't want *distressing news*," she said adamantly. "I just want to take my son out of this place. I want to take him home."

"He's no longer here," Mr. Stevenson said quickly.

Mary stared at him. "You've moved him someplace else."

Dr. Tanner sighed and finally looked at her. "No, Mrs. Sinclair. We didn't move him. He's not here because, well, because—he passed away almost a year ago."

Charles stood just as she swayed on her feet. "Mary . . ."

"Passed. Away." She said the words out loud, but they made no sense to her. Dr. Tanner was speaking again, but she couldn't hear anything above the blood pounding in her ears. *He's passed away . . . dead? Died? No. My baby? No, no, no, no, no . . .*

". . . and the cause of death was ruled to be congenital heart failure. Probably a defect he was born with and never detected until it was too late," Dr. Tanner finished.

*Defect? Not my boy. No defects . . .*

"I'm very sorry for your loss," Dr. Tanner said.

"Very sorry," Stevenson echoed.

"You're sure it was Jack?" Charles asked.

"Maybe another boy in the facility that looked the same or . . ."

*That's right, Charles, tell them they're wrong. They're so wrong!*

"We're sure. We have other children here, but no one with his particular—challenges," Dr. Tanner said. "There's no doubt it was your—Jack."

Charles was talking again . . . *legal things* . . . questions she should be asking, but she couldn't talk. *Am I breathing? I must be breathing. . . .*

Their voices were so very far away. She was standing in the same room they had entered, but the walls were closing in on her and the floor felt like rubber beneath her feet—or was it her legs that felt like rubber?

*Jack's gone. . . . This is why I've never trusted you, God. Can I go back to yesterday, when I didn't know—when I had hope. . . . Charles is asking something . . . answer him.*

"Mary. Let's sit down," he was saying. "Can you get her some water?"

"She's had a bad shock," she heard the doctor say. *Bad shock—bad life—bad mother, bad, bad, bad mother . . . now I know. Now I know. . . .*

Her mind cleared enough to fasten onto something. "I want to see where he was."

"Oh no . . . that's not possible—"

"I want to see where my son lived until he died," she said in a voice devoid of any emotion. "And I want to see it right now."

• • •

They entered the children's ward with Dr. Tanner. Mary immediately covered her nose. Charles expelled a breath that expressed more than words as he stood next to her. She gazed around the room, at the bars on the windows, the beds stretching in two long rows. The stench cut right through her and made her stomach turn.

"It's all my fault," she whispered.

"Okay, let's go now," Charles said in a low voice. "You don't need to put yourself through this."

"I put *him* through this." She walked a few feet into the room. An alarm rang in the hall.

"That's for me, and I really need to go," Dr. Tanner said. "If you've seen enough . . ."

"Mary?" Charles asked.

"Not yet." She shook her head firmly.

Dr. Tanner looked agitated. "I'll be back," he said, finally dashing out.

Mary moved slowly through the room, noticing the children, who seemed to be unaware of her presence. A teenage boy was lying on a table in the middle of the room, his gaze on the ceiling above him. Mary stopped beside him.

"Hello."

"I don't belong here," he said flatly, never turning his gaze from the ceiling.

"Did you know my son? He had dark hair like you—but he was very quiet and never said a word. Maybe you were his friend?"

"I don't belong here."

"Hello, you!" a girl's voice came from behind her, and she turned to see twins—eleven, maybe twelve years old. They stood with their hands clasped, swinging their arms between them.

"Hello," Mary answered. "I'm Mary."

"I'm Louise and she's the other me," the girl said, nodding her head in her twin's direction. "She's the me I can't be."

The girls started to skip in unison, circling round the table where the boy lay. "Johnny, Johnny, Johnny, you're stuck, stuck—stuck," Louise chanted.

"Stuck, stuck, stuck, Johnny, Johnny, Johnny," her sister chimed in.

"Maybe you knew my boy?" Mary suggested, determined to keep her voice even and calm.

"Mary," she heard Charles say behind her. "They don't know . . . they probably can't remember. . . ."

"He has dark hair and beautiful eyes and is very, very quiet and still," Mary said as the girls kept skipping.

"Yupper. Quiet, quiet, no talking kid. He was gonna be my husband, but now he's dead—deader than dead, dead, dead," Louise sang as she skipped with her sister over to the last bed by the big window. "He slept in this bed, bed, bed. . . ."

"Bed, bed, bed," her sister mimicked.

Mary sucked in her breath and moved slowly to

the bed. The twins jumped up on it, then off. She sat down on its edge by the barred window and tented her hands in front of her face, pressed her fingers against her mouth, and was very still.

*He slept in this bed, looked out this window, wondered where I was. . . . He was alone in a place that smells of vomit and urine, and not one person here knew where he came from. . . .*

She felt herself rocking back and forth, arms crossed now over and around her waist, eyes on the view out the window of a world that no longer held her son.

"Mary?"

She stared through the bars. "This was my nightmare. This was the reason for using the gift—so that he'd have enough money to never have to endure a hell like this when I died. And now I find out my nightmares were nothing compared to this."

She felt his hand on her shoulder and turned away from the window.

"Is there anything I can do?" he asked.

"You can find out where he is. Find out where they buried him. You can do that," she said through lips so stiff they barely moved.

Charles was so heartsick and worried and felt so guilty he thought he'd die from it. It was twilight, and the headlights of the car were just starting to show in the dimming light. He took his eyes off the road and looked across the seat at Mary for the fiftieth time since they had found the simple white headstone in the cemetery a mile from the Rock River Poorhouse. "Jack, Born (approx) 1930—Died—1939. Rest in Peace."

Charles had wept when they found the grave, but Mary had stood stoically, then traced the date of death with her finger slowly—twice. She turned and walked away. Got into the car and hadn't spoken a word since. She was calm . . . too calm.

"Mary?" he said, knowing she wasn't going to answer him but needing to try anyway. "I'm going to investigate the poorhouse. Get some answers—petition for Jack's medical records. Anything I can get to help piece together . . . what happened."

To his surprise she turned her face from the window. "We know what happened." Her voice was devoid of emotion. "Jack was thrown away—and then he died."

"But I still want to find out—"

"It doesn't matter anymore, Charles. It just—doesn't—matter."

She turned back to the window, and he focused on the road. "We'll be home soon," he said.

"I don't have a home," she said quietly. "But then, I don't need one anymore."

It was easy for Charles to imagine Jack sitting at the window at the Rock River Poorhouse, easy to picture how still he must have been—how he could sit for hours at a time staring at nothing. It was easy because Mary had been doing the very same thing from a chair in his kitchen for three days. She rarely took her eyes off the limited view through the small window. She wouldn't eat, barely slept, rarely spoke.

Charles walked over to the chair where she sat and knelt beside her. She gave no sign that she knew he was there. "Mary, I'm making lunch. Will you eat something, please?" he asked.

She didn't answer—didn't even blink.

"Mary. Did you hear me?" Nothing. Charles shook his head and stood to move to the stove. "I'm going to make you some soup."

"No, don't," she said in a monotone.

He was encouraged that she'd even spoken to him. "You must eat, Mary. Can you do it for me?"

She shook her head. "I can't."

"Yes, you can. And you're going to," Charles insisted.

"I won't."

"At some point you're going to have to stop neglecting yourself, punishing yourself."

"That's all I deserve."

He walked back to the table and pulled out a chair to sit down by her. "No, Mary . . . you don't. You were a wonderful mother. You're a wonderful person."

"You don't know anything about me, Charles. And what you do know . . . is a lie."

"I know how much you loved Jack," he said, "and I know you would have done anything on earth for him."

She offered a tiny ghost of a smile. "I did. That much is true. And I should have known better. I should have known that Jack would pay for my mistakes, because anytime I love someone—it ends up badly. It's been that way ever since I was a child."

"You're not making sense," he said carefully.

"Yes, it makes sense when you have proof." She knit her fingers together and looked down at her hands. "There is a wake of damage a mile wide in my life—starting with my own parents."

"You're not responsible for their breakup," he argued. "You were only a little girl."

"A little girl who saw her father with another woman and then told her mother." She was talking fast, as though she couldn't hold it back anymore. "You have no idea how much I wish I hadn't done that. It unraveled everything that my parents had—all because of something I . . . I saw. . . ."

"It wasn't your fault. . . ." he tried again.

"They couldn't stand to look at me after that," she said, her eyes vacant. "My dad couldn't be in the same room with me."

"Because of his guilt . . ." But Charles knew she wasn't even hearing him.

"And my own mother told me not to touch her when I reached for her one day. She told me I was demon-possessed, the same as Mr. Osterstrom, a man from our church."

"People say cruel things when they're in pain."

Mary must have heard him, for she answered, "So was I, and I wanted it to stop." She paused and turned to him. "It wasn't an accident that my hands were burned, Charles. I put them in boiling water one day while my mother was canning. I did it to myself. I wanted the demons to go away."

Charles couldn't speak.

"Don't feel sorry for me. Like I told you, I destroy everyone around me."

"That's not true," he said, his voice ragged.

"It is—everyone who comes in contact with me suffers. My parents divorce, my son born deaf and mute, my foster parents—and there were *many* of them—troubled by my troubles. Even Jerry might have been a different man without me. The Edmundses' home turned upside down, Agnes in prison because she met me—"

"Because she's a thief."

"You don't see your daughter because of a letter with my name on it—"

"That's not your fault either. . . . It's mine, Mary."

She rushed on, "My son is dead because I encouraged the use of a gift that ultimately left him without a mother to protect him!"

"You need to stop this now, do you hear me?" He could barely refrain from shouting.

"I'm toxic—poison. But it's all right now. I've got no one left to hurt. I'll live or die alone. Like I should have in the first place. Like God intended."

"You think God is punishing you?"

She nodded with huge, sad eyes. "I'm not a good person."

"None of us are. Look what I did to my own family. The letter was forged, but the information was accurate," he said. "I did the terrible thing I was accused of. I was a weak, self-indulgent man who can never undo what I did—but I will regret it every day for the rest of my life."

She stared at him. "Pathetic, aren't we?"

He nodded his head. "Broken, Mary. Looking for someone or something to fix us. But, Mary, I've been wondering about the One who made us. . . ."

"He can't fix my Jack! He can't fix the fact that I'll never hold . . . or see him smile. Never tell him—never tell him . . ." She choked on the word.

"Tell him now," Charles said.

"There's no point."

"There is. You need to tell him."

She shook her head. "He lived his whole life not hearing me. It doesn't matter what I'd say now."

"It does matter! If he was here, I'd have so much to tell him," Charles said. "I'd say, 'Jack . . . I'm so sorry! So sorry that you got caught up in something you didn't understand. So sorry that you lived in a world where something like this could happen to you!'"

Mary pushed her chair back and stood. "It won't change anything for Jack." She retreated into the small living room and sat on the couch.

Charles went to sit beside her, aching at the hopelessness in her eyes. He had to will himself not to look away. "Maybe doing that can change something for you," he finally said. "Talk to him about things the two of you shared—tell him what's in your heart."

Mary just shook her head.

"Maybe, for the first time, he can hear you."

He could see the tiniest flare of hope in her expression as she thought about his words. Her lips trembled. "I loved him so much," she whispered. "I want to hold him again. I want to lie in the snow and make angels and ride the merry-go-round in Brewster Park." She closed her eyes. "*Jack.* I miss you so much, and I want you back—just like you were. You were my greatest gift, and I'm so sorry. . . ." Her voice broke. She opened her eyes and looked at Charles. "It's too hard. . . ."

He saw such abject pain in her eyes that his own filled with tears. "I'm so sorry, Mary—I can't tell you how sorry—"

"I know."

"I care about you, Mary," he said, "and I always

cared about finding Jack." He was very still as she stared into his eyes. He saw a question in her expression and worried that it was doubt. She didn't look away, and then he was aware that she was peeling off her glove. Slowly she raised that hand and pressed it to his cheek. He reached up and tenderly covered her hand with his own.

He heard the swift intake of her breath as their hands connected, and he saw a flicker of surprise in her wide eyes.

"Mary . . ."

She swayed, and he leaned toward her to steady her, but she moved back on the sofa.

"Are you all right?"

She nodded, made a fist with her bare hand, and tucked it against her side as she bent to retrieve the glove on the floor.

"I think I need to splash some water on my face," she said in a shaky voice. "Maybe even a shower."

He nodded slowly. "Of course. I'll finish making that soup and have it ready for you when you get out."

He saw her studying his face again. What was she thinking? Had he intruded too far into her grief? The last thing he wanted to do was to cause her any further sorrow.

"Mary? What is it?"

She shook her head. "Go ahead and make the soup," she said. "I'll try and eat."

Relieved, he watched as she stood, picked up her overnight bag, and found her way into his small bathroom.

Charles turned the heat down under the soup and listened for the shower. It was still running and had been for at least twenty minutes. *Twenty minutes . . . the hot water lasts barely five minutes for me. . . . Maybe I should check on her. . . .*

He knocked on the bathroom door, reluctant to intrude on her privacy but beginning to have an uneasy feeling.

"Mary? Everything all right?"

He expected to hear the water go off—but the shower continued to run. He knocked again—louder this time.

"Mary!" he called. "I'm just making sure you're okay. . . ." He waited and the water still ran. "*Mary!* Answer me!"

*Something's wrong . . . something's wrong . . . never should have left her alone! What was I thinking?*

"Mary—either you answer me right now, or I'm coming in there! I'm serious!"

He jiggled the doorknob and knew before he tried it that it would be locked. He pounded hard on the door.

"Mary! Mary! Just say a word—just my name! Mary!"

He backed up, turned sideways, then hit the door

hard with his shoulder, hollering when the pain told him it was his *bad* shoulder—and it burst open. The shower curtain was pulled across the tub—and the window was wide open to the summer night.

"Mary."

Charles yanked the shower curtain back to expose the empty tub, turned off the water, and ran from the bathroom—through the apartment and out the door.

Mary had simply vanished. It was several hours later when Charles finally gave up and tried to accept the fact that Mary didn't want to be found. He was worried sick about her. She was too weak, too vulnerable, to be alone. His mind conjured up all kinds of torturous images—where she might be, what she might do. . . . He shook away that thought as best he could.

He had failed to find Jack before it was too late—and now he had failed to find Mary.

# Chapter Forty-three

*Chicago, Illinois*
AUGUST 1940

HANK'S DINER WAS BUSY, reflective of heavily traveled Madison Street in downtown Chicago. Ceiling fans lent a buzzing undertone to the bits and pieces of conversation across the room. Mary wasn't even aware of those around her. She was sitting at a long, pale yellow Formica counter situated against the windows to the street. A cup of coffee and an untouched piece of toast were in front of her. It took all her energy just to keep herself upright on the stool—she idly watched a man running to catch a taxicab. She couldn't imagine ever running again, ever sleeping again, ever caring about anything again.

A waitress reflected in the glass in front of her floated in and out of Mary's sight as she worked the patrons, bringing them water, food, menus, along with lighthearted banter.

"Warm up your coffee, doll?" the waitress asked from behind.

"No thanks," she murmured.

"Can I get you anything at all?"

Mary shook her head. "No. I'm fine."

"S'cuse me for sayin' so, sweetie, but you don't look fine," the waitress said. "Looks like you could use a night out on the town. A handsome man who'll bring you a dozen red roses and a box of chocolates. In fact—"

"I have to go." Mary put two dimes down on the counter and slid off the stool.

She stood on the sidewalk and felt the crush of the city's activity—pedestrians moving around her, cars honking and backfiring, the clang of trolley cars, buses rumbling past filling the air with the smell of diesel fuel. All Mary wanted was to be left alone—the invisible woman.

With no particular destination in mind, she started up the sidewalk. The heat rolled in waves off the pavement as she moved along with the tide of people. She remembered walking along that same street with her son, remembered how good it felt to have his small hand held in her own, remembered how Jack could suddenly have his attention captured by something Mary wouldn't have noticed. She remembered Jack's head tilted way back looking up . . . up . . . up.

Jack was gone, and there was no point to anything—no reason to keep on . . . living.

Nothing had changed—yet everything had changed for Mary when she stepped out of the elevator on the top of the Babcock Towers Observatory. Several others were lined up along the edge of the roof, protected by the fancy steel barrier and enjoying the view. She moved slowly toward the edge. Her legs felt so heavy her shoes seemed to be made of lead, and it took all her energy to keep putting one foot in front of the other. She had to get to the spot that had so entranced her son.

*Oh, Jack! Look how beautiful it is up here! No wonder you wanted to do this!* She felt too weary to try and make sense out of it all. *My life has no meaning—what's the point anymore? I've messed it all up—from the time I was old enough to open my mouth. Made choices and mistakes that hurt the people I loved. Jack. Jack most of all . . .*

She stopped next to the barricade and looked over the edge at the flagpole jutting out from the building. There were the birds, the birds that made Jack smile. *No more of those wonderful, fleeting smiles.*

Without conscious thought she lifted one foot and wedged her toe into the latticework. *Just like Jack.* She gripped the top of the barrier and watched as one of the pigeons on the flagpole seemed to step off the metal into space. He floated for a moment and then spread his wings . . . *Jack! Look at that. . . . Oh, God, can't he be here? Why?* The bird spiraled down toward the ground, and Mary's eye was drawn to a billboard on the side of a tall building across the street: "Repent from Sin and the Kingdom of Heaven Is Yours!" it called to her.

*Repent from sin? I repented . . . I begged . . . I prayed. And it led me here—to this rooftop.* Random thoughts and phrases whirled through her mind. *Thou shalt not bear false witness. . . . Remember the Sabbath, to keep it holy. . . . Thou shalt not kill. . . .* The terrible memory of Charles at the other end of that gun . . . *I could have killed him. . . .*

She looked down at the sidewalk below, at the tiny figures hurrying along with their busy lives. *Thou shalt not kill. . . . But what if I already feel dead? I used to believe in heaven—do I still? I believe in hell because I'm there. . . . If there's a hell, doesn't that mean there must be a heaven? Jack is in heaven.*

Heaven with Jack sounded so good . . . so wonderful to be in a peaceful place with her son where they'd both be safe and happy. Mary tested her weight on the foot wedged in the latticework— then lifted her other foot and fit it in a space just above it. *You've taken everything from me, God. Is this my punishment? Is this the price I pay for misusing the gift? But I was doing it for the very son you gave me—for the boy with big brown eyes and a beautiful smile that you allowed to be deaf and mute. He trusted me! And finally . . . finally . . . finally I trusted you, and look what happened! Here I am—alone again.*

"Hey, lady! You should get down from there—it isn't safe."

*Climb over the railing . . . step off the roof—over in seconds. Thou shalt not kill. You've taken it all from me, God. . . . Thou shalt not kill. . . . I can be rid of this ache in my soul that won't go away.*

She watched as the wayward bird returned to the flagpole—back to its family. Back to the fold.

"Lady! C'mon, get down," the voice was closer, insistent.

Mary pulled her top foot free of the latticework. *I don't want to stay . . . but I will. I don't want to believe in you . . . but I do. I can't live my life without Jack . . . but I am.* She placed both feet solidly on the roof of the observatory and turned away from the edge. Vaguely aware of people staring at her, she felt her legs trembling as she moved toward the elevator—and stepped inside to ride back to the street and the endless days of the rest of her life.

Mary came out of the Babcock Towers and paused on the street. She was right back where she'd been when she first arrived in Chicago—broke, and needing a job. *Today's the day we're gonna find a job, Jack!* She shook her head at an overwhelming sense of hopelessness. *I've got only three dollars, though. . . .*

She searched windows of the businesses she passed, hoping to see a Help Wanted sign posted on the glass. A trash can held a discarded newspaper, and she reached for it to check the classifieds. She noted the headlines first—"Millions Visit New York World's Fair" . . . "Battle of Britain—R.A.F. on Offensive" . . . "Concert in Lincoln Park Free to Public" . . . "Circus Boy Sleeps With the Lions." She looked at the picture under the last headline. *The sun must be hitting the page and playing tricks. . . .* She angled the paper out of the glare and stared at the photograph. A little boy with a dark fringe of hair across his forehead. Wide, dark eyes that looked into the camera without giving away what he was thinking.

*"Jack . . ."* she whispered. Her legs would not hold her, and she clutched at the edge of the trash can for support. *He's alive—he's really alive!* She held the paper close to look at every detail of the picture, then quickly devoured the short article under the picture.

*Circus . . . Chicago's South Side . . . Limited engagement ends tonight. . . . Hurry, hurry, hurry!*

Mary nearly ran through the bustling midway toward the entrance to the Bixby Brothers' Spectacular Show. She could hear music and applause wafting out of the big top and looked around wildly. *Where to start? How to find him in this mass of people?*

She spotted a man seated on a tall stool behind an ornate ticket window. "How long till the show is over?" she asked breathlessly.

"Judging by the tunes, ma'am, I'd say another fifteen minutes or so," he said. "You're in time for the grand finale—the boy who sleeps with the lions."

*Jack, Jack—he's talking about my Jack!*

"Here," she said, sliding a quarter through his window.

"You sure you don't wanna wait and see the whole show? We do it again in three hours—"

"No—I've waited long enough." She snatched up the ticket stub and dashed through the entrance.

Her eyes began searching the second she entered

the arena, but there were so many people—so many faces. *I need to be high enough to see everything.* . . .

She found a seat midway up in the grandstand, right in front of the center ring. The clowns were just ending their act. The crowd applauded enthusiastically, and the clowns took several bows.

Mary opened the paper again, just to be sure, and stared at the picture. *Jack* . . .

A hawker selling large pink clouds of cotton candy on paper cones moved along the row below her, and she had to crane her neck around him to see the ringmaster step into the center ring.

"And now!" A thunderous drumroll, then, "The Bixby Brothers' Spectacular is proud to present our grand finale—the *pièce de résistance* of our show—Boris and his jungle cats. And"—another drumroll—"the lionhearted boy who sleeps with the lions!"

The crowd erupted into enthusiastic applause. Mary felt as if her heart was trying to leap from her chest. She leaned forward as Boris came through the performers' door brandishing a long whip that produced loud cracks in the air. Behind him came a train of three cages on wheels—each holding a huge lion. Behind them, four clowns in tuxedos carried a platform balanced on long bars across their shoulders—and seated on the platform was a boy looking around in wide-eyed wonder at the spectators. He was dressed in a suit with a red jacket and tan pants, and he wore a small top hat. The crowd was clapping and chanting, "Lionhearted, lionhearted!"

Her world stopped, the crowd disappeared, and the only thing she saw was *Jack!* Her son was alive and well! She was terrified it would turn out to be a dream, a trick of her own mind. She did not take her eyes off him as his clown entourage circled the big top with their precious cargo.

She shakily stood and stumbled over spectators' feet, knocking over a box of popcorn to get to the aisle and the steps downward. She finally made it to the sawdust floor under the grandstand just as the clowns carried Jack out a flap at the back end of the tent.

She shot through the same back-end flap and ran smack into the chest of a large man, arms crossed over his chest. He put big hands on her shoulders and physically moved her backward. "Whoa there, missie. This area's off-limits."

"I have to . . . see someone," she insisted, craning her neck around him. She glimpsed Jack being drawn into a group of performers congregating outside another tent and saw a tall, thin man reach out and ruffle his hair.

"You can't go over there," the man said firmly. "If you want an autograph or something, you'll have to wait on the midway with everyone else."

"You don't understand. The . . . the lion boy. He's my son!"

She tried to move around him, and he grabbed her by the arm. "Yeah, and I'm the giant that lives at the top of the beanstalk." He hauled her back. "You're not losing me my job 'cause of some daffy—"

"That isn't necessary, sir. Let her go."

Mary's breath caught. She turned and saw Charles just a few feet away. Their eyes met and held for a long moment. He offered a small smile and held up the newspaper. She let out a choked laugh and held up her own.

"Get outta here—both of you," the man growled.

"You need to let her pass." Charles stepped closer.

"Nope. Can't do it."

"She's not lying about her son," Charles said. "I'm sure you don't want to be part of a kidnapping charge."

The big man scoffed and shook his head. "I ain't some First of May who doesn't know the score, mister. People'll say all kinds of things to get into the backyard of a big top."

Even though Charles was half his size, he grabbed the big man's arm. "No one is going to stop her from getting to her boy—not you, not anyone. Run, Mary!"

While the two men scuffled, Mary sprinted past.

Jack was standing beside the tall, homely man, and she stumbled to a stop just in front. She ached to hold him, to pull him close and never let him go again, but she made herself wait. Jack stared at her with those beautiful eyes, the ones she had thought were closed forever. She looked for any sign in his gaze that might convey any recognition, any sign that said he'd forgive her for being away for so long.

"Hey, lady. You can't be here," the tall man said.

She took a step closer, and he put a hand on Jack's shoulder and drew him back.

"Hey, Felix! What's going on here?"

"Where's Boyd? Ain't he on security?"

"Somebody haul her outta here."

"She's scaring the kid."

Mary struggled to find her voice, to get out a single coherent sentence. She looked at the tall man someone had called Felix. "I'm—his— mother!" she finally said. "His mother."

Jack hadn't moved a muscle.

"Felix here would know his own kid's mother, lady!" someone nearby yelled scornfully.

Tears welled in Mary's eyes. "They told me he was dead," she said through trembling lips. "They told me at the Rock River Poorhouse that Jack was . . . dead."

Felix's jaw dropped, and he stared into her face as she inched closer.

Boyd, the big security guy, barreled toward them with a gash above his eye and his lip already starting to swell. "Listen, lady! I already told you—"

But Felix had his hand up. "Hold on," he said. "Give her a minute."

She nodded her gratitude to Felix, then saw that Charles had come to stand just a few feet away. He was holding a handkerchief to his bleeding nose, his lip was split, and his shirt torn, but she could see the joy radiating from his eyes.

Mary turned back to Jack as Felix moved his hand from the boy's shoulder and stepped away. She held her breath, crossing the last few feet and dropping to her knees in front of her son. *This is real. This is Jack. I'm not dreaming. . . . I'm not crazy. Thank you, God, thank you, God, thank you. . . .*

"Oh . . . Jack," she said, tears flowing down her cheeks. He stared at her, and she pulled off her right glove. Slowly, she reached out and touched the tip of his nose, ran her finger up the bridge and formed a heart around his face.

"I love you, little man," she whispered.

She saw it then. The light of recognition in his eyes that told her more than words could ever say. He smiled—wide, joyful, and stepped into her arms.

Mary nearly collapsed with happiness, relief, gratitude, and profound thankfulness for this wonderful gift she held tightly against her. She looked over his shoulder at Charles, on his knees, weeping tears of joy right along with her.

• • •

THERE ARE MOMENTS IN ALL OUR LIVES that live forever—moments so pure that while they are recalled, we are actually transported to that very time to relive the emotions all over again. The realization that the beautiful woman kneeling before me was my mother was such a moment for me. I can recall exactly how her hair smelled and the rough skin of her finger drawing a heart around my face; I can feel her quick, emotional breaths against my neck and feel the blanket of love that dropped over me . . . and stayed over me for the rest of my life.

The set of circumstances that brought Charles and my mother together were the same set of circumstances that made it difficult at first for them to admit they were in love. Like all of us, they were both broken people —souls who had lost their trust in God and who needed healing from deep inside before they could find a life together. After I was found, they both entrusted their secrets and sins with Pastor Martz. He slowly and carefully led them back to that place of grace, where forgiveness was theirs for the asking. My mother eventually was able to forgive my father. After their divorce was final, he remarried, and we never heard from him again.

Charles and Mother discovered their own new beginning with hand-holding and whispered endearments, dreams shared and fears abandoned. I was eleven the spring my mother married Charles, and the three of us began a new journey as a family.

It turns out that Agnes had been right about three things: There *are* providential moments in life if we will only learn to recognize them; the big house on the shore of Lake Michigan could be gotten for a song; and it would turn out to be a wonderful place to live.

My parents' marriage was dedicated to God, our family—and to service. Mother and Charles never forgot what they saw the day they visited the Rock River Poorhouse, the children who had been left there to exist in a place devoid of love. They made it their mission to shut down the children's ward and bring to justice the staff who had violated the trust of those children.

The idea to provide a place, a true home, for the unwanted and unloved children like those who had been all but forgotten, grew from something the pastor said to my mother: "This gift is much bigger than anything you've ever dreamed." They bought the house on the shore—Mother had learned there was no deed in her name as Agnes claimed—and poured their energy into restoring it back to the beautiful place it had originally been. Charles practiced enough law to pay the bills, and my mother finally found what she believed was the true purpose of the gift—a way to "see" the children who yearned for love and needed a place to be their special selves. When she found them she gathered those children close and brought them home. Over the course of my life, I have played with more children than I can count; watched my parents shower love on the unlovable; and held the skeins of yarn while my mother knitted countless stockings for the big mantel in the living room she had envisioned at Christmas.

Besides my parents and myself, there were several staff members who stayed in the house over the years, but the only other adult who ever called the place home was Felix.

He had become my mother's friend for life when she'd learned his reasons for taking me from the poorhouse. He had held her hand while she cried over the things he told her— but she'd insisted on hearing them. He had confessed how much he loved me by then, how much he was going to miss me. Felix had done the best he could with me, and my mother was forever grateful. He retired from his life with the circus when I was a grown man and came to live at our house. There were times on the porch when I sat next to Felix—

special moments when I could feel the bumpy ride of the train cars over the tracks and smell the roasting peanuts that we ate together in our tent. I loved Felix Stanhope and was there when he passed away nearly fifteen years ago, peacefully in a feather bed with a handmade quilt and friends around him.

Charles's devotion to my mother was evident in everything he did and said—but we both knew there was a stone of sadness in his heart in the early years of their marriage. My mother understood it and gave him the gift of never discounting it by trying to talk him out of it. She knew all too well the pain of missing a child. We never spoke of it, of course, since speaking of things always remained impossible for me, but I knew instinctively what pure moment Charles held in his heart until the day he died—because I was there to witness it.

I had just turned twenty that summer. There were children playing in the yard, running and laughing and teasing my mother with worms they were finding in her garden. I was sitting by Charles, who was busy pruning some of the many hedges that made a natural fence along the side of the lawn, when a sleek car pulled up. Charles stopped and put a hand over his eyes to shield them from the sun, and the three of us watched as a beautiful young woman stepped out. She had long blond hair and wore a simple gray skirt and pink blouse. Charles took a couple of steps toward her, and though I couldn't hear it, I know he whispered his daughter's name. I saw the look that passed between my parents. No one knew better than I all the things that can be said with just one look—all of the love and fulfilled wishes and dreams that one partner has for the other. After years of writing letter after letter of apology, years of missing her birthdays and Christmases, Charles crossed the lawn toward his precious Stephanie. He took her on a tour of the house, let her see for herself the love that had been poured into the lives of other people's children, even as he longed to see his own. The forgiveness that came from Stephanie took away the sad stone from his heart, and they spent years together making up for all those they had lost. My mother's joy at his reunion with Stephanie was a moment I know she could and did recall until she passed away when I was already a man on the precipice of old age.

I grew up in a time when white gloves graced the hands of stylish women—those who attended teas and parties and fund-raisers. But the only *real* lady I ever knew to wear the gloves was my mother. The hundreds of white gloves she wore throughout her lifetime took on the daily routine she lived: They got dirty as she worked the soil, got wet when she dried a child's tears, were stained red when she baked cherry pie, and smelled like the Jergens lotion that was always on the skin of her hands beneath the material that kept them from accidentally being seen by the world.

My mother never doubted that the gift of prophecy was from God, though she always regretted the way she'd allowed it to become distorted during that period in our lives when fear over my future took precedence over faith. Over the years there were others who found their way to the house on the lake, hoping to leave with a prophetic verse about their own future—but she told them all the same thing before she turned them away. "The gift isn't meant for those who can ask for a chapter and verse—it's meant for the children who don't have a voice."

It had never occurred to me that my mother wouldn't be with me until the end of my life—but as she so magnificently demonstrated, it had occurred to her. The home I lived in had long since been paid for, and Olivia Edmunds had been instrumental in setting up a fund that had grown over the years to pay for the care of the children who passed through its doors to live with love. The caretakers of the house always came with a heart for the children. Stephanie Westerly was the first among them after Charles went to join my mother in heaven.

I had chosen the round turret for my bedroom when I was just a boy; I couldn't voice my preference, of course, but the act of moving a chair near the window and sitting down was all my mother needed. The view outside that window has been a panorama of passing time: new spring flowers pushing through the earth, summer days carpeted with children playing on emerald grass, winter snow that made everything gleam still and white—and glorious fall foliage that never failed to inspire me.

Thinking about sitting there, I recall another moment in my life with clarity—the last chapter and verse my mother and I ever wrote together. I was a grown man, and I know she saw the surprise in my eyes when she took my hand, pressed a pencil against my palm, and proceeded to guide me through the words of forty-six, thirteen, two: "If I have the gift of prophecy and can fathom all mysteries and all knowledge, and if I have a faith that can move mountains, but have not love, I gain nothing."

For a while after my mother's passing, a few still made the pilgrimage to our home, hoping to find answers in the form of a chapter and verse from me. But they always left empty-handed.

So, you see, I wasn't able to tell them that the gift of prophecy had never been mine at all. It had always been my mother's. As I said in the beginning, you should focus on my mother—she's where the heart of this story lies.

God took me home one evening while I sat in my chair and watched the sunset. I slipped from this life to the eternal life, where not only could I look upon my mother's ageless, beautiful face, but I could hold her perfect hands and finally say the words in heaven that she never could hear from me on earth . . . "I love you."

# Acknowledgments

The authors greatly appreciate Pastor Cliff Gregory for all the time, counsel, and help he provided in the early stages of our novel. We were blessed to have had some great resources for our research and would like to sincerely thank Dr. Clint Arnold, Biola University; Dr. Timothy Warner, Freedom in Christ Ministries; and Dr. Mike Pocock, Dallas Theological Seminary, who generously gave us insight into some difficult and thought-provoking questions. Our gratitude to friend and mentor Carol Johnson for her editorial acumen. And last but not least, we are thankful to Luke, who became the seed of inspiration without even knowing it.

## FROM MICHAEL

The process of writing this book was made infinitely easier because of the love and support from my wonderful family. To my children, Ashley, Brittany, and Austin, I am grateful every day that I'm your father. And in the words of Mark Andrus, to my wife, Sharee, *you* make me want to be a better man.

# FROM CINDY

Lots of appreciation goes to my loving family and amazing friends for all their support during this endeavor. A special thanks to Michael Landon for inviting me on this particular journey of novel writing. To Christy Cooper, who has read each new draft with enthusiasm, many thanks! I don't have to look far to find the gifts that God has given me. Grandchildren, Delaney and Brody, I adore you! Nicole, Josh, and Danielle, you've grown into incredible people and I'm so proud of you all. And Jimmy, for everything you are, and all that we have together . . . thank you.

**Michael Landon Jr.** is all about stories and storytelling. His father's *Little House on the Prairie* television series established the Landon name with family-friendly fare, and Michael carries on that tradition. This is captured in his very successful *Love Comes Softly* movie series based on the novels by Janette Oke and, among other recent film projects, *Saving Sarah Cain*, *The Last Sin Eater*, and *The Velveteen Rabbit*. The parallel paths of book and film both provide their contrasting rewards and challenges, and readers and film watchers alike will be enjoying Landon projects for a long time to come. Michael and his wife, Sharee, make a home for their three children in Austin, Texas.

**Cindy Kelley** is married to her high-school sweetheart. (Their early dates included flying to various cities for lunch so he could clock flying hours.) Devoting herself to raising their three children, she also served as a Lamaze instructor and birth coach. A lover of reading since childhood, she more recently has been able to pursue her dream of writing. Though this is her first novel, she has collaborated on screenplays with Michael Landon Jr., including some *Love Comes Softly* films as well as *The Velveteen Rabbit*. Cindy and Jim make their home in Tucson, Arizona, and are enjoying their new role as grandparents.

## Center Point Publishing

600 Brooks Road ● PO Box 1
Thorndike ME 04986-0001 USA

(207) 568-3717

US & Canada:
1 800 929-9108
www.centerpointlargeprint.com